MW00416347

"Kelli Stuart is a master at the care and handling of the characters who people her novels. She writes them with sensitivity, cultivating them with dignity and seeing them through their troubles with empathy and integrity. In *A Silver Willow by the Shore* we meet three generations of women who we come to love, ache alongside, and learn to find hope with. In the reading, we become part of their family, wishing the very best for them as they overcome past hurts and secrets, and observing them realizing their great need for one another. For readers of The Nightingale and The Light Between Two Oceans. A beautiful, gentle, triumph of a book."

~ Susie Finkbeiner,
author of *All Manner of Things*

"A deep, contemplative novel built around three generations of women asking the same timeless question: 'Who am I?' The answer unfolds with Stuart's trademark attention to history and hauntingly beautiful prose."

~ Jocelyn Green,
author of *Between Two Shores*

"*A Silver Willow by the Shore* is more than a story, it's a tapestry. Love woven with grief. Brokenness threaded with redemption. The secrets we hold close and the choices that become a part of us. Kelli Stuart's gifted pen breathes vivid life into both past and present--from the bitter hardship of survival in a Siberian gulag, to the shadow-world of Soviet Moscow, to a Tennessee family struggling to rediscover the meaning of hope. Layered, deeply moving, and ultimately inspiring, this is a novel that will linger in your heart far beyond the final page."

~ Amanda Barratt,
author of *My Dearest Dietrich:
A Novel of Dietrich Bonhoeffer's Lost Love*

*"I know her. She is me...or she was me.*

*She's the me who survived something terrible.*

"In *A Silver Willow by the Shore*, Kelli Stuart brings readers into the heart of humankind's greatest resource: the strength of women. Three generations—Elizaveta, Nina, Annie—each faced with the turmoil of her time. Choices and circumstances the others could not imagine. One woman caught in the middle: could she have survived the crippling poverty of her mother's post-war Russia? Would she be able to navigate the social pressures that come with her daughter's modern day freedom? The contrast drawn between Cold War Russia and unfettered modern America draws a stark, unbreakable line, and we see that a simple change of time and place does nothing to dislodge the roots of pain forged in sacrifice. And yet, two resounding themes repeat: new life carries hope and new love restores strength. The subtle nod to cultural mysticism adds a fourth light, protective layer to the narrative. *A Silver Willow by the Shore* gives us a story steeped in secrets, stubbornly held from one generation to the next, across continents, across ideologies. Stuart draws you in while keeping you just a word away from full revelation. It's my favorite kind of story—where shadows remain after the final page."

~ Allison Pittman,
author of *The Seamstress*

"Kelli Stuart has crafted a deep and meaningful story spanning three generations—grandmother, mother, and daughter. Each of these women has her own secrets and her own narrative, but all three of their journeys are intricately connected. In *A Silver Willow By The Shore*, Stuart delves into the richness of Russian culture, and the harsh past of the Soviet Union. This novel weaves in the depth of love and the depth of loss in a powerful way that will leave the reader pondering long after the last page is turned."

~ CATIE CORDERO,
author of the Roaring 1920's Series—
*Ramble & Roar* and *Marvel & Mayhem*

"I knew that Kelli Stuart could write. I read her first book *Like a River From Its Course*, and in it Kelli courageously revealed the love, fear, horror and sorrow of some of our species' most hideous times and crimes. But when an author writes a first novel and blows us out of the water, one always wonders if she will ever produce anything that good again. Well she has! Her new book, *A Silver Willow by the Shore*, may even trump her last amazing work. This time we plunge into the lives of three exceptional and exceptionally brave and yet damaged women, and live with them through very real dilemmas, dangers, and damages. Yet, despite all the blows that mankind can throw at them, they survive and thrive. I began reading this book one morning and I couldn't stop. Despite my rather busy life, I read it cover to cover in two days, and it was worth every moment spent! I wept with them laughed with each character, and in the end rejoiced. This is a job well done and a book worth celebrating."

~ Douglas Gresham,
Producer of *The Chronicles of Narnia* and author of *Lenten Lands: My Childhood with Joy Davidman and C. S. Lewis*

"Stuart guides us seamlessly through three generations of women: daughter, mother and grandmother. But it's not only a story about Annie, Nina, and Elizaveta—it's also a story about memory, about things passed down, and about how every generation must make a way for themselves, through their own hardships. It is, in other words, a story about all of us. A wonderful read."

~ Shawn Smucker,
author of *Light from Distant Stars*

# A
# SILVER
# WILLOW
## by the
# SHORE

*Kelli Stuart*

# KELLI STUART

*A Silver Willow by the Shore*
© Kelli Stuart, 2019

Published by Fine Print Writing Press, a division of Fine Print Writing Services, LLC, Tampa, Florida.

All rights reserved. No part of this book may be reproduced, stored in a retrieved system, or transmitted in any form or by any means—electronic, mechanical, photoshop, recording, or otherwise- without written permission of the author or publisher, except for brief quotations in reviews.

Distribution of digital editions of this book in any format via the Internet or any other means without the author and publisher's written permission of by license agreement is a violation of copyright law and is subject to substantial fines and penalties. Thank you for supporting the author's rights by purchasing only authorized editions.

This is a work of fiction. Any representation that resembles a person living or dead is purely coincidental. The persons and events portrayed in this work are creations of the author.

Cover and interior by Roseanna White Designs
Cover images from Shutterstock

ISBN 978-0-578-50430-8

Printed in the United States of America

*For my dear friend, Sveta.*
*You are an inspiration.*

*A silver willow by the shore*
*trails to the bright September waters.*
*My shadow, raised from the past,*
*glides silently toward me.*
Anna Akhmatova

# ELIZAVETA

*Keep it hidden. Share as little as possible.*

I know when someone's holding a secret. There's a certain nuance that cannot be fully disguised when one is harboring hidden news. Most people wouldn't recognize it, but I do. Of course I do. I've lived my entire life in whispers.

She steps into the room, and I see it. The secret trails its scent behind her, heavy and thick. It weighs her down, a prisoner's chain clamped tight around her soul. She moves like a shadow, quiet, as if the very breath escaping her lungs might draw our eyes in her direction. Her eyes flit to my face for only a brief instant before turning down. She runs her hand over her hair self-consciously, the long braid hanging limp down the middle of her back. Her hair is still wet, and I cluck my tongue at such carelessness.

She turns her back to me and faces her mother. The two speak in murmured tones. I can't hear them, but even if I could, translating their harsh syllabic dialogue is still difficult. So I sit mute, and I take in the sounds, the gestures, the unspoken words that shimmer between mother and daughter. And I fight the memories.

They haunt me. Though I've spent a lifetime rearranging the facts, I still can't seem to escape the images. They move through my head in the quiet moments like a mirage. Real or fake? Even I'm not sure anymore. But I'm old, and I'm tired, and I no longer have the energy to fill my days with meaningless tasks to keep the secrets at bay. So they chase me, and they are catching up.

I can't speak of the memories, of course. Not to anyone. The key to keeping a secret is to replace the hidden news with something different, and then to make yourself believe the new story. Roll the facts through your head until they've muddled the reality of events. This is what I've done. What I've *tried* to do. This is what she'll try to do.

Keep it hidden. Share as little as possible. She and I are not so different after all. We're both rewriting our own history.

# ANNIE

Annie flips her head up, her hair falling in cascades over bare shoulders. Picking up the brush, she rakes it through her golden strands, smoothing them out until they hang long and straight down to the middle of her back. With shaking fingers, she lays the brush back down and runs her hand over her stomach. Water falls off her hair in shimmering droplets onto the tile floor behind her. Those are the tears she refuses to shed.

Another wave of nausea hits and Annie rushes to the toilet, leaning forward just as her insides find their way out. When finished, she pulls the towel off the floor and wraps it around her trembling body.

Stepping into her closet, Annie glances at her clothes and sighs. Today is the first day of school, her senior year. Today is exciting.

Today *was* exciting.

Sinking down onto the floor, Annie leans her head against the wall. Her mind drifts to the test buried in the trashcan. One little stick that changes everything; just two small pink lines is all it took.

"Annie!"

The call from her mother pierces Annie's thoughts, and with a sigh, she pushes to her feet and dresses quickly: jeans and a plain white t-shirt, boring and bland so she won't stand out.

"Annie!" her mother calls again.

"Coming!" she calls back. Her voice comes out angrily, but she doesn't mean it. Mostly she's just tired.

Quickly weaving her hair into a long braid that hangs down her back, Annie glances again at the mirror. Soft, blue eyes look back at her, and they tell the story. Squeezing them shut, she takes a deep breath.

"They can't know," she whispers. "No one can know."

"Anastasia!" This time it's her mother's turn to sound angry. Annie grabs her bag and her phone, and then quietly makes her way down the stairs. When she enters the kitchen, she feels her grandmother's stare drilling a hole through the air between them. Glancing up, she briefly makes eye contact, then shifts her eyes away, reaching up to smooth her still-damp hair.

"Baba is staring at me again," she murmurs to her mom. Nina glances over her daughter's shoulder at her mother sitting tall and stern in the corner.

"Well," she answers, raising one eyebrow, "if you'd talk to her every once in awhile maybe she wouldn't have to stare at you like that." Nina's accented English comes out thick.

"Whatever," Annie mutters. Nina tosses a wary glance at her daughter, then pushes a bowl in her direction.

"Eat your breakfast before it's spoiled," she says.

Annie looks down at her feet and doesn't see the way her mother looks at her, full of longing, wishing she knew and understood her daughter.

"I'm not hungry," Annie says, biting her lip to keep it from quivering. Her stomach churns at the bowl of *kasha*, a sticky oatmeal that her mother insists on serving her because "*it'll make your bones thick.*"

"Of course you are hungry," Nina responds with a tight-lipped smile. "It will make your bones thick and your brain strong."

Annie flops into the chair and shovels three large bites into her mouth. With a gag, she manages to swallow half of it before spitting the rest out.

"Oy, *Nastia*! What is the matter?" Nina tosses a towel at her daughter who wipes her mouth with trembling hands. Pushing back from the table, Annie grabs her book bag and heads for the door.

"My name is Annie!" she barks over her shoulder before stepping out and slamming the door behind her. Drawing a deep, shaking breath, she takes in the sights around her. Their small townhouse sits nestled in a thick, Tennessee suburb just outside of Knoxville. Low lying fog hangs all around her, like the sky is constantly fighting off tears. The last heat of summer causes mountain moisture to kiss her skin and send shivers down her legs. She reaches into her bag and pulls out her phone, the screen lighting up and framing her pale face. She punches at the last number dialed—the only number she's dialed in weeks.

"Hey," she says, the phone pressed tight against her ear. "Can you come get me?" She forces back the lump in her throat. "Yeah I'm fine," she says, pushing her mouth into an insincere smile and blinking hard.

# NINA

*"A dream is wandering at night,*
*A nap is following his way.*
*A dream is asking, 'Dear friend,*
*Where shall we now stay?'"*
Russian lullaby

Nina stands still for a moment, staring blankly at the table in front of her. Her daughter's last words roll through her head. "*My name is Annie!*"

Swiping a weary hand over her eyes, she pushes herself back from the table, grabbing the discarded bowl of *kasha* and heading to the sink. She can feel her mother's eyes piercing through the room.

"I don't want to talk, Mama. Please. *Ne nado*," Nina says, immediately flipping back to the language of her youth, the words flowing over and off her tongue like a comfortable friend.

"What did I say?" Her mother's words are braided with accusation, the pointed look in her eyes further exacerbating Nina.

"Oh, Mama, not now," she says, her words laced with fatigue.

"If not now, then when?" Elizaveta Andreyevna squeezes her hands tight in her lap, pursing her lips at her daughter's admonition. "I am an old woman," she says, letting the hurt permeate her words. "I could die any moment, so I cannot wait to say things." Leaning back, Elizaveta smooths her skirt out over her legs.

"Besides," she murmurs. "I *didn't* say anything...but if I was going to say something, I would say you shouldn't let your daughter speak to you that way. And what is this 'Annie'? Such a crude sounding name for a girl."

Elizaveta goes on muttering while Nina finishes cleaning the kitchen. She tunes out her mother, a skill she's long since mastered, but the few words she ingests kick around in her head. She frequently hears this complaint from her mother, and it always sends her back to the same memory.

It was six years ago, when Annie was eleven, that she'd barged through the front door of their home, tears streaming down her face.

"I don't ever want to be called Nastia again!" she'd sobbed, flopping onto the couch with all the drama a preteen could muster.

Nina sat by her daughter that day, letting her cry all her tears dry. She'd stroked her hair and whispered soft words of comfort in her beloved Russian language. She quietly sang her the lullaby that her own mother had sung when Nina was just a child, humming it in the still spaces of the night when Nina couldn't sleep:

> *A dream is wandering at night,*
> *A nap is following his way.*
> *A dream is asking, "Dear friend,*
> *Where shall we now stay?"*

> *"Where the house is warm,*
> *Where the baby is small.*
> *There, there we will stay,*
> *Lull and hush the baby-doll."*

"They were all making fun of me," Annie sobbed, shaking off her mother's gentle words. "They called me 'Nasty.' They said I'm a nasty girl because my name means nasty. Mama, please," she sat up and stared hard into her mother's eyes, the tears gleaming bright on her soft skin. "Please don't call me Nastia ever again. I don't like it. I don't want that name."

"Okay, I will call you Anastasia, then," Nina said with a gentle smile, but Annie shook her head.

"No," she replied, stubbornness setting tight into her jaw. "That name is too Russian. You can call me Annie. That's my new name."

"But my darling," Nina crooned. Annie pushed away from her mom and stood up.

"No. My name is Annie from now on. I am an American girl, and I want an American name." Turning on her heel, she'd run from the room, stomping up the stairs and slamming her bedroom door so loudly that Elizaveta had hurried from her own room clutching her chest.

"Is the house falling down?" Elizaveta had asked, for of course she was always certain that doom awaited them in this adopted country.

Pinching the bridge of her nose, Nina suppresses a smile at the memory. Her mother and her daughter share a flair for the dramatic, despite their continual insistence that they have no common traits.

"And now you laugh at me," Elizaveta grumbles, reaching up to smooth her silver grey hair back out of her pinched eyes. At ninety years old, Elizaveta has a weathered face, coarse and wrinkled. She bears a hard look about her, mouth drawn down and eyes constantly revealing deep sadness. There's something hidden behind those eyes—something that Nina has spent a lifetime trying to figure out.

Shaking her head, Nina turns back to her mother. "I'm not laughing at you, Mama," she says gently. "I'm just...remembering something."

Elizaveta leans forward and slowly, gingerly, pushes to her feet. She stands silently for a moment, willing her legs to hold her broad frame steady. Her hand trembles on top of her cane as she leans heavily into the polished wood. She shifts her gaze to her daughter's face.

"Remembering is dangerous," she says, her voice a whisper.

# ANNIE

Annie leans her head back against the seat, her icy cold hands clenched in her lap. Toby fiddles with the radio as he navigates his car up and down the hilly back roads. He glances over at Annie and takes in the sight of her. She looks small, tucked into the ripped leather seat as though she hopes it might swallow her up.

"You okay?" he asks. The question sounds awkward coming from him. He isn't usually one for small talk—it makes him uncomfortable.

"Fine," she answers. "Just tired. And sick of dealing with my mom and crazy grandmother."

Toby offers a lopsided grin. "Rough morning?" he asks. He pulls out a pack of Marlboros from the console and holds the box up facing her with one raised eyebrow. Annie shakes her head, the scent of the unlit cigarettes making her stomach turn. Toby shrugs and drops the box back into the cup holder between them. His sandy blond hair falls around his ears, wet at the tips. Annie wants to reach up and run her hand through his hair, but given the new circumstances she feels awkward and uncomfortable. The secret she holds has already opened up a chasm between her and everyone else.

"You know, mothers usually love me," Toby says sticking a cigarette between his lips. "I could stop by and turn on the Toby charm. I bet your grandmother would dig it."

Annie offers him a small smile and shakes her head. "You haven't met *my* grandmother," she answers.

Toby sighs and pulls up to a stop sign. He lights his cigarette, squinting at Annie as smoke unfurls from the orange tip. She rolls down the window to let it escape.

"Seriously," he says, exhaling heavily. Smoke creates a haze between them and Annie swallows hard against the bile building in the back of her throat. "We've been together for six months. You ever gonna introduce me?"

Annie leans the side of her head against the seat and looks back into his bright blue eyes. He has the type of look she imagines her mom would appreciate. He's tall and thin, clean cut, but not too pretty. He's fiercely independent, much like Nina. He moved out of his house the day he graduated high school and has been supporting himself ever since. Of course, his lack of education is a strike against him that Annie knows can't be overcome, and so she must protect him...protect *them*.

"I..."Annie's voice falters. She clears her throat. "I just like to keep my home life as far away from the rest of the world as I can."

Toby glances out the windshield, thinking briefly before answering. "Sure. Whatever." He inhales deeply and pushes his foot down on the gas, taking a sharp turn as he crests the hill overlooking Annie's school. He's frustrated, and this frustrates Annie.

"You don't understand," she mutters, turning her face away from him.

"You're right," Toby says, pulling the car into the parking lot. "I don't understand because you won't explain it to me. All you've told me is that your mom is controlling and your grandmother is a crazy Russian." He puts the car in park and leans back taking one more drag on his cigarette before flicking it out of the window.

Annie closes her eyes and takes in a few deep breaths, a

wave of nausea rolling over her once again. Toby narrows his eyes and shakes his head.

"I gotta get to work," he says. Annie pushes the door open and steps out. She watches as Toby squeals the tires and peels out of the parking lot.

# NINA

*Moscow! You, with your concrete walls;*
*I hear your cry, but I cannot answer.*
*Still, I haven't forgotten.*

M ama?" Nina calls out from the doorway. "Your doctor's appointment is in twenty minutes; we're going to be late!"

A few minutes later, Elizaveta swings the door wide and steps into the hallway. Nina suppresses a cough at the intense odor of perfume as she takes in the sight of her mother. Elizaveta has put on her "going out" dress, the one she saves for leaving the house. The dress engulfs her, hanging to just above her ankles. Nina stifles a smile at the bright red flowers that adorn the dress, standing out against the dark, navy fabric. As her mother has aged, the placement of the flowers has begun highlighting her sagging chest in ways that are more comical than flattering. Nina and Annie both tried giving her different dresses, but Elizaveta staunchly refuses any offer of new clothing.

"Psh!" she scoffed the last time Nina brought home new clothes for her to try. "Russians do not need to fill their closets the way that Americans do. I am perfectly fine with the clothes that I have. Why would I need such excess?"

Taking in a deep breath, Nina reaches out her hand to

steady her mother's shaking frame. Grabbing Elizaveta's elbow, Nina guides her toward the back door, her mother's shuffled steps painfully slow.

"I'm not a child, *dochen'ka*," Elizaveta snaps, pulling her arm away. "I can walk on my own."

Nina drops her hands to her side. "I know that," she says, fighting to mask the hurt in her voice. "It's just that we need to move a little faster."

"Oy," Elizaveta replies with a wave of the hand. "The doctor will wait. Americans are always in a hurry. Everyone wants to rush from one moment to the next. This country needs to slow down."

Nina draws in a deep breath. It's been more than a decade since her mother moved to America, into her home, and she's found daily reasons to complain about this new land. At first it made Nina laugh listening her rant on and on about the excessive capitalism and overwhelming American way of life, but it quickly began to wear on her patience.

"And please do not drive so close to the edge of the road, *Ninochka*," Elizaveta mutters on. "Last week, you nearly flung me off the side of a cliff when we turned a corner."

Nina slowly lets the air out of her lungs. Elizaveta watches her through narrowed eyes.

"Okay, Mama." Nina says, a forced cheeriness raising the pitch of her voice.

As quickly as they can, the two women make it to the car. Nina helps her mother buckle her seatbelt, and then she slowly backs down the driveway. Pulling out onto the road, she takes in the sights before them. The fog lies low today, shadowing the top half of the trees. It makes the path before them look mysterious and alive, as though an adventure waits on the other side of the haze. Nina sighs happily. The view from their little home at the top of a hill never ceases to amaze her. It is a haven, an oasis after all those years growing up in the bowels of Moscow.

To calm her mother's frayed nerves, Nina pushes play on the stereo system and the sounds of Tchaikovsky's *Eugene Onegin* fill the car, the soaring vibrato of the soprano singing the famous Letter Scene snaking its way beneath Nina's skin. She glances at her mother and observes the way that Elizaveta's eyes close and her mouth moves with the words. Whenever Nina questions her mother's ability to love, she simply plays Tchaikovsky and reminds herself that somewhere under Elizaveta's tough exterior is a woman who feels deeply.

The car ride is short, and they soon arrive at the doctor's clinic nestled in a long strip-mall. Nina slows to a stop, parking in the closest open spot. She takes in a deep breath and checks herself quickly in the rear-view mirror before pushing open her door and walking to the other side of the car where Elizaveta sits quietly in her seat, eyes still closed, a small smile having turned up her thin lips.

"Mama?" Nina asks, touching her mother lightly on the shoulder. Elizaveta jumps and turns to look at her daughter.

"Do not scare me like that!" she exclaims. Nina bites back a laugh. She reaches in to help her mother stand, but Elizaveta refuses to take her daughter's hand. She slowly pushes to her feet, gripping the side of the car. When she finally straightens up, she looks up at Nina proudly. Nina steps to the side and lets her mother shuffle independently to the front door. The two women walk into the waiting room, and Nina approaches the front desk.

"We're here to see Dr. Shevchenko," she says. The receptionist glances up, peering out at them through black lined eyes. Her hair hangs long and shiny over slender shoulders. She's wearing a tank top that reveals a large tattoo covering her shoulder. Elizaveta clucks her tongue.

"Mama," Nina whispers. She offers a small smile to the girl behind the counter.

"He'll be right with you," the girl answers with a slight roll of her eyes. Nina bites her lip to keep from clucking her own tongue.

Elizaveta shuffles to a chair in the corner and sinks into it. She rests her hands on her cane in front of her while staring at the receptionist.

"Why does she paint on herself like that?" she asks. "It's crass. And what is it supposed to be? Is it a flower? Or is it a clown? I can't tell."

Nina picks up a magazine and tunes Elizaveta out. She pretends to read, but really she's thinking about all the years she spent trying to understand her mother. They were years of silence in a world that bustled with energy. Staring at a picture of some movie star whose name she doesn't care to remember, Nina lets her mind drift back to the day she told her mother she was moving to America.

"You will end up begging for food on the street," Elizaveta had sniffed the morning that Nina had informed her of the decision to marry an American man and leave the country of her youth. "That man will abandon you, and you will have to live alone under a bridge. With the cats."

It was 1985, and Nina was twenty years old. She'd met Andrew when he visited Moscow as a student from an American university. He was a teacher of Slavic history in America, so he'd come to Moscow with a language immersion program. Nina was also a student at the university, trying hard to wrap her mouth around the English language, the beautiful, round sounds so different from her native dialogue. When Andrew showed up with his bright blonde curls and perfect white teeth, something stirred inside Nina, something that she realized later had been there all along, waiting for her to discover it. She suddenly felt a deep desire for adventure. While she'd always been curious about America with its endless supply of blue jeans and glamorous movie stars, she really knew nothing about the strange land across the ocean.

"Capitalists are not trustworthy," she'd heard all her life.

"They worship money, and this makes them greedy, self indulgent, and dangerous."

She heard whispers on the street, the wagging tongues of the generation before her hissing out stories of traitorous Soviets who immigrated to America only to be robbed and left for dead under bridges. "You go to America, and you will die sad and alone," they whispered, eyes darting left to right as they acknowledged the one thing that wasn't to be mentioned, the stain running through the undercurrent of the Soviet utopia—people were leaving.

That defectors would die sad and alone was the caution she heard most frequently from the suspicious elders on the streets. Even her mother whispered the words when they were home alone, as though the walls had ears and would squire her forbidden warning into the public square for all to hear. Her mama liked to add on the part about cats, as if somehow *that* would make the American experience so much more demeaning.

But Andrew changed all that. He was strong and self aware, completely confident in himself in a way that was different from the boys she had grown up with. Nina would steal glances at him when she thought he wasn't looking, the sight of this tall American so strange against the backdrop of her university. He stood out against the cracked walls like a vision of perfection in a flawed painting. Nina stared furtively at him, trying to be discreet, and marveled at the way he worked to speak and understand her language. He seemed genuinely interested in learning the nuances of this foreign land, and when he spoke, she felt her heartbeat quicken as he tried to pull together his Russian sentences with the proper case endings. For weeks after he first arrived, Nina was careful to sidestep him and the other Americans with him whenever they happened to share a corridor. She tried to be invisible, a silent observer of the foreigners that she was supposed to fear, but instead found fascinating.

Ultimately, her attempt at invisibility failed due to Andrew's natural curiosity and her paper-thin shield. It was the
magazine *Noviy Mir*, New World, that brought them together,
or it was the appearance of *Noviy Mir* at any rate. The quintes-
sential Russian journal read by Soviet students was ultimately,
and perhaps ironically, the catalyst for shooting her life onto a
brand new trajectory.

Nina was leaning against the wall that day as she waited
for her friend Tamara after classes and had pulled out the latest, tattered issue of *Noviy Mir*, slowly opening it up so that she
didn't give away what was hidden. Tucked inside the journal
was the real magic, the secret she and several of her friends
were concealing. The pages were worn, the print small, but
Nina didn't care, because those words made her feel truly alive.
On that particular day, Nina was reading Vladimir Nabokov's
*The Gift*. Tucking the printed pages into the magazine was
the perfect ruse, sure to keep Nina off the radar of sharp-eyed
teachers. So many of them were sold out to the Soviet cause,
completely unaware that she and her peers were looking beyond the propaganda and seeking out answers to life beyond
what had been drilled into them.

It wasn't her first banned book. Nina had recently finished
reading a tattered copy of Bulgakov's *The Master and Margarita*
and, completely baffled by the confusing and wild tale, found
herself with an appetite for more. Nina wanted some justi-
fication of love, since her mother insisted that such a thing
was only a flighty instinct that chased the uneducated. After a
morning spent translating passages from her Russian textbook
into English, sweating over the declensions, and trying once
again to remember what constituted a present perfect partici-
ple, Nina found solace in this simple act of rebellion.

She whispered Nabokov's words that morning, letting
them glide over her tongue as she attempted to understand
and dissect their meaning. She had never been the smartest
in her class, constantly a disappointment to both her teachers

and her mother as she received only average marks in school. Nabokov's prose didn't make sense to her, but there was something magically romantic about it, and so she read the sentences over and over, hoping someday to tap into the hidden meaning that eluded her.

"I didn't realize *Noviy Mir* was so compelling."

She'd jumped at the sound of his voice, nearly letting the magazine slip from her hands.

"Yes," she answered, almost in a whisper, the word feeling as foreign as it sounded slipping past her parted lips. She fumbled with the pages, slamming them shut and pulling the magazine to her chest, squelching the forbidden words, holding her secret close.

Andrew smiled, and Nina's knees shook. "I'm Andrew Jamieson," he said, reaching out his hand. She stared at it a moment before slipping her hand into his in an awkward shake.

"Nina," she replied. And that was the beginning. It was innocuous and small, not at all glamorous like she imagined interactions must normally be between worldly-wise Americans. But it was the beginning, and it was a nice beginning as stories go.

For two weeks it became their unspoken habit. Nina stood in the corridor pretending to read *Noviy Mir*, and Andrew walked by, pretending that it was a coincidence to run into her. Finally, he asked her if they could take a walk outside the grey walls of the foreign language university. He asked, and Nina's heart soared, but then it sank. To walk on the streets with this man, this *American* man, was not something that would be looked upon favorably. She could just hear the tongues of the babushkas on the sidewalk clucking as she walked past with the tall American and his perfect teeth, voice a little too loud as he tried to carry on a conversation in Russian. She'd looked into his eyes in that moment, at war with herself for both wanting and fearing being alone with him.

But all she'd seen was an eagerness that no one had ever

shown her before. Andrew made her want to be brave, and bravery didn't seem so terrible. With the pages of banned books seared into her conscience, Nina made the only choice that seemed natural. She said yes.

She'd gone for a walk with him that day, a walk that ended in a long and passionate kiss. That was the walk that tore through her heart, through all that she'd ever known or believed or understood. It was the walk that made her think leaving the borders of the concrete prison that was Moscow might be within reach.

At the end of another month, the end of weeks of walks, of stolen kisses in dark corners of the city where the prying, watchful eyes of her Soviet comrades couldn't chastise her for such foolishness, Andrew asked the question that exploded with possibility.

"Would you like to come to America?" he asked, his face close to hers, hot breath on her cheek. "You could come and study English there, and I could show you my country the way that you've shown me yours." She'd pulled back in surprise, locking eyes with this man who had to be dangerous. He was an American, after all.

But Andrew wasn't a threat. He was safe, and so that day, hidden in an alley in Moscow, in the district outside Mitino where her mother would be waiting for her in their tiny apartment, Nina had made the choice to deny her birth country and enter the new and foreign world that belonged to a man that she felt certain she could eventually love. It was the ultimate act of rebellion, not against her country, but against her mother.

Shaking herself from the memory, Nina lays the magazine back down on the table in front of her. Impulse had been the driving force of her youth, but it had definitely given her some great memories. Of course it wasn't so easy as hopping on a plane to America back then. Andrew had to marry her in order to bring her back, a sacrifice more than he'd bargained for in that passionate moment on the street. And with the paperwork and mandatory waiting period, it had been a full year before she could leave—a year of living in tension with her mother. There were long nights of arguing and tears before Elizaveta finally gave up, laying on the guilt as thick as fresh honey as she walked Nina to the minister's office to sign the papers giving her permission to marry a foreigner.

Nina chuckles and shakes her head. Impulse may have brought her here, but it hadn't turned out quite so horribly as had been predicted all those years ago. Of course, her marriage to Andrew hadn't lasted, just as her mother had told her it wouldn't, but there had been a mutual respect between the two of them that closely resembled love for a little while, and that was enough for Nina. She had also made sure she never owned a single cat in the years since she arrived.

"Ms. Mishurova?"

Nina looks up at the young nurse trying desperately to pronounce her mother's name. She turns to Elizaveta and finds her deep in thought, a lost and pained look masking her pinched face.

"Mama?" Nina touches her mother's arm. Elizaveta pulls herself free from the hidden visions of her mind. "The doctor is ready to see you now."

Elizaveta pushes herself to a stand and shuffles to the nurse standing at the door. Nina stands up behind her, studying her mother quietly. She senses a change, a softening in Elizaveta that she's longed for all her life. Her mother wants to tell her something, and after all these years of waiting, Nina is suddenly unsure if she's ready to hear it at all.

# ELIZAVETA

*The trees whisper nightmares.*

We settle back into the car after meeting with the doctor, a handsome Russian man with a voice that melts into his words like warm honey. I gave Nina several pointed looks while we were in the office, willing her to look at him and see what has been so obvious to me from the first time I met him.

I watch her again now, nervously fiddling with the mirrors, avoiding meeting my eyes. She flips on the radio, filling the car with the sounds of some American band that seems to have recorded their music inside a tin can. She taps her fingers on the steering wheel as she turns her vehicle down the winding road that will lead us back to the house.

I take in the blurry image of the woman I raised and feel a pang of remorse at years that have grown between us, pushing us away from one another to the point it seems impossible to ever bridge the gap. I lean back and think of my own mother, the way she used to stroke my hair back off my forehead and whisper prayers in my ear at night before bed. I remember the sound of Mama reading in the darkness, her voice barely above a whisper because the words she read were dangerous. They were words of freedom, the lyrical prose of those who would dare speak against oppression. My mama whispered those hallowed words, reading them from a small book by the light of the moon then hiding them in the folds of her skirt when the protection of the darkness fled with the sun.

I wish my daughter held such memories, but I know they aren't there. Something inside me broke a long time ago, and it erected a wall that separates me from everyone else. I grip the seat belt across my chest and turn my face away from her toward the window, trying to shake the images that threaten to spill from my memory.

The horizon buzzes by the car faster and faster as we pick up speed. We crest a hill before the nose of the car tilts back downward, a thin back road leading us deeper into the surrounding trees. They are still thick and green, not yet thinned out by the chill of the winter. They form a canopy that hovers over us on either side, whipping by the window and leaving me off balance.

This stretch of road is the most frightening part of the drive. It reminds me of the place I long to forget completely. The earthy scent of the wooded landscape wars to upend the memories I so carefully curated those years I lived in Moscow. I replaced fresh air and open spaces with concrete buildings and busy sidewalks so that I could feel safe. This place that Nina has made her home is not a haven, not for me. It is too open, too fresh. I feel exposed between these leafy walls. They are too much like my nightmares.

"I'm going to drop you at home and get you settled before I go back to work, okay Mama?" Nina says. She glances at me out of the corner of her eye. I nod once so she knows I heard her, then lean my head back against the seat and close my eyes.

Mama's face floods my mind the moment I begin to drift off, and I snap my eyes back open, looking around wildly. The sound of tires spinning on gravel jars my senses as I quickly reorient myself to my surroundings. It's been happening more lately. When I close my eyes, I see her—my mother. She looks back at me, but I cannot read the expression on her face. I never look at her closely enough to know what she thinks or how she feels. I pull myself away as quickly as possible, wrestling the memories back to the place I tucked them away so long ago. But they're chasing me, these visions, and the pursuit leaves my nerves frayed.

"Here we are," Nina says. Her voice is bright, her words infused with a forced cheeriness. I glance up at the small home that I now share with Nina and Annie, and I'm momentarily overwhelmed with emotion.

When I moved here, my plan was to redeem the years I had lost with Nina. I didn't really understand that you can never get the past back. It simply trails behind you like the tail of the moon's reflection on the surface of a pond. You can neither change the past nor hide it. You can only try to run away from it.

Nina opens my door, and I jump. Looking up, I blink at the sight of her face in the mid-morning sunshine. She helps me to my feet and steadies me, then steps back and lets me shuffle past on my own, her arms hanging awkwardly by her side. We enter through the front door, and I inch into the kitchen, then stop and turn back to her.

Nina steps to the fridge and opens it up. "There is some lunch meat in here, Mama," she says. "And we still have apples and oranges. Will that do for your lunch?"

I nod my head in response. Nina straightens up, turning to look at me. She's still small and thin, age having found favor with her over the years. Her hair hangs thick over narrow shoulders. She shifts from one foot to the other, then takes in a deep breath.

"Okay," she says, clasping her hands together. "You'll be alright then?"

I nod quietly. I want to offer her some kind of smile or encouragement, but words get locked up on my tongue, an occurrence that's happened more frequently over the last several months. Nina glances at her watch, then looks back at me and clears her throat.

"I've got to go," she says. She turns to leave and calls over her shoulder. "I'll see you tonight!"

And then she's gone. I am alone again, and the silence wraps around me like a fist, slowly and methodically squeezing the breath right out of my lungs.

# ANNIE

Annie slouches down in the back of the room, her sweatshirt pulled tight around narrow shoulders. The teacher drones on and on about school policies and procedures, but Annie has long since tuned him out. All she can think about is how hungry she is. An hour ago, the thought of food made her stomach turn, and now she would eat cardboard to settle the hollow feeling inside.

"Pull out your student manuals and read through them for the remainder of the period," the teacher says. What was his name? She hadn't been paying attention when he introduced himself. She opens the manual to page one and tries to focus on the words, but they all seem to swim together. Reaching into her backpack, Annie grabs a pencil and does the one thing that soothes her.

Moving her hand in the slightest of strokes over the page, she lets the calming rhythm of the pencil ease the tension in her back and neck. She doesn't know what she's drawing. She never does when she begins. She just lets her fingers move, and when they stop she can see the results.

The noises of the room begin to fade, and her intense hunger subsides as the pencil moves slowly, up and down, across the page, dark shades here, and the wisp of a shape there. The minutes tick by, but Annie doesn't notice. She doesn't think about anything. She just draws.

She jumps when the bell rings. The boy sitting next to her snickers. Sliding out of his seat, he glances over her shoulder.

"Someone you know?" he asks. Annie snaps the book shut, hiding the picture she hadn't even had a chance to study yet. He raises his eyebrows and holds up his hands in mock surrender.

"Sorry," he says, a wry grin spreading across his face.

"Forget about it," Annie mumbles. She shoves the manual into her backpack and stands up. The room begins to spin, so she grabs the desk to steady herself.

"You okay?" the boy asks. Annie glances at him and blinks hard. She nods her head as everything slowly settles.

Moving quickly, she heads for the door. The boy catches up with her.

"I'm James," he says. "I'm new here. My dad got a transfer from Milwaukee if you can believe it. Senior year, and I'm starting a new school."

Annie doesn't respond, mainly because she isn't used to anyone talking to her. She prefers anonymity. She hasn't had a real conversation with anyone besides Toby in a long time.

"So...do you talk, or are you mute?" James asks, raising one eyebrow. Annie sighs.

"I'm Annie," she says. Her voice catches in the din of the bustling hallway, and she wonders if he even heard her. She can feel him grinning beside her, though, so she turns and looks at him briefly.

"Hi, Annie," he says, holding out his hand. She takes it hesitantly. "You should keep drawing," he continues with a grin. "You're good at it."

He turns and disappears into the throng of students hustling through the halls, all trying to find their second period. Annie pulls her backpack off her shoulders and digs out the manual. She opens to the first page and studies her picture carefully.

It's a picture of a little girl sitting by a lake. Ripples of water seem to dance in the invisible breeze. Her face is turned up toward the sun, a small smile pushing her lips upward. She has her knees pulled to her chest, her arms wrapped around her legs. Between her fingers, she holds a small flower. Annie stares at it for a long minute until the bell breaks her concentration. She quickly tears the page out of the book and crumbles it up, tossing it in the nearest trashcan.

Turning around, she rushes toward her next class, all the while wondering why on earth she would have drawn a picture of herself as a child.

# NINA

*Winter's fist clamped tight and cold,*
*But still we labored on.*

"Mama, Annie, I'm home!" Nina hangs her coat on the hook by the door and steps into the house. It's quiet. "Mama? Annie?" She walks into the kitchen and flips on the light, then sets the grocery bags heavily on the counter. The countertops are clean, the sink empty. Nina smiles. Her mother cannot stand a dirty kitchen. A dish left in the sink sets Elizaveta's tongue clucking in an almost rhythmic succession. Years ago, before Annie grew sullen and withdrawn, she and Nina would leave dirty dishes strategically placed throughout the house and make a game of how long it would take Elizaveta to find and clean them all. They'd huddle on the corner of the couch, pressing their fists to their mouths to suppress their giggles.

Nina's smile fades. It's been a long time since she laughed with her daughter.

Walking to her mother's room, Nina knocks lightly. "Mama? Are you okay?" she asks.

She turns the knob and pushes open the door. Her mother's room is dim, a small lamp by her bed the only light illuminating the small space. The walls are a pale grey, and above her full size bed Nina hung two large prints of Moscow. The first is an old black and white photo of St. Basil's Cathedral that she'd found at a flea market years after moving to America.

The second is a picture of the street she and her mother lived on for the entirety of her youth. Nina had taken the photo with a small camera that Andrew gave her when he returned to Moscow to marry her. The quality was poor, but it didn't matter. The fuzzy photo matches her memories.

Nina studies the photo, soaking in the sight of the small market that stood on the opposite corner from where she and her mother lived. Hours and hours, the two of them stood in lines at that market, waiting to purchase whatever produce might be available when they reached the front. If Nina closes her eyes, she can still hear the sounds on the street outside her home—the trolleys clanging in the distance, the babushkas on the corners selling headscarves or table linens. Sometimes they'd stand out there with a box of puppies, selling them to anyone who stopped and expressed even the slightest interest. Nina had begged her mother for a puppy when she was younger, gazing longingly at the squirming little balls of fur from the line while her mother grasped her hand.

"Don't be silly, Nina," her mother would chide. "What would we do with a dog? I am working all day, and you are in school. And besides, then we would have to stand in another line just to get food for the dog. I will not stand in more lines."

Nina opens her eyes and stares a moment longer at the picture, crossing her arms tight over her chest. Her childhood memories are comprised of standing next to her mother in lines. She turns to look at Elizaveta who sleeps soundly in her chair in the corner, a book in her lap. Her chin rests on her chest and she breathes slowly.

Nina creeps forward to study her mother more closely. She glances down at the book in Elizaveta's hands and recognizes her mother's scrawling handwriting. It's not a book, but a journal. A pencil lies in the crease. Very slowly, Nina leans forward to study the page. At the top is a picture, small strokes of the pencil form the outline of a fence. Stretching across the top of the fence are circular loops with sharp edges, barbed wire. And between one of the slats of the fence, Nina sees a single eye peering out. She bites her lip as she studies the picture.

It's been years since Nina saw one of her mother's drawings. She didn't even know Elizaveta still put pencil to paper. As a child, she used to watch her mother in fascination when she drew, because she never seemed to realize what she was doing when she began. Peering beneath the small drawing, Nina reads the words her mother has scrawled across the page.

*"My earliest memory is cold. I remember feeling terribly cold all the time. My mother used to tell me to think of warm things, and I would be warm, but it never worked because I didn't know anything but the cold. And I hated it."*

Elizaveta lets out a snore causing Nina to stand up sharply. She quickly backs out of the room and closes the door behind her. Resting her hand on the doorknob, Nina pauses for a moment, ingesting the words she just read. She closes her eyes and her mind drifts to her childhood, to the year when she was seven years old and a particularly cold winter had settled upon Moscow, clamping down on them with an icy fist. Rations were low, and Nina and Elizaveta had to wait in longer lines than usual for whatever produce might be available when they finally got to the front. Her mother always hoped to get some butter, but they could never seem make it to the front of the line before it disappeared. Many evenings, Nina and her mother left the market with nothing more than a bar of soap, a small tin of tea, and maybe a loaf of crusty bread if they were lucky.

"I'm cold, Mama," Nina would whine, pulling against her mother's vice-like grip on her gloved hand.

"It's okay, *Ninochka*," her mother would answer. "You simply have to think of warm things, and you will be warm. Quick, let's think of warm things together." And they'd take turns listing all the warm things they could think of: Fire, borsch, a summer night, a cup of hot *chai*. They'd make their list as the line crawled along, and somehow it had worked—Nina had felt warm.

Or maybe she'd just forgotten the cold.

She pushes herself away from the door and turns toward the stairs. When she reaches the top, she pauses at Annie's door. Nina can hear her daughter moving around in her room and she lifts her hand to knock on the door, then stops, fist poised but unable to initiate the contact. Nina wants to go in, to ask about her first day of school and see how she's doing, but she knows her questions will be met with biting, mono-syllabic answers. She decides to wait until dinnertime to speak with Annie.

Nina walks to her own room and changes quickly out of her work clothes, hanging up her skirt and jacket carefully. She loves her job in the medical clinic. Though she's a disappointment to her mother, her work as a Physician Assistant is fulfilling, and it gives her the flexibility she needs to raise Annie.

"You said you were going to America to become a doctor," her mother had complained when she found out what her daughter did for a living.

"Well, Mama, that was the plan. But plans change. Besides, working as a doctor would have taken me away from Annie, and I didn't want to leave her alone."

"Like I left you alone," Elizaveta had replied.

Nina pads back down the stairs to the kitchen and unloads her groceries. She sets to work cutting vegetables and marinating meat, trying to escape the nagging feeling that something is off in the house. While communication has never been strong between herself and her mother and daughter, lately it's felt even more strained.

"Do you need help?"

Nina looks up to see her mother stepping into the kitchen, back hunched as her feet whisper across the wooden floors. Her grey hair has been smoothed back into a tight bun, and her eyes squint in the bright, overhead lights.

"No, but you can keep me company," Nina answers with a smile. Elizaveta sits in one of the chairs at the counter and looks hard at her daughter. She opens her mouth to speak, then closes it quickly.

Nina puts the vegetables in the skillet and smiles as they sizzle in the oil. "I always loved that sound," she says, glancing at Elizaveta. "I remember listening to you cook when I was little. Something about the sound of vegetables cooking has always made me feel excited." She pinches off a stalk of fresh dill and tosses it into the skillet, inhaling deeply as the comforting aroma fills the room.

Elizaveta's face softens. She remembers those days, too. She can still hear Nina's squeaky voice asking if dinner was almost ready. "It will be ready faster if you help me," Elizaveta would reply, and Nina danced into the kitchen, her blonde curls bouncing with delight. Those were the happier memories, the ones Elizaveta didn't mind falling into. She only wished there were more of them.

"I remember," Elizaveta says. She glances around the kitchen. "Where is Nastia? She should be here helping you."

"It's Annie, Mama," Nina replies with a sigh. She waves her hand. "She's resting in her room. I'm fine down here." But inwardly, Nina knows her mother is right. Annie should be helping. She should be doing more around the house. She should be more present.

"What do you mean, "resting"?" Elizaveta clucks her tongue. "What does that child need to rest from? From thinking? You rest from thinking and you die. No, she should be here in the kitchen helping you."

Nina drops a small pile of chopped carrots and onions into the simmering dish, hoping that if she doesn't respond her mother will grow tired of talking and stop.

Unfazed, Elizaveta shakes her head. "Americans," she mutters. "They want everything easy and fast. Just think of the food they buy! Drive up to a window in your car and someone throws a sandwich at you as you drive by. I don't even think it's real food. It's plastic made to look like food because you don't want to take the time to prepare food the right way—food that was grown in the ground, not made in some laboratory."

"Hey, Mama?" Nina interrupts. "Would you cut up these potatoes for me?" She shoves a pile of potatoes toward her mom and hands her a knife. Elizaveta stops talking and sets to work cutting. Nina pours herself a large glass of Pinot Grigio and bites her lip, not knowing whether to laugh or cry at her mother's rant against the fast food industry. She thinks back to the horrified look on her mother's face the first time she drove her through a McDonald's and has to stifle a chuckle.

"They wrapped this meat in bread and put it in paper, and they want me to eat it?" Elizaveta had asked. "How do you know this is real meat? Really, Nina. I raised you to be a smart girl. How can you trust anyone who instantly hands you food through a window? Especially someone who smiles like that? Why was she smiling at me? Why do people smile so often in this country? How can you know what they're thinking when they constantly smile?"

Glancing at Elizaveta as she cuts the vegetables, Nina shakes her head. As much as her mother rails against American customs, she has a feeling that inwardly Elizaveta is really impressed with it all. Because despite all her complaints, in the eleven years since she moved to the U.S., she's never once asked to go back home.

# ELIZAVETA

*I am the child of a kulak. I am a kulak. No one can ever know.*

You mustn't make a sound," Mama crooned in our ears. "Think of something warm, and you will be warm."

The problem was that we were so young, my little sister and I. We whimpered in the corner of the frigid barracks, the wind howling through the open slats. We didn't even know what warmth was, so we had nothing of which to think. But my older brother remembered warmth, and he would whisper the warm things into the air, then I would try to grab them, hoping they could offer me some comfort.

"Borsch, fire, a summer day in the garden." On and on he'd offer his list, and I would lay my head on Mama's breast and listen to her heart, wondering if life was always this painful.

My papa had gone ahead of us to Siberia, disappearing in the night before I could ever have the chance to memorize his face. They told us to leave all our possessions behind. We were to be relocated along with the other 'kulaks' of the land. I didn't know what it was to be a 'kulak' back then. I just knew it made my father bad—it made me bad.

But Mama was good—at least that's what I believed then. Even though Mama was a 'kulak' like the rest of us, she had a heart that whispered kindness like a litany of grace. Every night, she read to us softly by the moon's light. On nights when the winter clouds snuffed out the moon's light, she simply spoke verses from memory and sang prayers over us all as we shivered beneath her sweet voice. Mama had smuggled one little book out the day we were forced to leave our home and sent to Siberia. It was a forbidden book, this New Testament. It went against everything that Father Lenin had laid out for our country, and Stalin himself would not stand for such rebellious stories. Even at my young age, I understood that mama's whispered words into the icy nights were dangerous. They were not the teachings of a true Soviet.

Mama read until we fell asleep, our stomachs hollow and noses red with cold. But somehow her reading brought the comfort we needed to rest. I think, perhaps, it was Mama's only rebellion in life, and it made her independent.

Of course, it was Mama's hidden book that saved us in the end. It was her book, and it was my skill with a pencil and paper that brought us out of that frozen hell. Mama gave me life twice—first through the natural act of bringing me into this world, and second through her fearlessness in the face of the worst that mankind had to offer. So who is really to blame in the end? Is it Mama, or is it me?

# ANNIE

nnie grabs her notebook and shoves it into her backpack, then pushes out of her seat. She heads out of the freezing room and makes her way to the cafeteria, arms crossed tight over her chest to stave off the frigid blast of the over enthusiastic air conditioning.

"Are they trying to freeze us all out of this God forsaken building?" she mutters as she rushes through the hall, hoping to get her blood circulating enough to feel her feet again.

"Who're you talking to, Picasso?"

Annie turns in surprise. He smiles and lifts his hand in a brief wave.

"What's up," he says with a lopsided grin.

Annie nods slowly. "Um, hi," she replies. She turns and continues walking down the hall. "Please go away," she whispers under her breath. He cocks his head to the side and stares at her as he rushes to catch up.

"Well..." Annie gestures in front of her. "I'm headed to lunch, so..."

"Do you remember me?" he asks, falling into step next to her. Annie sighs.

"Yes. You're the guy in my first period class. John? Jim? Jason?" She looks at him for some help, but he only stares back in amusement. "Well, I remember *you*. I just don't remember your name," she says, cheeks hot.

"James," he responds. "I just wanted to see how long you'd keep guessing."

Annie smiles, despite her annoyance. She shakes her head and tries to toss a glare at James.

"So I guess you probably have a class to go to now, huh?" she asks.

"Oh, no. I'm headed to lunch, too," he responds. "I figured we could keep each other company since I don't know anyone at the school yet, and you sit alone."

"How do you know I sit alone?" Annie asks.

"We have the same lunch period. I just told you that," James says. His eyes sparkle. "The cafeteria isn't that big, Picasso."

"Don't call me Picasso," Annie says. The two step into the cafeteria, the din of 300 students reverberating off concrete walls.

"Why not?" James asks. "I can't get that picture you drew out of my head. It was so lifelike. Where'd you learn to draw like that?"

Annie steps into the line and grabs a tray. She grimaces at the food choices before them: greasy pizza or something resembling chicken and gravy.

"First of all, Picasso was a painter, and I just draw with a pencil. You really can't compare us to one another." She reaches in and grabs the pizza, sliding it on her plate and swallowing hard at the bile already gathering in the back of her throat.

"And I didn't *learn* to draw like that. I just do it. I always have. And I usually don't let anyone see what I draw, so maybe we could stop talking about it."

James lifts his hands in mock surrender. He grabs two slices of pizza, and then slides his grey tray down the line next to Annie's.

"Sorry, Picasso."

Annie looks at him in exasperation. He grins. "I really am sorry, but I've been thinking of you with that name for a week now and it's stuck in my head!"

Annie rolls her eyes and walks to the cash register. She grabs a bottle of water and gives the cashier her student ID number. When she and James have both paid, they make their way to a table in the back corner of the cafeteria.

"You don't *have* to sit with me, you know," Annie says. "I don't mind sitting alone. In fact, I kind of like it," she says pointedly, eyebrows raised. James smiles again, and Annie notices a small dimple on his right cheek. She flushes and looks down quickly.

"Well, maybe I don't like sitting alone, Pic...uh, Annie," he finishes as she tosses him a withering stare. He takes a bite of his pizza, the grease dripping down his fingers. Annie fights a gag and picks up her own piece. It goes limp the second she lifts it off the tray. Her stomach churns and growls at the same time.

"So, Annie isn't your real name, is it?" James asks, wiping his hands and mouth. Annie takes a tiny bite off the end of her pizza and chews carefully.

"What do you mean?" she asks. "It's not a fake name."

"I know," James smirks. "I mean, I heard the teacher call your full name on the first day. Your name's Anastasia."

Annie puts her pizza down and swallows hard. She nods, but doesn't speak.

"Cool name," James says. He takes another bite. Annie looks at him curiously as he chews his food.

"I hate it," she says. She immediately regrets her words because now an explanation will be expected, and she wants to keep her conversation with this boy to a minimum.

"Hate it?" James asks. "Why would you hate it? It's unique and interesting. It's the name of a mysteriously vanished Russian princess. Who wouldn't want a name like that?!"

Annie snorts.

"What?" James asks.

"Well, for starters, Anastasia Romanov didn't mysteriously

vanish. There's actual evidence that she died right there with the rest of her family. I didn't take you for a Disney guy."

James grins and shrugs his shoulders.

"And second, the name Anastasia hasn't made me unique so much as it's made me confusing to people. So I prefer to go by Annie. Just Annie. *Not* Picasso."

"Yeah, well, I got that," James answers. He starts in on his second piece of pizza. Annie looks at her food longingly, wishing it didn't look and taste so unappealing. She takes a long drink from her water bottle to try and quell the hunger that's gnawing at her.

"So what's the real story behind your name, then?" James asks. "How'd your parents settle on it?"

"Not parents," Annie answers. "Just mom. My mom happens to be Russian, thus my Russian princess name." She smiles grimly, her lips spread in a thin, forced line.

"So your dad had no say in the matter?"

"I don't have a dad," Annie says. She picks her pizza up again and forces herself to take another small bite.

"No dad?" James' eyes widen. "So what, were you like miraculously conceived or something?"

Annie rolls her eyes. "My dad died before I was born. It's been just my mom and me my whole life. Nothing miraculous."

Annie puts her pizza down and stares at her plate for a minute. She finally looks up at James who is studying her intently. "I don't usually talk about myself or my family with people," she mutters.

James wipes his hands on his napkin and leans forward, his elbows pressing into the table so that it tips slightly toward him. "No worries," he says. "Your secret's safe with me."

Annie looks at him for a minute, oddly taken with this strange new boy. "So," she says. "What about you?"

"What about me?" James replies.

"What's your story?" she asks.

"Well, *my* story is a sad one—a total conversation killer."

James crumples up his napkin and tosses it on his plate. Annie waits.

"My dad and I moved down here from Milwaukee in July. He got a job transfer, which was fine with me because both of us were ready to leave and start fresh."

Annie looks at him intently. "Start fresh from what?" she asks.

"My mom and sister were killed in a car accident last December. Christmas Day, actually. Not so merry." He offers her an apologetic smile. Annie opens her mouth, but can't think of anything to say so closes it again.

"Yeah, you don't have to say anything," James says. He leans in toward her. "I don't usually talk about my family to people, either," he confesses, the words settling between them into a heavy silence.

Annie stares at her plate and realizes she can't eat any more. The bell rings, and the sound of chairs scraping against the tile floor fill the already noisy room. James stands up and grabs his tray, then reaches for Annie's.

"You done?" he asks. She nods. "Not much of an eater, huh?" he remarks. Annie shrugs.

"The pizza tastes like melted plastic," she says. James grins.

"Totally," he says with a laugh.

Annie picks up her backpack and stands up. The room begins to spin, and she grabs the back of the chair to steady herself.

"You okay?" James asks. He puts down the trays and grabs her elbow. Annie shakes her head and pulls away from him.

"Fine," she says with a thin smile.

"You also get dizzy a lot," James remarks. He picks the trays back up and walks to the trashcan, tossing the contents in, then setting the trays on top. Annie shrugs.

"I probably just have low blood pressure or something," she says. She tries to keep her voice light.

"Yeah," James replies, watching as she moves slowly on her feet. "Probably."

"Well..."Annie says. She glances at the clock. "Guess we better head to class." James nods. He adjusts his backpack on his shoulder and gives her a big grin.

"See you tomorrow, Anastasia," he says with a wink. She opens her mouth to correct him, then closes it again. Somehow, her name coming from his lips sounds nice—pretty, even.

"Tomorrow," she replies. James turns and disappears into the throng of students rushing to class. Annie feels her cell phone buzz in her pocket. She reaches back and pulls it out. Glancing down, she sees the text from Toby.

"*Pick u up today?*" it reads. "*Wanna hang?*"

Annie slowly puts the phone back into her pocket and turns toward her class. She doesn't answer the text.

# NINA

*Autumn buds as
winter shakes off
summer's heat-soaked
kiss.*

Nina leans back in her chair and lets out a long breath, releasing the tension of the morning. Glancing out the window, she takes in the beautiful, late summer day, her mouth turning up in a slight smile. September is looming. After September comes October, and October has been her very favorite time of year since she moved to Tennessee.

Back in Russia, Nina would lament the coming of October because it brought with it the beginnings of blustery winds that led into frigid winters that never seemed to end. But October in Tennessee feels like a gift. The air grows crisp and cool, and the leaves fill in the backdrop making it seem as though the world itself were nothing more than a painting. Nina glances at the wall, at a print that her daughter gave her last year for her birthday.

*"I'm so glad I live in a world where there are Octobers."*

The scrawling letters were painted in vivid hues of red and orange. Nina looks intently at the framed quote, and she feels her happiness melt into an ache. That was the last time it seemed she and her daughter exchanged genuinely caring words with one another.

"It's a quote from the book we're reading in literature class," Annie had said when Nina held up the print and examined it. "We're reading *Anne of Green Gables*, and as soon as I read that line I knew you needed to hang it on your wall."

Nina rubs her eyes. Lately the strain between she and her daughter has grown to the size of a chasm, and she can't figure out why. Annie had always been hard headed, but never insolent and rude. Sometime in the last year, something happened. Nina shakes her head and looks down at the file on the desk in front of her, forcing herself to concentrate on the words. She jumps when her cell phone rings.

"Hello?" She says, tucking the phone between her shoulder and her ear while she folds up the file.

"Nina?"

The voice on the end of the line is warm. Nina immediately recognizes it as Doctor Shevchenko, and her heart flutters in her chest. She's thankful no one else is in the room.

"Yes. Hello! Hi there, yes," she stammers, her cheeks growing warm. There is something about this man that sends her into fits of embarrassment.

"Hello," Dr. Shevchenko replies, an evident grin filling in his greeting. "Do you have a moment?"

"Oh, sure!" Nina tucks her hair behind her ear and sits on the edge of her chair. She immediately jumps back up and walks to the window.

"I'm getting some of the results back from your mother's lab work, and I have a few concerns," he says.

"Concerns?" Nina sits back down slowly.

"It's nothing that will put her in severe danger," he says quickly, "but I need you to be aware of what's going on so you can take a few measures to help her."

"Okay," Nina swallows hard. She rubs her hand over her chest, baffled by the tightness that settled there so quickly.

"The lab results show high cholesterol, which has been the case for some time now, but it has jumped significantly since the last time you had her in. Her blood pressure was up as well, and when I was speaking with her she seemed to be struggling to retrieve a few words."

Nina nods. "Yes, I've noticed that lately." In truth, her mother's slower responses had been a bit of a relief to Nina, so she'd not thought much of it. Now she feels foolish for not being more concerned.

"I don't really think that any of these issues are alarming at this point, but I would like to run a few more tests, and I think we need to change her cholesterol medication. How is her diet?"

Nina closes her eyes and leans her head back. "I think it's okay," she answers. "She doesn't eat vegetables. She says American vegetables taste like they were grown in a lab."

Dr. Shevchenko chuckles on the other end. "Well, she may not be too far off in that assumption," he replies.

"She does like fruit, though." Nina continues. "And she hasn't quit eating meat yet, though she's threatened to do so. She stopped eating chicken about six months ago because it tasted like rubber. I believe her words were, 'If I want to gnaw on a tire, I will go out to the garage and eat the car.'"

Dr. Shevchenko lets out a full laugh this time, and Nina feels her heart skip a beat. Her mother has been seeing this man once a month for six months now, and after spending time in his office the other morning Nina has no plans to change that routine anytime soon.

"Your mother reminds me of my grandmother," he says, his voice laced with a kindness that makes Nina's heart race.

"How so?" Nina asks.

"My grandmother was Russian to her very core. When my parents brought her to the States, she was certain we were all conspiring to lead her to a slow death. The convenience and ease of the country terrified her."

Nina smiles. "Yes, that does sound like my Mama."

"It's understandable how they'd feel that way," he answers. "My grandmother was very secretive. She told us once of the people she knew who disappeared in the middle of the night. Her uncle was sent to a Soviet gulag for telling a joke that offended his neighbor. My babushka was programmed to be suspicious of everyone."

Nina is quiet. She lets his words roll around in her head for a moment, digesting them. She snaps back to reality when his voice pierces her thoughts.

"Nina? Are you still there?"

"Sorry, Dr. Shevchenko," she replies, pulling herself back into the conversation. But as she does so, she grabs a pen and writes on the Steno pad in front of her, *'Soviet gulag.'*

"Please, call me Viktor," he says. His voice sounds different—a little huskier and hesitant. Nina glances up as one of the nurses strolls into the break room.

"Of course," she stammers. "Viktor." She swallows hard, willing her hands to quit trembling. "So would you like me to bring her back in this week?"

Viktor clears his throat. Does he sound embarrassed? "Yes, that would be great," he answers. "Can you get her in on Friday morning?"

Nina nods her head. "Yes, Friday morning will work. Thank you for calling and letting me know."

"Okay, then," Viktor replies. "Until Friday."

"Yes," Nina answers, her voice barely above a whisper. The phone goes quiet, and she sets it down on the table in front of her. She looks back at the note on her Steno pad and feels her mouth go dry as she remembers Viktor's words.

*"My babushka was programmed to be suspicious of every-one."*

Tapping her fingers on the table, Nina lets her mind drift to her childhood. They were years spent in silence, her mother quiet and reserved. If Nina spoke too loudly, her mother jumped and looked around the room. It was as though she was always waiting for someone to enter, but whom, Nina could never quite figure out. When she pried, she was quickly shut down, told that children don't ask questions. One conversation in particular had never left Nina's memory.

She had been thirteen years old, trapped in the hormonal abyss of the teen years, and feeling completely abandoned by her mother. Elizaveta worked long hours as a research technician at a medical lab, which meant Nina was usually on her own for most days, and many evenings as well. One night, she'd waited up for her mother to return home.

"You're still awake?" Elizaveta asked when she walked through the door. "Why do you sit here in the dark, child?"

Nina could still remember the fear that had settled in her stomach when she asked the question that had been bothering her for years.

"Where is my father?" She asked. Elizaveta stopped in the hallway, her eyes frozen as she stared at her daughter. In that brief moment, Nina had seen terror flash through her mother's eyes, but she didn't care. In those days, she didn't care much about how her mother felt.

"Why do you ask?" Elizaveta replied.

"Why *wouldn't* I ask? It seems like something I shouldn't even *have* to ask." Nina crossed her arms and leaned back in the chair she'd been sitting in for hours. She'd arrived home after a day of being taunted by two girls she thought were friends. They'd called her a bastard child, the daughter of a whore who couldn't name her father if she had wanted to. Nina had responded by kicking one of the girls so hard she'd fallen over. A teacher at the school saw the incident and took Nina inside, making her spend the rest of the afternoon standing up in front of the class, her cheeks enflamed with humiliation and anger.

"I am tired, *Ninochka*," Elizaveta had responded. "I will not have this conversation tonight."

"Yes, Mama," Nina hissed. "You will tell me his name at least. I won't go to bed without it."

Elizaveta had drawn herself up and stared hard into her daughter's defiant eyes. "Then I suppose you will not be sleeping tonight, *detka*," she answered back, her voice hard. "I will see you in the morning." Just before she left the room, she turned back to Nina. "Oh, and please, *Ninochka*," she said, her voice humming with frustration. "Put on your *tapochki* or your feet will freeze, and you will get pneumonia and die."

Nina leans back in her chair and rubs her temples. Like any decent Russian mother, hers was always certain they were moments away from pneumonia. Half of Nina's childhood was spent bundling up against the elements, certain that imminent death waited around every icy corner. She takes a deep breath and glances up at the clock. Her break over, she stands and stretches. Nina tears the paper off the pad and sticks it in her pocket, wondering when and if she can make it to the library to do a little research.

# ANNIE

Annie bolts up with a cry. Her foot is pulled back at an angle, the cramp in the back of her leg tying her calf in knots. She slides off the side of the bed and limps around her dark room, taking in deep breaths, trying to loosen up her leg. She jumps when the light flips on.

"Are you okay?" Nina stands in the doorway, her hair askew and eyes squinted as she takes in the sight of her daughter hobbling in circles. Annie's sheets are crumpled in a heap in the middle of the bed, which sits against the wall of a room that's still decorated for a little girl. Nina had been meaning to update Annie's décor, to remove the wallpaper border with pink flowers and paint the walls a more grown up color. But there never seemed to be enough time or money, so she'd continued to push the task off. Now it's almost comical watching her daughter limp around the room, a nearly grown young woman trapped in a little girl's world.

"Fine," Annie says through gritted teeth. She rolls her ankle around feeling the muscle beginning to release tension. "I just got a cramp."

Nina rubs her eyes. She walks to her daughter and grabs her elbow. "Come sit down. Let me look."

"I'm fine, Mom," Annie says, pulling her arm from her mother's grasp. "Geez, it's just a cramp."

Nina drops her hand and swallows hard against the hurt

that threatens to bubble to the surface. Annie sits on the edge of the bed, exhaling loudly.

"Sorry," she mumbles. "I'm not really awake. But I'm fine. It already feels better."

Nina nods and studies her daughter a moment. She reaches out and places the back of her hand on Annie's forehead. For a brief moment, Annie leans into her mother's touch rather than pulling away. "You're very pale these days, my dear," Nina says gently, moving her hand up and over the back of her daughter's head. "Have you been feeling okay?"

Annie softens to her mother's touch, allowing it to comfort her for only a few seconds. She has fleeting memories of being sick as a small child and curling up in Nina's lap. Her mom would croon old Russian folk songs into her ear and rub her face until she fell asleep. It always made her feel better. But this isn't an illness that can be cured. Annie shakes her head and pulls away once again from Nina's touch. She lays slowly back in her bed.

"I'm just tired. There's a lot going on." She glances at her mom and feels panic well up inside as she sees the way Nina studies her features. "I probably need to drink more water or something," Annie says. "I think I'm just dehydrated."

Nina nods. "Yes, that is a possibility, but I wonder if it could be something more. You should come in with me to the office one day this week and we can run a blood test. It could be mono. We should have you checked."

"No!" Annie cries out, then winces. "No, Mom," she repeats, forcing her words to come out softer. "Really. I'm fine. I just need to sleep and stay hydrated. And I probably need more protein. It's okay."

Nina sighs and shakes her head. "I'll get you a glass of water," she murmurs, turning to leave the room.

"Thank you," Annie says, her voice small and soft, hovering in the chasm between them. Nina pauses and studies her daughter for a moment more.

"Of course, *dorogaya*," she says quietly. *My darling.* The term of endearment catches in her throat, and Nina moves quickly from the room to escape the emotion. There's a nagging pit in her stomach that she can't shake. Her daughter is hiding something from her, she can tell. She's spent a lifetime living in the shadow of secrets. She knows them when she sees them. She just wishes she could figure the secrets out.

# ELIZAVETA

*Exile. It is an ugly word, and a wretched way to live.*

I wake with a start and immediately pull the covers up to my chin. I heard a cry. Who was it? There is a knocking sound above me. My eyes shift up and down, left and right, trying to discern what is causing the sound. I hear muffled voices, and I shut my eyes tight, then open them back up. The small night-light in my room casts shadows across the walls, and suddenly I am a child again hovering under the sheets of our small home in Ukraine. The fire in the hearth dances across the dark walls, as I lay warmed from underneath by the oven that mama keeps lit. Dima and Tanya lay beside me on our little bed, and I hear Dima's breathing grow unsteady.

Another knock, louder this time. Peeking out, I see Mama's small, wooden broom leaning stoically against the opposite wall. Next to it is a bucket full of melted snow, which Mama will use tomorrow to clean the floors. There's a small table in front of the fireplace, and a rocking chair sits beside it. Dried mushrooms hang from the ceiling, strung across the room like a banner. We collected them during the autumn months, and now Mama uses them to make soup. She plucks mushrooms from the string each night and peppers them into the pot simmering over the fire, stirring and blending together a meal that may not fully satiate the rumbles of our stomachs, but which is sufficient enough to satisfy us.

Against the wall next to the door is a bench that Papa made for us. It's roughly fit together from pieces of wood that Papa gathered when he splintered the chicken coop after our chickens were killed by wild dogs. It was his way of comforting Mama, who was devastated that we would no longer have eggs to gather for our morning meals. Papa made this bench just tall and wide enough for Mama's *skrynia* to fit beneath, the worn box nestled like a puzzle piece between the bench and the floor. Inside her *skrynia*, Mama keeps all the linens and clothes, and the torn rags she has acquired, which have been wound up into a thick ball. They are the clothes that my brother, sister, and I have grown out of. Mama has torn them into pieces, and from those pieces she will knit us new blankets to keep warm. Before sliding her treasure box into place, Mama always covers it with her embroidered *rushnyky*, the dainty towel that she says makes the house look more like a home.

Our one room cottage sits at the edge of our village, the large trees behind us stretching far beyond what my young mind can comprehend. I don't like the woods behind our little house. Dima told me that Baba Yaga, the witch who steals little children and boils them for supper, lives back there. I make sure to never go beyond the fence line toward those fearsome trees, but stay instead wrapped in the safety of our small garden, which blooms bright and happy with sunflowers in the summertime, their stalks pointing toward the sky like they are asking for a hug from the sun perched high. I love to wander through the *sunyashiki*, and when they bloom full and bright Mama plucks some of them from their stalks and wraps them into a wreath that she sits atop my head like a crown of praise.

Another bump outside our door and my eyes shift across the wooden room, a knot growing in my stomach. I take in all the sights, stitched together in my memory like one of Mama's blankets, and I begin picking at them, unraveling to this particular moment. I'm frightened, and I whimper softly.

"Shh, *dochinka*," Mama whispers in my ear. Her voice sends a shiver down my spine. "Don't move. Don't make a sound." She glances behind her, then pulls up the small icon of Saint Maria holding the Christ child and slips it under my pillow. "You will keep this safe for us," she says. "Keep your head down no matter what happens."

She pushes to a stand and steps away from the bed as I burrow beneath the covers. I can feel the wooden icon beneath my thin pillow, and I'm scared. Peeking one eye over the top of the sheet, I see Mama standing next to the fire. It crackles behind her leaving her petite frame nothing more than a silhouette. She smooths out her dress, the embroidered flowers on her apron glowing in the firelight. Grabbing the headscarf that hangs over the back of her chair, Mama quickly ties it around her head, tucking it behind her ears and covering her thick hair. She looks young, illuminated by the light, her bare face revealing both strength and fear.

Another figure moves toward the door. This one is taller. Stronger. He is my father, though I cannot see his face, and how I wish that I could because that would be the last time I saw him, and I was left with nothing to chase but a shadow.

There are muffled voices at the door, and I hear my Mama draw in a sharp breath, though her shoulders remain high and proud. My brother and sister huddle in the bed next to me. Tanya sits up, and Mama's hand quickly waves her back. Dima pulls our little sister back into his arms and she cries, the sound of her indignation piercing the darkness and filling the shadows.

Papa turns and casts one quick look back at Mama.

"It will be okay," he says. His voice is calm. I may not have a memory of his face, but those final words lock deep inside my consciousness and never leave. They work their way out when the shadows start to close in on me.

Mama kisses her fingers gently, then holds her hand up toward my father. Papa sucks in a deep breath and lets it out long and slow.

"Tell the children I love them," he says, and then he is gone. It's as though he has been swallowed by the fog of the night. His voice hovers over us all, mixing with Tanya's wails and Mama's soft sobs. I take it all in, hiding the memory in the recesses of my heart, not knowing that this one moment in time is only the beginning.

The next morning is when the real nightmare begins. That's the morning that they come back for us. They come when the earth is still covered in a hazy grey from the night, and they stand in the doorway barking orders. They pull all our possessions out, dragging them into the yard and rifling through them callously. Mama's *skrynia* is split wide open, her beautiful towels tossed in the mud. The men laugh as we pick through our things, choosing only what we can carry with us.

"You won't be back, so make sure you take only what is necessary," one of them says. He grins at me, his yellowed teeth jutting out awkwardly, and his eyes revealing pools of deep hatred. He steps back and as he does so, his booted foot comes down on Mama's icon of Saint Maria, splitting the wood down the middle. Throwing his head back, he lets out a howl of laughter, kicking the broken pieces to the side. I watch him as a mixture of fear and intense anger bubble up inside my young chest.

Mama moves quickly, wrapping up the warmest clothes we have in a bed sheet and tying it into a *katomka*, a satchel to hang around Dima's shoulders. She wipes off one of the towels as best she can and fills it with a few of the rags, then ties it around my shoulders.

"Keep this safe, *dorogaya*," she whispers, her eyes shining. "We will need these to stay warm."

She picks up Tanya, who sits whimpering in the doorway of the house, and she nods stoically at the men in our front yard. We follow them past our little home that stands in front of the field where the sunflowers will bloom, but we will not be there to greet them. We follow them past the fence that connects to the barn where our horse, Zvezdochka, watches us with sad eyes. I kiss my hand and hold it out to her, tears pricking my eyelids. She blinks and takes an unsteady step toward me, then stops and watches as we march past.

Our cow, Zorka, stands in the field behind the fence, her head turned toward us as though she is trying to figure out why we are walking away from her at this morning hour, rather than toward her. Her pointed ears flick back as she studies us.

Just as we pass the corner of the barn, Druzhok, Dima's dog, comes bounding forward, his tongue flapping as his ears bounce up and down. His fur is matted, pinned to his sides from an early morning romp in the woods. Druzhok doesn't need to fear Baba Yaga. She only likes to eat children, Dima told me, so dogs are safe. Dima kneels down and holds onto Druzhok, sobbing into his neck as the dog squirms in his arms, his tail tapping against the soft earth. He thinks we're here to play.

"Leave the dog, boy!" the man with the yellow teeth demands. He grabs the *katomka* and pulls hard, yanking Dima to his feet. Druzhok crouches low, growling softly at the man who only grins in return. He turns to his comrades.

"What do you think about having dog for dinner tonight?" he asks. The men laugh, and before we can comprehend what's happening, the man pulls a gun from his waist and shoots Druzhok. My eyes dart to Dima who stands mute, tears still streaking his dirty face, his eyes wide with horror and mouth open in a silent scream.

I squeeze my eyes shut. This isn't real. This didn't happen. This isn't my past. A sound outside my door snaps me out of the hidden memory, and I jump, trying to pull myself back into the present moment. I blink several times, disoriented. I hear water running and want to sit up to see what's making the sound, but my body doesn't move quickly like it did before. Instead, I lick my lips and call out.

"Nina?"

The water turns off, the silence suddenly deafening.

"*Ninochka*?" I call again. I slowly push myself up in the bed, sliding back so my head rests on the headboard. My hands are shaking and I blink heavily, trying to push back the vision of Dima's face. It is too much, this memory—too painful. I swallow hard and jump when my door opens. Nina pushes her head into the room.

"Are you okay, Mama?" she asks. I nod.

"I didn't know who was out there," I answer.

"I'm just getting a glass of water for Annie. Can I get you anything?"

I shake my head. "I'm fine. What's wrong with Nastia?" I ask.

"It's *Annie*, Mama," Nina responds, her voice laced with fatigue. "She woke up with a cramp in her leg. I think she just needs some water."

I narrow my eyes and take in the dim sight of the girl I raised—a girl who is now a woman. It's quiet for a moment before she moves.

"I need to get this up to her," she says softly. "You sure you don't need anything while I'm up?"

I shake my head again. "I'm okay," I answer, but the tremble in my words betrays me. Nina takes another step into the room. I hold up my hand, shaking fingers telling her to stop. "I am fine, *dochka*," I whisper. "I just heard you out there and it startled me. I thought perhaps someone was breaking into the house."

I can almost hear the soft smile that turns her lips upward. Nina thinks me paranoid. My fears humor her, and I let it be so. It's a peace for me to know that she doesn't fear the shadows like I do. As terrible as it was for me the day she left Moscow, I know it was the best thing. She was far away from the dangers, far from the darkness. She was safe.

"Okay, Mama," she says gently. "I'll see you in the morning."

"*Da*," I reply. "In the morning."

Nina closes the door softly, and I listen as her feet pad up the stairs next to my room. The shadows on the wall are taunting me again, only this time with a different memory. They're reminding me of the one thing I wish that I could truly forget— the most dangerous secret of them all. This is the truth I've tried to convince myself was a lie, because if I can believe this part of my story, then perhaps Nina will never find out.

She can never know she's not really my daughter.

# ANNIE

**A**nnie sits down at the table and scans the room. She stares at her salad and the odd blob on the plate beside it that she thinks is supposed to be chicken, and she swallows hard. It's getting a little easier every day to eat, although pregnant or not, she's pretty certain this meal would turn her stomach.

Glancing up again, Annie looks around the room. She tries to do so discreetly, not wanting anyone to notice. With a disappointed sigh, she leans down and pulls the book out of her bag. Today, her Literature class will finish their unit on *Catcher in the Rye*, and not a moment too soon. This hasn't been her favorite novel. She flips it open and leans over the book to read.

" *'Don't ever tell anybody anything. If you do, you start missing everybody.'* "

Annie looks up, and despite her efforts to play it cool, she feels a smile turn her mouth upward. James stands over her glancing at the page. He shifts his eyes to hers. "Sounds like that Holden Caulfield guy is on to something," he says with a smile. He slides into the seat next to her and opens up a brown paper bag.

"You're not really going to eat that stuff, are you?" he asks. Annie shrugs.

"I was planning on it," she replies.

James shakes his head. "Sorry. Wrong answer. The food

here is nasty, so I packed my own, and since it's been grossing me out to see you sit here day after day pretending to eat that stuff, I packed enough for both of us."

Annie feels her cheeks grow hot. "You didn't have to do that," she says.

"I know," James answers. "I wanted to. So here's your chicken salad sandwich and bag of potato chips." He slides the sandwich and chips to her, and she smiles again.

"Isn't this the same thing you ate yesterday?" she asks, pulling the sandwich out of the plastic bag.

"Yes. Yes, it is," James deadpans. "And the day before that, and the day before that."

"How do you eat the same thing over and over like that?"

James shrugs. "My dad hates to cook," he begins. "So rather than get creative in the kitchen he has simply picked his five favorite foods and focused on those: spaghetti and meatballs, potato casserole, baked chicken and rice, hamburgers, and chicken salad. Every Sunday, he picks one of those meals and he makes enough for both of us to eat for the rest of the week. I either have to tolerate eating the same thing over and over, or I have to grocery shop and cook myself, and I haven't gotten tired of it enough to take that drastic measure yet."

Annie nods. "Well, if you could only eat five things, I suppose those are the best you could ask for."

James smiles at her. "Yep," he says. "And every once in a while, Dad will throw in peanut butter and jelly sandwiches, and a box of macaroni and cheese just to mix things up a bit."

Annie laughs. "I've only eaten macaroni and cheese once in my life," she says. James stops mid-bite and looks at her, horrified.

"How is that possible?" he asks. "I thought you were American."

Annie gives him a pointed look. "I am," she retorts. "But my mother and grandmother are Russian, remember? And one of the few things they agree on is that eating American macaroni and cheese is basically the same as dredging the bottom of a trash can for your meal. Their words, not mine."

James shakes his head. "Is there a Russian macaroni and cheese?" he asks.

Annie shrugs. "Sure. We eat macaroni with cottage cheese and a little sugar mixed in. Or sometimes my mother puts a little milk and sugar in with the noodles. We like our macaroni sweet." She offers him an embarrassed grin.

James sighs. "I am going to fix this problem of yours," he says.

Annie shrugs. "Whatever. I don't think I've really missed out on anything. I hardly need Kraft macaroni and cheese to function in life."

James drops his sandwich and leans back, clutching his heart in mock shock. Annie rolls her eyes, chuckling at his overreaction.

"Okay, before I walk away from this table for good, let's change the subject. What do you think of the book?" He thrusts his head toward *Catcher in the Rye*, still open beside her elbow. Annie glances at the book, and then back at him, her nose crinkled.

"I'm not a fan," she replies.

"Why not?" he asks.

"Well, first of all I think it's boring," Annie replies. She pops a chip in her mouth and chews for a moment, studying James' reaction to her statement. "You think I'm wrong," she says after swallowing.

James shrugs. "No, I don't think you're wrong," he replies. "You're entitled to your opinion. I just don't share the same opinion. I think the book is awesome."

Annie bites down into her chicken salad sandwich and chews for a moment before responding. "Okay, so you think it's awesome, and I think it's boring. What am I missing?"

James smiles and leans forward. He runs the back of his

hand over his mouth before speaking. "What's the second reason you don't like the book?" he asks.

"What?"

"You said 'First of all, it's boring.' So what's second?"

Annie puts her sandwich down and picks up the book, flipping through it slowly. "He's whiny," she answers. "He sounds like a brat just throwing a tantrum because life is hard."

James nods and leans back. "I can see how you would think that," he says.

"What does that mean?" Annie asks.

"You're a realist," James answers. "You see things in black and white. Things either are, or they aren't. You're not going to be the kind of person who concocts a fantasy to wish away a portion of her life."

Annie swallows and brushes her palms against her jeans. She blinks hard for a minute, composing herself against his assessment of her. "What makes you think that?" she asks softly.

James smiles, and then shrugs his shoulders again. "I just have a sense," he says. He takes another bite of his sandwich. "I could be wrong, though," he says, his words muffled from the food in his mouth.

"So, what?" Annie asks after a moment of silence. "You're not that way? Are you wishing away your life?" As soon as she says the words, Annie regrets them. She thinks of James' mother and sister, and she wishes she could take her comment back.

"Sorry," she mumbles. "That sounded really insensitive."

James shakes his head. "No, it's okay," he says, but she can hear the tremor in his voice. "It's true. I see Holden's point. Growing up sucks. Facing reality sucks. I wouldn't mind going back to childhood and staying there for a while."

Annie thinks back to her childhood, to the years before her grandmother came when it was just her and mom. She tries to remember a time when she wasn't self-conscious, wasn't constantly afraid of being found a fraud. She can't remember it, though, and this frustrates her.

"Yeah, well you're not so wrong about me," she says to James. She picks up her sandwich and forces herself to take another bite. James was right. Things simply are the way that they are. She glances back at the book and shakes her head. Perhaps she has more in common with Holden than she wants to admit.

They eat in silence for several minutes until they're interrupted by Annie's phone buzzing on the table.

TOBY

Annie snatches the phone, hoping James didn't see the name. She stands up quickly. "I'm just going to take this call," she says. He nods, but doesn't look at her.

Stepping away from the table, she puts the phone up to her ear.

"Hey," she says quietly.

"Hey yourself," Toby answers. "You haven't called me back. Everything cool?" Annie glances over her shoulder at James who is cleaning up his lunch mess. He nods his chin in her direction, and she raises her hand in a self-conscious goodbye.

"Annie?"

"Sorry," she focuses back on the conversation with Toby. "What did you say?"

"I asked if you wanted me to come get you out of school?"

"Get me out of school?" She asks. She glances up at the clock. "I still have three hours left," she says.

"I know," he answers. Annie hears the smile in his voice. "I just thought it might be fun if I busted you out. We could drive up to Lookout Mountain and, you know...*look out*?"

Annie rolls her eyes at his innuendo.

"We haven't really...you know...been together since that one time," Toby continues. "Let's just go have some fun, you know?"

Annie closes her eyes for a brief moment, and pulls in a

deep breath. She prepares to tell Toby no, but then she opens her eyes and catches sight of her book on the table and she remembers James' words. *"You're not the kind of person who concocts a fantasy to wish away a portion of her life."*

And in that split moment, Annie wills herself to imagine that life could be different—that she could be impulsive and fun...and *not* pregnant. She could be the girl who skips school and fools around with her boyfriend.

"Sure, why not," she says. She forces herself to smile as she walks over to the table and gathers her things.

"Wow, really?" Toby asks, the surprise in his voice bringing a genuine smile to her face. "I did *not* think you'd say yes," he says.

"Well, I did," Annie replies. She throws her backpack over her shoulder and gasps as a wave of nausea rolls over her again. And just like that, she remembers what's real. She's pregnant.

"So I just need to clock out here at work, and I can come get you," Toby says. "I'll pick you up in the back parking lot behind the dumpsters?"

Annie takes a deep breath and forces herself to laugh. "Toby!" She says, her voice a little louder than she intended. "I was just kidding. I can't leave. I have a test in 6th period that I can't miss. Sorry, I thought you knew I was joking."

"Oh," Toby says. Annie can hear the frustration in his voice. "Yeah, sure. I knew you were kidding. I mean, God forbid you skip a test, right Annie?"

"Toby," she begins, but he cuts her off.

"No, whatever. It's fine," he says. "It was stupid of me to ask. I knew you'd never go for it."

With a sigh, Annie lowers the phone as the line goes quiet. The bell rings, and she rushes from the cafeteria toward her next class. She glances up at the stairs and notices James watching her from above. She smiles and he smiles back, and suddenly the world feels very, very complicated.

# NINA

*No silence is quite so profound
as that of unspoken words.*

Nina lowers herself down and pulls her sweater tight around her shivering shoulders. "Why do they keep it so icy in here," she murmurs as she slides the book toward her. She glances at the clock on the wall. She has forty-five minutes before she needs to head back to work. The library is quiet this time of day. Except for a young mother with her two children looking calmly at books on the oversized chair in the corner, there is no one here. Nina smiles at the little girl nestled close to her mother's side. A trip to the library used to be Annie's favorite thing as a small child. Every Saturday morning, Annie clamored into the car when Nina said it was time to go get new books, chattering all the way there. When they arrived, Nina reminded her to speak in whispers. Then the two of them would enter into what felt like a holy space and spend the morning wrapped in stories.

Nina loved reading to her daughter in those days. She filled Annie's mind with every whimsical tale that she could find, thrilled at the vast selection available at their fingertips. Her own childhood had been spent reading *Karllson on the Roof* and *Pinocchio*, the only two storybooks her mother could get her hands on. In school, there were other books to read, but nothing like the selection she and Annie found at the local library where a new adventure waited for them every week.

Nina shakes off the memory and flips open the book before her. The trips to the library ended around the time Annie decided to change her name. A lot of things changed those days. Her once happy, excitable daughter had slowly morphed into a despondent, surly teenager. And perhaps it was normal. She knew that these teenage years were meant to be trying. But there seemed to be something more, something lying beneath the surface of it all. If she could just find her way to the source of Annie's anger, perhaps she could find the girl who used to snuggle close and smile wide.

Nina focuses her eyes on the words of the book in front of her, forcing herself back into the present moment. *"The years of terror under Stalin's regime are forever etched in the minds of the men and women who survived them. For many, those are the years that dictated who they would become later on in life. They looked back on the horrors, the unknowns, the hunger and fear, and they determined never to be so vulnerable again. They learned to operate in quiet and communicate in code. They spoke in whispers, because that was the only thing that felt safe."*

Leaning back, Nina runs her fingers through her hair. She thinks back again to the years of her youth, to the many questions that she asked her mother. "Where are my grandparents? Did you have brothers and sisters? Why don't we go to a *dacha* for the summer?"

She peppered her mother with question after question, but the answers never really satisfied.

"Your grandparents died in the war."

"I was an only child."

"We don't need to retreat to a *dacha*. We can stay right here in the city."

Nina finally quit asking her questions, realizing that she would never get more than skeletal answers. But now, as she continues to read, she feels a shiver run up her spine.

*"A large swath of survivors from Stalin's reign were a group known as 'kulaks'. These were wealthy peasants considered enemies of the state. 'Kulaks', or 'kurkuls' in Ukrainian, were a special threat to the communist state. 'Kulaks' were blamed for everything wrong in the USSR, from famines to illnesses, and this justified their treatment by the government."*

Nina takes in a deep breath, a weight settling on her chest. Tucking a bookmark into the pages of the book, Nina slowly pushes to a stand and walks to the front desk to check it out. She fights the urge to drop the book and run. Something tells her that she's following a trail that will open doors. Either that, or she has opened up a can of worms she may never be able to close.

# ANNIE

Annie leans back, settling uncomfortably in the crook of Toby's shoulder. She stares at the screen, completely uninterested in the movie. Toby's hand moves lightly up and down her arm, and she shivers. He leans down and kisses the top of her head. Annie pulls away. Toby sighs and slides his arm out from under her. He grabs the remote and points it at the TV, freezing the frame just as Tom Cruise begins crawling up the outside of a Dubai skyscraper. Annie looks up at him, his eyes extra blue in the glow of the television.

"What's up with you?" he asks.

Annie shifts, swallowing hard. "What do you mean?" she asks.

"I mean, you're, like, a million miles away. You ignore half of my texts; you're apparently repulsed by my touch. I practically had to beg you to come hang out tonight. What's up?"

Annie is silent a minute, then shakes her head. "It's nothing," she lies. "I've just been tired lately."

Toby sighs, running his hand through his hair. "Look," he begins, "I know things...happened a couple of months ago. I'm sorry if you felt pressured, or if you weren't ready, or whatever. I'm not here to make you do stuff you don't wanna do, 'kay? Stop making me feel like such a creep."

Annie feels her cheeks grow hot. Her hand unconscious-

ly drifts to her stomach. It's still early in the pregnancy. She
doesn't have to say anything yet.

"I just..." Toby leans back with a sigh. "I like you, Annie,"
he says. "But if you don't feel the same then you need to just
tell—"

"I'm pregnant," Annie blurts out. She immediately regrets
the words, and the silence that follows her announcement hovers heavily over them. Annie feels like she's standing beneath
a waterfall trying to breathe through a straw. Toby stares at
her, his mouth slightly open, the color slowly draining from
his face. He swallows hard and stands up, walking a few steps
to the kitchen in his tiny apartment. He pulls a beer out of the
mini fridge and pops it open, taking several long gulps. Annie
stares at her hands, now crossed over her flat stomach. She
shouldn't have said anything.

"You're sure?" Toby asks, leaning against the wall. His
broad shoulders slump inside a rumpled white t-shirt that
hangs, untucked, over his baggy jeans. His hand grips the can,
knuckles white.

Annie nods. "I'm sure," she answers. Her voice is timid,
laced with shame.

"When...? Um...how far?"

Annie shrugs. "I guess I'm about two and a half months,"
she says looking up and meeting his eyes. It was only the one
time, an afternoon of passion after a particularly stressful
morning spent deflecting the judgmental eyes of her grandmother. Annie had called Toby that Saturday and asked him to
come pick her up. She told her mom that she was studying with
her friend, Natalie. She didn't even know anyone named Natalie, but that didn't matter. She'd made her mother so jumpy
over the last year that Nina was willing to say yes to almost
anything if it meant avoiding confrontation.

She'd gone to Toby's and let herself be swept away by
what she thought was the perfect rebellion. Sleep with your
hidden boyfriend to get back at your overprotective mother

and tongue-wagging grandmother - it seemed like the perfect assertion of her free will. But afterward, Annie had been overcome with shame. That wasn't how she'd wanted her first time to be. She'd always pictured herself waiting until marriage, feeling as though that would be the perfect gift she could give to the man she loved.

She didn't love Toby. She'd only realized it that day two and a half months ago.

"What're you gonna do?" Toby asks.

The question floats between them and lingers for a moment, whispered words full of weight and meaning. Annie slowly shakes her head. "I don't know yet."

"Have you told anyone?"

"No. Just you." Annie looks up at him, her eyes filling with tears. "I don't know how I can possibly tell my mother this," she whispers. And for the first time since she took the test, she cries. The tears rake their way down her smooth, thin cheeks. Toby takes a step toward her, then stops. Both of them stare at one another, fear weaving its way through the dim room.

"What do I do?" Annie asks.

Toby doesn't answer, and in his silence, Annie realizes what she knew all along. She's alone.

# ELIZAVETA

*Moscow. My heart longs for Moscow.*

I've only ever loved one man. He was a good man, a kind man. I'm certain he would have loved me forever if I hadn't destroyed it all with my lies. But then, what were my options? If I'd been truthful, he never would have even considered me to begin with. And so perhaps he and I were destined to fail.

I tried hard to be the perfect citizen, the upstanding communist that my country dictated. I followed every rule, abandoning anything that would stain the name I created for myself. I enrolled in the Russian National Medical University, easily passing the entrance exams thanks to a natural ability to learn that I had somehow always possessed. I kept my head down, distancing myself from others as much as possible, avoiding study groups and quiet off-to-the-side meetings of students who glanced around furtively as they discussed politics. Everyone was afraid to speak then, not just me. It seemed I was simply better at staying quiet than all the rest.

Pulling myself free from the memories, I shuffle from my room into the kitchen and shake my head at my daughter's carelessness. She was in a hurry this morning, bustling through the house and out the door without turning off the coffee pot or rinsing her dishes. I reach for a sponge in the sink and my arm cramps, a jolt of pain coursing through my body. I gasp and slump forward onto the countertop, swallowing hard against the nausea that rolls over me whenever this happens. It's been occurring more frequently lately, though I haven't told Nina. It would only make her fuss over me as though I am a small child incapable of caring for myself. She forgets that I've long been independent, that she left me alone to fend for myself more than twenty years ago. And, of course, she does not know how long I was alone before that.

The moment passes, and I straighten back up, gulping in deep breaths before lowering myself on the stool in front of the sink. I turn the water on and let it run until steam rises, then plunge my hands into the scalding stream. I wince for only a moment before settling into the pain. My hands occupied, I'm instantly transported back to the day Nina left, so many years ago.

I didn't go with her to the airport. It was my final rebellion, one last attempt to control her. Not that it would have mattered. At that point all the arrangements had been made. She had renounced her Soviet citizenship and married an American man. She had signed the papers stating her intention to desert her country and move to the United States. I had protested and yelled and fought her on it every step of the way, until finally I stopped. She needed me to sign papers in the court allowing her to marry and leave, and I did so because it became apparent that I would lose her either way. If I refused, she would still leave me, and she might never come back.

Nina had packed up her suitcase the week before her departure, utilizing all twenty kilograms that she was allotted, folding what she could of her culture and heritage into a small, hollow square. There were no tears from her that final morning. She was stoic, steady in her resolve to leave the life I had so carefully curated. How desperately I wanted to stop it, but the only way to do that would have been to tell her the truth, and that was a risk far greater than sending the girl I'd raised into the mouth of the American beast. So I kissed her cheek goodbye that morning, blinking hard against the tears that threatened to spill on my own cheeks, and she had nodded resolutely at my cold *dosvedonya*.

"I will write you as soon as I land," she said. "It will be okay, Mama. In fact, I think it will even be wonderful."

"Yes, well you must at least promise me that you will be very careful," I had replied, my words clipped. "Wear warm clothing, and don't forget your *tapochki* in the house. I don't want to hear that you caught American pneumonia and died."

"Okay, Mama," she answered with a sigh.

"And do not sit on the concrete. I hear they have many concrete benches in America, but don't sit on them. They will make you infertile."

She'd smiled at me then, a wry smile laced with impatient amusement, and it took my breath away. Despite my horror at her choice, I felt the smallest prick of pride nip at the base of my brain. She was strong, this girl I raised. She was forging her own path in the world, so different from the way I had done it. She wasn't acquiescing, as I had. She was striking out on her own, and it hurt so badly.

I watched her from the window of our small flat, careful not to let her see my face from the street. She stepped into her friend's car without so much as a glance back at the place she'd called home for twenty years. That was the day that I began washing dishes in scalding hot water, boiling it in the communal kitchen of our flat, then carrying the bowl into my small kitchen and plunging my hands in as I winced in pain. Perhaps it was my own punishment for having so obviously and desperately forsaken the child I had raised.

That was also the day that I began to feel the cold again. It seeped into my bones through memories I had long worked hard to stifle. The cold was a nagging reminder of the years I had spent a lifetime trying to escape. And so the hot water became like a balm to my frozen soul. It was my hiding place, the place where I tried to keep those icy visions from blowing back, but it never really worked, because there is a single truth that I cannot escape no matter how often I plunge my hands into a basin of steaming hot water: Nina doesn't know. She doesn't know her own story, and that is my fault.

I close my eyes and take in a deep breath. Of course, there is much about her life she has willingly hidden from me as well. There are so many questions I want to ask. I want to know about the decade that Nina lived in America before I arrived. What did she see and experience? What did she do? Why did she split with Andrew, and who was Annie's father?

Nina refuses to talk with me about the details of what happened between her and Andrew, though I suppose it doesn't matter. I knew that morning she left for the airport that the marriage would never last. It was so foolish and impulsive, but Nina had been a stone wall, impervious to reason. I'm not really disappointed that she left Andrew. He was a nice man, but hadn't been right for her.

But who was the second man? Who was it that Nina loved so much she was willing to bring a child into the world? Nina will only tell me that his name was Richard, and that he died of cancer before Annie was born. Besides those two details, she never speaks of him—not even to Annie.

Pulling a towel out of the drawer, I dab the water from my reddened hands, the brown spots of age a contrast to my heated skin. I lean against the counter and mull over the nagging thought that pricks at my conscience.

The walls that separate me from Nina are my own doing. I built them and hid behind them, and it is too late to climb over now. The life of quiet that I so carefully set up for Nina and I all those years in Moscow was a farce. It is I who taught her to whisper, and no amount of heat can stave off the bitter cold of that truth.

# NINA

*Ah! The foolish bravery of youth.*
*I miss it.*

Nina stares at herself in the mirror, turning her chin from left to right. She picks up a tube of lipstick and slowly applies it, hoping that today will bring the miracle of fuller lips that she's always wanted. She straightens up again and takes in the sight.

Her thick brown hair has been straightened and sprayed, and now hangs stiff over her shoulders. She's applied more makeup than usual this morning but was careful not to overdo it. She pulls her shoulders back and holds up her chin, then smiles at herself in the mirror. Her soft, hazel eyes crinkle at the edges when she smiles. They've always done that, apparently. But it wasn't a feature she noticed until Andrew pointed it out to her all those years ago.

Nina smiles at the memory. The day she arrived in America was one of the most terrifying days of her life. She had so many emotions as she timidly walked off the plane. What if he didn't show up? What if she got lost, or she found herself alone in the big, bad capitalist land of opportunity? What if her mother was right and she really did end up living alone on the streets...*with the cats?*

But Andrew had been there. He stood just outside the door

as she exited the customs line, a large bouquet of flowers in his hand, and when she stepped out and blinked at the bustling noise of the new land, he'd grabbed her and kissed her. Right there in public, he had kissed her and she'd pulled away, terrified. What if they were seen? What type of public chastisement could they receive for such a blatant and ridiculous display of emotion?

No one seemed to notice them, though. People buzzed on by, oblivious to this break of public protocol. Many of them rushed into the arms of their own waiting loved ones. That was the first moment Nina realized she had a lot to learn about this new country.

"Are you hungry?" Andrew asked, grabbing her hand and walking her away from the crowds of people at the gate. Nina was so taken by all the sights, the brightness of this new land, that she couldn't translate his question in her head, so she simply stared at him blankly.

"*Ty golodna?*" he repeated himself, this time in Russian. Nina nodded her head slowly.

"I didn't eat on the plane," she said. "I couldn't recognize the food."

He threw his head back and laughed. "Come on," he answered, sweeping his hand over her shoulder and leaning on her a little. "I'm going to introduce you to your first American meal."

Nina had been so smitten with him in that moment. He was natural and easy with her, as though they had known each other for years. Really, though, this man was a stranger to her. Even though they were married, she knew so little about him. But in the first few moments of that first day, she felt great hope that perhaps she hadn't been as foolish as her mother had so boldly claimed. Perhaps she'd even made a good decision.

Nina followed Andrew out of the airport into the bright American sunshine. The hot summer air swelled around them, thick and stale, reminding Nina of home. She swallowed hard against the pang of fear that kept threatening to choke her, and she stopped in front of a large gold car as Andrew fumbled with the keys. He opened the back door and slid in her suitcase, then gently guided her to the passenger side and opened the door for her. Nina slowly ducked into the seat, reminding herself to not let her mouth hang open in fascination. This was the nicest car she had ever seen.

In actuality, she had only been on a handful of car rides her entire life, and traveling by car had been one of the things she most looked forward to in this new land of freedom, where everyone drove their own vehicle.

"Buckle up," Andrew said. When Nina blinked at him in confusion, he chuckled. He reached over her lap and grabbed the seatbelt hanging beside her, crossing it over her waist and sliding the buckle into the latch. She felt panic swell for a moment. Why would she need to be strapped into a car like this? How fast was he planning to drive? Her body tensed at all the fears that instantaneously raced through her mind. Andrew still leaned over her, his face close to hers. His lips lightly grazed her cheek then he leaned back into his own seat and strapped himself in.

"Don't worry," he said with a grin. "This is just a safety precaution." She cocked her head, trying hard to decipher his strange words. "Safety." "Precaution." They were words without a translation, and the confusion balled itself into a lump at the base of her throat.

Ten minutes later, after Nina finally unclenched her hands, which had clamped down around the seatbelt, Andrew pulled into a parking lot in front of a restaurant. Nina blinked up at the giant, yellow 'M' on the front of the building. Andrew swung the car around the corner and got into a line behind another car. Nina looked at him quizzically.

"Uh..." she began, attempting to say her very first English words in America. "We get food? Here?" She pointed at the building outside Andrew's window. He smiled, white teeth gleaming in the American sunshine. He smiled a lot, a trait that Nina quickly realized was not unique to Andrew, but rather to America.

"Yes," he replied. "Only we're not going inside. We'll order out here, and they'll give us the food in the car."

Nina worked hard to digest the information he'd just given her. All the words alone made sense, but put together they sounded like nonsense.

She watched as Andrew stuck his head out the window and spoke to a voice in a box, then blinked curiously as they drove around the corner to a small window where a young man with a pimply face leaned his head out and asked for payment. At the next window, a woman reached her hand out and handed Andrew a bag. Nina watched all of this happen with great interest. None of the people in those windows seemed at all intrigued by this process. They acted as though it were perfectly normal to pass food through windows into the hands of strangers.

Andrew pulled away and handed Nina the bag. The smell made her stomach rumble, and Andrew grinned. "Eat," he urged. Nina opened the bag and looked inside. There was a bag of what looked to be long, yellow sticks, and something wrapped in foil. Andrew reached over and shoved his hand in the bag, grabbing a few of the sticks and putting them in his mouth. She watched him chew for a moment then glanced back in the bag.

"What it is?" she asked. Andrew grinned again, completely enamored by her innocence and beauty. She was like a lost little doe in the middle of the city.

"It's a hamburger and French fries. An American staple," he said. Nina had nodded even though she had no idea what he'd just said.

She tentatively reached into the bag and grabbed one of the yellow sticks. It was hot and greasy. She placed it at her lips then took a small nibble. She chewed for a moment, trying to process this new and strange food. It tasted a bit like the potatoes her mother use to fry in oil.

"It is potatoes?" she finally asked, and Andrew had thrown his head back in laughter. He nodded as she took another bite.

"Do you like them?" he asked, reaching into the bag and taking another handful. He put them all in his mouth at once as Nina watched carefully. She nodded, finishing her French fry and swallowing. She found she genuinely did like the taste, though the texture of this hand-held potato left her a little wary.

She pulled out the foil package and slowly unwrapped it. Inside lay what looked to be meat in between two pieces of the whitest bread she had ever seen. At home, her mother only served black bread. White bread was a delicacy that Nina had only enjoyed once before, thanks to the attention of a boy in her class when she was in the 8th form. But his white bread, a pale brick called *kirpich*, had been stiff and stale, not soft like this. She picked up the meat and bread and held it gingerly between her delicate fingers.

"This is hamburger?" she asked Andrew. He glanced at her with a glimmer in his eye and nodded. Very tentatively, she took a small bite, chewing the strange food carefully.

"Well," Andrew asked after she swallowed. "What do you think?"

Nina sat still for a moment letting the lingering taste register. She turned toward him shyly. "I don't know," she answered. He returned her smile.

"You need to try a bigger bite," he urged. Nina took a larger bite this time, and immediately she felt a tightening in the back of her jaw as the unfamiliar flavor assaulted her. She looked at the hamburger and saw a red paste dripping out the side. She swallowed hard and examined the burger closely.

"What it is?" she asked, pointing to the paste oozing from the bread. "This red?"

"That's ketchup," he replied. "It's a tomato sauce."

Nina stared at the ketchup quizzically. It looked very different from the tomato sauce at home, brighter and thinner. And it tasted different, too. It was tangy, sharp against her tongue. Nina took another tentative bite and chewed for a moment, then swallowed quickly.

"Do you like it?" Andrew asked, his face eager. Nina forced her mouth to turn up into as sincere a smile as she could and nodded unconvincingly.

"Yes," she lied. But she knew she could not take another bite of this hamburger for fear she might get sick. Andrew chuckled beside her, and she hesitated to look his way. She did not want to insult the man who had done so much to bring her to this country, and she feared she had already blown her chance to make it work in the first hour.

"It's okay if you don't like it," he said. She glanced at him from the corner of her eye. "I won't take it personally."

Nina smiled at him gratefully and placed the hamburger in his outstretched hand. He took a large bite as she watched with great interest. Seeing her large, inquisitive eyes looking at him brought a smile to his face once again, and this time she genuinely smiled back. He dropped the burger back into the bag on her lap and reached over, brushing his thumb along the corner of her eye.

"Your skin crinkles when you smile," he said. Nina blushed at this intimate touch. "I like it," he'd continued, his voice a little softer this time.

Nina pulls herself back into the present and glances into the mirror, taking in her reflection once more. Would Andrew still like what he saw if they had somehow made it work? If the glaring differences between their cultures and backgrounds hadn't split wide a chasm between them, would they have somehow been able to remain a family? The newness of it all had worn off so quickly. Within a year, the flirtatious smiles and stolen public kisses waned, leaving nothing but strained conversation. There was often a tired silence between them, and it had terrified Nina. She couldn't handle the uncertainty of it all, which coupled with an intense sense of failure. Her mother had been right after all. The relationship would never last.

Nina sighs and grabs her handbag off the end of the bed. The irony of it all is that she's never had a conversation with her mother about the circumstances surrounding her divorce. She never gave her mom any information on how her first marriage fizzled and faded, like the end of a movie reel that went from grey to black when the show was over. And though it was no secret that she had remarried and had her child with another man, she and Elizaveta never went in to the details of those missing years between leaving Moscow and Elizaveta moving to the States. Nina couldn't figure out how to bring up the brief and sad love story she shared with Richard Abrams, a man she married shortly after her divorce to Andrew was finalized.

Richard was the real love, different from that which she'd felt for Andrew. But cancer is a wretched beast. Cancer doesn't care if you're newly married or if you're pregnant. Cancer will sneak in and steal the man you adore right out from under your nose leaving you alone to raise a daughter in a foreign land. Cancer will render you a divorcee *and* a widow in one fell swoop, and somehow prove that your mother was right after all.

Nina couldn't handle the aftermath of telling her mother the whole story, so they simply never discussed it. When Elizaveta tried probing Nina for details of Annie's father, Nina brushed past her with simple platitudes. She told her that Annie's father was a good man who died too young, and made it clear the subject was closed for discussion. Elizaveta finally quit asking, though on occasion she made sure to mention what a pity it was that Annie had no father in her life, a comment so laced with irony that Nina couldn't help but stare incredulously at her mother when she brought it up. She, Elizaveta Mishurova, had never spoken of a man, and Nina had no male influence her entire childhood, so her mother's overly righteous insistence that Annie should have a male role model was laughable at best.

Moving out of the shadows of her memory, Nina heads downstairs to find her mother and daughter sitting at the breakfast table—the very table she'd sat at the day Richard told her he was terminally ill, and she'd broken down as she told him she was expecting a child. The cancer took him quickly, never affording him the opportunity to see his daughter. And the pain of it all had caused him to shut her out in his last few months of life. He'd pushed her away, and she'd watched it all happen from the sidelines as his mother nursed him out of this life. When it was all done, she'd left Nina alone, never attempting to meet her only granddaughter.

Nina looks between her mother and her daughter, and shakes her head at the uncomfortable silence between them. Annie's shoulders are hunched over her cereal bowl. With one hand she raises the spoon to her mouth, and in the other she holds the box of cereal up, reading the back for the umpteenth time. Elizaveta sits across from her, hunched over her cup of chai. She stirs it slowly, her spoon clinking against the side of the cup to a beat. Nina smiles as she remembers a platitude she heard frequently as a youth.

"*Russians make the loudest sound with a spoon while stirring their tea.*"

Elizaveta's eyes bore into the cereal box that blocks her from seeing her granddaughter's face. The two mirror one another in every way, and Nina nearly laughs at loud.

"Good morning," she says, forcing a smile. She bustles past them and grabs a coffee mug from the counter. Pouring herself a cup, she turns and faces the two, who look up at her warily.

"Annie, I need to head into the office early this morning. Why don't I drop you off on my way so you don't have to take the bus."

Annie shrugs, and Nina isn't sure if it's a 'that's okay' or 'don't bother' shoulder shrug. She doesn't feel like deciphering it, so she moves on.

"Mama," she begins, switching from English to Russian. "I've left you a *buterbrod*, and some *vinigret* in the refrigerator. Remember I'm coming home at eleven today to pick you up so we can go back to Vik—Dr. Shevchenko's office this afternoon." Nina brushes past her mother, ignoring the narrowed eyes that work to discern why she nearly called the doctor by his first name. She grabs her keys and gulps her coffee down quickly.

"Ready, Annie?" she asks. Annie rolls her eyes and slides out of her chair. She grabs her bag and walks to the door. Nina sighs at her daughter's retreating figure. She looks back at her mother whose pinched face shakes. It appears her mother is fighting back tears.

"Mama?" Nina asks as she takes a step toward the usually stoic old woman. "Are you okay?"

Elizaveta holds up her hand, waving Nina off as she turns back to her breakfast. "I am fine," she mutters taking a bite of the thick, black bread slathered in butter. After Elizaveta moved to America to live with her, Nina began buying the black bread again at a local European deli in order to quell her mother's constant berating of the "useless" white fluff that Americans insisted on wrongly labeling "bread."

"You look too thin. You should eat something so you don't die," Elizaveta says to her daughter without looking up. She takes another bite, then she grabs the other slice of bread from her plate and holds it out. Nina silently takes the bread from her mother. It smells like home, like her past.

It smells like secrets.

# ANNIE

Annie's hand is moving slowly across the paper. She doesn't even know she's doing it, the drawing so ingrained in her that it comes out as an extension of her very breath. Her pencil moves back and forth, lightly here and darker there, shading in the white spaces until they begin to take shape. But she doesn't see the shape. Her eyes are glazed over, and though one might assume her inexorably zoned out, she is actually quite tuned in as the teacher drones on and on at the front of the classroom. He's dissecting the different branches of government, offering an explanation for each that Annie quickly digests and tucks away in her subconscious, knowing full well that she will be able to extract it when the next test rolls around. And all the while James watches her carefully, completely enamored by the quiet girl with the ever-moving pencil. He tries to see what she's drawing, but can't without leaning across the aisle and giving away his silent observation. So he simply takes in the sight of her, the way her long, blonde hair hangs in soft waves over her shoulders, tucked behind her ears to reveal the milky complexion of her cheeks.

"Mr. Davis, perhaps you'd like to quit studying Miss Abrams long enough to explain to me the difference between the Judicial, Legislative, and Executive branches of our government?"

James snaps to attention, his face immediately growing hot

as the class snickers around him. He sees Annie slink down in her seat, and he fights the urge to look at her as he stammers out his best explanation of the differences. Mr. Jacobs sits on the edge of his desk, an amused look worn on his smug face. Annie closes her notebook, hiding the picture she'd begun to draw without even realizing it.

"Good enough," Mr. Jacobs replies, a smirk stretching his mouth out like the Cheshire Cat. "Keep your eyes forward for a little while, 'kay?" he says. James slides down in his seat and fights the urge to say something smart in reply.

When the bell finally rings, Annie shoves her notebook in her bag and makes a mad dash for the door. James quickly gathers his notebook and books, shoving them into his bag and rushing after her. He winds his way through the bustling crowd of students, looking for Annie. He turns toward his next class and rounds the corner, running hard into her. She's leaning against the wall, face set in a frustrated scowl, when James nearly trips over her feet.

"Hey," he says, and he blushes for the second time, still embarrassed by the incident in their shared class. "Sorry about that back there," he continues.

"Why were you staring at me?" Annie demands. Her voice comes out hard and biting. James blinks.

"Why?" she repeats.

"I don't know," James says. "I just saw you drawing, and I was curious what you were creating this time."

"Well it's none of your business," Annie huffs. She shoves away from the wall and walks toward her next class. James hustles to catch up with her.

"Yeah, I know it's none of my business," he responds. "But I'm sort of fascinated by your talent, and by the fact that you don't even seem to know you're talented. It's like a subconscious thing. It's weird...and...kind of cool."

Annie stops and turns to him. Her eyes are brimming with tears. "You can't do that," she whispers.

James takes a step toward her, but she moves away from him, her head shaking side to side. "Annie, what's wrong?" he asks.

She swipes her hand over her eyes and shakes her head. "You can't get close to me," she replies. "I can't handle it. And you really can't look at my drawings. They're personal. It's like reading my diary. You just can't do that."

James nods and holds up his hands in surrender. "Okay. I'm sorry," he answers. Annie sniffs and jumps as the bell rings. She looks at him, her eyes red-rimmed and shining. She looks lost.

"See you later," she murmurs. She turns and rushes down the hallway. James waits for a moment to give her space then follows behind her. The halls are nearly empty now, the echoes of chaotic chatter bouncing off concrete as students disappear into classrooms. James watches as Annie stops before her next class. She yanks a notebook out of her bag and tears a page out of it, crumpling it up roughly before dropping it in the trash-can outside the door. She disappears into the classroom just as the second bell rings.

James watches her go, a knot in the pit of his stomach. He walks to the trashcan and glances inside at the crumpled paper. He reaches in to pull it out, then stops and stands back up, balling his hands into fists. With a sigh, he turns and makes his way down the hall to class.

# NINA

*Russian women are too strong for tears.*

Nina glances at her mother briefly as she guides the car toward Viktor's office. Elizaveta's head droops to the side as the hum of the car's engine overtakes her. Moments later, she falls into a deep and fitful sleep.

Nina swallows hard over the feeling of concern that has formed a knot in her throat. Her mother acted strange today—distant and confused as Nina helped her get from the house to the car. It was as though Elizaveta was trapped between two worlds.

Nina steals another look at her mother. Elizaveta's eyes, circled by deep wrinkles, twitch and her mouth moves as she sleeps. Nina turns down the radio and listens, trying to discern the whispered dreams of her mother, but she cannot make out any words. She pulls into the parking lot and slows to a stop in front of Viktor's office. She gently puts the car in park and glances at the clock. They're a few minutes early, so she pulls out her book and opens it up to read, hoping that this short nap will make her mother more agreeable inside.

"Mama!"

Nina jumps as her mother's voice comes out in a ragged gasp. She turns to see Elizaveta still sound asleep, eyes squeezed shut but hands gripped together vice-like and white-knuckled.

"Mama, *prosti menye.*" Forgive me.

Nina gulps as her mother begs forgiveness. Her breathing grows more uneven, small gasps lifting up over cracked, dry lips, inhaling her plea and exhaling panic. Nina feels her heart constrict, the vulnerable words pulling out the oxygen and replacing it with choking dread. She reaches over and gently puts a hand on her mother's shoulder.

Elizaveta's eyes open wide, and she takes in one long, sharp breath. She looks around wildly, trying to determine her whereabouts, to reconcile the piercing sunlight with the darkness and fear that pervaded her dreams. The warmth of the car stands in stark contrast to the frozen memory of her slumber.

"We're here," Nina says. She tries to force a smile into her words, but they come out strained.

Elizaveta's heartbeat slowly begins to even out as her eyes focus on Nina. "I was sleeping," she murmurs, and Nina nods.

"Yes," she replies.

Elizaveta pushes herself up and reaches for the door handle. Her hands shake, and her breathing still sounds uneven.

"We can wait a few minutes, Mama," Nina says. It happens quickly after that, the next few moments a blur of confusion. Nina finds herself dashing into the building, yelling at the tattooed receptionist who blinks up at her with infuriatingly callous eyes. Moments later, Nina and Viktor are at Elizaveta's side, attempting to steady her as she screams in the passenger seat of the car, her spotted hands covering her face.

"What happened?" Viktor asks, reaching across Elizaveta to release the seat belt.

"I don't know," Nina answers, her voice wavering under the strain of the moment. "She had fallen asleep and was dreaming. She woke up and spoke to me clearly, then I put my hand on her shoulder and she tightened up and started screaming."

Viktor leans down and speaks soothingly to Elizaveta, his flawless Russian cutting through the terror.

*"A flower - shriveled, bare of fragrance,*
*Forgotten on a page - I see,*
*And instantly my soul awakens,*
*Filled with an aimless reverie"*

His voice is honey, the harsh syllables of their native language soft and gentle coming from his mouth. He speaks the words of Pushkin into Elizaveta's suffocating discomposure, and it becomes an instant balm. Nina watches as her mother slowly lowers her hands and looks at his face, the dark of her eyes shrinking back with her receding terror. Viktor gently touches her hand, and when she doesn't pull away he slides his hand up to encircle her frail wrist, measuring her pulse as he continues to speak quietly, the poem falling from his lips in a calming cadence.

He stops and offers Elizaveta a soft smile. She covers his hands with her own and peers intently into his eyes.

"Dima?" she whispers. "Dima, is it you?"

Nina puts her hand over her mouth and blinks hard at the sight of her mother so disoriented. Viktor remains calm.

"No, Elizaveta Andreyevna," he replies, calling her by her formal name as their shared culture demands. "I'm Dr. Shevchenko."

She blinks twice, then drops his hands. Her confusion thickens, and Nina takes in long, slow breaths.

"Do you know where you are?" Viktor asks.

Elizaveta purses her lips and nods once. Nina squats down next to Viktor and grabs her mother's hand.

"Mama, let's go inside with Dr. Shevchenko and let him have a look at you, okay?"

Elizaveta pulls her hand away, her jaw set in the usual line of stubbornness. "Yes, *khorosho,*" she murmurs. "Fine. But I don't need to be coddled like a child."

Nina knows immediately that her mother is back, and she exhales deeply, the knot in her stomach hardening as she processes all that transpired.

"Of course you don't," she replies. She steps back and lets Viktor help her mother to a stand. It's clear that he is the better person to handle this moment.

"Elizaveta Andreyevna, would you like Nina to come with us into the exam room, or should she wait out here?" he asks. Nina's eyes snap to his face, hurt welling up in her chest at his suggestion.

"She will wait here," Elizaveta answers, the relief in her voice palpable. Nina nods and stands frozen as Viktor guides her mother toward the front door of his office. He glances back at her over Elizaveta's silver-grey hair and offers an apologetic smile. She watches until they're safely inside and she's certain she can no longer be seen. Then she leans forward on the front of her car and puts her head in her hands.

"Don't cry," she whispers. "*Ne plach.*" She blinks back the tears that threaten to fight to the surface. She can hear her mother's voice in her head from when she was a child.

"Russian women are too strong for crying, *Ninochka*," her mother would say when Nina came home teary-eyed over a skinned knee or hurt feelings. "We are above all the tears."

Nina had long since learned to stifle emotion, to hold it at bay out of sheer determination, and today wouldn't be any different. She stands back up and draws in a deep breath, then turns and walks slowly to the pharmacy next door to the clinic.

"I won't cry, but I can smoke," she mutters, pulling open the door and stepping into the refreshingly cool building.

# ELIZAVETA

*There is no room for individuality in a truly great society.*

I saw him so clearly. His face materialized before me soft and young, and I could reach for him, but I could not touch him. My hand flitted through the air, and I caught only a memory.

The doctor asks me questions, but I can't quite seem to make out all that he's saying. His words move in and out of the room like flies at a picnic. They are a distraction, and so I ignore them. I think only of Dima.

We were young, huddled together in the bare, wooden schoolroom at the internment camp outside the gulag. We knew Papa was somewhere inside the camp, but we hadn't been permitted to see him. Every day before school, Dima and I walked along the line of the fence that separated us from the real prisoners and stared at the faces of those on the other side, hoping for some glimpse of Papa. We saw men and women walking around, all wearing the same brown prison uniform on their bodies and a haunted look on their faces. No one moved quickly behind that wooden fence topped with barbed metal that twisted and curled its way around the perimeter like a wretched sneer. We pressed our faces against the wood, hoping for some sign that he was really in there, but we never saw him. I didn't even know who to look for, but Dima did, and he insisted that he saw nothing.

I remember how icy cold my hands were, and even now I feel the urge to ball them tight into a fist, nails digging into flesh, hoping to stave off the cold that pierces through flesh and muscle and settles tight inside the bones. It was Dima, my protective older brother, who always grabbed my hands and rubbed them between his own, hoping that the friction between his thick hands would heat up my thin, frail fingers.

We arrived at the small building that housed the schoolroom, and I still remember the feeling of relief when we stepped inside. It was warmer inside those walls, insulated somewhat from the raging winter by planks of wood that actually met, a thin, black line of some sort of sealant keeping the outside elements at bay and offering us a few short hours of freedom from the cold. We sat in our seats, and I scooted as close to Dima as I could. He never minded when I pressed up against him.

The teacher walked into the room and greeted us in her taut, high-pitched voice, the nasal tone so grating that even now I feel it run down my spine. She stood before us, her pudgy hands clasped in front of her pouch of a stomach. Her crisp, brown jacket was buttoned tight over her abdomen, the buttons straining against her girth. The navy blue skirt hung nearly to her ankles, longer than on most of the other officers due to her oddly short legs. Her hair was always pulled into a severe bun at the nape of her neck, and her navy beret sat crooked on her head at such an uncomfortable angle I sometimes found myself tilting my head when she spoke to try and straighten it out in my mind. I could never quite decide how old Valerya Sergeyevna was. I didn't know if she was quite old, or perhaps quite young and merely aged poorly. Either way, I found her to be the ugliest woman I had ever seen.

"Good morning," she said, her eyes scanning the room with obvious disdain.

"Good morning, Valerya Sergeyevna," we intoned. We

were a room full of children, imprisoned and found guilty for being born in the wrong place at the wrong time. We were *kulatskoye otrodye*, the children of '*kulaks*', and Valerya Serge-yevna reminded us every day just how offensive our very lives were to her. Even then, I sensed that she must have been under some terrible punishment to be forced to breathe the same air as us.

"You are a disgrace to our society," she said each morning before drilling us in the ways of the proper Soviet. "There is no room for individuality in a truly great society. The collective can only achieve greatness if we all acquiesce to the whole, together as one."

I didn't know what acquiesce meant. Even now I struggle with its meaning. The word swims through my consciousness leaving only confusion and frustration in its wake.

"You're here because your families, your parents and grandparents, were violent enemies of socialism. They didn't care about the collective whole. They were *selfish*, and that selfishness made them dangerous. They are the worst our society has to offer, and there is little hope for them. But you all can change your own destinies. You can redeem yourselves by simply renouncing your families. If you admit their harmful activities, and your guilt by association, then the future can change for you. Acquiesce to the greater good. Fall in line with our great nation. This will save you from the ugly and deserved path of your parents."

She said this, and her words were beginning to sink in. I found myself angry with my father for his individuality. I grew increasingly bitter toward my mother for her quiet sto-icism and her whispered rebellion. She continued to read the dangerous words at night—poetry and quoted scriptures—all of which were expressly forbidden, and as she spoke it seemed her words were lifted up by the howling wind and sent out over the camp, her rebellion floating over all of us like a blan-ket of guilt. She needed to...to *acquiesce*.

All of our lessons in school reiterated just how terrible we were, how guilty by association, and the bitterness grew inside my childish chest, crackling like fire fizzling in the icy winds that seemed to never stop. But not Dima. He didn't believe a word she said, and he muttered under his breath throughout each lesson. Sometimes he'd let out a defiant laugh only to be struck across the cheek and sent to stand in front of the class. Valerya Sergeyevna had no patience or time for rebellion, and she let Dima know by her refusal to look at him or speak to him. Their only communications were the repeated slaps she doled out, sometimes deserved, and sometimes just because she felt like it.

There were days when I also received the brunt of Valerya Sergeyevna's anger. On the days that Dima remained passive, unwilling to engage with her in debate, she elicited his rage by coming down on me. The worst was the day she caught me drawing. I didn't even know I was doing it. She was speaking, and my hands just started moving over the page, the tiny stub of a pencil I'd been given working in thin strokes to create an image. When she slammed her hand on the table in front of me, I snapped my eyes to hers, then quickly shifted them back down to my paper. I had drawn a picture of a woman standing beneath a tree. The picture was crude, not perfectly drawn, but well done enough to see that the woman stood up straight, almost as if in defiance, her hands hanging by her side as if preparing to run. I had drawn the woman's back, with no face to help me discern who she might have been, but somehow I felt that this was a woman that I knew, that perhaps had I been given the chance to finish the drawing she would have been recognizable to me.

"What do you think you're doing?" Valerya Sergeyevna screeched, snatching the drawing from my hands. She crumpled it up into a ball and tossed it over her shoulder, then brought her hand down across my cheek with a vicious crack.

Immediately my eyes filled with tears as I huddled down in my seat.

Dima flew up out of his chair and stepped between the enraged teacher and me, his eyes flashing.

"Don't ever touch her again," he hissed. Tall for his age, Dima stood eye to eye with the stout woman, her fleshy eyes blinking furiously over bright, red cheeks. She reached up and grabbed Dima by the ear, dragging him to the corner where she shoved his face into the wall.

"You'll stay there the rest of the day, you little worm. And if you don't learn to shut up, I'll have you and your sister sent to the other side of the fence where they know how to deal with trash like you." Spittle flew from her fat lips. She turned back to the rest of the class, all of us stunned, too frightened to move. Smoothing her stiff jacket back into place, she took in a deep breath and instructed us to write our names 100 times followed by "is an unworthy *kulak child.*"

That afternoon as we trudged home, the icy path crunching beneath our feet and bellies grumbling with no hope of satisfaction, I stole glances at Dima from the corner of my eye. His face was set in a hard stare, hands shoved deep into the pockets of his frayed pants. His hair had been shaved the day we arrived at the camp, and it was starting to grow out in tufts that sprouted up around his head. They had cut off my braids the day we arrived as well. Dima said my shorn hair made me look older, but I never really did believe him. I knew I must look as strange with my haircut as he looked with his.

"What is it?" he finally asked me after I opened my mouth and snapped it shut for the tenth time.

"Why do you make Valerya Sergeyevna so angry?" I asked softly.

"Because she's a liar," he answered. I grabbed his elbow and stopped walking, peering up at him through the dim, grey sky. I blinked twice, trying to formulate the words in my young brain. Dima was my older brother, wise and protective. He was the one who tried to make me laugh when the days felt too long and brutal. When Mama dragged herself into the barracks after another long day of working, hauling trees and branches that the loggers brought in onto carts to be shipped away to the good Soviets, Dima was the one who massaged her hands and feet. When Tanya sobbed into her thin blanket at night, begging for food to fill her empty stomach, Dima sang songs into her little ear until the sobs softened, and she drifted into a fitful sleep. Dima was good. But the things he said were bad.

"How is she a liar?" I asked. "She's here to teach us to be better so that our country will like us again."

Dima snorted and shook his head. He was twelve, so grown up and mature. At only six years old, I lived in constant confusion, doubts gnawing at my stomach with thick precision.

"She's not teaching us anything. She's just making us feel bad, telling lies about our family. Papa is not the enemy, little one." Dima leaned down so that his eyes could look into mine, and those are the eyes I saw again today. They were clear and pure, free of malice. "Our enemy wears a uniform." He stood back up, his eyes still locked on mine. "Don't believe a word she says."

If only I had listened to him.

# NINA

*She feared nothing,*
*Or so I thought.*
*She was my mama.*

Nina sits on the curb next to her car, rolling a cigarette through her fingers. It's been years since she quit smoking. She stopped the day she found out she was pregnant, suddenly acutely aware of how her actions might affect someone else. But now, for the first time in nearly eighteen years, she finds herself craving a cigarette. It's as though the ghost of her past settled upon her the moment her mother started screeching. All the wondering and confusion she'd felt growing up as the daughter of Elizaveta Andreyevna Mishurova squeezes at her heart like a vice, and her hands tremble as she looks at the rolled tobacco in her hand.

Her mother had never cared for the habit, which only fueled Nina's desire to smoke as a young woman. Many nights, she lit up just before entering their small flat so that she could walk in the door and finish smoking inside, relishing the way Elizaveta's mouth would tighten into one long, thin line. Perhaps she'd never really loved the habit of smoking, but rather the power it wielded over her mother.

The door to the clinic opens behind her, and she stands as Viktor steps out. "Would you like to come in now?" he asks.

Nina takes in a deep breath, then lets it out slowly, the air in her lungs feeling stifled and starched, tight like it's being pushed through a narrow hole. She nods, and he holds out his arm toward the door. Nina drops the cigarette into her purse and offers him a wry grin.

"I haven't had one of those in a long time," she says sheepishly. Viktor offers a gentle smile in return.

"Well, as your doctor I can't recommend that you have one, but..." he pauses and Nina stops in front of him, looking up into his dark eyes. "But as your friend, I can certainly empathize with the desire," he says. Viktor's voice has a low husk to it. Nina's heartbeat quickens as she locks eyes with him.

"*Ahem.*"

They jump and turn to the tattooed receptionist who pokes her head out from behind the door that leads to the exam rooms. Viktor clears his throat and steps back so Nina can walk by.

"Yes, Alexa?" he asks, strolling to the front desk.

"The patient in Room 1 just yelled something at me in Russian. I'm not sure what she said, but she sounded pissed, so..."

Viktor and Nina rush past her and push into Exam Room 1 where they find Elizaveta pacing back and forth from one wall to the next, muttering under her breath. When they walk in, she turns and plants her hands on her soft, wide hips. She's readjusted her headscarf, tying it tightly under her chin. With her pinched, wrinkled face she looks like every stereotypical picture ever painted of the Russian babushka. Nina almost laughs, but is quickly sobered by the look in her mother's eyes. It is a mixture of terror, anger, and fatigue.

"Why would you leave me here?" she demands, her eyes not on Viktor's, but on Nina's. "You leave me alone, and then send in the crazy girl with the drawings on her arms to check on me. You are trying to kill me!"

"Mama," Nina begins, taking a step forward. "I'm not trying to kill you. You weren't alone that long."

Elizaveta holds up her hand, silencing Nina. "I don't want

to hear it," she responds. "I would like to go home. I am tired, and I need to rest."

Nina glances at Viktor with raised eyebrows. He sits down on his swivel stool, his long legs stretching out in front of him. Crossing his arms over his chest, he looks at Elizaveta for a moment before speaking.

"Elizaveta Andreyevna," he says, "it has been a very long, hard morning for you. I'm concerned about you returning home right now. I'd really like to have a few more tests run to make sure that your health is strong."

"Psh," Elizaveta interrupts. "I am fine. There is nothing wrong with my health. I'm only tired and want to go home."

Viktor takes in a long, deep breath and nods his head. "Absolutely, I understand," he replies. "And you're right, you do need some rest. How about this." He sits up a little and slides his chair forward so that he's sitting in front of her, their eyes almost level with one another. "How about you go to the hospital right now and let them run their tests. I will call ahead and make sure they understand you are an outpatient, which means they will not keep you overnight. If they need to run more tests you can return Monday after you've had a chance to rest."

Elizaveta shakes her head. "No. I will not go to the hospital. I go to the hospital and I die. I won't die under the noses of incompetent American doctors."

Nina sighs. "Mama," she says, but stops immediately when Elizaveta glares at her, the hurt in her eyes brimming bright in the very center.

Viktor reaches out and grabs Elizaveta's hand, covering it with both of his. She looks back at him and suddenly looks so small and frightened. Nina blinks hard against tears that prick at the corner of her eyes.

"I promise," he says gently, "that the doctors there will take excellent care of you. I will speak with them myself, and as soon as I finish seeing the patients on my schedule, I'll meet you there so that I can tell you exactly what they're doing. Okay?"

"I can be there, too, Mama," Nina says. "I took the rest of the day off work today, so I can stay. I want to help you." Nina wishes she didn't sound so childish. It makes her feel foolish. Elizaveta narrows her eyes at her daughter, and then returns her gaze to Viktor. She takes a deep breath and pulls her hand from his.

"Fine," she sniffs. "I'll go to the hospital for these tests, but I will not stay any longer than is absolutely necessary. Understood?"

Viktor nods and smiles, "I would not expect it," he says. He reaches for his notepad and scribbles out a series of notes, handing them to Nina.

"Take these with you. I'll call them now and ask them to have a room prepared for her when you arrive, okay?"

Nina purses her lips and nods her head, overwhelmed by the confliction of her mother's hostility mingled with Viktor's kindness.

"*Spasibo*," she says, her voice trembling. Viktor nods. As she takes the slip of paper from his hand, his fingers linger on hers for a brief moment. A tremor runs up her spine.

"It's going to be okay," he says. "We'll figure out what's going on."

Nina nods. Together they turn to Elizaveta, who looks back and forth between the two of them, blinking slowly. She studies Viktor for a lingering moment, and then turns her eyes to Nina.

"You need to marry this man," she says, and Nina's face grows instantly hot.

"Mama!" she exclaims.

"Do not 'Mama!' me," Elizaveta replies. She pulls her handbag up, tucking it into the crook of her elbow and turns to open the door. Looking back, she offers her daughter a pointed look. "He is the man you and I have been waiting for."

Nina offers Viktor an embarrassed smile and ducks her head. Elizaveta shuffles out the door and the two are left momentarily alone.

"Sorry about that," Nina stammers, switching back to English. Somehow she feels better able to mask her embarrassment behind the syllables of her American language.

Viktor grins, amusement dancing through his eyes. "Don't be sorry," he says with a smile. "She is like every Russian grandmother I have ever met in my life, and I'm starting to love her for it."

Nina blinks and clears her throat awkwardly. "So...um...I will see you later? At the hospital?"

Viktor nods, and she turns to leave. Nina catches Elizaveta's eye across the room and bites her lip. She can sense her mother's approval, and doesn't quite know how to feel about it. She watches as Elizaveta tries to push open the door of the clinic, and the image immediately sobers her. Her mother, the formidable woman who raised her, the one made of iron, unshakable and strong, is now old, frail, and unable to leave on her own.

# ANNIE

Annie stands on the curb and holds her hand over her eyes, shielding them from the glaring sunlight. The sidewalk hums around her with kinetic energy, everyone buzzing in anticipation of the upcoming homecoming dance. Annie catches snippets of their conversation, all of it swirling around her in a haze, reminding her of just how different she is—how separate from the rest of the world.

"You okay?"

Her shoulders tense when he steps up beside her. Taking a shallow breath, she shrugs before answering.

"Fine," she mumbles. She feels him looking at her, but can't bring herself to return his gaze.

"Sorry again," James says quietly. He steps in front of her, blocking the piercing sun so that she can lower her hand. Her arms hang awkwardly by her side.

"It's no big deal," Annie responds. "I shouldn't have freaked out like that. It's just..." she stops and swallows, a lump suddenly making it a little harder to form the words. She sighs before finishing quietly. "I'm not quite myself right now."

James cocks his head to the side slightly and gives her a crooked smile. "Well, fine," he says. "I'm glad to know that you don't really have it all together. I was starting to think you were a robot." He grins, and Annie smiles back, her mouth turning up involuntarily. It's a relief, this natural emotion. The smile feels so comfortable, like a breeze blowing through on a hot, summer day.

"I'm not a robot," she says, a hint of amusement dancing through her words. James nods and puts his hands in his pockets.

"Well, good," he says. "Then we can still be friends."

Annie chuckles, and James smiles back at her, rocking back on his heels. He clears his throat and glances up at the sky.

"So..." he begins, his voice cracking. "Um...are you...I mean...were you, or I guess would you like to go with me to Home—"

Annie hears the putter of the car engine before she sees it, the familiar rumble thickening the air around her. She glances to her right and sees Toby's car sweep around the corner. She looks back at James with wide, apologetic eyes. He glances at Toby's car, and then back at her.

"Oh..." he says. He clears his throat, his face flushed. Stepping back, he moves away from the curb just as Toby pulls up in front of Annie. Toby gazes up at her through the window.

"Hey," he says. There's a grit to his voice. He glances at James, and then back at Annie, suspicion shadowing his face.

Annie steps forward and grabs the handle of the door, pulling it open and sliding into the seat in one, quick move. She glances back out the window at James who stands slumped and dejected. Raising her hand, she offers a half-hearted goodbye. He nods his head, then turns and disappears into the throng of students still milling around the pick up line.

Annie leans her head back and takes in a deep breath.

"Who's that?" Toby asks. He shifts the car, moving it from 1$^{st}$ to 2$^{nd}$ gear with a loud grind. Annie shrugs her shoulders.

"Just a guy I know," she offers, trying unsuccessfully to keep her voice light. "He's helping me in lit class. Some of these books we're reading are crazy."

Annie leans forward and unzips her backpack. Her hands tremble as she reaches in and grabs the newest literature book.

"Have you read this?" she asks him, hoping that this change in subject will be enough to diffuse the tension in the air.

He grabs the book with a sigh and holds it up, shifting his eyes back and forth between the road and the cover.

"*Of Mice and Men*," he reads. He hands it back to her. "Yeah, I read that in high school. Didn't get it. All I remember is that there's some big buffoon of a guy who kills a puppy, and then gets offed by his friend. Total downer."

Annie looks down at the book, running her hand over the outside. She thinks of the conversation she had with James last week when they discussed this upcoming book. "You'll love it," he'd said. "It's short, but there's so much meat to the story. It's thematically rich."

She drops the book back in her bag and turns to Toby with a strained smile. "Oh," she cracks, her voice thin. "Well, I guess it's good that it's a short book then, huh?"

Toby shrugs, and the two of them fall silent. Annie glances out the window and watches the landscape roll by. Her mind drifts to the days of her youth when she and her mom would escape to the mountains for long weekends, renting a cabin and spending entire days exploring the magic of the trees. They'd run uphill until their lungs felt like they'd burst, then find a log to sit on, both of them heaving and laughing at one another.

It was in the forest that her mother had spoken most freely and intimately, offering Annie a glimpse into her heart that she didn't normally see in the day-to-day grind of every day life. It was as though the mountains held her mother's whispered secrets, the bits of her past that she normally locked away, and she was free to share those secrets only beneath the protection of the trees' canopy. Annie closes her eyes and remembers the last trip they took together to the mountains. They'd spent the morning cutting their way through the fog, the cool, early spring air sweet and fresh after a frigid winter. They'd stepped carefully on the backs of rocks, tiptoeing across slick creek beds to explore new and unseen corners of the forest. As the final moisture burned from the air, Nina had Annie sit beside her at the crest of a hill and the two of them watched as the sky faded from grey to crystal blue.

"Your grandmother is moving to America," Nina had said that morning. Something about the way she said it, the doubt and strain in her voice, made Annie's heart constrict.

"She'll be coming to live with us," Nina said. Annie had turned and looked up at her mother, their eyes locking for a moment, and Annie knew immediately that this was going to change everything. All they'd known, everything they had enjoyed, would be different now that the grandmother she barely knew was coming to stay. Annie had heard stories of her grandmother, and she'd spoken with her on the phone. This was not welcome news.

That was the last time Annie and her mother had gone to the woods. When Babushka moved in, everything changed, and even now as she watches the trees move in and out of view through the changing landscape, Annie feels the weight of that overwhelming loss.

Toby rolls to a stop at a stop sign and glances at Annie out of the corner of his eye.

"So..." he begins. He clears his throat nervously.

"Did you, like, decide what you're gonna...do...about the, um..." he glances at her stomach, then back up at her, his eyes distant. "The situation?" he finishes.

Annie swallows hard, her hand running self-consciously over her stomach. "No, not yet," she answers.

"Have you even thought about it?" Toby asks. Annie bristles at the edge in his voice.

"Yes, Toby," she snaps. "I've thought about it. In fact, it's pretty much *all* that I think about *all* the time." She blinks back tears and turns her face away from him. Toby sighs in frustration.

"Hey," he says. "I'm sorry, alright?" Annie turns back and

stares at him incredulously. "I'm just freaking out a little, An-nie. You know? I'm not exactly ready for this."

"Right," she snaps, blinking hard. "And I am?" She draws in a trembling breath.

Toby shoves his foot down on the gas, peeling away from the stop sign and across the quiet intersection. "So if neither of us are ready, then why don't you just...you know...end it? I'll go with you." He jerks the wheel to the right, taking the next corner a little tighter than usual.

"Will you slow down, please?" Annie asks, glancing out at the curved road ahead of them.

Toby pulls his foot off the pedal slightly and steals a glance at her from the corner of his eye. "So did you hear what I said or what?" he asks.

"Yeah, Toby, I heard you," Annie responds. Her heart pounds as the gravel beneath Toby's tires flips behind them, knocking against the bottom of the car.

"Toby, slow down!" Annie cries again, her voice raising to a yell. Toby lets out a growl of frustration and slams on the brake, yanking the wheel hard so that they skid to a stop on the side of the road. He turns to look at her, his eyes wild, fear dancing across his normally handsome features. Annie draws in short, shallow breaths. She shifts in her seat so that she is looking directly into his eyes.

"Toby," she starts, forcing her voice to stay calm despite the continued pounding in her chest. The tears are dry now.

"I don't expect you to be ready for this. Let's face it, you and I both know I'm alone. This is my problem, not yours. So I'll figure it out, okay?"

"What, so I don't get a say in the matter?" he spits back at her.

Annie shrugs. "Do you have an opinion?" she asks.

He opens his mouth, then closes it again, his shoulders slumping.

"It's just..." Annie stops. She reaches out and puts her hand on Toby's wrist, squeezing it tight. "I can't do...*that*, Toby," she says. Her voice is quiet but firm. "I can't end it. I just can't. I've thought about it. I've done the research. But, *I can't do it.*" The pitch of her voice raises and Toby pulls back.

"So then what?" Toby asks. His voice is softer now, but there's still an edge to his words that pricks at Annie. "What're you gonna do?"

Annie shrugs. "I don't know yet," she replies.

"Yeah, well, listen Annie. I am barely making ends meet right now, okay? I can hardly pay my own rent. There's no way I can support you and a kid."

Annie glares at him. "I get that, Toby. That's why I told you you're off the hook. This is my deal. I'll figure it out, okay?"

"Whatever," Toby mumbles. He grabs the stick and shifts the car into gear, pushing his foot down on the gas and peeling out onto the street. He doesn't see the car coming around the bend, and by the time he registers the sound of the horn, it's too late.

The last thing Annie hears is metal grinding and a scream filling in the empty space above her head.

# ELIZAVETA

*I am haunted, and I deserve it.*

I sit in the stiff bed, back rigid, face pressed into a stubborn, hardened stare. Blinking hard, I fight against the smell that haunts me more than anything else. Death has a very telling odor, the draining of life settling in the air, suffocating the senses. It's a smell that never quite escapes the consciousness, and even now all these years later, the memory of it sends a wave of nausea over me. Fear tickles the back of my spine. Death is coming for me. I know it, and I'm not yet ready.

The doctors poked and prodded for far too long, asking questions that didn't make sense even after Nina translated them. I cannot relax until Viktor Shevchenko arrives. As soon as he steps into the room, I feel myself settle into the pillow.

"Good," I bark as he steps to my bedside. "I'm glad you're here. I think it is time for me to go home. These doctors, if they really *are* doctors, don't believe anything I say. They think I'm just a crazy old woman. Tell them I am done. There's nothing wrong with me."

Nina looks at Viktor and he nods. "Okay, Elizaveta Andreyevna," he says gently. "I'll go talk with the doctor on shift and see what he says. If he's satisfied, I will ask him to be finished for the day, okay?"

I nod at him with one, slight move of my head. He gives

Nina a small smile then leaves the room, the door slowly closing behind him.

"Mama." Nina's voice cuts through the air, slicing the silence and causing my heart to skip a beat. I shift my eyes to her, willing them to focus on her face. Blinking hard, Nina takes a few steps forward. I lean back on the thick pillow and pull the scratchy hospital sheet up a little higher.

"Mama, who is Dima?"

This is the only question left, and Nina waited until we were alone to ask it. I glance at the door, willing it to open. Of course, now those annoying young doctors choose to give me space, no one charging through the door trailing his long, white coat behind him on the wings of his own pride. The door remains shut, confining me inside with nothing but my lies to protect me, thin veil that they have become. The stories shimmer like a mirage, softening a bit as if beckoning me to tear the sheet away and reveal the truth.

Nina sits down on the edge of the bed, and I jump at the movement. I shift my eyes back to Nina's face. She stares back at me, bright, a longing for answers swimming in the center. I open my mouth to speak, then close it again.

"Mama," she repeats. Nina reaches out her hand and rests it lightly on the sheet that covers my leg. Her touch feels cold. I jerk my leg away.

"Who is Dima?" she asks again, pulling her hands back and clasping them together in her lap.

"I don't know what you are talking about," I answer. The lie feels bitter on my tongue, sharp and painful. Nina looks at me for a long moment before pushing herself up off the bed. She picks up her purse and sweater, tucking them into the crook of her elbow.

"I need to use the bathroom," I say, breaking the silence between us. I blink hard at the pain running through Nina's eyes.

Nina reaches down and puts her hand under my elbow, steadying me as I stand to my feet. "Your clothes are hanging up on the back of the door," she says quietly. "Do you need me to help you dress?"

I lift my chin and shake my head no, then turn to shuffle into the bathroom leaving my daughter behind. I close the door, placing a barrier between myself and her questions, and I turn to look in the mirror.

My hair stands in wild tufts around my head, bright silver shoots reaching out as if trying to escape. I turn on the sink and wet my hands, smoothing the renegade hair back into place. Standing up, I blot my face dry with a small towel and stare at my reflection in the mirror. I gaze into the eyes of an old woman. They're bloodshot and buried in wrinkles. Turning my head from side to side, I study myself closely. Once, not so long ago it seems, I was a pretty woman. Not beautiful, but pretty enough with large, brown eyes and delicate features. My lips had been naturally pink, and my thick hair had been my crown. But time has a way of fading more than just memories.

As I stare at my reflection, the image before me swims until I no longer see my own face, but that of my mother. Her face is smooth, not confined by the weathered signs of a history of lies. As I take in the peculiar sight, the air behind me shimmers. I blink, and when my eyes open my sister is standing behind me. I clasp my hand over my heart and whirl around, coming face to face with Tanya. She's exactly as she was the last time we saw one another so many years ago. Tanya looks hard at me, accusing and angry.

"Tell the truth," she says. Her voice sounds like the wind, the words blowing into my ears and whistling through my soul. "Stop lying."

My hands tremble as I try to form words in reply. This isn't real. It cannot be real. But it feels so very real. Tanya glares at me.

"Say it!" she yells. "Say it now, out loud. Who is Dima? SAY IT! You owe it to him to say it out loud!"

"Dima was our brother," I whisper to the woman swimming in and out of my sight like a vision in the hot light of the desert sun. "He was our brother, and he loved us. He took care of us until the day that he vanished."

Tanya shakes and disappears. My mouth opens. I reach into the air before me hoping to catch the vision, longing to touch her, to know she was real, but my hands come back empty, and I slump against the sink, the pain of those spoken words trickling down my weathered cheeks.

"Dima was my brother only until I turned fifteen years old," I continue with a tremor. "And then he was the enemy. He was the escapee. He was the hunted. Dima was a traitor."

I reach my hand up and cover my mouth, trying to trap the words before they can fill the room.

# NINA

*There is no dissonance quite so abrasive
as that of an unwelcomed secret discovered.*

Nina closes her eyes and rubs her temple. A headache has formed behind her eyes, and she longs for a soft bed and a dark room so she can sleep away the stress of the afternoon.

"Mama?" she calls, leaning in toward the bathroom door. "Are you okay?"

Elizaveta pulls open the door and steps back into the room. She has smoothed her hair back with water, and her dark dress now hangs over her thick body instead of the hospital gown.

"I am fine," she says, her voice shaking.

Nina guides her back toward the bed and lowers her down onto it. "I'm going to go find the doctor and see what we need to do before we leave, okay?" she says. She doesn't look her mother in the eye.

"*Khorosho,*" Elizaveta responds, her voice just above a whisper.

Nina turns and walks into the hall outside her mother's room. She blinks, adjusting her eyes to the bright, white lights and bustling noise that surrounds her. She turns toward the nurse's station, then stops as her phone begins buzzing in her pocket.

"Yes?" she answers. Her voice comes out harder than she intended. She takes a deep breath to try and calm her frazzled nerves.

"Hello, is this the mother of Anastasia Abrams?" The voice on the other end is gentle, her thick, Tennessee accent dragging out the syllables of her words.

"Yes." Nina presses the phone to her ear and steps to the side, leaning her shoulder against the wall.

"Ma'am, I am sorry to be calling with this news, but I'm afraid there has been a car accident, and your daughter was involved. Her injuries are not critical, but the young man who was driving the car sustained serious injuries. Your daughter has been taken to University of Tennessee Medical Center."

Nina shakes her head. "I'm sorry," she replies. "I think that you are mistaken. My daughter rides the bus home from school. She does not ride in a car with a boy." Nina grips the phone tighter to settle the trembling in her fingers.

"Ma'am, I am sorry to be the one to tell you this, but I am afraid it *was your* daughter in the car this afternoon. Can you get to the hospital okay?"

Nina looks around at the bright lobby with its silver-white walls and floor to ceiling windows. Two doctors walk past her, discussing something in murmured tones. She pinches the bridge of her nose and shakes her head slightly.

"Yes, I can get to the hospital," she says. "I will be right there."

"Great," the woman on the other end says. Her voice is warm, like fresh honey. "When you arrive, head to the Emergency Room, and we will direct you from there."

Nina drops her phone into her purse and rushes down the hall, bursting into the lobby of the hospital. She pushes through the door that leads to the next wing and runs into Viktor.

"Oh!" she cries as he reaches out his hand to steady her.

"I'm sorry," he says. Nina shakes her head.

"It's not your fault." She looks around him. The Emergency Room is across the roundabout outside the door.

"Is everything okay?" Viktor asks. His hand is still on her elbow.

"No, everything is not okay," Nina replies. Her words are stiff and clipped. She purses her lips and looks at him. "I just got a phone call that my daughter, Annie, has been in a car accident. She was in a car. With a *boy*. And they had an accident, and she is at the Emergency Room right now." Nina pushes past him and continues her walk toward the ER.

Viktor furrows his brow in concern and moves quickly to follow her. "I'm sorry," he says, stepping up beside Nina. "What can I do to help you?"

"Nothing," Nina replies, pushing through the hospital door into the bright, afternoon sunshine. Her hands shake as she makes her way toward the building that holds her only daughter, injured and alone. Viktor gently places his hand on her elbow.

"Why don't I stay with your mother for a bit while you go to your daughter," he says.

Nina glances at him from the corner of her eye and slows down. "Fine," she answers, her voice a little softer. "That would be very helpful. Thank you. Could you get her and bring her to me?"

Viktor offers a kind smile and a nod. "How about I take her to get something to eat first so that you can have some time with Annie?"

Nina blinks. "That would be fine, yes," she says, turning and walking more quickly now. Viktor slows and watches her go, her steps sharp and determined, the terrified gait of a mother fighting fear.

Nina pushes through the door and heads toward the front desk, her shoes squeaking across the freshly mopped floor.

"Hello, I am Nina Abrams. My daughter Anastasia was brought here after a car accident."

Nina swallows hard over the words. What was Annie doing in a car, and who was this boy she was with?

"Yes, ma'am," the receptionist says. "I'm the one who called you. I can't believe how quickly you got here!"

Nina considers offering an explanation but doesn't feel like it, so she remains quiet, staring at the receptionist with impatient eyes. The woman behind the desk clears her throat.

"Yes, well," she says glancing down at the manila folder in front of her. She opens it up and reads the paper inside. "Your daughter is in room 109," she says. "It's just down this hall, fourth door on the left."

Nina nods and turns on her heel. She rushes down the hallway and throws open the door to room 109. Annie sits in a bed against the wall, her arms crossed over her chest. She has a bandage over her forearm and a thick Band-aid over her left eye. She looks small in that hospital bed.

"*Privyet*," Nina says, suddenly feeling quite tired. She walks to Annie's bedside and sits down gently. Reaching out, she runs the back of her hand over the bandage on Annie's face, her fingertips barely brushing against her daughter's skin. Annie looks away from her mom, staring down at the blanket that covers her legs.

"What happened?" Nina asks.

Annie shrugs. "I was in a car accident," she says. Nina drops her hand and narrows her eyes, studying her daughter's face. She waits for Annie to explain further.

Annie sighs. "I was in my friend Toby's car," she replies. "He pulled out onto the road quickly and didn't see another car coming around the corner, and they hit us. He was hurt pretty badly." Annie's voice quivers. "He wasn't conscious when the ambulance arrived," she continues.

Nina nods. She runs her hand over the blanket that covers Annie's legs. "And who was this boy?" she asks. "This Toby?"

Annie sighs. "He's the...boy that I have been dating," she mumbles.

Nina opens her mouth to reply, but stops when the door opens. A young doctor walks in, her light brown hair pulled back in a stiff ponytail. She is short and stout with a broad face and indifferent eyes.

"Hello, are you Mrs. Abrams?" she asks. Nina stands and nods.

"I'm Dr. Hewitt. Can I have a word with you out in the hall?"

Nina looks quizzically at the doctor, then glances back down at Annie who has turned her face to the window, avoiding any eye contact.

"Yes, of course," Nina murmurs, following the doctor out the door and into the hallway. Dr. Hewitt holds a chart in the crook of her elbow and turns to face Nina.

"Your daughter is lucky," she begins. "The accident could have been much worse. She'll need a few stiches in the cut on her arm, and we'll put a liquid Band-aid over the cut on her forehead. Both should heal up fine. She likely will also experience some neck and back pain in the next few days. This is to be expected."

A young man in blue scrubs walks past them carrying a metal tray in his hands. He pushes into Annie's room as Nina watches, growing more agitated.

Nina nods. "And the boy who was driving the car?" she asks.

Dr. Hewitt nods. "Yes, his injuries were a little more severe, as the other car hit him directly. But he is awake and is being treated. He's stable."

Nina nods. "This is good," she says. She straightens the purse on her shoulder. "So when can I take Annie home?" she asks.

Dr. Hewitt nods. "As soon as we finish stitching up her arm, she will be free to go. I just have a few papers for you to sign. But first, Mrs. Abrams, I need to tell you," Dr. Hewitt pauses and turns so that she is facing Nina squarely. "When Annie arrived, she told us that she is pregnant," she says.

Nina doesn't register her words at first. They seem to bounce past her, and she stares at the young woman standing before her in a long, white coat.

"I'm sorry," she responds with a shake of her head. "What did you say?"

"Annie is pregnant," Dr. Hewitt repeats. "We ran an ultrasound right away, and she's roughly 12 weeks along." The doctor looks up at Nina. "She'll need to start seeing a doctor regularly."

Nina steps back and stares at Dr. Hewitt with wide eyes. She draws in a long, shaky breath and nods her head slowly. "Yes, of course," she says.

Dr. Hewitt holds out her clipboard. "If you could just sign right here," she says gently, "then you and Annie are free to leave as soon as they finish with her arm."

Nina takes the pen and unevenly signs her name. Dr. Hewitt hands her a sheet of paper.

"I've written the name of several OB-GYNS that you can call if you need a recommendation," she says. "I also gave Annie a picture of the ultrasound if you want to ask her about it."

Nina nods and backs away. She turns and puts her hand on the doorknob to Annie's room. Tears prick the corners of her eyes and her heart races. She bites her quivering lip and straightens her shoulders, then takes a deep breath and enters the room. Annie lay back on the bed, her long, thin legs stretched out in front of her. The young man in blue scrubs leans over her arm, working quickly to close the cut. Annie looks so young, like a little girl who can't find her way back home.

"Oh, Nastia," Nina whispers. A tremor pulses down her neck and through her shoulders, working it's way out her fingertips. She stares at her only child, the little girl who was her whole world for so long. Nina does not know the girl lying before her in that bed. She is someone entirely different.

Annie turns toward her mother, and her face crumbles.

"Mama," she whispers. Nina, heart tearing in two, rushes to her daughter's side and engulfs her in a desperate embrace.

"Easy, easy," the man in scrubs says, holding Annie's partially sutured arm steady.

Annie buries her face in her mother's neck and sobs. Nina strokes her daughter's hair, small pieces of glass pricking at her fingertips, a reminder that love can cut deeply, and unexpectedly.

There are no words spoken between mother and daughter. Only the desperate embrace of two people who once depended on each other for everything, but who lost that dependence in the shuffle of life. Nina doesn't know where to begin or what to say, nor does she trust her voice.

The young man finishes, gently washing Annie's arm and wrapping a bandage around the wound as mother and daughter grip one another in pained silence. Annie's tears subside, and she pulls away from her mother as the nurse pushes back and stands up.

"Alright," he says, glancing from Annie to Nina and back again. "You're good to go. Just keep that cut clean and change the bandage regularly, okay?"

Annie looks up at him and nods, swiping away the tears from her cheeks. He brushes past Nina who gives him the slightest nod of acknowledgement before he leaves the room. Her eyes shift back to her daughter.

"Annie," she begins, voice breaking. Annie looks away. The moment of tenderness flees almost as quickly as it came. Nina watches her daughter retreat back into the shell she has constructed for herself. Annie draws in two long, jagged breaths, blinking hard and drying her cheeks with the back of her hand.

"Can we not talk about this right now, Mom?" Annie asks. Her voice is flat, all emotion swallowed and tucked safely away. "Please?" She stares at her mom, fear and desperation mixed together in her bright eyes. Nina tilts her head to the side and blinks.

"If not now, then when?" Nina asks. She blinks away her own tears, and swallows against the exasperation that threatens to replace the compassion she had felt moments ago. Annie turns her face away from Nina's, her mouth set in a stubborn line.

"You are pregnant." The words tumble painfully off Nina's tongue. "I assume this Toby is the father?"

Annie swings her legs to the side of the bed and stands up. "Mom," she says, her voice now steady. "I don't want to talk about this right now, okay? I just don't."

They lock eyes and stare at one another for a long moment. Just as Nina opens her mouth to speak, the door behind her flies open and Elizaveta walks in followed by Viktor.

"How is my granddaughter?" she asks. Her gaze shifts to Annie who stands awkwardly by the bed, cradling her bandaged arm in her hand.

"Oy, you are alive. This is good." She turns to Nina. "And why was she in a car without you?" she asks. "Whose car was she in? How did this happen? You should know these things. She is your daughter."

Nina shifts her gaze to Annie's face, which has stiffened. *Yes*, Nina thinks, the lump once again burning her throat. *I should know these things because she is my daughter.*

Viktor steps to Nina's side. "I'm sorry," he says softly. "I tried to stall, to get her to come with me to the cafeteria, but she insisted that the food would kill her. She just wanted to be here with you."

Nina shifts her gaze to him. "It's alright," she answers. Viktor takes in a deep breath.

"Do you want me to stay?" he asks.

Nina shakes her head. "No," she replies. "Thank you but we will go home now. Annie is fine."

*She's not fine, she's pregnant.*

Viktor nods. "I'll call to check on you all later," he says.

Nina offers one, quick nod. Viktor reaches out and gives her hand a gentle squeeze, then turns to Elizaveta.

"I will be leaving you now, Elizaveta Andreyevna," he says. She turns to face him, squinting through the dim light.

"I'll call with the results of your testing in the next few days."

"Fine," Elizaveta responds. "And I assume you will be calling Nina to take her to dinner?"

"Mama, not now," Nina interjects, her voice cutting as she wars against all her pent up emotion. Elizaveta draws back her shoulders and glares at Nina.

"Goodbye," Viktor says gently. He nods at Annie, then turns and leaves the room.

Nina stares at her mother and daughter, the space between all of them wide, like a chasm. "Come on," she says with a sigh. "Let's go home."

# ELIZAVETA

*Much can be done to flee the memories,*
*but it's the silence one cannot fight.*

I watch the trees as they move past us, the fading sunlight peeking occasionally through the branches and kissing the center of my eyes. The sky is streaked in hues of red and gold, purple and yellow and vibrant orange all rolling together to give one a sense of majesty. I don't remember seeing such sunsets as a child. Were they there and I missed them, or did they simply not exist then?

I lean my head back and shift my eyes forward. Nina clutches the wheel beside me, her knuckles white. The radio, which usually plays all manner of nonsense that the Americans call music, is silent. I hear only the sound of gravel crunching beneath tires as we make our way back toward the place we call home—a place that doesn't feel like home at all.

Nina glances repeatedly at Annie in the rearview mirror. What passed between mother and daughter is not known, but the tension I feel is something that is so familiar. I felt the same tension with my own mother so many years ago. I remember the way she studied me—the way her eyes searched mine, longing for some sense of understanding of who I was and what I was thinking. Nina searches Annie's face the same way. She is a mother who longs to see into her daughter's heart.

My eyelids grow heavy, but I fight the feeling. I cannot shake the visions of Dima and Tanya. If I close my eyes, they may come back, and I don't know that I can handle seeing them again today.

Nina turns into the driveway and pulls up the small hill, slowing the car to a stop. We sit in silence for a very brief moment before she turns off the car. Annie pushes out of the car and slams the door behind her, causing me to jump.

"*Bozhe moi*," I mutter. Nina sighs.

"I'll help you inside, Mama," she says. My daughter's voice is weary, and there is a sadness there that I haven't noticed before. I look at her, trying to make out her features in the dimming light, but my eyes fail me. I cannot see her eyes to read them.

Nina steps out of the car and walks around to my door, opening it and grabbing my elbow to steady me as I stand. Normally I would wave her off, but not today. Something tells me that right now she needs me to let her help. Somehow, in this brief moment, I know enough not to fight back.

We walk slowly inside, my legs feeling shaky beneath me. Age is an unforgiving foe and doesn't ask permission before taking things from you from your looks to your sight—even the simplest act of standing on your own two feet.

When we get inside the house, Nina helps me out of my coat and hangs it up for me. We stand and stare at one another awkwardly for a few moments.

"I think I will go change my clothes," I finally say. She nods her head.

"Do you need anything?" she asks.

"No, I'm fine on my own," I respond.

Turning slowly, I shuffle to my room and close the door behind me. I stand still for a long moment, my hand on the doorknob as I remember all the years that have swollen the space between Nina and me. They were quiet years when she lived with me at home, but when she left the silence grew suffocating. The silence was why I finally had to leave—why I had to do the thing I swore I would never do. I had to leave the land of my youth, the home that had molded me in all the good and bad ways, and I had to come here, to this foreign, loud world filled with colors and smells that were as unfamiliar as the language. I had to come because I couldn't stand the silence.

I didn't realize that it would follow me here.

# NINA

*A toast to love, to happiness,
to a life that's full and free,
is given then with great finesse
but it can never be.*

Nina collapses onto the couch, pulling up her slippered feet and tucking them underneath her. The house is quiet. She hears the shower running upstairs and the familiar shuffling and puttering of her mother behind her closed bedroom door. Nina grasps her mug of hot tea between her hands and lets her mind wander back to her eighteenth birthday.

She'd come home late that night, having spent the afternoon drinking with her friends in the ditch behind the courtyard of the school. They'd taken turns offering toasts in her honor, draining a bottle of port that her friend Pasha had stolen from his grandfather's liquor cabinet.

"May your future be bright!" her friend Marina had giggled, the liquor pushing its way immediately to her head.

"To your health!" Evgeniy said with a wink, making her heart flutter. He was her first love, the boy she thought she would marry until she later found out he was the love of several girls around town.

"May you get out of this hell hole and find peace in another land. And may you prove your mother wrong." Pasha's eyes locked with Nina's as the alcohol made the ground around them swirl and dance. She looked at him and clinked glasses, then poured the searing hot liquid down her throat. The memory burns. She takes a sip of her tea, wishing she could go back to that moment so long ago when the future seemed so very hopeful. Even then, as a young girl trapped behind the Iron Curtain, Nina had a sense that her life would look different. She craved adventure and longed to experience the world that her country, and her mother, worked so hard to hide from her. When she drank to Pasha's toast, it was as though a bit of magic swam through her, convincing her that her life would be different. But right now, she finds herself unsure. Perhaps his toast had not been a blessing, but rather a curse.

Nina puts her mug down on the table next to the couch and rubs her eyes. She's suddenly exhausted. She leans her head back for a brief moment, then opens her eyes and sits back up to find Elizaveta standing in front of the couch. Nina yelps in surprise.

"Mama!" she gasps. "You scared me! I didn't hear you."

Elizaveta has changed into her nightdress, a long cotton gown that makes her look twice as large as she is and hangs to just above her feet, which are covered in the thin, white slippers that she refuses to replace despite Nina's many attempts.

"I'm sorry," Elizaveta replies. "I did not mean to."

"No, it's okay," Nina says. She pushes herself to a stand and gestures for Elizaveta to sit in her place. "Would you like something to eat?" she asks.

Elizaveta waves her hand in the air. "I am fine. I don't need to eat as much as Americans need to eat. I survived the war, you know. Didn't eat for months, but I survived because I'm strong, and my body knows how to conserve its own fuel."

Nina closes her eyes and counts to five before reopening them and offering her mother a thin-lipped smile. She's heard this story a thousand times, always with some kind of variation. Sometimes it's that Elizaveta didn't eat for a year, sometimes she went only days with no food. Today it is apparently months. And predictably her mother always mentions the cold.

"It was also devastatingly cold. Not what the Americans call cold here, of course. This is practically the tropics compared to the cold of the war. No, the cold I survived was the kind that you felt in your bones. It was the cold that made your teeth ache, and there was no escaping it."

They settle into uncomfortable silence. Nina has no response for her mother's ramblings, so she stands still, staring blankly at the wall of the kitchen where Annie's kindergarten picture hangs slightly lopsided over the table. She had gotten a pair of scissors the night before picture day and cut her bangs painfully short. Nina tried to slick the fine little sprouts of hair back into a bun, but it didn't work, so she'd finally combed them down flat against her forehead where they fell about a quarter of an inch below her hairline. Annie's wide smile revealed a large gap where her two front teeth used to be, and her eyes sparkled with childish curiosity and mischief.

Nina thinks about that little girl—the way the light would dance in her eyes when she told a story, her lisped words tumbling out of a mouth that couldn't seem to keep up. Nina remembers when laughter and tenderness were the pillars of this home they shared.

"Nina!"

Nina turns her face to her mother and looks into her eyes. "I asked you a question," Elizaveta says.

"Sorry," Nina says rubbing the back of her neck. "I was distracted. What did you ask?"

"I want to know when you will see Viktor again," Elizaveta responds.

"Oh, I don't know," Nina says. She grabs her mug and walks to the kitchen, pouring a little more hot water into her cup and settling in another tea bag. "We didn't talk about it."

"Oh, *Ninochka*," Elizaveta says with a sigh. "You must act

fast and not lose that man. He is the one you have been waiting for."

"Mama," Nina says, annoyance now creeping into her voice. "I..." she breaks off and lets her head drop for a moment, fighting back another wave of emotional fatigue.

Taking a deep breath, she looks back up at her mother. "I haven't been waiting for anyone," she continues, the words quiet. "I'm perfectly fine with my life the way it is right now." But even as she speaks, Nina knows that's a lie. Her teenage daughter is pregnant, her nagging mother is ailing, and she's got a family background that doesn't make any sense. The truth is, she knows her mother is right. Viktor is the kind of man that one doesn't let get away, but Nina can't decide if the fact that he meets her mother's approval is a positive, or a strike against him.

"Oh my darling," Elizaveta says leaning forward just slightly. "Are any of us ever really happy in this life?"

Nina takes a long drink, then sets her glass down and grabs a new glass, filling it with water. "I need to go check on Annie," she murmurs.

"What's wrong with the girl?" Elizaveta calls out. Nina stops, immediately formulating an explanation that doesn't involve telling her mother the truth.

"Nothing," she says with a small wave of her hand, a gesture so similar to Elizaveta's that Nina almost cringes. "She'll be fine." Nina turns and walks quickly up the stairs, ignoring her mother's narrowed, knowing eyes.

# ANNIE

L ying back against her pillows, Annie stares at the pictures in her hand. The first is a picture of her and her mom taken years ago at Nina's office Christmas party. Annie keeps the photo under her mattress, pulling it out occasionally to remind herself that she once felt happy.

Nina's arm is around her daughter's shoulders, and Annie leans into her mother's side. Their mouths are open, both of them mid-laugh. What they were laughing at, Annie cannot remember, but this photo, captured in a single, brief moment of time, reminds her of the joy of laughing out loud.

Annie lays the photo down and stares at the second image. This grainy black and white photo is evidence of the truth she's carried silently for months, and she blinks back tears. She traces her hand over the fuzzy silhouette of the child in her womb—proof of its existence. She closes her eyes and thinks of the way her mother embraced her today. It was the first real connection she'd felt in a long time.

At the knock on her door, Annie quickly shoves the pictures under the pillow and turns on her side, closing her eyes.

Nina comes in silently and walks to her daughter's bedside. Her room smells fruity, the scent of Annie's shampoo lingering in the air. Nina sets down the mug of tea on the bedside table, then sits softly on the edge of the bed.

"I know you're awake," she says. Annie opens her eyes and

shifts them to Nina. The bandage over her left eye is already peeling away at the corner. Annie has re-wrapped her stitched arm in fresh gauze. Mother and daughter hold one another's gaze for a brief moment before Annie looks away. She traces the pattern of her quilt with her finger, taking in shallow breaths through the thick, tense air.

"How are you feeling?" Nina murmurs. "Are you in pain?"

"I'm fine," Annie confesses. She slowly pushes herself up and leans back against her pillows. The corners of the pictures push out from beneath her. Nina reaches over and takes hold of them, sliding them out from beneath the pillow. She looks first at the picture from the Christmas party, and a fresh wave of emotion courses through her. She remembers that night. The man who took the photo was one of her colleagues and he'd just told them a joke.

"What's black and white and red all over?" he called, holding the camera up to his eye.

"I don't know! What?" Annie replied.

"A penguin with a sunburn!" he yelled, and Annie had collapsed into her mother's side in a fit of giggles, which set Nina laughing as well.

She shifts her gaze to the other picture. She stares at it closely, studying the small profile, the tiny legs kicked up above a round and forming abdomen. She closes her eyes briefly as the doctor's words from earlier in the day run through her mind once more.

*Pregnant. About 12 weeks.*

"Are you ready to talk about this?" Nina asks. She holds up the ultrasound.

Annie shrugs. She crosses her arms over her midsection and leans her head back, closing her eyes. As quickly as the tenderness came, frustration replaces it and Nina sighs.

"That's not an answer, Nastia," she responds.

Annie's eyes snap open. "Fine," she replies. "Then, no. I'm not ready to talk, alright? What do you want me to say anyway, Mom? I screwed up. I ruined everything. I destroyed your image of my perfect future. I've embarrassed you. Babushka will now be even more ashamed of me than she already is, and she will know for certain now that *you're* a failure, which I'm guessing is the most disturbing piece of the whole puzzle for you, isn't it? Is that enough talking for you?"

Annie turns her face, immediately regretting the horrible, hurtful things she said to her mother. Nina stands, her knees shaking and weak. The lump in her throat swells and she stares at her daughter. Impulsively, she leans forward and places a firm kiss on the top of Annie's head. She lays the two photographs down on the bed before turning and moving quickly to the door, closing it behind her and blinking furiously against the tears that threaten to spill on her cheeks.

Annie rolls back over just as the door clicks shut, preparing to call her mother back. She stares at the white door, the large puppy poster on the back hanging slightly crooked and frayed at the edges.

"I'm sorry," Annie whispers into the void of space. She covers her face with her hands to muffle her sobs.

# NINA

*Nothing cures an aching heart*
*quite like a scalding cup of chai.*

Nina makes her way shakily down the stairs. She glances at her mother, who still sits stoically on the couch.

"I'm going to make some more chai," she says, her voice thick. She clears her throat. "Would you like some?"

Elizaveta nods her head once. Nina fills the teapot and sets it on the stove. She's reaching for two mugs when her phone rings on the counter beside her.

Nina grabs it and answers without even looking to see who it is, grateful for the distraction from her mother's probing stare.

"*Allo?*" she answers.

"Hello yourself." Nina's hearts skips at the sound of Viktor's voice. She turns her back to Elizaveta and lowers her voice.

"Hi, sorry," she murmurs. "Sometimes I forget to make the switch from Russian to English." Her face flushes as she sets the mugs on the counter. She turns her back to her mother.

"It's alright," Viktor chuckles. "I wanted to give you some of the results from today's tests."

Nina stops moving and presses the phone more firmly

against her ear. "Oh?" she replies. "I didn't realize you would have them so quickly."

"Well," Viktor begins. He clears his throat. "It will be a few days before we get any definitive answers, but overall it seems she is in fairly good health. For her age, and as little exercise as she gets, as well as her sparse diet, she is in as good a shape as we could hope for."

"But," Nina injects.

"But there was the episode this afternoon, and the fact that she is struggling to retrieve words. There is still some concern about dementia." Nina takes in a long, deep breath as Viktor continues.

"For now, I think it's best that we urge her to make a few lifestyle changes."

"Like what?" Nina asks. She removes the whistling teapot from the stove and pours the steaming water into the waiting mugs, watching as the bags of tea float lazily to the top of the cup.

"Well, for starters, she needs to be moving around a little more. I know that it's hard for her, but even if she could just take a few laps around the kitchen table every day to increase the circulation in her legs, that would help."

Nina swallows hard, knowing that this suggestion will be ruefully scoffed by her mother. "What else?" she asks.

"I'd like to start her on a vigorous round of vitamins to increase some of the positive effects in her bloodstream and memory, and she needs to stay consistent with her cholesterol and blood pressure medication."

Nina's mouth stretches into a thin-lipped smile. "You obviously haven't spent enough time with my Mama," she says, sarcasm dripping from her words. "I will let you be the one to give her those instructions. She'll dismiss me with one, quick wave of her hand if I try."

She can hear the grin in Viktor's voice as he replies. "Fair enough," he says. "I've got a way with Russian mothers, you know."

"Yes, you do," Nina murmurs. Viktor clears his throat on the other end of the line.

"So that's all I have for now, but like I said I'll have a more comprehensive report in a few days. Now...how is your daughter doing?" Viktor asks.

Nina draws in a deep breath and closes her eyes, the vision of Annie pressed back into her pillow looking angry and sullen filling her mind.

"She's...fine," Nina says. She suddenly feels very, very tired. "She will be fine."

There's a pause at the other end of the line before Viktor clears his throat and continues.

"I didn't only call to talk about your mother, Nina," he says. She can hear the nerves in his voice, and her heart starts beating a little more rapidly. "I know it's been a long day for all of you, and I was going to wait to ask, but...well, I can't wait." He coughs nervously. "I was wondering if we could meet sometime soon? I'd like to see you. Alone. Without your mother watching." She can hear the smile in his voice.

Nina feels her shoulders relax as she considers meeting with Viktor. She turns to hand her mother her tea, and Elizaveta's eyebrows shoot up, almost disappearing into her hairline as her eyes bore into Nina's, and immediately the muscles seize back up as reality sets in. She cannot meet with this man. Not tonight - maybe not ever. Not under the steady gaze of Elizaveta Mishurova.

"That's very kind of you to ask," she says, turning her back again and lowering her voice. "But I'm not sure when I'll be able to get away. There is just...a lot going on these days." Nina walks out of the room, pushing open the front door and stepping out onto the porch to get away from her mother's persistent stare.

"Of course," Viktor says, and Nina cringes at the disappointment in his voice. "I understand. It's not a good time."

There's an awkward pause as Nina tries to come up with the right words to say to smooth over this bumpy conversation. Finally, Viktor clears his throat.

"Well then," he says. "I'll let you go. Feel free to call me if you need anything at all."

Nina nods. "Yes, of course I will," she answers. "And...perhaps another time will be better," she offers. Her voice sounds timid, unsure of how to proceed with this man whom she wants to know, but can't find the space in her already muddled life to fit in.

"Yes," Viktor said. "Perhaps. Good night, Nina."

The line goes quiet and Nina pauses for a moment, contemplating the potentially terrible decision she just made. With a deep breath, she turns around and steps back into the house, walking back into the kitchen to grab her mug of tea.

"Was that Viktor Shevchenko?" Elizaveta asks. Nina nods slowly.

Elizaveta raises her eyebrows. "Well good," she replies. "I knew he would call. He is a good man. A good *Russian* man, and the good ones always call right away."

Nina takes a sip of her chai and offers her mother a barely discernible nod of the head.

"Did you know," Elizaveta continues, "that Russian men are actually *smarter* than men of other nationalities? It's true. It's a scientific fact, actually."

Nina bites her lip and glances up at the ceiling, taking note of a vent that needs to be cleaned out.

"So what did he say?" Elizaveta asks.

"He wanted to check to see how you and Annie were doing," Nina replies, choosing her words carefully. Elizaveta looks hard at her daughter.

"Is that *all* he wanted?" she asks. Nina takes in a deep breath and shrugs her shoulders.

"Yes, that's it," she replies. She takes a drink of her tea, letting the scalding hot water work its way past the tightness in her throat. Unable to stand the intensity of Elizaveta's gaze, Nina takes a deep breath and pushes to a stand.

"I'm going to take a shower and go to bed," she says. "It's been a long day." She leans forward and kisses Elizaveta gently on the cheek.

"*Da*," Elizaveta murmurs, watching her daughter turn toward the stairs. "A long day."

# ELIZAVETA

*Love, they say, is the emotion of the weak.*
*Why then did it make me feel so strong?*

I watch her leave, trailing behind her a scent of doubt. She's pushing Viktor Shevchenko away, but she doesn't really want to. I can tell. I'm old, but I still remember that feeling of hopefulness and bright-eyed desire. I felt it for Igor, and the memory of his youthful face, the eyes that drew me in and held me captive for ten years, pulls me back into a time that felt both infinitely more complicated, and yet also so much simpler than today.

Igor was the only man I ever loved. I met him just as I was beginning to give up on the prospect of love. There were men before him, but they were the type of men that only used me for a short time, got from me what they wanted, then discarded me like a mangy pup on the side of the road. But not my Igor. He was gentle and kind, a good man who loved me fiercely until the day he discovered my lies.

I was twenty-nine when I first caught his eye, a research technician at the Russian National Research Medical University in Moscow where he came on staff to teach fresh-faced youth barely grown out of the young Komsomols. Handsome and quiet, he immediately became an attraction to every single woman inside the university walls.

Life was, of course, different then. We were still dealing with the effects of the war, still reeling from the devastation of those long, dark years when death became the constant bedfellow to us all.

I was rebuilding in more ways than one, meticulously erecting walls around myself meant to keep anyone from getting too close. I'd forged a new path all on my own. I had to. It was the only way to survive. The choice had been presented to me so clearly since those early years trapped in the icy winds of the gulag: Family or State. One had to choose between the two, and each choice came with consequences. To choose Family over State meant that I would live in constant fear of rejection. I was the child of a *kulak*—a half-citizen considered dangerous by my government due to nothing more than the geography of my birth and my father's refusal to bend to the will of the oppressive NKVD, the police bent on upholding their beloved Stalin's Five Year Plan. This status barely registered me as a citizen, and it was drilled into my head that a *kulak's* offspring had little to no prospects in life. The child of an enemy of the state did not deserve to be educated the way that a good Soviet was educated. And so, with the echo of Valerya Sergeevna ringing in my ears, I did the only thing that seemed logical at the time—I chose State.

Dima, my wayward and lost brother had long since chosen Family. He'd gone before me, fleeing what he called a wicked and traitorous government. He'd spoken viciously and boldly against the enforcers of State, generating backlash that dogged not only him, but the rest of us as well. I begged him to keep silent, to simply go along with the unit. I tossed around the ever-elusive term "acquiesce" as if I understood it, and our conversations grew more heated with each passing day. I was fifteen when my entire world exploded.

Dima came home frantic that last day. He grabbed a bag

and shoved in a shirt and pair of pants, three potatoes, and a loaf of mama's rye bread. All the while, he barked orders at Mama and me while Tanya hovered in the corner, trembling.

"They'll be here soon, and they will be looking for me. Don't talk to them. Say nothing, do you understand?" He stared at us. Mama nodded, but I just looked back in disbelief.

"What did you do?" I asked.

"That doesn't matter," he barked. "I simply stood up for what's right." He rushed to me, grabbing my arms and squeezing so tight that tears sprang to my eyes. "Don't trust them," he hissed. "I know you want to, but you can't. They are lying to you. Do *not* trust them."

Moments later, he rushed out the door and disappeared in the tall, yellow grass of the field. Sunflowers danced in his wake, as if bidding him a joyful goodbye. The rest of us were left to pick up the pieces. We had to put back together all that he'd torn apart, suffering long, cruel days of questioning by the NKVD agents who wanted us to confess to Dima's crimes. We were to admit our part in his traitorous activity, his blatant dissidence. Why they didn't just arrest us and throw us into the gulag to suffer the same fate as Papa, I do not know. Mama insisted it was the protection of her God—the God she spoke of rebelliously in the barracks of Siberia—the God she prayed to unashamedly morning and night—the God I begged her to forget, to leave behind lest we find ourselves in greater danger than before because of her open faith.

"I prayed that their eyes would be blinded, and that they would be unable to follow through with their usual protocol," she whispered after a particularly grueling day of questioning. She stroked Tanya's hair back off her face as she spoke, and I swallowed against the anger that threatened to drown me.

"God has protected us, *dochenka*," she said as she grabbed my hand. "He has answered my prayers." I pulled my hand from her grip, though, because her words were too foreign and dangerous. The NKVD officers never returned to our home after that day. It was as though they simply forgot about us, though I suspect that they caught Dima and killed him, thus losing interest in our family altogether. I never knew for sure, of course, but I'd grown used to living in the unknown by then.

The day that Dima left was the day I decided I would never trust Family again. We were not a unit, but rather each individuals looking out for ourselves. Mama clung to her faith, and Tanya clung to Mama. I chose to cling to the unit that I could see and grasp. It seemed, on the surface, that that was the easiest choice of all. I didn't realize that it would require such deep sacrifice. Dima broke my trust in Family, and I never thought I'd get it back again—at least not until I met Igor.

It was decidedly un-Soviet to fall in love, actually. The moment I found myself longing for Igor, desiring his presence, was the moment I began to doubt my decision to walk away from Family. Because to renounce the ones you love means you must forevermore keep everyone else at arm's length. This is what I did with Igor. I kept him just far enough away to prevent him ever knowing or seeing the real me, but I let him in enough to find those lines between Family and State blurring until I could no longer figure out why I'd separated the two in the first place.

Igor never even knew my real name. He didn't know that I was the daughter of a man who died behind the barbed fence of a gulag labor camp, sentenced to work for betraying the motherland. He didn't know that I was the sister of a boy who spoke so vocally against our government that he was eventually chased out of town, never to be seen or heard from again. He didn't know I was the daughter of a woman who read banned poetry and proclaimed her loyalty to an unseen, forbidden God.

He knew nothing about me, but he loved me, or he loved the image that I allowed him to love. For ten years, I held my secrets, stealthily shrouding them in vague speech and half stories. At night, after Igor went to bed, I'd reach into the drawer beside me and pull out the identification papers that I'd had falsified so many years earlier. I would read the name over and over, *Elizaveta Andreyevna Mishurova*, and I would recite the details of my rewritten history. I was the only daughter of intellectual parents, both of whom died in Leningrad at the end of the war. I was loyal to country and sound of mind. I had no siblings and no living family connections. I was alone, and I was a servant of the State.

I recited these facts over and over, hoping to one day believe them. During the daytime hours, when the sun shone brightly and people's eyes were blinded to the truth, I was able to almost make myself believe the story. But at night, under the watchful eye of the moon, I felt exposed. I'd watch Igor's chest rise and fall, his even breathing a clear sign that he had nothing to hide, no secrets to fear.

This is why it was so very surprising the day my sister showed up at our door. Tanya came in the middle of the day on a Sunday afternoon. Igor and I had been lying in bed, reading lazily, something so rare, as we normally spent our Sunday afternoons walking in the park or visiting the theater. But that day he wasn't feeling well, and we decided to stay home. When we heard the knock, I was so relaxed that it didn't even occur to me to be startled or afraid. I threw open the door and blinked in surprise, the image of her standing there foreign and strange. It was like a splotch of paint accidentally dropped into the middle of a serene landscape painting.

Her eyes were red, swimming with pain. She held in her arms a bundle, clutching it tight to her chest as her chin trembled in a rhythm of fear. I didn't even know what to say, so I said nothing, my heart racing, completely unaware that Igor had stepped into the hallway behind me.

"Can we help you?" he asked, and I jumped, the sound of his voice slicing through the air like a blade.

Her eyes shifted from my face to his, and then back to

mine. She jutted her chin toward me. "You can't," she whispered, "but she can."

Igor turned to me, and in that moment I knew that I would lose him, that all the lies and the secrets would now be exposed and would tear through us in one quick motion.

"Do you know her?" he asked. Still I didn't answer, because what could I say? There were too many words and not enough all at once.

I looked back at her and swallowed hard. "What..." my voice failed me. I shook my head, cleared my throat, and tried again. "What do you want?" I asked.

She thrust the bundle into my chest, and instantly a wail erupted. Igor and I both looked down, stunned, at the tiny face swaddled tight in layers of dirty blankets. Little fists pushed up out of the top of the swaddle, fighting for freedom. I took a step back, horrified at what I was seeing.

"I want you to take her," Tanya said, and as she did so a sob escaped her throat. It was a deep, guttural sound like the tearing of muscle from bone, so heart wrenching that I wanted to clap my hands over my ears and block it out.

"I...no. I can't!" I responded, backing away as she moved toward me, holding the screaming child out like a sacrifice.

"You have to take her!" she sobbed. "Take her now. You *must!*"

Igor stepped between Tanya and me, pushing the baby back toward her and spitting out his words.

"I don't know who you are," he seethed, "but you have no right to come to our home and demand we raise your bastard child. Get out of here you crazy woman."

Tanya rocked the baby close to her chest, sobbing as she gently kissed the little one's face. She looked back up at me, and I shifted my eyes down, unable to take the accusation.

"It was horrible for us when you left," she whispered.

My entire body tensed up as her words took root. "Mama died in that place. She died because of you. And I have been alone ever since." Tanya's voice broke, each syllable coming out in a pain-filled gasp. "But do you want to know what the final words were that she said to me the last time I saw her?"

I couldn't answer, couldn't breathe.

"She asked me to find you and to tell you that she forgives you."

Tanya buried her face into the blankets, the child in her arms now bright-eyed and silent, looking up as though fully aware of the moment's weight.

"How...did you find me?" I asked, my words no more than a gasp. She looked at me, disdain swimming through her eyes.

"I have my ways, sister," she hissed. "I knew you would find your way here, and of course you chose *that* name."

I swallowed hard, muted by the anger in her voice. She glanced down at the baby in her arms, tiny squeaks echoing from the blanket. Her face softened.

Tanya looked back at me and shook her head. "I can't raise this child," she said, tears welling up in her eyes. "I'm alone. I have no one to help me, no job, no way to provide for her. I cannot be the one to raise her because if I do, I will fail." Her eyes bore into mine. "Please," she whispered. "I need you to take her and raise her. I need you to give her a chance in this world. She'll have no opportunity in my care, but you can give her what I can't. Please."

I heard her voice, but it entered through my ears as though traveling first through a tin can. The sounds echoed, and as I tried to make sense of them the room began swaying. I tried to pull it all together, but I couldn't figure out the ceiling from the floor, and then everything went black.

⬥

When I woke, I found myself on the couch, Igor sitting in a chair across the room. His legs were crossed, a cigarette in between his fingers as he watched me closely. I sat up and looked around, wondering for a moment if it had all been a dream.

"I sent her away," he said softly. My eyes shifted to him, and I felt the breath pull from my chest in a gasp.

"Oh," I answered.

"She was your sister," he said. He drew the cigarette to his mouth and pulled in deeply, slowly releasing the smoke until it formed a momentary film between us, blurring the space that now divided him and me. That was the day that I began hating the smell of cigarette smoke.

"Yes," I answered, and the truth tasted like a bitter root.

"Yes?!" he exploded. He stood up so quickly that the chair behind him flipped over. I shrank back onto the couch as he advanced toward me, fire in his eyes. "You have a sister who is very much alive and a mother who did not actually die in the revolution, and you have nothing else to say?" He was now leaned down over me, the mingling of anger and betrayal so palpable that I felt the air between us light up. I didn't know what to say, or where to start. I opened my mouth, then closed it again.

"What is your name?" he asked, this time his voice quiet.

"My name is..." I hesitated. For a moment I didn't know how to answer. And then I made a choice.

"My name is Elizaveta Andreyevna Mishurova," I answered, raising my chin slightly.

He pushed himself back and stared down at me in disgust. "Liar," he said, spitting out the word like it burned his tongue.

I was about to speak again, to tell him that I was sorry, that I had become who I said I was and couldn't go back. I wanted to ask him to forgive me, and to trust me, but before I could say anything there was another knock at the door. Both of us froze.

"Are you expecting anyone else today?" he asked, sarcasm weaving through the words. "Your uncle, perhaps? Your long lost cousin? Or maybe your dead papa, resurrected?" Neither one of us moved.

I stared at him and he at me until the silence between us was broken by soft whimpers. He growled in disgust and stormed to the bedroom, slamming the door behind him. I pulled myself from the couch and walked heavily to the door, preparing the words that I would say to Tanya. "I cannot keep the child," I whispered as I approached the door. "I cannot keep the child. It doesn't belong to me. You must find another way."

I pulled open the door, ready to tell her the news, but no one was there. My eyes shifted to the floor where the child lay alone on the cold concrete, her whimpers quickly escalating into wails. A note was pinned to her blanket:

*You have to raise my daughter. You owe this to me, and you owe it to Mama. I pray to God that you take care of my baby. Raise her well and keep her safe. Her name is Nina.*

I slowly picked the child up and wrapped the blanket around her a little tighter. I brought her into the apartment, the feel of her little body against mine uncomfortable and awkward. I couldn't breathe, each inhale shallow as I tried to move the air through my constricted lungs. I walked into the bedroom where Igor sat sullenly on the bed. He looked at me, then down at the child.

"She left the baby," I said, my words hollow. Igor looked away, unable, or perhaps unwilling, to speak.

Two days later, Igor was gone, and Nina and I were alone.

# ANNIE

A nnie lays her book down slowly and stares out the window. The sun sits high now, the morning fog having long since burned off. She blinks back tears as she runs her hand over the cover of the book, tracing the title with her nail while digesting the story.

She closes her eyes, trying to force the image of George and Lennie from her mind, the outcome of their friendship too painful for her to process. Annie's stomach growls. Her mother is at work, and her grandmother should be down for her afternoon nap, so she pushes herself slowly up off the bed and waits for the room to stop spinning. She stands up and makes her way softly to the stairs. Taking care to avoid each creak, she walks quickly past her grandmother's closed door, her heart pounding. She glances nervously at the door, listening intently for any sounds behind the thin wood separating her and the woman who makes her feel unendingly scrutinized.

She tugs open the fridge and suppresses a small smile. Her mother has left two meals, each in its own container, and each labeled. She pulls out the container that says "ANNIE" and pulls it open. Inside is half a turkey and avocado sandwich, sliced apples, a small water bottle, and three Hershey Kisses. Shaking her head, Annie pulls out the sandwich and takes a bite. Immediately the rumbling in her stomach subsides and she feels her head begin to clear. She unwraps a Hershey Kiss and walks over to the wall opposite the kitchen. She grabs a photo album off the shelf and pads to the couch, settling down with the picture book and her lunch.

Annie takes a bite of her sandwich, then sets it down on the table next to the couch and opens the album. She stares at the pictures, trying to will some emotion to the surface. She feels nothing as she looks at the photos—no joy, no sadness. She feels only a numb sense of loss, as though somehow she once had all those things and they're now forever gone.

She runs her thumb over the picture of her and her mother sitting in front of a waterfall, the mist rising around them, fogging the photo so that it appears they're sitting in a haze. Her mom's arm is clasped tight around her shoulder, and Annie is leaned into her. It looks comfortable and safe.

This was the last photo taken right before Mama told her that Babushka would be moving in. Annie and Nina had walked along the path and come upon the waterfall, the sound of the water rushing down around them in thunderous plumes.

"Let's take a picture right here!" Nina had said with a laugh. Little droplets of water had settled in their hair like dew drops on a misty morning. Annie sat on the rock, goose bumps rising on her arms and legs, while her mom set up the timer on the camera.

"Ready?" Nina called out, and Annie nodded her head. She remembers smiling, and she thinks she felt happy. She might have even laughed.

Nina pushed the button and turned, slipping over the rocks and falling into Annie. Throwing her head back, she'd let out a hearty laugh and put her arm around her daughter's shoulder. "Smile, my darling," she'd said, her mouth close to Annie's ear. "This is a moment worth remembering."

With a sigh, Annie turns the page and looks at the next set of pictures. They were from her twelfth birthday. The photo shows Annie sitting at the table, two other girls sitting awkwardly next to her. Sarah and Isabelle, two girls who had been her friends for about ten minutes in grade school but who spent the whole of middle school ridiculing her mercilessly. Before her stands a large cake iced in bright turquoise icing, and standing behind her, hands gripping the back of the chair, is Babushka. Annie's smile in the photo is stiff and forced, as are the smiles of her guests. Those girls didn't want to be at Annie's party any more than she wanted them there. They rode the bus with her to school every day, both of them living in the same townhouse complex. Nina had insisted on inviting them to celebrate Annie's birthday.

"You only turn twelve once, darling! This is a big deal. Soon you'll be a teenager and you will be too cool for parties. Let's make this one fun!"

Her mother hadn't understood that Annie didn't like those girls. They were into makeup and boys. They loved listening to music over reading books, whereas Annie would be content to never have human interaction outside of the beloved characters in her favorite novels.

Sarah and Isabelle stayed long enough to eat a piece of cake that day, and they barely spoke a word to Annie. They gave her a joint gift; a tube of lip-gloss and a Christina Aguilera CD that Annie threw away the minute they were gone. The entire hour was uncomfortable and awkward, and as soon as they left Annie retreated to her room and opened up her tattered copy of *Harry Potter* and let herself get lost in Hogwarts. She read until her stomach started grumbling and she got up off the couch and headed down the stairs toward the kitchen. That's when she heard her mother and grandmother talking, their voices raising above one another as the thick syllables of Russian bounced off the walls of the house.

Though Annie pretended not to understand her mother's native language, the truth was she understood everything. Her mother had insisted on speaking to her only in Russian for the first eleven years of her life until Annie refused to respond.

She wasn't so quick to forget the melodic harmonies of the language that defined her family background.

"You are losing that girl," her grandmother said. Her voice had floated up the stairs and into Annie's consciousness, and Annie immediately understood that they were talking about her. She sank onto the stairs and listened in.

"Mama, she's twelve years old. This is a confusing time of life. I'm not losing her." Nina's voice sounded weary...doubtful.

"Oh, *Ninochka*, surely you are smarter than that. Can't you see anything? Your daughter has no friends. She is quiet and sullen, and she stays locked up in her room most of the time. Those girls didn't want to be here today, and Annie was miserable."

Annie remembers the way her eyes filled with tears at her grandmother's assessment of her, and how in that moment she realized that the grandmother she didn't really understand or care to know seemed to understand her better than her own mother.

"No, Mama, you're the one who doesn't understand. Annie is just going through changes. She's hormonal, and this is all natural. She'll come out of this, trust me."

"And tell me, please, how it is you know so much about raising a child when you've never done it before?" Babushka had responded, her voice softer now, and laced with accusation. "I'm the only one in this room who has actually raised a child before. Surely that means my opinion counts for something."

"Mama," Nina responded, her voice thick with a barely constrained anger. "You didn't raise me. I raised myself, remember? I celebrated my own birthdays, I dropped myself off at school, and I made my way home each day alone. I spent those long summer days alone while all of my friends were at their dachas in the country. I laid under the table in your research lab, and I read the same books over and over because they were the only two you gave me to read. I taught myself about boys, about love, and about heartache. I grew up in silence not because I wanted it, but because it was all I had. So please, Mama," Nina's voice had been laced with pain, "please don't tell me that I don't know anything about raising a teenage girl. I raised me."

Annie sighs and leans her head back against the pillow behind her. She wonders how her life would have turned out if her father had lived. She knows very little about him, her mother always tight-lipped and secretive. When Annie asked, her mother gave vague, pat answers.

"He was a good man. He would have loved you. He was quiet and thoughtful." She would offer these lame details, then quickly change the subject. And after Babushka came to stay with them, her mother made it clear she did not want to discuss Annie's father at all. There was a history there that Annie didn't understand, and the holes in her past left her tired and confused.

Her eyes drift back to the album and settle on a photo taken a few months later, right after Babushka came to stay. They had gone out for ice cream, but Babushka hadn't wanted any. Annie sits awkwardly next to her grandmother, squinting up at the camera, the ice cream cone in her hand melting and dripping down her wrist. Her grandmother had fussed over her that day, mortified at the mess she was making, imploring her to eat quickly so that she didn't ruin her shirt. It had been so stressful that Annie couldn't finish her ice cream cone, and when she threw it away her grandmother tutted over her wastefulness. Annie sets the book down and grabs the container with her half-eaten sandwich. She stands to walk back to the kitchen and freezes when a knock on the front door breaks through the silence.

Wincing, she glances at her grandmother's door, hoping that the sharp-eared woman doesn't come bursting out demanding to know what was causing such a commotion. Annie walks quickly to the door and pulls it open. She stops short when she sees James.

"I...what are you doing here?" she asks. She steps outside and pulls the door closed behind her.

"You haven't been in school for a couple of days, so I decided to come check on you," he replies. He holds out a half-empty box of Kleenex. "I thought you might be sick, so I brought these as a sort of get well gift." He takes in the sight of the bandage over her bruised eye, and the gauze wrapped around her arm and his eyes fill with concern. "But you're not sick, are you?" he asks. He drops his arm, the box of Kleenex hitting his side. "Are you alright?" he asks, his brow furrowed.

"I'm...yes, I'm okay," Annie answers. "We were in a car accident. Toby and I were—the other day. It's okay, though. We're both okay."

Annie thinks of Toby and wonders if he really is all right. She still hadn't spoken to him since the accident, though the hospital told her that he had been discharged yesterday.

"How did you know where I lived?" she asks looking up at James.

James shrugs. "There's this nifty little thing called the internet," he answers. "I just did a couple of quick searches and this address popped up. Oddly enough, there are not many Anastasia Abrams in east Tennessee."

Annie offers a weak smile, then the two stand in awkward silence. James clears his throat.

"So," he says. "Are you really doing okay?"

Annie shrugs. Not knowing quite how to answer, she nods her head slowly. "Yeah," she says. "Just a little sore."

James nods. "I'm so sorry," he says and they stare at each other. "So that guy who picked you up the other day...that was Toby?"

Annie's heart skips a beat. She nods.

"Is he...I mean, are you guys together?"

Annie takes in a deep breath. "We have been together, but I don't really know what we are at this point."

James' mouth turns up slightly, a look of relief passing through his eyes. Annie looks away, unable to elaborate any further.

"So I finished *Of Mice and Men* this morning," she says, quickly changing the subject. James raises his eyebrows. He steps forward and leans his shoulder against the doorjamb. Annie turns to face him, her back now to the sun.

"What'd you think?" he asks.

"I don't know," Annie replies. She reaches up and runs her hand through her hair, suddenly self-conscious about how she must look after a morning spent in bed. "I wish that Lennie didn't have to die, that George didn't pull the trigger," she says finally. "But I don't know if there could have been another outcome. It had to be that way. It makes me sad." She turns toward him and blinks back tears. "I'm just really, really sad." She blinks hard against the tears and lets out a short, embarrassed laugh as James reaches over and plucks a tissue from the box and hands it to her. "Thanks," she says, dabbing at her eyes.

James pushes himself away from the wall and pulls Annie into his arms. It's impulsive, and for a moment she tries to pull away before relaxing into him. She puts her head on his shoulder and blinks back tears, both comforted and horrified by this tender moment. She squeezes her eyes shut, then pushes away. She swipes the tears off her lashes and shakes her head.

"I'm sorry," she says again with a slight laugh. "This is so silly. It's just a story. It isn't real."

James cocks his head to the side. "I don't know," he answers. "Maybe it's fiction, but don't you think that the emotion you feel over the story only goes to show that you're human? And haven't we all had to make horrible decisions like George? Don't we all realize that one action sends a ripple effect that can completely and totally alter the future? Maybe the sadness is what makes the story so *real*. Because any one of us could be George, ya know?" He looks out and squints into the afternoon sun. "At any given moment, we're all seconds away from a life-altering choice."

The two stand in silence for a long moment, each lost in their own thoughts. Annie is so wrapped up in the moment that she doesn't hear her mother's car turn into the driveway. It's only when the garage door hums behind her that she whips around.

Nina turns off the car and stares out the window at her daughter and the strange boy standing on her front step. A flash of anger consumes her, and she throws open the door.

"Who are you?" she demands, slamming the car door behind her. Her sharp steps click indignantly on the concrete as she walks firmly toward the couple. Annie's eyes flash at her mother.

"Mom, this is a friend. He's in a couple of my classes at school, and he noticed I was absent, so he came to check on me."

Nina doesn't look at Annie, but instead keeps her eyes trained on James' face. "So, is it you?" she asks. "Are you Toby?"

"Mom!" Annie steps forward, horrified.

James looks quizzically from Nina to Annie. Nina steps a little closer. "Is it you that did this to my daughter?" she asks, her teeth clenched.

"I...I'm sorry," James replies taking a step backward.

"It's nothing, James," Annie says. She steps between him and her mother. "My mom is a little confused right now." She stares hard into Nina's eyes. "Mom," she says quietly, "please. This is my friend James. This is *not* Toby."

Nina shakes her head. "My seventeen year old daughter turns up pregnant, and I come home to find her with a strange boy. I am not permitted to be suspicious?"

Annie drops her head, her cheeks turning a deep crimson. She turns slowly and raises her eyes to James who stands rooted in place, eyes wide.

"I should go," James murmurs. He walks slowly down the steps, passing by Annie and Nina without looking at either of them. Annie watches him get in his car and pull quickly out of the driveway, his red taillights disappearing over the crest of the hill.

She turns to her mother, eyes bright with tears of humiliation. "I hate you," she whispers. Nina steps back, stunned by the heat in her daughter's words.

"Annie," she says, but Annie turns and storms into the house slamming the door behind her. Nina sits down slowly, her head sinking into her hands. She's there for what seems like an eternity when she hears the door open behind her.

"Annie?" she asks, spinning around and jumping to her feet. "Oh. Hi, Mama," she says. Her voice is flat, numb. Elizaveta stares back at her daughter.

"It's noisy out here today," she says. Her voice is not accusing or angry. It's gentle. For a moment, Nina wonders if, perhaps, her mother might understand what she's going through. "What is Nastia upset about now?"

Nina takes a deep breath. "It's nothing, Mama. She's still sore from the accident, and I interrupted her talking with a friend from school. She just got frustrated with me. It's my fault."

Elizaveta clicks her tongue. "It is always your fault," she says. "Perhaps the girl could take a bit of the blame for these difficult times."

Nina opens her mouth to argue, then closes it again. She can't give her mother all the information she needs to understand what's happening right now. She simply isn't ready to talk about it.

"Viktor is going to stop by this afternoon to discuss the results of your test, Mama. He'll be here around 5:00 after he leaves his office. I have to get back to work, but I wanted to let you know so you could be prepared."

Elizaveta pushes herself up, leaning lightly against the cane in her left hand. She nods her head. "Alright."

Nina turns and heads toward her car. "I'll be home around 4:30. I'm going to pick up something for dinner tonight, so don't worry about pulling any food out of the refrigerator, okay?"

"I assume you will ask Viktor Shevchenko to eat with us as well?" Elizaveta calls out. Nina turns and looks at her mother.

"I...I didn't plan on it," she said. "He was just going to stop by to talk with you. I'm sure he will want to leave quickly."

Elizaveta raises her eyebrows. "Are you really sure of that?" she asks. "Why would the man want to leave quickly? To return to his empty house? *Ninochka*, please. You must be smarter than this."

Nina's shoulders slump in resignation. "*Khorosho*, Mama," she sighs. "I'll ask him to stay for dinner."

Elizaveta nods her head in approval and turns to go inside. "Good girl," she says. Nina slides into the front seat of her car and sits in the quiet for a long time. Her knuckles turn white as she grips the steering wheel of the car, swallowing hard against the lump in her throat that threatens to dissolve. Finally, muscles aching and sore, she starts her car and puts it in reverse, slowly backing away as her failures tighten like a vice around her.

# ELIZAVETA

*There is no emotion quite so strong*
*as that of a mother's love.*

I remember precisely the day I began to love my daughter— the day I actually began to think of her as mine and not as a burden thrust upon me. She was three, and we were in the midst of one of the coldest winters that I had experienced since my childhood in the prison holding camp. I'd taken Nina with me to the store where we waited in the icy cold with the hope of buying some milk and tea leaves. Finally, an older gentleman near the front of the line had offered me his spot because Nina cried so bitterly from the cold.

"You need to get your little one home and warmed up," he'd said as we ducked into the store. The tea was gone, but I'd managed to find *ptichye moloko* and a small wedge of cheese. I paid for our items and, tucking the creamy cake and cheese under my arm, I rushed back to our little flat at the edge of Moscow where I'd piled Nina under a blanket and offered her a lump of bread and a slice of the cheese, but she refused. She wouldn't even take a bite of the cake I tried to give her.

That's when I noticed how red her cheeks were. She was burning with fever. I pulled off her *valenki,* the winter boots that she would soon outgrow, and watched as the balled up newspaper that I'd stuff inside to keep her feet warm rolled out. Her feet were icy cold, and I worked quickly to warm them up, rubbing them between my hands and cursing myself for not getting her new *valenki* earlier.

For a week, I nursed her. I took two days home from work, visiting the children's policlinic, but the doctor prescribed medicine that I didn't trust, and he asked too many personal questions, which made me nervous, so I chose to treat her myself.

When I called into work the third day, I was met with sharp reprimand from my supervisor at the research lab, so I bundled Nina up and brought her with me. She wheezed from the fluid in her lungs, and cried on and off throughout the day, causing my co-workers to scoff at me for bringing her along. But I had no one to help me in those days, and the nursery school refused to take her with such a high fever. So for the rest of the week she came to work with me, and I endured the frustrated rants of my colleagues.

Only one showed us mercy. Olya, the woman who worked at the table next to mine, offered assistance where she could, rocking Nina when she grew agitated and confused due to the high fever, and offering me a little extra to eat from her own lunch during our midday breaks.

"Your daughter is very sick," she told me that Friday as I prepared to head home, exhausted from the length of the week. "You need to bring her fever down and get her to loosen up some of the congestion in her lungs." She gave me three mustard patches that her mother had given to her that morning.

"My mama said to heat these with hot water and put them on her chest for thirty minutes at a time. But don't put them directly on the skin or they will burn her. Put a rag beneath the patch and then apply it. You can use each patch twice. And have her drink hot water, and then twenty minutes later, cold water. Repeat that all day long tomorrow. This little girl is dangerously sick." She squeezed my arm then. "Take care of her," she whispered. "Get her fever down. You will be okay."

She hadn't said that Nina would be okay, though, and the absence of that reassurance terrified me.

That was when the fear set in my heart. It settled there like an icy weight, choking out the breath in my body. I took her home that afternoon and held her on the couch, fighting panic that pulsed through me. I swallowed hard against the wild, frantic strangle in my throat, and in the quiet hours of the evening as I rocked her back and forth, an involuntary prayer lifted from my lips, hammering its way out of my soul over and over and over.

"Please," I whispered to my mother's God—the One in which I had convinced myself I did not believe. "Please, please, please." I didn't know what else to say, so I continued my litany of pleading for hours with Nina in my arms. That was the first time it dawned on me that I could lose the little girl I had so reluctantly taken charge of, and if I did, I might lose myself. She was a piece of the family that I had abandoned, and she was a salve to my guilt. But more than that, I had come to enjoy her presence without even realizing it. I needed her.

I didn't leave Nina's side for the next forty-eight hours. I covered her body in cool rags, replacing them constantly as her hot skin warmed them. I put the mustard patches on her chest as directed, and despite the fact that I used a rag to protect her skin, the patch still burned leaving a blistered red square over her breast. I rubbed her feet with vinegar to lower the fever, and I forced small sips of hot tea into her mouth while she slept. I was exhausted by the end of the weekend, but it was worth it as I noticed a vast improvement in her breathing after the fourth treatment.

On Sunday evening, her fever finally broke. She lay in sweat covered sheets, and for the first time she spoke to me coherently, her big, brown eyes looking up at me clearly.

"I'm hungry," she croaked, her voice hoarse from a week of coughing. I gave her a piece of bread and a cup of hot water mixed with raspberry jam, and I watched with relief as the color began to return to her cheeks. She was so small, then, petite and thin. Her short hair was cropped around her face, and as strength began to return to her features she looked like a cherub. She drifted off to sleep shortly after eating that night, and I pulled out my drawing pad and pencil.

I hadn't drawn much at all since Igor left. While drawing had once been an unconscious escape from reality, after the incident with Tanya I found it to be a painful reminder of the life I'd left behind. But that night, as relief flooded over me, and the fear that had threatened to engulf me began to dissipate, I needed to feel the pencil in my hand.

I sat on the chair across the room and I watched her sleep, her face relaxed, chest moving up and down without a rattle, and I let my hand move across the paper. I didn't think about what I was drawing. I simply let it happen the way I'd done as a child. Drawing had once saved my life, and perhaps that night it did again, because as I drew, I let myself imagine that I could be the mother that she needed. I gave myself over to the feeling of love that I'd kept at arm's length for so long. And when I was done, I looked down and studied my drawing.

I'd drawn Nina. I'd drawn her lying on the couch, her cheeks full and soft. Her hand was curled on her chest, and her face looked peaceful, angelic. In the corner of the page, I wrote "Nina. February 2, 1968. My daughter."

Blinking my eyes at the memory that's stilled me, I push myself up off my bed and move stiffly to the closet. Reaching toward the shelf in the back corner, I pull out a small, metal box. I sit on the bed and hold it in my lap, slowly pulling out the few, precious items that I keep locked away. There are Nina's birth papers, which I had to have falsified shortly after Tanya left. It hadn't been easy finding someone to help me, but a friend of a friend finally agreed to print out papers for the baby left in my charge, not asking questions about whose she was or where she came from. I pull out the birth notice and read the name at the top: "*Nina Igorevna Mishurova. Born January 17, 1965. Mother Elizaveta Andreyevna Mishurova.*"

Though I never spoke to Igor again after he left, I managed to keep a part of him with me forever by ascribing his name to the baby. When the man who created the identification papers for me asked her name, that was the only name I could think of to offer her. I couldn't give her my father's name, and I didn't know her father's name. And so she carries with her still a piece of the man who loved me until he realized he didn't know me.

With a sigh, I set the paper aside and pull out the small shoes that Nina wore to her first day of primary school when she was six. I'd made sure to dress her neatly that morning, her crisp, black dress with the white, lace collar looking so bold on her tiny frame. I'd tied two giant bows in her hair and given her firm instructions not to ruin her shoes or white knee socks, because they were the only pair she would have for the school year. The first day, she'd jumped in a puddle of mud on the playground and come out of the school sobbing because she had disobeyed me. She was so repentant and upset that I couldn't even get angry with her. We'd gone home and washed the mud off her shoes and socks together. I run my hand over the faded stain on the side of the shoes.

I reach back down into the box and pull out a yellowed sheet of paper. Unfolding it, I hold it up, studying it in the light. It's the picture I drew of her the day her fever broke. The pencil lines are faded now, blurred by time, but the drawing is still discernible. And despite all the years that have passed, I find my heart swelling at the sight of her puckered face, little lips parted slightly as she breathed peacefully for the first time in days. I didn't birth her, but I raised her, and I love her with a fierceness that often surprises me. I only wish that she knew.

Finally, I glance back down at the remaining items inside my box of memories. There are my own papers—the ones that gave me the name that became my identity. And there are the letters, which I cannot bear to read. Finally, beneath those is the small book that brings a quiver of fear to my heart.

It was my mother's book—the one that she read from during those icy nights in Siberia. This was the book that saved our lives, but it was also the book that made me hate her so many years ago.

It contained the dangerous message of faith that had defined my mother—the message that made me question and doubt everything she said or did. I had not touched that book since the day I lay it inside this box, had not opened it, not because I was frightened of the words inside, but because those words had made me frightened of her. I run my finger lightly over the worn leather cover, and a chill runs down my spine. This one little book made me do a terrible thing. I kept it all these years so that I wouldn't forget how easy it had been to do the unthinkable. I kept it to remind me why I had to leave, and why I was never able to go back.

# NINA

*Only she who does nothing makes no mistakes.*

Nina puts away the last of the dishes and watches as Viktor talks quietly with her mother in the corner. She glances up as Annie comes down the stairs and enters the kitchen.

"Did you get enough to eat?" Nina asks. Annie grabs a cup from the cabinet and tosses her mother a glare. She fills it up with water and turns to head back upstairs. Nina sighs and wipes down the countertop.

"Is everything okay?" Viktor asks walking into the kitchen. He sits down at a stool opposite from Nina. She glances at him briefly, then looks away.

"Yes," she replies, her voice flat. "She's just...she's a teenager." Nina blinks hard.

"Your mother told me she's been home from school since the accident. Is she still experiencing any pain?"

Nina looks at him again, desperately trying to mask her emotions. "No, I don't think so," she answers. "I think she just needed a few days to get over the shock. I'm going to send her back tomorrow."

Viktor nods. He glances over his shoulder at Elizaveta who sits silently in the corner studying them. "She is a bit formidable, isn't she?" he says. Nina offers a wry smile.

"Well that's an understatement. How did she take your recommendations?"

"She didn't really say much, actually. She just nodded her head. I was prepared to recite a little Pushkin to soften her up, but I didn't need it," he says with a crooked smile.

Nina lets out a genuine laugh, releasing some of the tension that knotted its way into her shoulders. Viktor smiles in return. He watches Nina closely, noticing the strain that never seems to leave her eyes. Even when she laughs, she looks wounded. He stands up and walks around the island to where Nina stands, and leans back against the counter, crossing his arms and letting out a long sigh. Nina grabs a rag and wipes the counter beside him to busy her hands.

"I would really like to take you out to dinner," he says quietly.

Nina glances over his shoulder at Elizaveta who is picking at imaginary fuzz on her skirt while look up repeatedly at the two of them.

"Is she watching?" Viktor murmurs.

"She's trying to pretend that she's not," Nina whispers. She can see her mother's mouth pinched tight in a grim line. Viktor's mouth stretches into a wide smile as he looks expectantly at Nina.

"Viktor," she begins, turning her back to Elizaveta and lowering her voice. "I just don't think I can. Things are...complicated right now."

"And the fact that your mother likes me and is pushing for this doesn't help matters, does it?" Viktor asks, his eyes searching hers. Nina opens her mouth to protest, then thinks better of it and shrugs.

"Look, I'm not asking for anything permanent," Viktor says. "Just a dinner. Alone. So that maybe you'll feel comfortable enough to really talk to me without your mother staring at the back of your head."

Nina glances back over her shoulder again and almost

laughs as Elizaveta quickly averts her eyes. She turns back to Viktor and takes in a deep breath.

"Okay," she says. "This is fine. But just one dinner, and do not say anything to my mama about it. Okay?"

Viktor holds up his right hand and nods firmly. "Deal," he says. "So...tomorrow night? Will that work?"

Nina nods her head, suppressing a smile. "Text me where and what time, and I will be there," she replies. He gives a discreet thumbs up before turning around.

"Okay, well I am going to head out," Viktor says, clapping his hands together lightly. He turns to Elizaveta who looks at him in return. "Elizaveta Andreyevna, I will see you in a week. I look forward to hearing how you're doing with your exercises."

She waves her hand at him. "I do not need you to remind me," she says. Then she turns to Nina. "I don't need it from you, either. I'll walk around the table a few times, but not with you two staring at me like I'm a child taking her first steps." She hobbles into her room and shuts the door behind her as Viktor stifles a laugh.

"She is definitely a tough bird," he says with a grin. He pulls his coat off the hook by the front door and Nina opens it, letting him step out into the fading evening light. The sky is painted in red and orange above the hills on the horizon. The air is crisp, and Nina can feel the impending winter working its way toward them. Viktor turns back to her.

"I'll see you tomorrow night," he says. Nina swallows hard and offers a thin smile. She watches as he walks to his car and backs quickly down the driveway.

Wrapping her arms tight across her chest, Nina looks out at the fading sky. She thinks about all her years in Moscow when she'd stand on the balcony of their little flat and try to watch the sunset. The skyline, cluttered with buildings, always seemed to hide it from her. As a teenager, she'd climb the stairs and push her way out onto the roof of her building, hoping to catch a few lingering moments of the sun before it hid behind the walls of brick and mortar, but it was never really enough. She was just chasing the sunset, but couldn't ever catch it.

The first summer she lived in the States, Andrew had taken her to a cabin in the mountains. He'd gotten them a little place as high up as he could, and on their first night there she stood at a clearing in the trees, and she watched as the sun melted into the horizon, for the first time catching hold of the moment when one day came to a close. She'd leaned into Andrew's chest and breathed in the scent of him, and she'd thought that perhaps that would be the grandest moment of her life. She wondered if life would always be as sweet as it had been in that split second when she stood in front of the sun-kissed horizon. But sunsets have a way of fading from view.

When Andrew quit coming straight home from work in the evenings, Nina would drive out to the highest point in the city and try to catch the sunsets, but they eluded her as they had in her childhood. When Andrew left, she stopped looking altogether.

It wasn't until she first took Annie to the mountains that she remembered the magic of seeing the day fade away. When Annie was five, the two of them stood at the highest peak in the Smoky Mountains, and Nina had picked Annie up.

"Look, darling," she'd whispered, pushing Annie's wispy blonde hair out of her eyes and pointing to the lowering sun. "This is a moment to make a wish."

Annie had closed her eyes, but Nina gave her a gentle shake. "No, my dear," she'd said. "This wish you must make with your eyes open. You have to wish just as the sun sinks into the earth. Then your wish will come true."

"I wish for a puppy," Annie had whispered moments later, lisping the words out through gapped teeth. Nina smiles at the memory. The next afternoon she and Annie went to the pound and picked out a roly little black and white dog that An- nie named Sunset - the dog that Annie loved dearly until her grandmother came to town and started sneezing uncontrollably. Annie had sobbed when they dropped Sunset off at her new home. It was one more reason for her to harbor bitterness toward her already difficult grandmother.

Nina sighs and walks back inside. She glances at the stairs and longs to run up to Annie's room, to pull her into her arms and apologize for all the ways that she's failed her. But the sky has grown dark, and the time for making wishes come true has long since faded away.

# ANNIE

Annie grabs her lunch tray and steps into the crowded lunchroom. She glances at the table in the back where James sits by himself, hunched over the table reading his book. Taking a deep breath, she walks toward him.

"Hi," she says, stepping timidly up to the table. James looks up, his sandy blonde hair falling over his forehead.

"Oh," he says. He clears his throat. "Uh...hi."

"Can...can I sit down?" Annie asks.

James takes in a deep breath. "Sure," he answers, gesturing toward the seat across from him. Annie sets her tray down and sits. For a moment they remain silent, each avoiding eye contact until Annie finally speaks up.

"I want to explain..." she begins.

"Listen, I..." James says.

They both stop and look at one another, an uncomfortable silence filling the void between them. "Go ahead," James says.

"I'm sorry you had to find out about my...um...situation like that," Annie says. She shifts her eyes around the room, avoiding James's gaze. "It's just, I haven't really told anyone about it. My mom just found out, and she's freaking out. Toby won't even talk to me. My grandmother will probably have a heart attack when she finds out. I just...I don't know what to do, and I'm sorry that I didn't say anything." Annie blinks back tears.

"Annie, listen," James says. He leans forward, pressing his elbows into the table and looking hard at her. "I get it. You and I don't know each other *that* well, and that's a huge secret. You don't owe me an explanation, okay?"

Annie nods.

James takes a bite of his sandwich. He holds up the other half and offers it to Annie. "Please take this," he urges. "I have no idea what that is on your tray, but I cannot let you eat it in good conscience."

Annie wipes her eyes and smiles. She takes the sandwich. "Thanks," she says. "I think it's supposed to be meatloaf." She glances down at her plate, and the brown lump of meat swimming in curdled, grey liquid makes her stomach turn.

"Uh, I think they're using a broad definition of the word 'meat' with that stuff," James says making a face. Annie smiles.

They fall into silence as they eat. Annie opens her mouth once to say something, then closes it and takes another bite. James watches her closely.

"So...do you want to talk about it?" he asks. His voice is gentle, offering her the freedom to decline, which Annie appreciates. She shrugs.

"I don't really know what to say," she says. "It's embarrassing." She looks around the cafeteria at the students milling about, happy and carefree. "I'm going to be *that* girl," she says softly. "I'm going to be the one they talk about when I walk by. I try so hard to make sure no one ever notices me, and pretty soon I'm going to be seen for all the wrong reasons."

She blinks back tears and looks at him. "It's just," she sighs. "It was one time," she mumbles. "One stupid time, and here I am."

She glances back at James who studies her silently. Blushing, Annie shakes her head.

"Sorry," she says. "You don't need to deal with this. I bet you wish you hadn't struck up that conversation with me on the first day of school, huh?" She picks at her sandwich, pinching little pieces of bread off between her fingers.

"Nah," James says. He leans back in his chair and crosses his arms over his chest. "I'm glad I noticed you that day." Annie looks up and meets his eyes. "There's no way I could have not noticed you, despite your attempts at being invisible. And let them talk," he swings his arm out toward the crowd. "Who cares what they think anyway, right?" Annie forces a smile, but inside she feels her stomach twist into knots at the prospect of her classmates beginning to notice the coming changes to her body.

"Most of these people will forget about you and me the day they leave high school. They'll never give us a second thought."

James leans forward again, his eyes boring into hers. "But I wouldn't forget about you, Annie. And this thing that you're dealing with? Your 'situation'?" He takes a deep breath. "It doesn't define who you are."

Annie puts her head down to hide the emotion that is swimming through her. She takes in several long, deep breaths before looking back at James.

"Thank you," she whispers.

"You're welcome...*Picasso*," he replies with a mischievous grin. Annie shakes her head and throws him a mock look of disdain.

"Now please finish the sandwich and let me throw away whatever that really is on your tray. I can't look at it anymore."

Annie laughs and watches as James walks to the nearby trashcan and dumps her plate of food, and for a brief, blissful moment she thinks that maybe things will turn out okay.

# NINA

*One thing is certain.*
*One thing I know.*
*Until I know her,*
*I'll know nothing at all.*

Nina tucks into the familiar corner of the library once again and flips open her laptop, waiting a moment as the screen lights up and the systems boot. It's quiet today. Fridays are always quiet, the end of the week lull leaving people a little less inclined to take solace inside the walls of the library.

Nina pulls her sweater tight around her shoulders, trying to stave off the frigid air that threatens to sink into her bones. She glances out the window, then grabs her books, computer, and bag and heads to the front desk. After checking out, she leaves and walks around to the back of the library to a bench nestled up against a tree. The reading nook is highlighted by a ray of sunshine, the early October air reminding her that though winter may be coming, there is still time to soak in the warmth of this autumn day.

She sits on the bench and leans back against the tree, then opens up her book and begins reading, typing interesting facts as her eyes scan the page. Her computer is now filled with notes taken from the very few resources she's found on Stalin's Russia and the bleak days when men and women went missing into the night, whisked away to the prison camps of Siberia never to be seen or heard from again. Nina stares at the question she typed in bold after reading about the peasant population of Ukraine that was heavily persecuted during those years. Nina knew the term *kulak*. She remembered her teachers in grade school drilling into them the notion that those peasants who refused to accept the greatness of the Soviet empire were a clear nuisance.

"The men and women who refused to acknowledge the perfection of this shared society were too selfish and bothersome to be a part of it," her fifth year teacher had intoned. "They were not fit to be citizens."

Nina traces her fingers over the question that has been plaguing her since she began studying more about the peasant class and the collectivization of the farms.

WAS MY MOTHER A *KULAK*?

With a sigh, Nina looks up and lets her mind wander, scanning the tree line as she tries to piece together any clues that might help her better understand the woman who raised her.

As she studies a hawk flying overhead, she slowly drifts back to her sixteenth birthday. She'd come home from school that day and gaped at the decorated flat. Her mother had taken the day off work, something Nina could not remember her ever doing before, and she had decorated the one room apartment with hand cut streamers, which she'd strung across the ceiling haphazardly. She'd made a huge bowl of *vereniki*, Nina's favorite dumplings stuffed with potatoes, and had a large *Prazhki* chocolate torte set in the middle of the table.

"What is this?" Nina had asked.

"What do you mean, what is this?" her mother huffed in reply. "It's your birthday, isn't it? This is your celebration!"

Nina had looked around, stunned. Her mother had never put this much effort and work into any celebration before.

"That's a lot of food," she said, glancing at the table. Beside the *vereniki* and torte there was a large plate piled high with *pelmeni* stuffed with meat, and next to that her mother had set a large loaf of black bread, a slab of butter, a small bowl of squash caviar, a plate of *kholodets*, the jellied, minced meat that Nina loved so much, a bowl of pickled cucumbers, and a jug of cranberry compote all filling the corners of the rickety table where Nina was accustomed to eating alone.

"It's not only for us," Elizaveta replied, and for the first time that Nina could remember she thought she heard a hint of excitement in her mother's voice. "I spent too much time waiting in lines and cooking to not share this meal," Elizaveta continued. Nina raised her eyebrows, too stunned to speak.

"I've invited your friends, my dear!" Elizaveta announced. "The ones you always speak of from school. I contacted the teacher and she gave them the message to arrive today at 5:00. Quickly, go make yourself presentable. You only turn sixteen once. Let's make it count."

Nina had retreated to the bedroom she shared with her mother, utterly confused and baffled by this strange event. A party? Her friends were invited? She'd pulled out her best skirt and top, slipping them over her slim frame and cinching the skirt tight with a braided, brown belt. The brown skirt was faded, fraying around the hem at the bottom. And the white, ruffled shirt was ill-fitted to her narrow shoulders. But that was the only dressy outfit she had. Her mother deemed it a capitalist mentality to fuss over clothing, and though Nina longed for more modern outfits, she knew she would never win that battle with her mother. So she compensated for her lack of style by teasing her hair a little higher that day, applying extra rouge to her cheeks, and slathering on the red lipstick that a friend had given her last summer.

When Nina walked back into the kitchen, Elizaveta took one look at her and clucked her tongue.

"I did not know you were going to dress as a clown," she muttered just loud enough for Nina to hear. With a roll of her eyes, Nina went to the balcony and looked out the window. Minutes later, a smile crossed her face as her three friends rounded the corner. Running to the door, Nina pulled it open and headed down the stairs to guide her visitors to the flat. It was the first time she had ever had friends over.

"Happy Birthday!" Marina screeched when she saw Nina, and the two girls jumped up and down, giggling and clapping. Pasha and Evgeniy took in the sight, then turned to one another and let out high-pitched squeals in mock excitement. Nina threw her head back at the two boys jumping up and down, clapping their hands in utter silliness.

"Come up!" she said, opening the door to the stairwell. "I have no idea what has gotten into my mother, but let's enjoy this evening before she comes to her senses!"

Marina and Pasha laughed and passed through the door, quickly heading up the stairs. Evgeniy stopped in front of Nina and held up a single, red carnation.

"Happy Birthday, Ninochka," he said. "I wish you health and happiness." Nina blushed and took the flower. She looked up in surprise as Evgeniy took a swift step forward, leaned down, and kissed her. His hand reached up and clasped the back of her head, pulling her tighter into him so that she finally gave in and returned the kiss. After a moment, Evgeniy pulled back and looked at her, his face still close. Nina's heart raced.

"I wanted to give you your present early," he said with a smirk. Grabbing her hand, Evgeniy pulled Nina inside and the two walked up the stairs hand in hand. When they got to the fourth floor, they met Pasha and Marina, both of whom stared at them with amusement. Marina locked eyes with Nina, one eyebrow raised. Her eyes twinkled, and she gave Nina a quick thumb's up. Nina blushed. She pushed open the door of her flat and gestured them all in.

"Mama!" she called. "Everyone is here."

Elizaveta walked out of the kitchen, a large smile pasted on her face. She had changed into her best dress, and piled her hair high on her head, a few brown tendrils falling around her flushed face. She took in the sight of the four young people, her eyes narrowing as they settled on Nina's flushed face. Her lipstick was smeared, and the boy standing next to her clearly wore what was missing from Nina's face. Her smile faded for a moment, then she pushed it back into place.

"Well, come in," Elizaveta said, gesturing to the set table in the corner. "Please, sit. I am just finishing up a few preparations in the kitchen, and then you may eat."

All four kids nodded, then made their way to the small sitting room where they settled on the couch, just a few feet away from the set table. Evgeniy and Pasha stared at the food, swallowing hard as they salivated over the coming meal.

"Your mother is a little intimidating," Marina whispered as they scooted up to their places.

"Tell me about it," Nina said with a wry smile. "I've lived with her my whole life."

"What about your Papa?" Marina asked.

Nina shrugged. "I don't have a Papa," she answered. "It's always just been me and Mama."

"Here we go," Elizaveta said, entering the room with a tray balanced in her hands. Nina gaped as her mother set it down on the table. It was her *faience*, the red and white tea set that she only pulled out for the most special occasions. It was, perhaps, the finest possession her mother owned. Nina had never been allowed to touch it before. She stared at her mother in wonder, desperately confused by her sudden enthusiasm to entertain.

Elizaveta set down the tea set. Balanced on the tray, she had also set a small jar of honey, a jar of cherry jam, and a bowl filled with chocolate candies that she'd picked up at the market that morning.

"Don't eat the *shokolad* yet," she murmured, gesturing to the bowl of chocolates as the kids settled themselves around the table. "It will rot your teeth to eat it before the meal." Evgeniy tossed Nina a humorous glance as she bit her lip, trying not to laugh.

"*Na Zdarovye*," Elizaveta murmured to each of them. "To your health." Her eyes lingered on Nina's for a brief moment, and Nina caught a flash of tenderness, so foreign and strange that she wasn't certain if she'd truly seen it or not. Then Elizaveta retreated to the kitchen leaving Nina alone with her friends.

Evgeniy held up his cup and looked across the table at Nina. "*Tvoye zdorvye*," he said with a grin. "May you be healthy," he repeated. They all raised their glasses and took a sip.

For the next hour, Nina enjoyed a leisurely conversation with her friends as they ate. Pasha and Evgeniy gorged themselves on *vereniki* with sour cream and bread while the girls nibbled daintily at their own meals. The conversation was interrupted occasionally by one of them offering a toast on Nina's behalf, a mealtime custom which Nina had never been offered before. Her face soon grew exhausted from the repeated grins.

At the end of the meal, Elizaveta came back into the room and picked up the *Prazhki* torte, a thick, chocolate cake that the boys had been drooling over for the entirety of the hour.

"I will cut this and bring you each back a slice," she said. Nina wiped her mouth delicately and offered her mother a genuine smile.

"Thanks, Mama," she said. Elizaveta smiled back at her daughter and nodded her head. When she'd left the room, Pasha leaned forward.

"Your Mama isn't nearly as bad as you've made her seem, Nina," he whispered. Nina shook her head and shrugged her shoulders.

"She's very different today," she murmured.

Evgeniy pushed back from the table and stood up, stretching his arms out to the side. "May I use the bathroom?" he asked. Nina nodded and gestured to the door to his right. He walked behind Pasha's chair and put one finger up to his lips. He pointed at Pasha and, with a twinkle in his eye, he yanked the chair out from under his friend causing Pasha to crash to the floor. The girls erupted into giggles as Pasha rolled to his knees and jumped up to his feet, turning to face Evgeniy who was doubled over in laughter.

Pasha cuffed Evgeniy on the back of the neck, his face red with embarrassment and anger.

"You stupid *kulak*! I'll get you for this!" Pasha sputtered.

Nina jumped at the crash, whirling around to see her mother standing in the doorway, her eyes wide. The tray was at her feet, chocolate torte splayed across the floor. A look of fear crossed Elizaveta's face, and was quickly replaced with anger.

"Mama?" Nina asked. "Are you okay?"

"The party is over," Elizaveta said. Her eyes were pinned on Pasha who stood mute. Evgeniy had straightened behind him and he fidgeted nervously.

"I'm sorry, Elizaveta Andreyevna," Evgeniy began. "It was my fault."

Elizaveta held up her hand, silencing the boy. "I didn't realize how late it had gotten," she said. Her voice bubbled with a barely restrained fury. "You all need to go home now before it gets too dark."

"Mama, please. They were only playing," Nina pleaded, pushing to her feet.

Elizaveta's eyes shifted to Nina's face. "I said the party is over," she said, her teeth clenched tight. Nina looked apologetically at her friends as they shuffled to the front door and put on their shoes. She opened the door for them.

"Thank you so much for coming," she murmured as they passed by silently. Evgeniy gave her an apologetic glance when he walked past, but Nina didn't have the energy to even smile in return. She closed the door softly and looked back at her mother who was now down on her knees picking up the shattered plate and crumpled torte.

"Mama?" Nina began.

Elizaveta held up her hand and shook her head. "I will clean this up," she said, her eyes remaining on the floor. "You may go rest." Silence engulfed both of them briefly before Elizaveta spoke again.

"Happy Birthday, *dochenka*," she said softly. The anger was gone from her voice. Monotone and soft, Elizaveta's words were masked, hiding any sign of emotion, and forbidding Nina from understanding what her mother could possibly be thinking or feeling.

Sitting up, Nina shivers. The memory has left her cold and sad, the confusion of that evening settling back on her grown shoulders as easily as it had so many years ago. She remembered going back to her room and sitting on the bed as tears streamed down her face. That was the day she was certain she would never understand her mother, no matter how hard she tried.

# ANNIE

A nnie punches the number and takes in a deep breath. She presses the phone to her ear and listens to the buzz. Finally, his voice fills her ear.

*"Yo! You missed me. That sucks, doesn't it? Leave me a message, and I'll call you back. Unless I don't want to call you back, in which case you won't hear from me."*

Annie fights the urge to roll her eyes. After the beep, she speaks quickly before she loses her nerve.

"Hey Toby, it's me." Her voice shakes. "Call me back, okay? I just want to know if you're okay." She tosses the phone onto her bed and walks to the window, looking out over the dimming landscape. Headlights pierce through the grey twilight, making the moisture in the air dance in swirls across Annie's line of vision until the beams of light turn and the dancing droplets disappear, fading back into the nothingness of the impending night air. Annie steps to the side of the window and watches her mother pull into the driveway and put the car in park. Nina sits in the car for a moment before pushing the door open and stepping out. Annie studies her from the safety of her hiding place.

It wasn't so long ago that she thought her mother the most beautiful woman in the world. She remembers sitting next to her in the bathroom, watching as she dabbed color across her eyelids, her cheeks, and her mouth. She'd laugh as Nina fussed at her hair, the Russian words spilling from her lips in a tangle of frustration.

"Be thankful for your amazing head of hair, my child," Nina would say. "Your father gave you a good gift when he passed that down to you."

The smile fades as Nina passes from sight. Annie hears the front door open downstairs, her mother's keys clanging into the bowl on the table next to the door. She closes her eyes and she can see Nina kicking off her shoes, slipping her feet into her slippers, hanging up her coat, and padding to the kitchen to start dinner, not even pausing for a moment to sit down and breathe.

Annie leans against the wall, her hand self-consciously rubbing up and down over her stomach. Her pants have gotten tight, though thankfully there still isn't a noticeable bulge. Annie wonders when it will start to be clear, when the whispers will start trailing behind her as she walks down the hall at school.

She walks to her bed and squats down, pulling out from underneath it a long, thin, plastic tub. Opening it up, Annie pulls out the stack of letters and sets them to the side. They are the letters her mother gave her on her sixteenth birthday. There are sixteen letters, one written for each year she had been alive. Her mom presented them all to Annie after they had celebrated her birthday quietly at their favorite Italian restaurant. Annie read them all that night before she went to bed, weeping over her mother's hopes and dreams, her longings for the perfect daughter that she felt she had birthed. She pulls out the letter that her mother wrote to her on her first birthday.

> My dearest Nastia,
>
> Today you are one year old, and I just can't believe it. This has been a hard year for me, for both of us really, though I suppose you will never remember this hard time. We were alone this year,

*my darling. Your father died just weeks before you were born, and you and I had to figure out how to do this life on our own. I had one friend from work who checked on us infrequently, but it was mostly just you and me. It was difficult, but we made it, and I will cherish these months that I had with you forever.*

*You are the most beautiful baby. I didn't get many photos of you this year, not nearly as many as I would have liked, but I made sure to take at least one photo every month so that I would never forget the way that you changed over the course of a year.*

*Oh my darling, I have so very many hopes for you. I hope that you will grow to be kind and free. I hope that you will be strong, that you will take charge of your life and live it fully. I hope that you will never be held back by circumstances, but that you will face each moment of your life with courage. And more than anything, I hope that you will always know how much I love you.*

*I grew up in a home where love was a foreign concept. I don't want it to be the same for you. I love you, my darling, and I will until the day that we're parted. May the path before you be filled with light, my Nastia.*

> *With great love,*
> *Your Mama*

Annie folds the letter and places it back in the box on top of the rest. They're all the same, though the tone of the letters changed after her grandmother came to stay. The writing was scrawled hastily across the pages in the letters that followed Babushka's arrival. Somehow her grandmother had infiltrated every crevice of their lives.

Annie reaches into the tub and pulls out the photo of her

mother and father, the only photo she's ever seen of the dad she never met. He sits next to Nina, his shoulder leaned into hers as they both grin up at the camera. His sandy blonde hair hangs over his right eye, his wide mouth stretched out easily and happily across a smooth face.

"Who took this picture?" Annie had asked her mother when she first discovered it. She was ten years old, digging through an old shoebox of photos one Saturday while waiting for her mom to finish making their weekly pancake breakfast.

"Where did you find that?" Nina had asked, her face turning white. She took the photo from Annie and ran her finger over it.

"It's my father, isn't it?" Annie asked.

Nina nodded. She glanced at Annie, then back at the photo. "I didn't think I had any pictures of him," she said softly. "I forgot about this."

"Who took it?" Annie asked again, holding her hand out for another glimpse at the man her mother spoke so little of.

"A friend of your father's," Nina replied. She turned her back to Annie so her daughter couldn't see the emotion fighting its way to the surface. "We were at a birthday party for one of his work colleagues. That was taken right before I found out I was pregnant with you." Nina took a deep breath and composed herself before turning back around and smiling at her daughter. Annie had blinked at her mother for a moment, then looked back down at the picture.

"How come you never talk about him? And why don't you have more pictures?" Annie asked.

Nina shrugged. "It's painful for me," she said, her voice quavering slightly. "I had so little time with your father, and I loved him very much. It makes me sad to talk about him, so I don't. As for the photos," Nina paused and stared at the wall thoughtfully. "After your father died, it was very difficult. I had no one to talk to help me process what happened. Grief makes you do strange things, my darling." Nina shifted her gaze to

Annie's face. "I threw away the only album I had with photos of your father and me."

Annie sighs as she runs her finger over the photograph. It's a little faded now, worn from years of her staring at it, touching her father's face and wishing she had more information. But she would never get more information on this man, not as long as her grandmother was around. Her mother locked up tight as soon as Babushka came to town. Annie gently places the photo back in the tub and pushes it back under the bed.

She jumps when the phone rings and swallows hard at the name that flashes across the screen.

"Hey," she says quietly, pressing the phone hard against her ear.

"Hey," Toby answers.

Annie takes a few big breaths in the cavernous silence that passes between them. She closes her eyes and waits for Toby to speak, but the phone remains quiet. Finally, she takes in a deep breath.

"Are you okay?" she asks.

"Fine," Toby answers. "My arm is broken, and I have whiplash and a concussion, but I'll survive. You okay?"

"Yeah," Annie answers. "Just a few stiches in my arm and a cut on my head." They both fall silent again. Finally Annie speaks. "I think we need to talk," she says. She hears a sigh on the other end of the line.

"Yeah," he answers, his voice resigned.

"So, do you want to talk now and get it over with, or would you like to meet and talk face to face?" Annie asks, annoyance clipping through her words.

"Look, Annie," Toby begins. Annie cuts him off.

"Oh come on, Toby. I'm not asking you to propose. I just want you to talk to me. This is kind of a big deal, you know?"

"Yes, Annie, I get that," Toby answers. His teeth are obviously clenched and Annie shakes her head in frustration. "I was trying to tell you that I can't right now. I don't have a car, remember? But my dad gets off work soon, and I'll borrow his car, okay?"

"Fine," Annie retorts. "My mom has some business dinner tonight, so I'll be free to meet while she's gone. Can you come around 7:00?"

"Fine," Toby replies.

"Fine," Annie replies with a sigh. She hangs up and tosses the phone on the bed, then glances at the clock. Walking to the mirror, Annie pulls a brush through her hair and straightens her shoulders. With a deep breath, she heads down the stairs to the kitchen.

Nina stands at the stove, a glass of wine in one hand as she stirs chicken and vegetables in the pan in front of her. Annie watches her for a moment, trying to decide how to begin a conversation. She still feels a knot of anger stir in her stomach when she thinks of the way her mother lashed out at James the day before. She considers heading back upstairs when Nina turns to face her.

"Oh!" Nina says in surprise. "I didn't hear you come down."

"Hey," Annie says with reluctance. Nina looks warily at her.

She puts down her spatula and gestures Annie into the kitchen. "How was your day?" she asks as Annie slides into a stool behind the counter.

"Okay," Annie answers. Nina takes a sip of wine, her eyes never leaving Annie's face.

"That's good," Nina murmurs. She sets her glass down on the counter. "Annie," she begins, "I'm..." she pauses, taking in a deep breath. "I'm sorry about yesterday. I'm sorry I said what I said in front of your...friend."

Annie blinks slowly at her mom. "He is just a friend, you know," she says.

Nina nods. "I believe you."

Annie clasps her hands in front of her and squeezes them

together, watching the way her knuckles turn white with the pressure. Nina pushes back to a stand.

"How are you feeling today?" she asks. The question is uncomfortable and hangs between the two of them like a cloud. Annie coughs nervously.

"Fine," she says.

Nina nods. "Good," she replies. "Still sore?"

Annie shakes her head no. Nina turns back to the stove. "Dinner will be ready in ten minutes," she says. "Could you make the salad?"

"Yes," Annie replies.

"You remember that I have a business dinner this evening, so you and Babushka will be alone for dinner," Nina says. Her eyes shift nervously to her feet, then back to Annie's face as she speaks.

Annie nods slowly. She waits a beat before the words come tumbling out of her mouth. "Mom, I'm going to meet with Toby tonight."

Nina stands frozen for a moment before turning back to her daughter. She narrows her eyes and stares at Annie. "What?"

Annie swallows and takes a deep breath. "There's just something that I need to do," she says weakly. Nina shakes her head.

"You will have to tell me what this is about, Annie," she says. Gone is the gentle patience from her earlier words. "You can't possibly think I will let you go out alone with that boy without more of an explanation."

Annie looks down at her hands and realizes that she doesn't have the energy to fight right now. She lets out a long deep breath before speaking, her eyes downcast, unable to look at her mother.

"I'm going to tell him that it's over."

Nina straightens up, the color draining from her face. She glances at Annie's stomach, then back at Annie's face.

"What's over?" she asks. "The pregnancy? Did you...have... an..."

"No! Mom! No." Annie runs her hand through her hair and takes a few deep breaths. Nina rubs her eyes, her hands shaking as she fights to regain her composure.

"I'm going to tell him that I can't be in a relationship with him anymore. It's just..."Annie takes a deep breath. "Too much has happened," she murmurs.

Nina turns and shuts off the stove, then walks around the counter and sinks into one of the stools next to Annie. The two are quiet for several minutes. Annie presses her lips together to keep them from quivering. Finally, Nina turns and looks at her daughter.

"I don't even know this boy you're meeting with," she says. Annie can hear the hurt in her mom's voice.

"I know," she replies.

"Why?" Nina asks. "Why did you hide him from me? Why did you hide everything from me for the past year?" She blinks hard against the frustrated emotion bubbling in her chest.

Annie sighs and leans back in her stool. She shrugs her shoulders. "I don't know, Mom," she says. "I guess..." she hesitates for a moment, trying to decide how to put the last year into words. "It's just...we're not exactly great at communication." Annie looks at her mom. "Why have you never shared more information with me about my father?" she asks.

Nina lets out a long breath, the years of secrets suddenly looming before her eyes like one long, ongoing mistake. She looks sheepishly at Annie and shrugs her shoulders. "I don't know," she answers. The two stare at one another for a long moment. Nina opens her mouth to speak, but stops when Elizaveta's door opens and her mother shuffles out into the kitchen.

"Is dinner ready?" Elizaveta asks. Nina looks into Annie's eyes, her gaze apologetic. Annie shifts her eyes back down to her hands. Nina sighs and pushes herself up from the counter.

"Not yet, Mama," she murmurs. "It will be soon."

Elizaveta looks from mother to daughter, her eyes narrowed as she takes in the sight of the two.

"Good evening, Nastia," she says. She takes a step toward her granddaughter. "You look pale, child. Are you still not feeling well?" She doesn't wait for Annie to answer before turning to Nina. "You should take her to see a doctor," she says firmly. "And she needs to eat. You must stuff her full of food so she can get stronger and fight off illness."

Nina presses her lips together and nods her head once. "Thanks, Mama," she says. She glances at Annie whose face has once again hardened.

"Mama," Nina says quietly, "you remember that I have a dinner to go to tonight, right?" Elizaveta sighs and nods her head. Nina glances at her daughter. "And Annie will be going out with a friend for a short visit, so you'll be alone for a little while, okay?"

Annie looks up at her mom, relief washing over her face.

Elizaveta lets out a long sigh. "So I will be eating my meal by myself, is that it?"

"No," Nina replies, and Annie winces. "Annie will eat with you. She's meeting her friend after dinner." She glances at Annie, eyebrows raised.

"I'll make the salad now," Annie says, tossing her grandmother a wary glance and forcing a smile. Nina stifles a sigh as she watches her mother and daughter look uncomfortably at one another. Her gaze settles on Annie's back, and for the first time a feeling of genuine relief washes over her. There was a moment of tenderness that passed between them. She glances out the window and takes in the sight of the sun sliding behind the trees, the sky lit up in an autumn sunset, the first she's seen in a long, long time.

# ELIZAVETA

*You can't move faster than your shadow.*

I remember exactly the day that I decided to lock away the past. I remember the chill in the air and the lilt of a bird floating on the wind above my head. I can pinpoint the moment in time when I made the choice to keep my memories hidden, stuffing them into a corner of my subconscious and willing them away, only to be haunted by them instead. I remember it now so vividly as I watch Nina and Nastia...*Annie*, move.

Mother and daughter float past one another in the kitchen, Nina stealing soft glances at Annie from time to time, a look of concern and heartache writing a story through her dark eyes, and I recall the feeling of pulling away from my own mother. I remember the way it felt when she looked at me, how she studied me so closely as she tried to figure me out, and the more she studied, the tighter I held my secrets until I couldn't hold her at bay any longer. She had figured me out.

The first secret I kept from my mother was during our second year in Siberia. I didn't tell her about the man's hungry eyes or groping hands. I didn't let her know what he said to me behind closed doors. I couldn't tell her these things because to do so would have meant sure death for us all.

Our situation had changed since our early days in the

holding camp. We were no longer living in the overcrowded barracks, trying desperately to survive the howling winter winds. Now we stayed in a small, brown house outside the camp. The house had a fireplace where mother could keep embers burning through the night to stave off the cold that still seemed to seep through the ill-fitting slats of the walls. We ate one full meal each day, and Mama often brought home enough bread and potatoes for us to eat a good breakfast in the mornings, too. We were warm and fed. But we were not safe.

Our placement in this little cabin came about by sheer luck and a little bit of quick thinking by my Mama. It happened in the spring of that first year, as the ground beneath us began to thaw and Tanya's cough subsided. We had survived the winter, and this made Mama brave.

Dima and I still trekked to the one room schoolhouse each day, where we continued to endure the abuses of Valerya Sergeyevna, whose every lesson reminded us of just how unwanted we were to our great and growing Soviet society. Despite the fact that she no longer had the protection of the wind to hide her whispered words of rebellion, Mama continued to read to us each night from her scriptures, the pages of her precious book growing faded and worn. It didn't matter, though. Mama knew most of the words by heart. It was her rebellion that ultimately saved us. Her rebellion got us out of the camp. My talent and my innocent youthfulness kept us in the good graces of the commanding NKVD officer.

The night he burst through the door of our shelter was the most fearful I'd felt since our arrival in Siberia. He ducked his head, crouching down into our dirty hole, and loomed in the doorway. There were a lot of us stuffed into that makeshift shelter, though fewer remained since typhus had swept through the camp. Many had simply disappeared, as though somehow they had never even existed. We were piled on top of one another, the shuffling cacophony of bodies forming an unwanted melody. But Mama's voice smoothed out the harsh rhythm. Everyone listened to her those nights as she read. The sound of her voice was peaceful, and some even found her words hopeful.

*"The light shines in the darkness, and the darkness has not overcome it."*

Mama spoke these words so boldly that people started to believe it. This is what we were listening to when he kicked open the door. I'd seen this man before. He was the Commanding officer in charge of our settlement. He visited the schoolroom on the first day of school and stood next to Valerya Sergeyevna who looked up at him with such admiration that she almost seemed to be drooling.

"You should all be grateful that you're here," he'd told us that day. He stood tall in the front of the room, legs slightly apart, his dark brown coat stiff and sharp. I took in the sight of his shiny medals hanging proudly over his chest, and the way that he spoke with such calm authority. There wasn't any bitterness or fear in his voice like I'd heard from most of the other men I had ever met.

"You are all being given a second chance—a chance to step away from the rebellion of your families and make a new life for yourselves. You should all be grateful that the Soviet power has been forgiving. They have allowed you, the children of *kulaks*, to be educated so that you can become good Soviet citizens."

I could tell that Dima remembered him that night he came into the barracks, too. He stiffened next to me, and I heard a small growl escape his throat. The commander picked his way through the mass of people huddled on the floor and stopped in front of Mama, who was standing in the middle of the room. She had lowered her book and now held it behind the folds of her skirt. His brow was furrowed as he leaned in to her. My heartbeat quickened and my mouth went dry. I could just make out his features in the moonlight that streamed through the small opening above our heads.

"What are you speaking, woman?" he asked.

Mama lifted her chin, but she did not respond. He reached down and grabbed her wrist, pulling her hand from behind her back. He snatched the book away and held it up to the moonlight, scanning the words.

"This material is forbidden," he hissed. Still Mama did not respond. I shrank back into Dima's arms, pulling Tanya with me into the shadows, away from the man who I knew could decide our fate with the snap of his fingers.

"You were reading this?" he asked.

Mama nodded, her head moving slowly down and then back up, her eyes never leaving his. He looked at the book again, then glanced down at us huddled by her feet.

"Are these your children?" he asked. He didn't wait for her to answer but took a step toward us. His eyes fell on me and they softened for a brief moment. I tried to be brave like my Mama, lifting my chin to return his gaze. But my lower lip started to shake, so I shifted my eyes back down.

He turned back to Mama. "Can you also write?" he asked.

Mama hesitated, then nodded again. He tucked the New Testament into his front pocket.

"Report to the front gate tomorrow morning and tell them you have an appointment to see Commander Nikolayev. Bring the children with you."

Mama opened her mouth to ask a question, but he held up his hand.

"Do not speak a word," he barked. "I could have you sent into the camp for this," he tapped his breast pocket, which held the book. "But I won't do that if you do exactly as I say. Tomorrow morning, go to the front gate."

Mama nodded once more and the man spun around, climbing out of our shelter and disappearing into the night. Murmurs coursed through barrack as people tried to dissect what had just happened. Some of them looked at us with pity, clucking their tongues and shaking their heads. I heard snippets of conversation that left me terrified.

*"Sent to the camp."*

*"Lose her children."*

*"What a pity."*

I squeezed my eyes shut and tried to block out their words as mama lay down next to me.

"Sshh...It's alright children," she whispered. "God will take care of us. Have faith, my darlings."

I wanted to scream at her to stop saying those things, but she was my mama and I loved her too much to contradict her. So I fell into a fitful sleep and waited for daylight to break.

The next morning, we arrived at the front gate where Mama spoke quietly with a young guard who eyed us all suspiciously. He stared down at us with steely dark eyes, his square jaw free of any stubble. He looked young, all smooth and clean like Dima. He was tall and thin, and I found myself staring, wondering how a boy came to be dressed like a man and if that would ever happen to Dima. The guard jutted his chin toward a small bench in the corner and told us to wait there.

Finally, after what seemed a lifetime of waiting, Commander Nikolayev arrived. He put us all in the back of his car and sped us past the barbed wire gate and out of the camp. For the first time in nearly a year, I saw a land outside the gulag holding camp. The grass was still brown, but I could see signs of life peeking through the trees, the ending winter giving way to a world waiting to bloom.

The car ride was short, perhaps only ten minutes, but long enough to ignite in my young heart a longing for more. I had forgotten what freedom tasted like, or perhaps I had never really known it at all. I remembered a feeling of awe at the expanse of the world around me, and I wanted more.

Commander Nikolayev established Mama as his personal secretary. She was responsible for typing and mailing all of his notices, setting his appointments, and keeping his calendar in order. She started immediately that morning, and Commander Nikolayev took me, Dima, and Tanya upstairs to a room above his office where he told us to be still and quiet.

"We will figure out what to do with you soon," he said. He glanced at me and winked, and a knot formed in my stomach. His stare didn't feel kind. It felt scary and dangerous. Dima saw his wink and he stepped in front of me, placing himself as a barrier between the two of us. The commander stretched his thin lips into a wry smile and offered Dima a terse nod.

"There are papers and pencils in the corner," he said pointing at a small table against the wall. "You can draw if you'd like. You will see your mother when she breaks for lunch."

He left us then, and Dima sat on the floor with Tanya, clapping his hands in front of her face and eliciting delighted giggles. He glanced at me, and I saw in his eyes the same hardness that had covered him in the schoolhouse under the glaring gaze of Valerya Sergeyevna. With a sigh, I walked to the table and sat down. I picked up a pencil and let my hands start moving across the page. As my fingers drifted back and forth, small strokes of the pencil filling in the white spaces, my mind wandered to the car ride here. I thought of the vast expanse of land that surrounded us, and I wondered if the whole world was this big and wide, or if this was the only place that existed and we were living in a small bubble. My tongue stuck out of the corner of my mouth as I colored, not even thinking about what I was doing. I didn't hear Dima and Tanya playing on the floor. I didn't think of Mama sitting at a desk downstairs, and I didn't notice the gnawing hunger in my belly. I let myself get swept away, my imagination dictating the world around me instead of the other way around.

It wasn't until the door to the room opened that I stopped drawing. I looked up to see a young woman standing in the doorway, a tray of dark, black bread in her hands. Beside the bread were three little cups, steam rising from them, dancing in tendrils up toward her kind eyes.

"My father said to bring you all something to eat," she said. She smiled at me, and I liked her instantly. Her face was soft and sweet. She looked young, perhaps only nineteen or twenty, and when she smiled, a small dimple formed in her cheek. Dima scrambled to his feet, brushing his hands nervously on his pants. The girl nodded at him, then walked to the table and set down the tray in front of me. She glanced at my paper and gasped.

"Did you draw this?" she asked, leaning over my shoulder. I nodded, my eyes frozen on the plate of bread.

"May I hold it?" she asked. When I nodded my consent, she picked the paper up and walked over to the window. She held my drawing up to the light and studied it closely. It was at this moment that I also got a good look at what I had drawn. It was a copy of the landscape outside the window. I hadn't realized that I was doing it, but there I saw the stroke marks of the paper outlining the rolling hills and trees that dotted the horizon. I'd drawn a few birds floating lazily in the sky, and small flowers dotted the forefront of the page.

The drawing was by no means professional. The unsteadiness of my young hand was obvious and apparent, but the image was a discernible copy of the outside world. The girl turned back and looked at me for a long time. She turned her gaze to Dima.

"Has she always been able to draw like this?" she asked.

Dima cleared his throat. "Yes," he answered, his voice cracking nervously. He blushed and coughed. "She loves to draw. She doesn't even know what she's drawing half the time, though. She just lets her hand wander on the page."

The girl looked back at me thoughtfully. She put the paper back down on the table and patted my head.

"You have a special gift, little one," she murmured. "We're going to see what we can do with this."

That was the beginning of my studies in the home of Commander Nikolayev. His daughter, Svetlana, met me and Tanya every morning after that, and she brought us back to her house where she had an art teacher come twice a week and give me lessons in drawing and painting. On the other days, she worked to teach me how to read and write, as well as how to cook, clean, and sew. Svetlana became more dear to me than anyone else had ever been. While Tanya played quietly in the corner, Svetlana taught me how to be a young woman.

Dima was sent to work back in the camp. Every morning, Commander Nikolayev drove him back inside the barbed fence where Dima was forced to work hard labor among men twice his age. He didn't complain, but he came home each day exhausted, too tired often to talk. He would only eat, shoving as much food into his mouth as he could without choking, then fall asleep on the floor in front of the fire.

This was how our life moved in our second year of captivity, and for awhile it was acceptable to me. I enjoyed our new arrangement, despite worrying about Dima during the days while he was gone. Two months into our move, however, everything changed.

It started the day that Commander Nikolayev returned home for lunch rather than eating at the office like usual. He sat at the head of the small table that he shared with his daughter, and ate his food slowly, staring at me as I shrank back as far as I could into the wooden chair. Tanya sat in Svetlana's lap, babbling and kicking her way through the meals while Svetlana told her father of all the things we accomplished that morning. And through it all, he stared at me and chewed his food.

A week after he began coming home for lunch, he also started returning in the late afternoons.

"I'll take the girls back to their Mama now," he told Svetlana. "The weather will begin to turn and it will be easier and quicker for me to drive them over there than for you all to walk." Svetlana didn't seem to mind this chore being taken off her plate, and so it was that I ended up sitting next to Commander Nikolayev in his car. It was a short drive to our little house outside the gulag, perhaps only five minutes. But a lot can, and did, happen in five minutes. Within a month, it became apparent that our stability and relative comfort outside the camp were all contingent on my willingness to cooperate with his wandering hands. If I kept quiet, we could stay where we were. But if I told anyone of the things he said and did to me, we would go back to our hole in the ground, and with another winter looming before us, I decided that secrecy was our only hope of survival.

On our third drive home, he slipped Mama's book into my hands just before I exited the car. I could still feel the heat of his touch on my body, and I trembled sitting next to him.

"This is the forbidden book I caught your mother reading, little one," he murmured. "This is the book that brought you to me." His lips turned up into the nasty smile that made my stomach churn.

"I'll give it back to you and let you decide what you want to do with it—what you want to do about your mother's rebellion."

That was the day that I began to resent my mother. I hid her book, just like I hid what was happening to me at the hands of Commander Nikolayev. I didn't really want to keep either secret, but what choice did I have?

I wanted my mother to figure it out on her own. I lay in my bed at night and willed her to sense the danger, but she didn't. She missed it all. For a long time, I blamed her for the things that happened during our time in Commander Nikolayev's care. But eventually I came to believe that it must have been my fault. I had her book, and I never showed it to her, never let her know I had taken it. Perhaps I was just as rebellious as she, and my punishment was the Soviet Commander with his wandering hands and hot breath.

At night, when the darkness left me terrified and alone, I accepted what seemed to be the only logical truth. What happened with the commander had to be my fault. Why else would it have happened to me?

I was just too good at keeping secrets.

# NINA

*Be ready! Always ready!*

Nina flips down the mirror and glances at her reflection, nervously fluffing her hair. She stares into her own eyes, shaking her head slowly.

"What are you doing?" she whispers. She closes the mirror and stares out the windshield at the restaurant in front of her. It's one of those quiet, intimate Italian restaurants that seats its patrons at candlelit tables and plays soft music in the background, all of which feels awkward and uncomfortable. She suddenly wishes she had suggested they just meet for coffee.

Nina's thoughts drift to her mother and how elated she would be at the prospect of this first date, and a tremor pushes through her body. Then she thinks of Annie going out with Toby, a boy she has never known but who has forever altered her daughter's life, and suddenly Nina is overwhelmed by it all.

"This is ridiculous," she mutters. "I can't have dinner with this man tonight." She reaches in to her purse to find her phone and text a hasty apology to Viktor when a sharp knock on her window causes her to yelp. She swings her head to the left and looks into Viktor's smiling eyes, and her throat tightens.

She drops her phone back into her purse and pushes open the door, stepping out into the cool, night air. "You startled me!" she says with a forced smile. Viktor smiles back, the lines around his eyes deepening in the handsome elegance that befalls men as they get older. His look is distinctly Russian, with dark eyes and a broad face. His brown hair is thinning just slightly, but still covers the top of his head. He's stronger than she realized, his crisp suit-shirt tucked neatly into black slacks. He is handsome, and Nina feels a blush warm her cheeks.

"You look lovely," Viktor says, holding out his arm so that she can tuck her hand into the crook of his elbow. Nina blinks, and offers a thin smile as she tries to push all thoughts of her mother and daughter out of her mind.

"Thank you," she says with a duck of the head. The two walk inside and get settled at a table in the back corner. It's dim and secluded, and when Nina sits down, her eyes dart from side to side. She tries to work out some excuse to shorten this evening, to get back to the life that so heavily presses down on her. Viktor watches her with a bemused expression.

"Are you alright?" he asks.

Nina looks up, almost as though she's surprised to still see him there. "What?" she asks. "Oh. Yes, of course. I just have a lot on my mind." She forces a smile and Viktor nods.

"You know," he says, leaning in to her. "This could be a nice evening away. We can talk about anything and everything that has nothing to do with your mother."

Nina smiles again, this time a little more freely. "It would be nice to leave it all behind for a little while," she concedes.

Viktor nods. "Consider me your reprieve."

Nina reaches out and takes a sip of the water in front of her, then takes a deep breath. She looks again at the restaurant, and her eyes crinkle in an unexpected grin.

"What is it?" Viktor asks, leaning forward so that the candlelight perfectly illuminates his own twinkling eyes.

Nina shakes her head. "It's...it's nothing," she says with a wave of the hand.

"No, come on. Something made you smile like that—what was it?" Viktor presses.

Nina takes a deep breath. Something about his gaze sets her at ease, and she finds herself slowly pushing back the thoughts of Elizaveta and Annie and settling into her evening.

"When did you come to the States?" she asks. Viktor leans his elbows against the table and looks up thoughtfully.

"Let's see," he begins, "I was 16 years old. My father worked as a Soviet diplomat. One evening he told my mother and I to pack one bag each, that we were going on a trip with him. We flew to Germany, and instead of leaving the airport as we were supposed to, we boarded a second flight to the United States. My father sought asylum with the U.S. government, and we never went back. That was in 1981, so I've been here thirty-seven years now."

Nina takes a sip of her water before responding. "Were you a part of Young Pioneers when you were in grade school?" she asks.

Viktor shrugs. "Of course. We didn't have a choice. Weren't you a Young Pioneer?"

Nina smiles and thinks of her days wearing the bright red kerchief around her neck, the pin of a young Lenin proudly displayed on her uniform. She remembers the thrill she felt when she was first inducted into the Pioneers, the communist training group required for all students beginning in the third grade. She'd watched as the teachers locked the door of the assembly hall after filing them all inside, ensuring that no student could leave until after they attended the mandatory meeting. It was so exciting at first. Her chest puffed with pride as the senior Pioneer member pinned her shirt and tied her kerchief. She'd recited the Solemn Promise at the start of the meetings fervently and pridefully, and when greeted by fellow Pioneers with the hearty *"Bud goty!* Be ready!" Nina returned the salutation with a firm *"Vsegda gotoy!"* Always ready!" And she was always ready...until it all got predictable and boring.

"Yes, of course," she answers. "I was just remembering one of the meetings I went to. I must have been 12 or 13. The Komsomol member who spoke was in her early 20's, and was one of those zealous inductees who took it all very seriously."

Viktor nodded knowingly.

"She spoke at the beginning of the hour about the horrors of capitalism, and how it would destroy us all if we didn't thwart its spread. I remember her specifically mentioning the capitalist's love of food, and how he would gorge himself on it at restaurants whenever he got the chance. 'This is why all capitalists are fat and ugly,' she told us." Nina raised the pitch of her voice to mock the girl whose memory is so seared into her brain.

"I was just thinking about how ironic it is that we are here preparing to gorge ourselves at a restaurant like a couple of capitalists. I guess the indoctrination didn't stick all that well, did it?"

Viktor laughs, a hearty sound that fills the room. He raises his glass of water and holds it toward her.

"*Tchestnoye pionerskoye,*" he says with a wink, stating the most popular Pioneer exclamation. The honesty of the pioneer. It was a confirmation that Pioneers never would or could tell a lie. Nina smiles and clinks her water glass on his.

"To capitalism," she replies, and they both drink.

The waitress approaches the table, and they order, Viktor indulging in a large steak, and Nina in a bowl of soup and a salad, unsure if he was planning to pay or if she should pay for herself. After placing their orders, Viktor leans back toward her.

"Well, I was never one to be appreciated or lauded by my teachers or group leaders," he says with a wry smile. "I was a bit of a troublemaker, much to my parents' dissatisfaction. And my grandmother thought me an outright menace to society until the day I called her to tell her I'd become a doctor. Apparently that white coat is magic." He smiles, and Nina nods in return thinking of her own mother's disappointment in her career choice.

"My father was a natural skeptic, though," Viktor continues. "He doubted everything, including the regime he worked for, and he voiced his doubts about the Soviet leadership enough at home that I knew better than to take anything they said in those meetings very seriously. Somehow, I think my father knew that part of my problem was simply that I was his son."

Nina nods. "I wish I could say the same. My mother hardly spoke to me while I was growing up, and I have no idea who my father was, so I can't say if I'm like him or not. So I didn't have anyone to help me grasp whether what I was saying was true or not. Mama asked me how my studies were, and chided me when I received poor marks in class. But she never explained anything to me in depth. It was like living in a walled off cave with her..." her voice trails off into an awkward silence as Viktor digests her divulgence of such personal detail. Nina clears her throat before continuing.

"My mama fell on the opposite end of the spectrum from your father," she said with a grim smile. "Elizaveta Mishurova made it very clear that to choose anything above State was a grave mistake in judgement." Nina takes a sip of her water and pauses, contemplating her next thought before speaking it out loud.

"I suppose that's why my choosing to leave the USSR and become an American citizen was so terrible for her. She swears she became an old woman the second I left home." Nina's eyes glaze over as she remembers her skepticism as a young girl. It all seemed so muddled and confusing. They were told that love was an emotion of the addled, a Western mentality that weakened the senses and made a person useless. And yet, as the group leaders and teachers spoke, Nina often found herself staring across the room at Evgeniy, the boy who had made her feel weak-kneed since she was barely old enough to write, and she couldn't reconcile the power of her emotion with the practicality of her training.

It wasn't until she was twelve, when her mother took her to see Tchaikovsky's famous opera based on Pushkin's *Eugene Onegin* live on stage at the famed Bolshoi Opera Theater, that Nina really began to question the indoctrination of her youth. How could such a beautiful story come from a place of cold impartiality? She remembered how mesmerized she was as she watched Galina Vishnevskaya bring the heroine, Tatyana, to life, her voice soaring above the audience and filling the room with hope, a feeling not common among her people in those days. And as the final strains of music began to die down, Nina had glanced at her mother and seen her swipe the tears from her eyes, and she knew, somehow, that everything her mother had been telling her up to that point had been a lie. Because to live without love was impossible. How could anyone listen to music, or read poetry, and not believe that love played a role in the makeup of mankind?

Nina suddenly becomes aware that she's drifted away from the conversation, and she clears her throat as she meets Viktor's eyes. She realizes that leaving behind her mother and daughter is an impossible notion, and she suddenly feels very tired. "Sorry," she murmurs. "I fear I am not good company tonight."

Viktor shrugs. "It's no problem. You looked lost in thought."

"Yes," she says. "I was just...remembering."

"Ah," Viktor says. He grabs a piece of bread from the basket that the waitress sets down in between them and tears off a small piece. "Memory can be a powerful tool," he says before taking a bite.

"Yes, well, my mother says remembering is dangerous," Nina replies. She draws in a deep breath, no longer wanting to discuss her mother or her daughter with Viktor. Shaking her head, she offers him an apologetic smile.

Viktor tilts his head to the side, studying her closely. "You know," he says, "you really have a lovely smile. You should use it more often."

Nina looks back at him thoughtfully. "Thank you," she answers. "I find that sometimes smiling is a little difficult. It feels like work. But..." she hesitates, afraid to offer too much of herself to this man. He waits for her to continue. "Well...nothing." She coughs as the waitress approaches their table.

*Careful,* she warns herself. *This life is already complicated enough. No need to drag him into the mess.*

The food arrives, and with a sigh of relief, Nina digs into her salad. They pass the rest of the meal exchanging safe, surface conversation, Nina careful to guard her answers and Viktor studying her closely, keeping his questions at a distance.

# ANNIE

nnie fidgets nervously as she sits at the table. She's pulled her coat tightly around her shoulders, the brisk night air tucking itself neatly into her frayed nerves, leaving her quaking with tremors.

Toby looks uncomfortably around the room, then makes eye contact with her. His face is bruised, his arm bandaged and held to his chest by a sling. His eyes dart left and right, as if he's looking for the quickest escape route. A weathered baseball cap is pulled low over his eyes.

"So..." he mumbles. Annie clears her throat.

"So..."

They sit in awkward silence for several moments before Toby stands back up. "I'm gonna get a drink. Want anything?"

"Hot tea would be nice," Annie replies. She smiles gratefully. "Herbal, please."

He nods his head uncomfortably. "Be right back."

A few minutes later, they stare at one another over heated mugs. Annie wraps her hands around her cup letting the warmth steady her racing heart.

"So," Toby begins again. "What's up?"

Annie stares at him for a moment, trying to formulate a response to his callous question. Toby shifts his eyes downward and stares at the black coffee in his mug.

"Well, first I wanted to see if you were okay," she finally answers.

Toby shrugs.

"That's not much of an answer, Toby," Annie says.

"Yeah, well, maybe I don't feel like talking about it, okay?" he snaps.

"About what?" Annie asks.

Toby sighs. "I lost my job," he mumbles. "I can't be much of a mechanic with no car to get me to work and my arm in a sling."

"I'm sorry," Annie murmurs. She reaches across the table to put her hand on his, but he yanks it away, crossing it over his casted arm and staring at her with dark, brooding eyes.

"I also had to move back home. My car is totaled, which means the only way I can get anywhere is to borrow my dad's car. And the only way I can do that is if I live under his roof again. So I'm back under his thumb, thanks to..." he stops abruptly and looks away.

"What, Toby?" Annie asks, her eyes flashing. "Thanks to me? So it's my fault then? All of it is my fault." She bites her lip to keep it from quivering.

Toby sighs and runs his hand over his eyes. "That's not what I meant," he says. "This all just got kind of...messed up."

Annie sits back in her chair and drops her hands to her lap. "Yeah," she whispers. They sit in silence for a long time, their drinks cooling in front of them. Slowly the coffee shop begins to empty.

"Ten minutes to closing, you guys," the barista says from behind the counter, breaking Annie's trance and yanking her back into the moment.

"So," Toby says quietly. "Now what?"

Annie takes a deep breath. "Now I think that you and I go our different ways," she says, the words tumbling out of her mouth. "I mean this isn't going to work, Toby. Not like this."

She gestures at her stomach, hidden beneath the table and her coat. "This is too much."

"And what about that?" he asks, pointing across the table. "What are you gonna do about it? Did you decide to end it?"

"No!" Annie wraps her arms around her waist protectively. "Why does everyone keep asking if I'm going to abort?!" she says, her words coming out louder than she meant. She ducks her head and glances at the barista.

"Sorry, Annie," Toby says. The frustration has returned to his voice. "I can't read your mind, you know." He leans forward and lowers his voice.

"You're pregnant with *my* kid," he says. "I just want to know what you're gonna do, and what you want from me."

Annie looks at him, and her eyes fill with tears. "I'm going to put the baby up for adoption," she whispers. "And I want to move on and pretend this never happened."

Toby leans back. He turns and stares out the window into the dark night. They're silent for a long time as each one lets the next steps settle.

"Okay," Toby finally says, his voice resigned.

"Okay, what?" Annie asks.

"Okay, I'll sign whatever papers I need to sign, and then you and I can move on and try to pretend this never happened."

He stands up and puts his good arm into the sleeve of his coat, tossing the other sleeve over his hurt arm. Reaching in his back pocket, he pulls out a pack of cigarettes, fumbling a bit to pull one out one handed. Finally, he sticks a cigarette in his mouth, letting it dangle from his lips. He looks down at Annie.

"C'mon," he says, his voice a little quieter, the edges in his tone smoothed out and weary. "I'll take you back home."

He turns and walks quickly out. Annie looks around, realizing she's the only one left in the coffee shop. The barista catches her eye, offering an embarrassed smile. She blushes and stands up quickly, grabbing her coat and rushing out of the building. She slides into the passenger seat of the car Toby is driving, and the two of them drive in silence. He pulls to a stop at the bottom of her driveway. Annie reaches for the handle, then pauses, turning to face Toby as he stares ahead, his face illuminated by the soft lights on the dashboard. She opens her mouth to speak, but finds there are no words left to say.

Annie steps out of the car and watches as Toby pulls slowly away, and for the first time in months, she feels relief.

# ELIZAVETA

*One never forgets the feeling of starvation.*
*It trails behind you, always unwelcome,*
*always whispering the memory.*

I stand and hobble across the room, my slippers whispering across the wooden floors. My gaze falls on the front door, hoping that it will open and Nina will come back home. The silence of this empty house suffocates me. I long for the noise of the outside world to drown out the memories.

The front hallway remains quiet, so I turn and pad back to my chair in the corner. I lower down slowly, wincing at the ache in my knees and stiffness in my shoulders. Leaning my head back, I think on my conversation with Nina from the hospital.

"Mama, who is Dima?"

Her question reverberates through my head as I sit in the lonely silence. It's not the first time she has probed me for answers. I remember when she was a teenager, trapped in the throes of self-discovery and determined to get answers to all of life's unanswerable questions.

"Mama, why have you never told me about your childhood?" she asked me once, her eyes searching mine, demanding a real answer.

I hadn't been able to speak right away, so stunned by the

boldness in her question. It was almost as though she already knew the answer, but was afraid to hear it confirmed.

"*Psh*," I'd finally replied, waving a shaking hand in the air to dismiss the question. "There is so little to tell—I've given you what you need to know."

"No, Mama, you really didn't," she'd replied, her youthful eyes flashing. "You never told me much of anything. I don't know your parents' names or where you grew up. I've never heard a single story about your childhood. You've only told me that you came from an intelligent family and your parents died in the Revolution." Nina had looked steadily at me that day, something new in her eyes.

My throat tightens as I think about all that I cannot share—the shame I've buried for so long. And now, alone in the quiet of a still house I repeat the answer I gave to Nina all those years ago.

"I am Elizaveta Andreyevna Mishurova," I whisper, my rote answer almost robotic. I feel all at once exhausted, as though the weight of my lies has suddenly become too hard to bear.

I lean my head back and think about the woman I raised. I can still see glimpses of the girl Nina had been, all bubbly and bouncy and full of questions. Somehow that spirit had been buried through the years. I blamed it on the influence of capitalism, the American way having seeped into my daughter's consciousness when she was so young and impressionable. But these days, as I watch Nina's slumped, defeated shoulders I feel a growing sense of dread that somehow I may be the one responsible for the dimming light in her eyes.

More and more, I want to share something of my past with Nina that may help repair some of the damage done, but I can never seem to formulate the words, and so they remain unsaid, stuffed and hidden away. I close my eyes, a heaviness pushing me into fitful sleep as sadness washes over me. There were so many opportunities to make things right. I missed them all.

# ANNIE

nnie opens the door quietly and hangs her coat on the rack by the door. She turns and sees her grandmother's door open. She cringes, hoping the old woman won't appear in the doorway demanding explanations for where she had been. She blinks hard and takes in a long, deep breath. When she hears no sounds, she tiptoes to her grandmother's room and peeks inside. Babushka is sleeping in her chair, her mouth hanging open to reveal a line of yellowed teeth. Her silver hair hangs down around her shoulders. She looks frail, and for a fleeting moment Annie feels regret at the lost years. She wishes she knew her grandmother better—wishes they could have connected. She's always had the sense that somehow Babushka knows more about her than she lets on, but her tough exterior made it unbearably difficult to decipher anything akin to genuine love.

Annie walks softly across the room and pulls a plush chenille blanket off the end of the bed. Holding her breath, she carefully lays it over Babushka's legs. She straightens up, then gasps as her grandmother's eyes pop open.

"Tanya?" Babushka whispers. She licks her lips and narrows her eyes. Annie stammers, trying to find the right, reassuring words.

"*Nyet, Baba*," she says. Russian always tastes funny on her tongue—like a sweet treat that has soured. "*Eta ya,* Annie...uh, Nastia."

Elizaveta's eyes slowly focus, the room around her coming into view. She looks at the blurry figure before her, slender shoulders hunched in defense as she takes a tentative step backward.

"Nastia," Elizaveta says with a sigh. Her hands grip the blanket around her legs. "*Spaseebo.*"

Annie nods, then clears her throat. "Well," she says, her voice timid. "Sleep good. Um...*Spi spokoyna.*"

Elizaveta nods, leaning her head back and watching as Annie's figure retreats. Annie closes the door gently, then looks up in relief as the front door opens and Nina steps inside.

"Oh!" Nina exclaims as she catches Annie with her hand still on her grandmother's door. "Is everything okay?" Nina hangs up her coat quickly and heads across the room.

"Yeah," Annie replies. "I was just...um...giving Babushka a blanket." She coughs nervously. Nina stands still and watches her daughter closely, the way her hands grasp and regrasp at her waist, her eyes downturned, cheeks flushed.

"How did it go with Toby?" Nina asks. She forces her words to come out slow and steady.

Annie shrugs, the lump in her throat making it difficult to formulate words. "Fine, I guess," she replies.

Nina raises one eyebrow. "Annie," she says softly. "Look at me." Annie shifts her eyes up to her mom, trying to compose herself.

"Annie," Nina prods, her voice gentle. Annie looks up at her mother, and she breaks. With a sob, she rushes to Nina and throws her arms around her, hot tears coursing down her cheeks.

Nina wraps her arms around her trembling daughter and pulls her in tight. Annie presses her face into Nina's neck, and Nina closes her eyes remembering the way Annie would crawl into her lap as a child and fall asleep in this same position.

Putting her arm around Annie's shoulders, Nina walks her to the couch and sits down with her. Annie lays her head in her mother's lap and Nina strokes her hair. "Ssshhh," she croons. Annie's shoulders heave as she releases months of pent up emotion and heartache. Nina closes her eyes and rocks gently back and forth as another memory slides over her.

She was eighteen years old and had stayed out all night long with Evgeniy, whom she'd been secretly seeing behind her mother's back. She hadn't meant to stay out all night, but she'd fallen asleep in Evgeniy's arms and hadn't woken up until the sun broke over the horizon. She'd rushed home, hoping to get back in before her mother rose and realized she'd been gone, but when she walked through the door, Elizaveta stood there, waiting, her eyes red rimmed and hair askew.

"Where were you?" Elizaveta had asked. Nina can still remember the sound of her voice. It had been laced with terror, the clipped words barely contained.

"Nowhere," Nina responded. In three swift steps, Elizaveta crossed the room and slapped Nina across the face.

"I have been up all night," she hissed as Nina glared at her, rubbing her burning cheek. "I have waited for you to return, and while I waited do you know what I thought?"

Nina didn't respond.

"I thought of every terrible thing that could have happened," Elizaveta continued. Her voice was slowly beginning to quaver, the anger subsiding and giving way to fatigue. "And do you know how I felt when I considered the worst possible outcomes?" Without waiting for a response, she shifted her eyes so that she was staring directly into Nina's. "*Toska*," she whispered.

Nina continues to stroke Annie's hair as she lets the memory marinate for a few minutes. *Toska.* It was an untranslatable word—a word that could hardly be conveyed in the English language. *Toska* communicated anguish. It was a soul-crushing heartache that couldn't be quelled. That one word in her native tongue communicated the height of despair. At the time her mother had used it, Nina had neither understood, nor appreciated, the meaning of *toska*. But that, of course, was before she became a mother.

Annie pushes herself up and wipes her eyes. Nina leans back and watches her daughter carefully. "So," she begins. "How did it *really* go?"

"I don't know how to answer that," Annie says, blinking back new tears that form in the corner of her eyes. "It was predictable, I guess." She looks at Nina, her big eyes full of regret. "Mom, I'm sorry," she whispers.

"Oh my darling," Nina responds, leaning forward and putting her hand on Annie's cheek. "I'm sorry, too."

Annie clasps her hands together in her lap and shifts her eyes away from the intensity of Nina's gaze.

"Mom," she begins, "I can't abort this baby. I just can't do it."

Nina nods. "Of course you can't. I wouldn't expect you to do that." She swallows hard, relief washing over her. Annie takes another deep breath.

"But, I also can't raise this baby. I'm not ready. I don't know if I *ever* want to be a mom, but I know for sure I don't want to be a mom right now." Annie looks back at Nina. Her cheeks are flushed and eyes bright. "I want to put the baby up for adoption," she says. The words fall out of her mouth quickly, and Nina takes a moment to put them in order and translate them properly.

"Adoption?" she asks. Annie nods.

Nina sits back on the couch and crosses her arms over her chest. She considers Annie's words, knowing that her daughter needs a confirmation that this is the right decision. And though Nina doesn't know how she really feels, she nods her head slowly and turns her lips up into a strained smile.

"Okay," she says. Her voice is tight despite her best efforts to sound neutral to the decision. "We will begin taking the necessary steps to take care of that."

Annie offers her mom a small smile and nods her head. "Thanks," she whispers. She pushes to her feet and takes a few steps toward the stairs before turning back and gazing at Nina.

"How was your evening?" she asks.

Nina feels her pulse quicken as she thinks of the dinner she shared with Viktor. She isn't ready to share this new development just yet. She takes in the sight of her only child, and swallows any notion of adding to her stress now.

"It was very nice," she lies. "I had a...productive dinner meeting."

Annie nods, then hesitates briefly before stepping forward.

"I've missed you, Mom," she says as she bends down and kisses Nina's cheek. She turns and walks quickly up the stairs to her room, leaving Nina alone on the couch to deal with her own emotions.

Nina leans her head back against the couch and thinks on the events of the last few days, a whirlwind of emotions swirling through her as she processes the newness of it all—of Viktor's attention and Annie's pregnancy. Of her mother's hidden secrets, and her own quiet contemplation. It all swirls together so quickly that she begins to feel dizzy. She closes her eyes and takes in a deep breath, and Annie's words swim through her head.

Adoption.

Not ready.

Nina draws in a long, deep breath and lets it out slowly as she focuses her thoughts on her daughter—the one person who has remained steady by her side for so many years. She whispers the word into the thin air.

"*Toska*," she breathes. And though a lump presses against the back of her throat, she refuses to let the tears fall.

# ELIZAVETA

*Sleep is the enemy of the haunted!*

It is sleep I fear the most. In the waking moments, I can better control the memories, pushing them around and stifling them in order to protect myself. But in sleep, I'm a slave to my mind and it terrifies me.

I lean my head back on my chair, my legs still covered by the blanket Nastia draped over them. What a rare, thoughtful act from my granddaughter. I've always known she was a girl given to gentleness, but there's a sadness that's covered her like a cloud for many years now. She's withdrawn, pulling into herself and away from the world. Nina doesn't seem to see it, but I do. I see everything.

My eyelids are heavy, and I fight the urge to let them fall. It's no use, though. I am as much a slave to sleep as I am to the memories waiting for me on the other side, and soon I feel myself drifting off. Too tired to fight anymore, I let go of the conscious world and slip into the past that's waiting.

Today, I fall into the memory of the night that Nina didn't come home. I remember the terror I felt, the cold that engulfed me when I imagined all the possible outcomes of her disappearance. But there was one possibility that had filled me with such dread that I became physically ill, heaving into a bucket in the corner usually meant for catching rain that dripped through the cracks in the ceiling above.

What if she had left on purpose? What if her not returning had been permanent? What if my daughter had left me behind?

The thought sent terror through my heart, and even now I feel it still. I sat in the darkened corner of our flat all night, hands shaking, imagining my life without the daughter who had been the only constant by my side. She was eighteen then, practically a woman, and distance had grown between us. But I had come to depend on her presence. It was a comfort, even in the quiet, tense moments.

And so on that long, dark night when I did not know if she would ever return home, I thought of all the ways I had failed, and I fought off the memories of my youth that shaped and molded the reality of that present.

Mostly, I thought of my mother. Perhaps that was the deepest pain of all, because in thinking of her I was confronted with a new truth that I had never considered.

I had been the embodiment of my mother's worst fear. I had done the unimaginable.

"*Toska*," I breathed into the stale air that night, and even now, in my slumber, I believe the word falls from parted lips. It was an unimaginable pain, the depth of anguish and fear pressing down on me until I felt heavy. But on that night, sleep would not come. I could only sit and stare at the door until the early morning sun turned the darkened night sky into a hazy grey.

That's when I heard her footsteps. The sound of her running up the stairs outside our door filled my soul with relief, but that relief was quickly replaced by an intense anger—a rage so deep I didn't think I could contain it.

She walked in, her hair mussed, lipstick smeared, and all my anguish and rage and terror rolled into a ball at the base of my throat. I hit her. It was one fast motion, happening before

I even knew what I'd done. She stared back at me, her face hardened and defiant as the word escaped my lips once more.

"*Toska.*"

I wake with a start, my eyes blinking wildly at the room around me. The house is still now, the nighttime having swallowed us all into the good and bad of our sleepy dreams. Slowly, I push myself forward, rocking slightly against the stiffness in my lower back. I push to my feet and shuffle unsteadily to my waiting bed, the covers turned down, soft pillows waiting to welcome me.

But there is no welcome in sleep.

# ANNIE

Annie drops her tray on the table and slides into the seat across from James. He looks up from his book with raised eyebrows.

"You okay?" he asks.

"I guess," Annie mumbles. She looks at the food on her plate: Chicken, mashed potatoes with a watery grey substance that she thinks is gravy, and stringy, limp green beans. She looks back up at James who holds out a sandwich in her direction, his eyes back on the pages of his book. With a sigh, Annie grabs the sandwich and takes a bite.

"So, what do you think about this book?" she asks, gesturing to the copy of *To Kill a Mockingbird* in his hand. He lays the book down and leans back in his chair.

"I think it's the best book ever written," James answers. Annie smiles and cocks her head to the side.

"The best book ever written?" she asks. "That's kind of bold, isn't it? Are you sure you're not just speaking in hyperbole?"

James shrugs. "Maybe," he answers. "I mean, I haven't read *all* the books ever written, so I guess there could be one or two other books that are better than this one." He grins back at her. "This is the best book *I've* ever read. I'm on my second pass through."

"Your second pass?!" Annie exclaims. "But we just got the book on Monday!"

"Yes," James answers. He grins at her and Annie feels her stomach flip. "And that's why I'm exhausted. I was up all night Wednesday. And here I am, starting it again."

Annie shakes her head. She stares at James quizzically as she takes another bite of the sandwich.

"What?" he asks.

"You're a strange person," she answers. James snorts.

"Trust me," he replies. "You are not the first person to think that. My father is completely confused by me—the son who would rather curl up by the fire and read a book than march around in the woods shooting things."

Annie stops chewing and waits a beat, letting his confession sink in. "I've never really heard you talk like that about your dad," she finally says. James shrugs. He puts down his sandwich and brushes his hands together.

"Yeah, well, now that the shock of the last year's event is wearing off, dad and I are falling back to some old habits. Unfortunately, we don't have my mother here anymore to act as a buffer."

"I'm sorry," Annie murmurs.

The two eat in silence for several minutes before James speaks again. "So," he says. "Have you read the book yet?"

"Well, I've only done the assigned reading," she answers. "I'm not quite as advanced as you are when it comes to all this literature stuff."

James smiles. He picks his book up and folds the page he's on, then slides it into his book bag. James stands and walks around to Annie. He leans down so that his mouth is close to her ear, and Annie feels goose bumps tickle down her arms.

"You remind me of Scout, you know," he says. Annie thinks of the spunky lead character in the novel and furrows her brow.

"I remind you of a six-year-old?" she asks. She shifts her head so that she can look directly at James. His face is close to hers, and she can see the light dancing through his eyes as he answers.

"Scout is courageous. She marches to the beat of her own drum, and she does the right thing, even when it's scary."

Annie searches his face, trying to discern if he's kidding, but she sees only sincerity in his eyes.

"I'm not that courageous," she mumbles, turning her face away from his. He leans in again, and Annie fights a shiver.

"You're braver than you think, Annie," he murmurs. He stands up and adjusts his backpack on his shoulder. "I gotta go early to class today," he says. "See ya."

Annie sits alone at the table for a long minute before pushing to a stand. She walks to the trashcan and dumps the uneaten cafeteria food, then turns and walks slowly down the hall, the sound of James' voice filling her head.

*"You're braver than you think."*

# NINA

*Give me a man who speaks in verse;*
*A man who tastes of treasured prose.*
*His lips, barely parted, drip*
*with the poetic language of love.*

I s everything okay?"

Nina looks up at Viktor in surprise, forcing herself to focus on his face. This dinner was a bit impromptu with Viktor calling her at work earlier and asking if she would join him at his house for a meal. It has been three weeks since their first date, and in that time they've managed to fit in several coffee dates, one lunch, and daily text messages and phone calls. But this is only the second dinner date, and it feels more intimate here in his apartment.

At first Nina had tried to decline, but he had persisted, and truthfully she found that she really did enjoy spending time with him. After a few brief, conflicted moments, she finally conceded. She called and had Chinese take out delivered to the house for Annie and her mother, sent Annie a quick text telling her she had another late meeting, and drove to Viktor's house before she could talk herself out of it.

She pulls herself back into the present moment and offers him an apologetic smile. "Yes, sorry," she lies. "Everything is just fine." She picks up her glass and lets her eyes drift across the room.

"Your house is exactly as I imagined it would be," she says. She looks through the lit candles at Viktor's face. He glances back at her curiously.

"How do you mean?" he asks.

Nina chuckles, and looks again at the small kitchen, which leads into a sitting area in front of a large plate window facing the backyard. The room is as orderly as any room she's ever seen, meticulously decorated, though Nina suspects that Viktor doesn't actually have an eye for decorating. It looks as though he saw a picture of a living room he liked, and he ordered every single piece from the picture and set it up accordingly. There isn't a painting on the wall that hangs crooked or a throw pillow that isn't evenly spaced from the next.

"It's very tidy," she answers. Viktor smiles.

"Yes, well, I do my best to impress," he says.

Nina takes a sip of the sweet, white wine then sets it back down. She leans forward and narrows her eyes. "So you're telling me it doesn't always look like this?" she asks.

Viktor shakes his head solemnly. "No, and promise me you won't go into the bedrooms. They are a nightmare. Mold everywhere, trash piled to the ceiling, all the junk I removed from this room shoved into the corners..." he smiles, and Nina grins.

"I pictured you to be a neat freak," she says.

"Well 'freak' might be a harsh word," Viktor replies with a grin, "But yes. I suppose your assessment wasn't too far off. I live alone," he says. "I don't have anyone to mess things up after I leave the house."

Nina nods with a smile. She inhales deeply, the smell of chicken parmigiana filling the room.

"It smells delicious," she says. Viktor pushes away from the table and walks to the stove, opening it a crack to check on the meal he is preparing for her.

"I'm glad you think so," he says, "because it's ready."

Several minutes later, the two of them settle into a comfortable silence as they eat the meal that Viktor prepared.

"You're a good cook," Nina murmurs.

"Thank you," Viktor replies. "My mother was most alive when she was in the kitchen. I spent a lot of time there with her and picked up a thing or two."

"Your mother cooked chicken parmigiana?" Nina asks, eyebrows raised. Viktor chuckles.

"Yes, I know," he answers. "Not a very Russian dish."

Nina grabs her glass and leans back, waiting for him to continue.

"When we moved to the States, my Mama was completely enamored with the variety of ingredients and foods available. I remember walking through the grocery store aisles with her as she blinked back tears at all the options. We didn't have a lot of money then, so every week she bought new ingredients and just started experimenting in the kitchen. Some of the most defining moments of my early years in the States revolve around the dinner table. That was when my parents relaxed, and when we could all just unwind a little."

Nina smiles and puts down her glass. She cuts off a large piece of chicken and puts it in her mouth, chewing slowly as she fights back thoughts of her mother and daughter once more. Viktor watches her closely. He puts down his fork and knife and leans forward.

"Nina," he says softly. He looks steadily at her, searching her eyes as she swallows nervously.

"Is everything alright?" he asks.

"Yes! Of course!" Nina leans back and waves her hand in the air as if to brush away his tender gaze.

"It's just that..." Viktor's voice trails off. "Well, you and I have spent a lot of time together over the last few months as I've looked over your mama, but it was never alone. And now that we've had some time together outside the office, I find that I enjoy being with you very much." He clears his throat nervously. "But, I don't want to be too forward," he says. "I am afraid I'm coming on a little strong."

Nina tilts her head to the side and looks at him quizzically, assessing how much she should let this man in to her increasingly broken world. She nods slowly.

"Yes," she answers.

"Yes?" Viktor replies. "Yes, I'm coming on strong?"

"No!" Nina responds. She laughs a garbled laugh as all the emotions of the last few days begin to bubble slowly to the surface. "No, I didn't mean you are coming on too strong," she says, trying to still the quiver in her voice. "I meant...yes...I enjoy being with you, too."

The swelling emotion begins to crack her tough exterior, and she blinks hard against tears that prick her eyelids. Viktor looks at her steadily, his dark, brown eyes filled with concern.

"I'm sorry," Nina says as she takes in a deep breath. "I fear that I am just not very much fun to be with these days." She wipes her mouth on her napkin. "There's a lot going on at home," she says. She shakes her head, blinking hard. Viktor reaches across the table and gently grabs her hands, engulfing them in his strong, warm palms.

"I'm sorry," he says. "Is there anything I can do?"

Nina shakes her head. "No," she finally answers. "I'm afraid I am alone on this journey."

Viktor squeezes her hand. "You don't have to be," he says. "I'm a good listener."

Nina is silent for a moment, wondering what she should say, when it suddenly occurs to her that she's so very tired of trying to hide words. She pulls her hands from his grasp and sits back, crossing them over her chest to stop the tremors. Viktor waits quietly, allowing her space to think and process her emotions.

Nina turns her head toward the window and looks out at the red sky, the sunset streaking the landscape with hues that pay homage to the fading autumn. It takes her breath away, the way the colors streak the horizon almost as if they're sending out a signal of hope just for her. Nina closes her eyes.

"Annie is pregnant," she says. *Toska.*

Viktor leans back in his chair with a long sigh. "Pregnant?" he asks. Nina nods and looks back at him, her eyes filling with tears. She blinks hard. Viktor looks at her carefully, his face so gentle and kind. She had forgotten what it felt like to be looked at like that.

"I'm so sorry," he says softly.

Nina looks down and tucks her hair behind her ears. "I just..." She stops and takes in a ragged breath. "I don't know what to do," she says. "I don't know what to say to her. She's scared and she seems so...alone." Nina looks back up, trying to ignore the look of concern in his eyes. "I spent my entire life alone," Nina continues, her voice quaking. "I *never* felt connected to my mother, *never* knew if she loved me or wanted me around. And I *never* felt like I could confide in her, so I didn't. I didn't tell my mother anything growing up."

Nina crosses her arms over her chest again to stave off the cold that seems to constantly engulf her. "When Annie was born, I was determined that our relationship would be different. I wanted her to know every day that she was loved and safe with me." Nina sighs. "There weren't going to be secrets between me and my daughter like there were between my mother and I. But..." she covers her mouth and leans forward, trying to stifle a new wave of emotion.

"I failed," she cries, turning to Viktor. "I failed her. I *did* keep things from her. I didn't tell her enough about her father. I thought I was protecting her by not sharing too much, but I only pushed her away like my mother pushed me away. My daughter has lived in the shadows for the last year. She hid everything from me, and it's my *fault*. I didn't fight hard enough for her. I just thought she needed space, but I should have been there. I *failed*."

Viktor stands up and walks around the table, pulling Nina

out of her chair and engulfing her in his arms. She presses her face against his chest and takes in long, shaking breaths, forcing the tears back, chastising herself for being so weak in front of this man.

"I'm sorry," she says again. "This is more than you asked for when you asked me out."

Viktor runs his hand down the back of her head, then pushes her back a little and looks in her eyes.

"Stop apologizing," he says. "Just listen to me."

Nina searches his face, taken aback by the firmness in his eyes.

"You did not fail," he says, his voice strong. "Nina," he puts his hands on her shoulders. Nina turns her face up, blinking hard. "I'm not a parent," Viktor says. "But I know for certain you have not failed your daughter."

"But I have," Nina interrupts. "Her life is ruined because I wasn't there. She didn't feel like she could talk to me. She had to run and hide, and that *has* to be my fault. Of course it's my fault. I was just too good at keeping secrets, and because of that, so was she."

Viktor cocks his head to the side. "Why does it have to be your fault?" he asks.

"Because I'm her mother!" Nina exclaims. She pushes away. "I should have known. I should have been there. She hid from me just like I used to hide from my mother, and that can only mean one thing." She stops and turns to look at Viktor, eyes wide. "I am like my mother despite all those years trying to run from her."

Viktor is quiet, patiently waiting for her to continue. Nina takes in long, deep breaths. She glances at him and shakes her head.

"You must think I'm crazy," she says. "I'm not sure why you'd want to get involved with me after this. I'm carrying more baggage than you could have possibly imagined."

Viktor steps to her side and puts his arm around her shoulder. He leans down and kisses the top of her head gently. Nina closes her eyes and leans into him.

"Lucky for you," he murmurs, "I don't spook easily." Nina looks up at him, some of the tension in her shoulders releasing.

"What am I going to do?" she whispers.

"Have you and Annie talked?" Viktor asks. Nina nods.

"We had our first real conversation in months a few weeks ago," she replies. "But it's still strained. We're both uncomfortable."

"What does she want to do?" he asks.

"She wants to put the baby up for adoption." Nina shakes her head. "I told her I would help, but I don't even know where to start," she says, her voice muffled. "I don't know what to do or who to call. What kind of mother am I?" Viktor turns to face her, smoothing her hair back off her forehead.

"I think you're being a little hard on yourself," he says. "And, also, *I* know who you need to talk to. I've had pregnant mothers come into my clinic who wanted to go with adoption. I have a very good adoption agency that I send those women to. I'll get you their number."

Nina blinks hard as fresh tears swell in her eyes. "Thank you," she whispers. She swipes her hand over her eyes and gives him a small smile. "You know," she says, "for someone who isn't a parent, you seem like you'd be pretty good at it. You know better than I do how to handle this situation."

Viktor shrugs. "I don't think that's true," he replies. "I'm just on the outside of all this, so it gives me a different perspective."

Nina nods and leans her head onto his chest. "I still have to tell my mother about Annie," she says with a groan. Viktor smiles.

"If I were you, I would wait awhile to talk to your Mama. Let some of the dust settle before you cross that road."

They stand silently for a few minutes before Viktor's stomach growls causing Nina to push back with an embarrassed smile. "You're hungry!" she exclaims.

Viktor waves his hand in the air. "I'm okay," he answers. His stomach rumbles again and Nina throws her head back, a genuine laugh filling the room and dusting off the heartache that had settled in the corners.

"I think we should finish our dinner," she says.

As the two settle back into their seats, Nina glances over at Viktor, and she feels her heart skip a beat. She realizes in that one, quiet moment that she is falling for this man fully and completely, and as she takes in his appearance through the dimming candles, she finds herself wishing she could stay with him forever.

# ELIZAVETA

*The secret keeper is always to blame.*

I push myself up out of the chair and steady my body, one hand gripping my cane while the other leans against the wall. When I feel like my legs are prepared to hold my weight, I slide my hand off the wall and shuffle away from the table. With a sigh, I begin to make one slow, painful circle around the table, remembering Dr. Shevchenko's urging to exercise more often. She comes floating into the room just as I finish my lap, and we both freeze, staring at one another through the haze of silence that always separates us.

"Hello," I say, the English word tasting strange on my tongue. She nods her head, a faint grimace washing over her delicate features.

"Hi," she says. She moves into the kitchen and walks to the counter. Opening up the box of Chinese food that a strange boy whose voice hadn't even changed yet dropped at our door, she glances at me. "Did you eat?" she asks. She speaks the words slowly, as though I am a small child. She doesn't know just how much of this language I actually understand. It's never really been the understanding that gave me trouble—it was always the communicating.

"*Nyet*," I answer. "I am not hungry now. You eat." I point to her, and she nods. I watch her closely as she scoops rice onto a plate, then covers it with what I believe is supposed to be some kind of meat swimming in a bright, orange sauce. She avoids my gaze, concentrating on filling her plate as quickly as possible.

It's a small motion that catches my eye—just a slight move of the hand over the top of her abdomen, but it's enough to draw my observation in tighter. I watch as she pulls a paper towel off the holder hanging beneath the cabinet, and notice how her shirt stretches just a little tighter around her narrow hips. And then it all starts to come together, like a puzzle in my mind that just needed the first piece to set the picture into motion. Her flushed cheeks and fuller chest. The nervous way she glances around the room, as though she may be caught in a terrible lie. The heaviness that has surrounded Nina since the day of the accident. I put all the clues into a reasonable order, and just like that, I know her secret. I know what she is hiding, and I feel my hand tremble, the cane quaking against the tile floor.

She glances up at me, her head tilted to the side. Our eyes lock for only a moment, but she shifts them away again. She grabs a roll from the basket on the counter, and puts her plate of food on a tray with a glass of water.

"Well," she says, awkwardly turning toward me, "I'm going to go back upstairs and eat. I have a lot of work to do." She turns and disappears into the stairwell as I sink down in the chair in front of me.

I feel an uncomfortable fluttering in my heart that works its way through my arms and down my legs like an electrical current.

"*Beremena*," I whisper. Pregnant. My granddaughter is carrying a child, hiding it from everyone, and the thought of it sends me spiraling to a time so long ago, to another life when I was a young woman with a different name.

And it is now that I know with certainty that I am partly to blame for her secret. If she knew my past, would she have made the same choices? My throat constricts at the thought, once again overcome by the memories of my past.

# NINA

*Ah! Pushkin. The words of my youth*
*that sang the language of love.*
*This transient life begs to bury*
*the feelings, but the knowledge*
*is firmly rooted.*

Nina fidgets nervously, twisting at her necklace as her legs bounce up and down in the stiff-backed seat. The room is quiet, the silence only broken by piano music playing faintly in the background. Annie sits next to her, staring stone faced at the wall across from them where a mural of pictures hangs in perfect symmetry. They are still-life photos of flowers and trees—nature scenes that Nina supposes are there to relax the mind.

"Are you okay?" Nina asks. Annie nods, but she doesn't speak. Her face is pale, hands clasped tight in her lap. Nina opens her mouth to speak again, but is interrupted when the door opens and a young woman walks out. Nina and Annie stand up slowly.

"Hello there," the woman says, her outstretched hand reaching for Annie as she looks gently into her eyes. "My name is Molly. I am the adoption specialist here. You must be Annie?"

Annie nods and reaches out, offering a limp handshake.

Molly turns to Nina. "And you're Nina, Annie's mother, right?" Nina nods and attempts a smile.

"Please, won't you both follow me?" Molly asks. She gestures Nina and Annie into the hallway and points to the open door on the right. "This is my office here," she says. Her voice is warm.

Nina and Annie enter the office and sink into two plush, blue chairs against the wall. Molly sits in a similar chair across from them and crosses her legs, her hands clasped in front of her.

"I'm glad to meet both of you," she begins. "Thanks for choosing *Lifesong* to facilitate your adoption." She shifts her eyes to Annie who looks around nervously. Molly's eyes soften.

"Annie, can you tell me how you're feeling right now?" she asks. Annie looks at her, then shifts her eyes to Nina. Her mouth opens and closes again. She shakes her head, blinking hard.

Nina turns to Molly. "We aren't quite sure what to expect out of this meeting," she begins. Molly nods her head.

"Of course," she replies. She turns to Annie. "In this first meeting, I just want to get to know you," she says. "I'll ask you a few questions about your pregnancy and about your decision to place the baby for adoption. Is that okay?"

Annie nods her head. Molly leans forward, meeting Annie's eyes. "Annie, I know this is scary," she says. Her voice is honey. "I want you to know that we're here to help make it less scary. We're going to answer all of your questions and walk you through each step of this process. You aren't alone. You have your mom's support, and that is such a gift. And you have all of us here in the office as well."

Nina blinks hard as she watches her daughter shift in her chair. She wants to reach out and scoop Annie up, to run back in time to the days when all it took was a hug to solve all the problems. Now, a hug isn't enough, and Nina's heart tears in two as she watches her daughter, a young woman now, straighten her back and jut out her trembling chin in determination.

Molly pulls a clipboard off the table that stands between them and grabs the pen from the top. "Do you mind if I ask you a few questions?" she asks. Annie shakes her head.

"Okay, good. First can you give me your full name?"

"Anastasia Elizabeth Abrams."

Nina blinks, remembering the day that she gave her daughter her name. She had been in the hospital for two days, and the nurses were preparing to discharge her but needed the baby's name to put on the discharge papers. Nina's friend and coworker, Jane, had come to help Nina get herself and her brand new daughter ready to go home.

"Do you have a name picked out?" Jane had asked as she cuddled the sleeping bundle to her chest while Nina looked befuddled at all the paperwork.

"I want to name her Anastasia," Nina mumbled.

"That's lovely," Jane answered. "And what about the middle name?"

"I don't know about a middle name," Nina answered. "Why do Americans use the middle name for their children?"

"Well, what's the middle name for in Russia?" Jane asked.

"In Russia, the child's second name comes from the father. It is the patronymic, and it's very significant. So a boy whose father's name is Ivan would get the second name Ivanovich. This shows that he is the son of Ivan."

"And what would the girl's patronymic name be?" Jane asked.

"Again, if her father's name is Ivan, then her middle name is Ivanovna."

Nina had looked at her newborn daughter in Jane's arms, small and frail like a tiny bird. "Her father's name was Richard. I do not know how to do the patronymic with a name like Richard."

Jane threw her head back and laughed heartily, startling the baby. She grimaced and rocked side to side before speaking again, this time more softly.

"Well, the middle name has less significance in America, I suppose," Jane said with a sigh. She walked to Nina's bed and sat on the edge. "Oftentimes, people give their children middle names after family. Like after a grandmother, or a sister. Do you have someone close to you that you'd like this little cutie to share a name with?"

Nina had thought carefully. "Well," she began. "My mother is not close to me, but she is the only family that I have. Her name is Elizaveta."

Jane looked down and studied the sleeping baby in her arms. "Anastasia Elizaveta is kind of a mouthful," she said, "but what about Anastasia Elizabeth?" Nina remembered looking at her daughter and repeating the name out loud, and it all suddenly made sense. As soon as she said the name, she recognized her daughter completely.

"Mom?" Nina pulls herself back into the present and looks at Annie. "Molly asked you a question," Annie mutters.

Nina looks at Molly. "I'm sorry," she says. "Could you repeat the question?"

"Of course," Molly replies. "I need a little background information on you if you don't mind."

"Yes, of course," Nina says, shifting in her seat.

"Okay, what is your full name?" Molly asks.

"Nina Igorevna Abrams."

"And what is your birthdate?"

"January 17, 1965."

"What is your nationality?"

Nina shifts slightly before answering. "I am Russian," she answers.

Molly smiles at her reassuringly.

"Do you have any history of serious illness in your family?" she asks. "Cancer? Mental health disorders? Heart problems?"

Nina stares at Molly, trying to make sense of the words. She shakes her head. "I don't know," she answers. "I know that my mother does not have any of these serious issues. But I don't know anything about the rest of my family."

Nina feels her cheeks grow warm at this confession to a woman who is a perfect stranger. She raises her chin and pushes her shoulders back, masking her embarrassment with a look of pride. At fifty four years old she knows so very little, even about her father. She knows only that his name must have been Igor based on her patronymic.

"It's okay," Molly tells her. "Knowing your medical history and your mother's is good." But somehow Nina knows it's not enough. She has so little to offer her daughter. She can't even complete a personal history.

"Okay," Molly says, putting her clipboard down and looking back at Nina and Annie. "Tell me, Annie, why you have chosen to place your baby for adoption?"

Annie looks down at her hands and bites her lip. She's silent for a few moments before finally speaking, her voice trembling.

"I can't do it," she whispers. "I'm not ready to raise a child." Molly nods and leans forward, her elbows resting on her knees. Her soft, brown hair is pulled into a loose ponytail at the base of her neck, and her eyes swim with compassion.

"It's okay, Annie," Molly says. "The choice you're making is one of the bravest choices any woman can make."

"It feels selfish," Annie confesses, swallowing hard. Molly shakes her head.

"Oh no, Annie," she says. She lowers her head to catch Annie's eye. "This is the most selfless decision anyone could make. You are brave."

Nina reaches over and lays her hand on top of Annie's. Annie flinches slightly, but doesn't pull away.

"Do you have thoughts about the type of people you might like to raise your child?" Molly asks.

Nina swivels her head toward Molly in surprise. The question feels bold and presumptuous, and Nina is ready to step in and stop the interview when Annie speaks.

"I've thought about it," she says. Her voice is steadier now. "I don't have specific thoughts. I just want to make sure that the baby is going to be loved."

Molly nods, and smiles. "How do you feel about the baby being placed with a family that already has children?"

Annie nods her head up and down vigorously. "Yes," she says, her voice firm. "I want this child to have siblings. I don't want it to be alone." The way she speaks this feels like a knife in Nina's chest. She had hoped at one point to have more than one child, too. But life didn't work out quite like she'd hoped.

After a few more minutes of talking, Annie's smiles come more freely. She quits clasping and unclasping her hands, and she looks much more comfortable speaking with Molly.

"I just have a few more questions, Annie, and this first one is an important one that you don't have to answer right away. You can think about it." Annie nods. "Are you interested in an open adoption if the birth family is agreeable to the idea?"

Annie pauses. "What does that mean?"

"Well," Molly says, leaning back, "it can mean different things based on the comfortability of the birth mother and adoptive family. But it usually means occasional photographs and correspondence so that you can see how your child is growing and developing. And as the child gets older, some adoptive families have met with the birth mother so that they can develop more of a relationship. What are your initial thoughts on this?"

Annie shakes her head. "No," she answers.

Molly nods. "I understand," she replies. "But please know this is not a decision we encourage you to make right away."

"I don't need to think about it," Annie answers. "I don't want to see the baby. Not even after it's born."

Nina looks at Annie closely, then shifts her eyes to Molly.

"That's okay, Annie," Molly says softly. "It's okay if you feel like that right now, and it will be okay if you want to change your mind later. We will discuss this all when we have you matched with a birth family."

Molly shifts her gaze to Nina. "You're taking her in regularly for prenatal checkups, correct?" she asks. Nina nods.

"Yes," she answers.

Molly nods approvingly. She turns to Annie. "And have you consumed any alcohol, drugs, or cigarettes since you discovered the pregnancy?" she asks gently. Annie snorts.

"I've never consumed any of that," she replies. "I'm hardly a party animal," she says, a wry smile turning up her mouth. Molly smiles in return.

"Okay," she says, standing up. Annie and Nina stand up with her. "Let's meet again next month. I'll have a few family files ready for you to look at by then. And, of course, you can both feel free to call me anytime if you have any concerns or questions. Does that sound good?"

Annie nods her head slowly. "I get to pick the family?" she asks.

"Well, I will pull the files of waiting families that I think would match your desires, and I'll let you read through them and, yes, choose the family that you want to raise your child."

Annie nods. "Okay," she replies. She looks at her mother, then back at Molly.

"What if I pick the wrong family?" she asks.

Molly walks around the table and puts her arms around Annie's shoulder. "You're not going to pick the wrong family," she answers. "You're going to pick exactly the family this child should have."

"How do you know?" Annie asks.

"You will have a mother's intuition," Molly responds. She

turns so that she is looking Annie squarely in the face. "Remember one thing very clearly, Annie," she says. "You *will be* this child's mother. You're the one choosing life for this baby, and making sure that he or she has the best chance at succeeding in that life. That's what mothers do. And so, when the time comes you have to trust your instincts. You have to trust that you will know the right family for the child you're bringing into this world. Okay?"

Annie nods again. Molly smiles in return.

"Okay, ladies," she says as she leads them back out of the office and to the lobby. "It was a joy to meet both of you. I'll see you again in a few weeks."

Nina and Annie wave goodbye and walk out of the clinic, the cold November air beating at their faces as they rush to the car. They slide into the front seats and sit in silence as the car slowly warms up.

"I liked her," Annie says.

Nina puts the car in reverse and slowly backs out without responding because deep down, she doesn't know how she feels about any of this.

---

"Mama?"

Nina knocks softly on her mother's door. It's quiet for a moment, then Nina hears the familiar stirring and shuffling behind the door that indicates her mother is awake.

"May I come in?" Nina calls softly.

"*Da*," comes the muffled response. Nina pushes open the door and enters her mother's room. It smells of stale perfume and age.

"Can I speak with you?" Nina asks. Her mother nods and gestures to the bed. Nina sits down and watches as Elizaveta slowly lowers herself into the recliner in the corner.

"How are you feeling today?" Nina asks.

"Fine," replies Elizaveta. "Old."

Nina smiles. "We need to go see Dr. Shevchenko again next week, okay? Just for a follow up."

Elizaveta nods her head. The two sit silently for several moments, Nina working up the courage to speak. There's so much she needs to tell her mother—she needs to tell her about Annie's pregnancy, and about her relationship with Viktor. The details of everything race through her mind as she works up the courage to speak.

"Mama," she begins. She stops, the words tangled on her tongue. Elizaveta stares at her daughter, her wrinkled eyes narrowed and her mouth set in a thin line. Nina takes a deep breath. "Mama, I need to tell you something," she says.

"You need to tell me that Nastia is pregnant," Elizaveta interjects quietly. Nina's eyes snap up, a look of confusion passing across her drawn features.

"How...how did you know?"

Elizaveta shrugs her shoulders. "A grandmother knows these things," she replies. Nina stands up and runs her hand through her hair. Elizaveta sees the tremor in her daughters' movements.

"How long have you known?" Nina asks.

"I have known for two weeks," Elizaveta answers. "I haven't said anything to either of you because it was clear you wanted to keep this information from me."

Nina notes the hurt in her mother's voice, and she instantly feels defensive. She opens her mouth to offer a sarcastic reply, but thinks differently of it and closes her mouth again. She learned early on not to argue with her mother. Another memory pushes into her consciousness.

She was twelve, and she'd been invited by her friend Alyona to go to their family's dacha for the summer. Nina had practiced her speech all morning, hoping her heartfelt appeal would convince her mother to say yes.

She approached the subject after dinner, when Elizaveta had processed her day and relaxed a bit.

"Mama?" Nina had asked. "I would like to ask you something."

"What is it, *Ninochka*?" her mother responded. She held a copy of *Pravda* in her hands, the national newspaper feeding her the most important headlines of the day, most of them involving America and its big, bad, capitalist abuse of the world.

"My friend Alyona invited me to go with her family to their dacha this summer and I really want to go, so can I please?"

Her mother had looked up at her then, her large, round glasses magnifying suspicious, brown eyes.

"Before you say anything, let me explain," Nina had continued. "Alyona's mother and grandmother will be there. Her father will come in July when he has his break from work. Her father works a very important job. For the government." Nina hadn't known if this was true or not, but she hoped it would impress her mother.

"Alyona said that we will get to have some enjoyment and adventures, but also that we will be working. We'll be responsible for gathering the mushrooms from the forest and helping harvest the garden. Her mother grows dill and potatoes in her garden, and also tomatoes, cucumbers, and squashes. And many other things, I believe. And we'll be working in the kitchen learning to cook and prepare foods. So I will be learning so many new things, and you won't have to worry about taking me into work with you every day, or leaving me home alone." Nina had stopped then, pausing to catch her breath. Elizaveta looked at her daughter for just a moment before turning her eyes back to her paper.

"No," she'd answered. Nina had stood stunned for a moment, unable to believe her mother hadn't seen the perfection of her proposal.

"No?" she'd asked. "Why?"

"Because I do not know Alyona's parents. I can't send you into the country with a family I've never met. It would be irresponsible. Plus, you don't need to be a burden to this family. You can stay here. With me."

"But...but, Mama," Nina had wailed. "They invited me! They don't think I will be a burden. They want me to come!"

Elizaveta had peered over at Nina. Her greying hair had been pulled back into a tight bun that day. She looked harsh and imposing, her lips caked with the remnants of rosy lipstick applied early in the morning and never freshened up. Her blue housedress pulled tight against her chest and expanded waistline, the white camisole stretching into awkward patterns against her mother's soft middle.

"No, Nina," her mother replied, her voice firm.

"No, Nina," Nina had mocked, raising her voice to an unfavorable pitch. "Do you not have a more original way of rejecting me?"

Elizaveta slammed her newspaper on the table and stood up quickly, her chair toppling onto the floor behind her. She leaned over the table so that she was only a few inches from Nina.

"Don't you speak to me that way ever again," she hissed while Nina blinked back tears of frustration.

"Mama, Alyona is a *good* girl. She is the top of our class. She's smarter than me. She can help me with the subjects that give me trouble in school. And she is very involved with the Young Pioneers. She's even responsible for the Pioneer room! She straightens the drums and flags and she organizes extra meetings so that we can all learn how to better serve our country. Her family is very loyal. Those things are important to you. Why wouldn't you want me to go with them?"

"Why do you insist on leaving me?" Elizaveta replied. She turned and righted her chair, sitting back down and picking up her newspaper. "Why are you not content to stay here with your mother? I am your only family, and you want to leave me?" The hurt in her mother's voice had formed into a poultice of guilt that settled on Nina's heart, joining the many other times her mother had used guilt to manipulate her.

Nina pulls herself out of the past and focuses back in on her aged mother who sits stoically across from her. There are so many things to say, so many words unspoken.

"I'm sorry we didn't tell you," Nina finally says, swallowing her pride. Elizaveta nods.

"When will the baby arrive?" she asks.

"The due date is May 1," Nina replies.

"And the baby will live here with us, I assume?"

Nina pauses and looks gently at her mother. "No, Mama," she replies. "The baby will not live here. Annie has decided to place the baby for adoption."

Elizaveta looks confused. "What does it mean, 'to place the baby'? She is giving the baby away?"

Nina shakes her head. "It's not like that, Mama. She just isn't ready to raise a child. She's young, and she wants to give this baby the best chance at succeeding in life."

"Psh," Elizaveta scoffs, waving her hand in the air. "If Nastia was ready to *make* a baby, then she is ready to raise one. And you will help her do that," Elizaveta responds. "She doesn't need to give the baby away. She can just live here and you will be her support. That's what good Russians do."

Nina cocks her head to the side and looks at her mother quizzically. "That's what 'good Russians' do?" she asks. "Mama, I don't know what that means." Nina draws in a deep breath. "Annie has made this choice on her own," she continues. Her voice trembles. "And I'm supporting her decision. I do not want you making her feel bad about this."

"What is this attack on me, *Ninochka*?" Elizaveta responds. "It's not Nastia who should feel bad, it's you. You should feel bad because you don't agree with her decision, but you're doing nothing about it. Why do you make me the enemy?" Elizaveta's voice is laced with hurt. Nina shakes her head.

"It's Annie, Mama, not Nastia," she says, teeth clenched.

"And you're not going to do this to me. Not this time. You're not going to turn the tables and make this all about me, because this *isn't* about me, and it isn't about you. It's about *Annie* and the choice she has made—a choice that I will support."

Elizaveta leans forward in her chair. She places her hands on top of her cane, staring intently at Nina. "A choice you support, but you don't understand," she says softly. "Have you told her how you feel, *Ninochka*?"

Nina sighs in frustration. "It doesn't matter how I feel, Mama. Annie doesn't need the pressure of trying to please me right now."

"Hmph," Elizaveta huffs. "You coddle her too much. Your goal has been to see her happy, but she isn't happy. She's sad, and she is lonely and scared, and all of that leads to too much introspection. She needs someone to remind her to think of others."

Nina stares at her mother in disbelief. "Do you really believe that?" she asks. Elizaveta sighs and studies her daughter closely.

"I'm an old woman," she says. "And I know what it's like to be haunted by the words that were never spoken."

They stare at one another for a long time without speaking. Finally, Elizaveta breaks the silence.

"Talk to her and tell her how you're feeling, *Ninochka*," she says. "You don't have to change her mind. But trust me when I tell you that the memories of hidden confessions are a weight under which you do not want to live."

"Mama, are..." Nina stops as her mother holds up her hand.

"I'm tired," Elizaveta says. She leans back against her chair and closes her eyes. Nina watches her mother for a few quiet moments before turning and walking slowly out of the room. She doesn't tell her about Viktor, deciding to protect that secret just a little longer.

# ELIZAVETA

*Idle thoughts are the downfall of the strong.*

It wasn't the same when we returned home. After four years in Siberia, we were released, sent packing as quickly and mysteriously as we had been brought. I was ten years old when the Commander walked into his house mid-morning, a scowl etching lines down his weathered face.

"I need the children," he told Svetlana. "I must take them right now."

For three years, our routine had been the same. Six days a week, my mother was at the Commander's disposal while Tanya and I spent our days in Svetlana's care. I practiced my reading and writing and drawing under Svetlana's careful and critical eye while Tanya played in the corner with the few toys they had been able to gather. On Sundays, we stayed inside our cabin and listened to Mama read from whatever book the Commander had let her borrow, oftentimes listening to the same stories over and over. When Mama tired of reading, she would walk around the small, wooden room with us quoting her scriptures. I once asked her why she talked so much during those long days.

"We need to keep our minds engaged, my darling," she answered. She pointed out the window at the white land that lay beyond our little cabin. A fresh snow had covered the ground, making it look pure and lovely, but only from inside by the fire. The icy cold transformed the land into a bitter vice when we left the comfort of our small home.

"As soon as we let our thoughts go idle, there's nothing left to do but lose our minds completely. The quiet and confinement will send you to places you don't want to go, my dear. And so you must always keep your mind engaged, keep it set on things above, not on the things of this earth which fade away."

Dima snorted from the corner of the room at this response. Sundays were his day off too, and he sat staring out the window, often speaking very little. The only one who seemed to be able to break through the wall he'd built around himself was Tanya. She'd crawl into his lap on those slow, quiet days and sit for hours, often falling asleep in his arms.

Dima had changed. The grueling labor had taken its toll on his young body, and his attitude had hardened even more. His back was bent, his hands rough and calloused. His lips were constantly chapped from the wind, and despite the fact that he tried desperately to hide it, he winced in pain each time he sat down or stood up from a chair. He was fourteen years old, trapped in the body of an old man.

"That sounds stupid, you know," he said that day. "*Set your mind on things above.* What does that even mean?"

Mama looked at him kindly. Her face was so soft and gentle, not etched with hardened lines like so many others around us. Her dress pulled tight around her round hips. It had once been a dark blue, but had faded in Siberia like most other things. Still, it made her look young and pretty. She had a kerchief tied around her head, tucked under her low bun and keeping all stray hairs away from her round face. Mama's eyes always looked kind, even when she wasn't smiling.

"It means that our time here on earth is temporary. But there's a new life that waits for us, if we choose to believe. There's a God who..."

"Oh, Mama, please!" Dima had shouted. "Don't talk to me about a new life or a God who supposedly cares. This life is all there is. This broken earth is all we have, and we *kulaks* are the ones who suffer for it."

Mama stood with her head held high as Dima glared at her. I simply watched the exchange between the two of them with great confusion. I knew that Mama's words were bad. They went against everything I had been taught in the camp school by Valerya Sergeyevna. Even Svetlana made sure I understood the importance of acquiescing to the greater good of the country. There was no higher power. There was only Father Stalin, and the NKVD, and the Soviet Union. These were the powers to which we had to submit. But my mother didn't agree, and this made her dangerous.

Of course, mama did not stop reading to us, nor did she quit quoting her scriptures. And despite my best efforts at tuning her out as a means of self-preservation, I found myself mumbling the forbidden words at night before drifting off to sleep. They were like a comfortable blanket that I wished I didn't need, but somehow still wanted.

*"Peace I leave with you, my peace I give you. I do not give to you as the world gives. Do not let your hearts be troubled and do not be afraid."*

I mumbled these words without even thinking about it, over and over at night because it was the darkness that I feared the most. In the dark, I couldn't escape the memory of Commander Nikolayev's wandering hands. The shadows of the night whispered his dirty words and reminded me of the way he smelled when he slid up close to me in the car. I'd feel the shadows closing in, and unconsciously speak mother's words into the darkness, and somehow they seemed to work. Sometimes, when the entire world was stilled with slumber, I reached beneath the slat in the wood beneath my bed where I had buried Mama's forbidden book of scriptures, and I would stand next to the window with the moon as my light, reading those words quietly to myself. I wanted to understand where my Mama's power came from - how she could be so unshaken by the life we were forced to live. But the words didn't make sense to my young mind. They were difficult to understand, and I wouldn't dare ask Mama to explain, because then I would have to tell her how I'd come to have her book. That was the secret I knew I needed to bury.

In the end, I would tuck Mama's book back into the floor. I'd lay in bed and think of the book hidden beneath me, and I would wonder why my mother did it. Why did she put us in danger this way? Why did she insist on filling our minds with these dangerous messages? And why did they bring such peace? I couldn't reconcile all the questions swirling inside my young heart.

When Commander Nikolayev told us to come with him that morning, I knew something was different. The look in his eye and the tone of his voice made all of us stop. Tanya edged closer to Svetlana, hiding behind her skirt while I stood frozen in the corner, pencil hovering above paper. I had been working on drawing portraits. Svetlana had asked me to draw each member of my family, and I had done well. She had been especially impressed with the drawing of my mother.

"You captured something in your mother's eyes," she'd told me when I showed her. "It's very unique." She'd held it up and stared at it for a long time before turning back to me. "You captured peace," she'd said quietly.

On this final day, I was staring at a blank page. The only person left in my family to draw was my father, and I had no image from which to work. It had been nearly four years since I'd last seen him, and my only memory was a shadow. My plan had been to pencil in a silhouette, but I'd never even gotten that far.

"What's going on, Papa?" Svetlana asked. She pulled Tanya up into her arms, my sister wrapping her thin legs around Svetlana's waist. Tanya had grown so attached to Svetlana that she would cry out for her in the evenings before bed. And the long Sundays trapped inside the cabin were often filled with attempts to distract Tanya so that she would stop asking when she could go back to Svetlana's house.

"It's time for them to leave," the Commander said, jutting his chin toward me. "They're being shipped back to their village."

"We're going...home?" I asked. He stared at me, his eyes dark, and gave a barely discernible nod. I glanced at Svetlana, who sat down and rocked my sister gently back and forth. Tanya whimpered in her arms, somehow understanding even more than I did that this new development meant a permanent change. Svetlana pushed Tanya's head back and looked into her eyes.

"You get to go back to your home, little one," she crooned. Her eyes shone brightly as well. Tanya's whimpers turned to sobs as she shook her head back and forth, her blonde curls shaking. Svetlana looked up at her father.

"Can't they stay?" she asked. "They have to be safer here with us than they will be at their home. And I can make sure these girls get a proper Soviet education. They won't get that in their village."

Commander Nikolayev shook his head firmly. "The orders have been sent down. The families of political prisoners who died in the camps need to leave to make room for the others coming." His eyes shifted to me. "There are other *kulaks* coming to take their place."

I met his gaze as my body went numb. "Political prisoners who died in the camps?" I whispered. My father was a political prisoner. "My papa?"

Commander Nikolayev turned his face away from me. "Get them dressed, Sveta," he barked. "We leave in ten minutes."

It all happened fast after that. Svetlana took us home where Mama, grim-faced and stoic, frantically packed up a *katomka* for each of us to carry on our backs. We had so little that preparing to leave took hardly any time. I rushed to the bed while Mama was busy sweeping dust out the door, and I pulled out the small book of scriptures. I tucked it into my shirt, determined to keep it hidden on our return trip home.

Dima burst through the door just as we finished bundling ourselves for the journey home. He stared at Mama, his eyes shining with grief. She reached for him, but he pulled away, shaking his head and wrapping his thin arms around his gaunt frame. I didn't know it then, but Dima had already left us. His body remained just a little while longer, but his spirit had been crushed long before, somewhere in the frigid wasteland where our father's body now lay lifeless and unclaimed. Without a word, we all filed out of the house behind the commander, *kulaks* forever branded as traitors.

A week later, we wandered back into our village. I didn't even really remember it, I had been so young when we left. The vague memories I had were brighter and bigger, but what we found when we returned was a dusty, barren group of faded houses. We had few possessions upon our return, only a couple of dirty bags with the toys that Svetlana gave to Tanya, two of my drawings, one book, and the limited ration of food that we'd been given when we were put on the train. Tanya had wailed the entire trip, stopping only to sleep when she wore herself out. Dima sat with his back tight against the wall of the rickety cattle car. We were pressed into the train with several other families, all returning to different parts of a land they called home. But none of us really knew what home meant anymore. We'd all forgotten, even the grown-ups.

When we got to the house that had once been ours, we found another family living there. Behind the house was a vast field, cornstalks standing tall in the setting sunlight. It was autumn, which meant the days were warm enough to enjoy the outdoors, but cold was settling into the night. I took in the sight of the withering sunflowers against the fence behind the small house, and tried to dig up some memory of this place, but it all looked new and strange.

"Go away," the woman occupying what had once been our home hissed, her blackened teeth bared beneath chapped lips. "You're not wanted here, traitors."

"Please," my mother begged. "We're tired, and it is getting dark. My children just need a place to stay out of the cold night air." The woman slammed the door. Our door. We followed Mama out into the knotted road, the chilled September air raising small shivers on our arms and legs. Tanya whimpered softly in Dima's arms.

"I don't understand, Mama," I said. "I thought that we were countrymen. I thought that we took care of one another."

Mama sighed and looked down at me with tear-filled eyes. "Unfortunately, my dear, most people are only looking out for themselves. I guess we can't really blame them, can we?" I shook my head because I knew that's the answer she wanted, but I didn't believe that. Of course we could blame them.

"But we don't have to live that way, my darling. We can be people who look out for others, and who protect one another." She knelt down and met my gaze in the fading sunlight. "Don't betray a fellow citizen in order to preserve your own comfort, dorogaya." She always called me darling when she wanted me to truly learn something. "Put others before yourself always, and you will see a reward."

She said this and I nodded, but after we visited three more houses and were turned away, I started to doubt her words. Finally, an old man gave us permission to sleep in his barn. As we buried ourselves in the hay, the stench of starving cattle searing our nostrils, it occurred to me that every single person who had turned us away was now going to sleep inside a warm cottage while we lay in the dirt. They had chosen self-preservation, and they were rewarded with warmth and the freedom from sharing their space with a strange and dangerous family freshly released from Siberia. Mama's words felt empty on that dark night.

They were confusing to me for many, many years, in fact. It's only now that I am beginning to understand my mother. And now it is too late.

# ANNIE

**M**erry Christmas."

Annie jumps as a box falls into her lap. She looks up at James and smiles. "What's this?" she asks.

"It's from your Secret Santa," he replies with a grin. He slides into his seat across from her and pulls out his lunch bag. He glances at her spread and raises his eyebrows. "So you've finally wised up and decided to pack your own food, huh?" he asks.

"Well, I hate mooching off you all the time, so I asked my mom to buy some real food for lunches. This was the best she could come up with." Annie gestures to her container of tomato and cucumber salad smothered in Italian dressing. Next to it is a chunk of black bread, an apple, and bag of dried fruit. James shakes his head.

"Here," he says. "Please, just take part of my sandwich. I can't watch you eat that stuff in good conscience."

Annie laughs and shakes her head. "It's actually fine. I like this food. It's...comfortable."

James shrugs and takes a large bite of his chicken salad sandwich. "So," he says, his mouth full, "you gonna open that or not?"

Annie tears the wrapping paper off the package and pulls out the most beautiful book she's ever seen. It's pale blue with green and red swirls splattered across the cover, surrounding an embossed image of a young girl with long, red braids.

"*Anne of Green Gables!*" she exclaims. She flips open the book and runs her hands over the words, then closes it again and takes in the sight of the cover. "It's so pretty," she breathes.

"I know you already have a copy," James says. "But this one just looked like it belonged in your hands, and really, we can't have enough copies of our favorite book, can we?" Annie looks up at him with a shy smile and shakes her head.

"I guess we can't," she says. "I'm sorry. I didn't get you anything," she continues with an embarrassed smile. James shrugs.

"I didn't expect it. I just saw that and thought of you. Don't feel bad. Promise?"

Annie smiles again. She hugs the book to her chest and nods. "Promise."

James clears his throat. "So, you asked your mom for better food, and she got it, huh? Does that mean you and your mom are talking more?"

Annie nods. "Yeah, I guess we are. It's still kind of weird and strained. My mom is totally dating that Viktor guy. She mentions him casually, like they're just friends or something, but she talks to him all the time and has at least three "business" dinners a week. I know she's serious about him, but she isn't saying anything to me, so clearly we haven't crossed some magical barrier where we tell each other everything. But maybe we're not supposed to, you know?"

"What do you mean?" James asks. He takes another bite of his sandwich.

"I mean, she's my mom. Are we even supposed to be close? She's certainly not close to her mom. The two of them hardly talk at all except to pick on one another. Maybe this is just normal mother-daughter stuff."

Even as she says the words, Annie knows she doesn't believe it. Something broke between her and her mother the day her grandmother landed on American soil. The distance between them extends beyond this one strained moment in time.

"I dunno," James says with a shrug. "You're talking to the wrong guy. My dad and I don't even know how to talk these days. He's wrapped up in work, which lets him escape the upcoming reminder of how life has completely changed. And I absorb myself in novels, or 'storybooks' as my dad so lovingly calls them, apparently to the severe detriment of all my other grades," he says with a grimace. "I'm not doing so well in Biology."

Annie puts her fork down and looks at James. It's December 20, the last day of school before they're released for Christmas break. In five days, James and his dad will mark the first anniversary of the car accident.

"Oh, James," she murmurs. "I'm sorry. This must be such a hard time for both of you," she says.

James stares down at his sandwich. "Neither one of us feels much like celebrating," he mumbles. They sit silently for a moment, James brooding and Annie working up the courage to make a huge offer.

"Why don't you guys come to our house for Christmas lunch?" she asks. As soon as the words escape her mouth she regrets them. She hasn't invited anyone over since her disastrous twelfth birthday all those years ago.

James looks at her through narrowed eyes. "Are you sure?" he asks. "Don't you think you should run it by your mom first? She might not want to celebrate under the cloud of sadness that my dad and I are dragging around."

"Oh, we don't actually celebrate Christmas at all," Annie says. "At least we don't celebrate it on December 25. We used to, but when my grandmother moved in she insisted we start celebrating the Slavic New Year and Christmas. It was just one more way she came in and changed everything."

Annie remembers the first few Christmases after her grandmother moved in when her mom would sneak into her room early in the morning on December 25, and the two of them would exchange presents through giggles because they were ignoring Babushka's rants against the "consumerist" American holiday. And then two years ago, they both just...forgot. They slept in and missed their secret gift exchange, awkwardly presenting the small treasures to one another that night before bed. Last year they didn't even try.

"What's the Slavic tradition?" James asks.

"Well in Russia, Christmas just isn't a very big deal, and it's not even celebrated on December 25. I don't know the whole history behind it. I think it was changed by Lenin or something since Christmas was too 'Christian.' Or maybe I'm wrong." Annie waves her hand, and James finds himself smiling at the way her face changes and moves as she speaks, her eyes dancing and hands fluttering.

"So we make a big deal of New Year's Eve. That's when Russian families put up their trees and decorate them. They tell stories of *Dyed Moroz*—that's Father Frost, the Russian version of Santa Claus—and his daughter *Snegurochka*. She's basically like this snowflake fairy. And there are all these stories of her and *Dyed Moroz* saving the Christmas tree from the clutches of *Baba Yaga*, the evil witch of the forest who likes to steal children and boil them for supper."

James' eyes widen. "Geez!" he exclaims. "You Russians have really spiced up the Christmas story, haven't you?"

Annie laughs. "It's a pretty big deal," she says. "Even though I grew up in America, I've always been kind of fascinated with my mom's Russian traditions. Of course, I'm not going to tell *her* that," Annie says. She offers him a sly grin.

"So that's New Year. What's the Slavic Christmas about?" James asks.

"Well, technically that's the day Russian's celebrate Christmas, but it's much more understated after the New Year's celebrations. We celebrate it on January 6, and we might exchange one more, small gift. And we'll have another big meal. Like, a huge meal." Annie says, holding her hands out wide to illustrate her point. "My mama calls it the 'Holy supper', and she and Babushka will make twelve different dishes."

James eyes widen again.

"Apparently the idea is that because Christ had twelve disciples, we should eat twelve different foods, and the foods are completely Russian. Vereniki, kutia, herring, vinegret, pampushki, compote."

James shakes his head. "I don't even know what you're talking about right now, but I'm completely fascinated."

Annie smiles. "Christmas dinner is the one time a year that my mom and grandmother seem to completely embrace their heritage. It's like they have to do these things...although the last couple of years things have tapered off a little. It hasn't been quite as big an affair." Her voice trails off.

Annie takes another bite of her salad and chews quietly before continuing. "Anyways, all that to say, we don't do anything on Christmas Day. So maybe you guys would want to come over? I promise not to let my mom cook too Russian of a meal."

James laughs. "I think it sounds great, even the Russian food. But I think you should ask your mom first." He raises his eyebrows. "She and I didn't exactly get off on the right foot the first time we met, you know?"

Annie blushes and nods. "Yeah," she mumbles. "This might be a terrible idea. My grandmother is crazy. Like, I think she legitimately might be crazy."

"Well, crazy doesn't scare me," James says. "But your mom makes me a little nervous. I mean, she does know that you and I aren't...um..." James glances at Annie's stomach, concealed by an oversize sweatshirt.

"Oh. Yeah," Annie clears her throat nervously. "She knows. I cleared up the confusion between you and Toby. And she's been supportive since I decided to, um, well I guess I haven't really told you, yet." Annie puts her fork down and looks at her hands. She glances up at James, her cheeks burning.

"Well, I'm placing the baby for adoption," she says quietly. "I've been reading files of prospective families, and the plan is to choose a family who can give the baby what I can't. Stability."

James puts his sandwich down and leans his elbows on the table, clasping his hands together. Annie can't look up at him.

"Annie," he says. His voice is soft. Annie glances up at him and takes in the sight of his eyes searching her face. "I think that's really cool," he says.

Annie blinks back tears. "You do?" she asks. Relief floods over her as weeks of trying to work up the courage to tell James this news unwinds.

James smiles. "I really do." He glances down at the table for a moment before speaking again. "My little sister was adopted," he says.

Annie raises her eyebrows. "Really?" she asks.

"Yeah. I was ten when my parents brought her home. They had wanted another child after me and hadn't been able to have one naturally, so they decided to adopt and...." he pauses, running his hand through his hair. He looks back at Annie, his eyes bright. "Annie, I will never forget the look on my mom's face when she walked through the door with Lily. It was...I don't know how to describe it. It was like the purest form of joy, you know? Like they had been waiting for this tiny person their whole lives, and there she was. We were all crazy about her. It was like we had been given the greatest, most undeserved gift."

He looks back at Annie who brushes away the tears before they have a chance to spill down her cheeks.

"You're doing something amazing, Annie," he says. "You're going to make someone's dream come true."

Annie smiles. "Thank you," she whispers.

James smiles back, and he leans forward again so that his

face is closer to her. "You're welcome," he says. "But you're still going to have to make sure that your mother and crazy babushka are okay with my dad and I coming before we cross the threshold of your doorway, deal?"

Annie laughs, wiping her eyes one more time. The bell rings and the two gather their things. Annie tucks her book under her arm and gives James a small wave. "Have a good afternoon," she says. James makes a face.

"I have Biology next," he says. Annie wags her finger at him.

"Pay attention," she says. "No reading during class."

"Ugh, but it's so boring," James complains. He reaches over and grabs Annie's backpack, pulling her to his side. Leaning down, he gives her a quick peck on the cheek. Annie's whole body grows warm, and she leans into him.

"See you later, Anastasia," he says. With a subtle wink, he turns and runs up the stairs. Annie watches him go, and for the first time she starts to believe what people have been telling her.

She finally believes that she might be brave.

# NINA

*Na zdorovya.*
*To your health.*

Nina opens up her mother's door quietly. She can hear Elizaveta in the bathroom humming loudly, the old Russian folk song quaking its way out of weathered vocal pipes. She smiles because she remembers her mother constantly singing when she was younger. She had a terrible voice, but she still insisted on singing loudly whenever she was in the bathroom, or cooking in the kitchen. She boldly belted out Soviet folk songs, and mercilessly hummed the national anthem. The most horrifying for Nina as a child had been the days following a trip to the opera when suddenly her mother believed herself to be in league with the famed Galina Vishnevskaya. She pranced through their small flat belting out the role of the soaring soprano while Nina huddled on the couch, hands pressed to her ears because it sounded like a cat being slaughtered. On occasion, the neighbor would come knocking on the door, a surly old man who always smelled of cheap wine and herring, and he would yell at her to quit her screeching, to which Elizaveta would respond by singing louder and longer.

Now, Nina finds comfort in her mother's shaky tune, oddly missing those moments from childhood. She reaches for the laundry basket, and as she leans down, her eye catches something in the open closet across the room. A small, metal box peeks out from behind the clothes hanging on the rack. Nina glances at the bathroom door, her mother's tune blending in with the running sink water. She tiptoes to the closet.

Pulling out the box, she gently lifts the lid and takes sight of the objects inside. The first thing she notices is a small pair of shoes that she recognizes from her childhood. Nina draws in a sharp breath at the sight of these precious objects from her youth. She runs her hand over the shoes remembering how upset she'd been when she'd gotten them dirty, certain that her mother would be forever disappointed in her.

She glances nervously at the bathroom door and pulls out the shoes. Beneath them are several folded papers, along with her Komsomol pin, which lay on top of the red kerchief she used to tie around her neck before grade school. She sets these larger items aside, relishing for one more, quick second the feel of her youth beneath her fingertips.

She reaches in and pulls out the papers. The first is a drawing that she has never before seen. It's a pencil sketch of a little girl lying on the couch, sound asleep, her hair matted to her forehead. Blankets are tangled around the little girl's thin legs, and her hands rest peacefully on her stomach. The picture is faded in spots, yellowed on the corner, but the drawing is so well done, so lifelike, that Nina almost thinks she sees the girl's chest rising and falling. Nina glances at the writing in the bottom corner of the page, and it takes her breath away completely.

"Nina. February 2, 1968. My daughter."

This was a picture of her, drawn by her mother. Nina runs a shaking finger gently over the edges of the paper. She blinks several times before shifting her eyes back to the bottom of the box. She reaches down and pulls out a stack of papers, slowly and gingerly unfolding the top sheet.

It's a letter, the scrawled language faint on the page. Nina squints, holding the letter under the lamp to make out the faded words. She immediately recognizes her mother's elegant handwriting, and she reads the words slowly.

*Dear Mama,*
*Forgive me.*
*Your daughter*

Nina folds the letter and lets it fall back into the box. She unfolds the second sheet of paper, and reads the same words. Over and over, she opens up letter after letter, each one asking for forgiveness. Sometimes the words are written shakily, as though the hand that looped them was unsteady. Others are written with darker, more sure handwriting, as though written in a fit of anger.

Nina counts up the sheets of paper. Fifty-three letters, all reading the same thing, fall back into the box. A tear slips from her eye before she has the chance to cut it off, and it drips onto the stack, spreading out across the paper, blotting her mother's hidden words. Who was this grandmother she had never known, and what happened between the two that caused her own mother such intense grief? Nina looks up at the bathroom door that separates her from the woman she has longed to know her entire life and a lump lodges tight in her throat.

The water in the bathroom turns off, and Nina quickly replaces the items, hands quaking as she makes sure to put them in exactly as she took them out. She pushes the metal box back into the closet and flutters from the room, closing the door behind her just as the door to her mother's bathroom opens. Nina leans her head against the door for a moment, waiting for her heart to slow down.

"Mom?"

Nina jumps and yelps, pushing away from her mother's door and running into the kitchen. Annie looks at her with eyebrows raised.

"Um...you okay?"

"What?" Nina asks. She looks at Annie with an air of confusion. "Oh, sure. Yes. I'm okay. I'm fine. Sorry, I was just making sure your, uh, grandmother was doing okay in her room. I was trying to be quiet. You scared me."

"Okaaaay," Annie says, her word drawn out. She looks skeptically at Nina.

"What do you need, Annie?" Nina asks. She moves to the stove and grabs the teakettle, turning toward the sink to fill it with water.

"Well, I...um...wanted to ask you a question," Annie answers. Nina turns the water off and puts the kettle on the stovetop, turning the heat to high and watching as the burner lights to a bright orange.

"Okay," she says, her back to Annie as she fights to control her emotions.

"Well, um, do you remember that day you came home and my friend James was here talking with me?"

Nina narrows her eyes and turns around, crossing her arms over her chest.

"I remember," she says.

"Okay, well James and I were talking at school today, and he and his dad don't have any plans for Christmas. They kind of want to just...skip Christmas this year. So I was thinking that since we never do anything on Christmas, maybe we could have them here? For a late lunch?"

Nina watches the way Annie twitches nervously as she speaks. "Uh-huh," Nina says. "And this boy, his name is James?"

Annie nods.

"Why is it that he and his father do not celebrate Christmas? Are they American?"

"Yes, they're American, Mom," Annie says, shaking her head. "It's just...well, James' mom and little sister were killed in a car accident last Christmas. It's going to be a hard day for him and his dad, so I thought maybe we could help distract them."

"Oh, that is a terrible pity," Nina says, shaking her head.

She pinches the bridge of her nose and draws in a deep breath. "It's very kind of you to think of them, Annie," she says, "but are you sure you want to invite company to our home right now?" she asks. "It seems there is a lot going on these days."

"I know," Annie says softly. "But I'm sure. I think it could be good for them. And maybe for us, too."

The kettle begins to sing behind them, and Nina turns to remove it from the stovetop. "Well, then, okay," Nina murmurs. "Let's do it. Perhaps I will invite Viktor over as well."

Annie looks up at her in surprise. "Viktor?" she asks. She offers her mother a crooked smile. "So you *are* seeing Viktor?"

"Oh, it's nothing," Nina says with a wave of her hand, but when she glances at Annie and sees the look of skepticism cross her face, she sighs.

"Okay," she says. "Maybe it's not nothing. He is a very nice man—a good man. He has been my only friend these last months, too. And he wants to meet you formally. You've met him as Dr. Shevchenko, but he would like you to know him as Viktor." Nina clears her throat. "Are you okay with that?"

Annie thinks for a moment, her blue eyes searching her mother's face. "Yeah," she says finally. "I think I'm okay with that." She glances at her grandmother's door, then looks back at her mom with raised eyebrows. "Will she be okay with that?"

Nina winces. "She will be more than okay. She'll be thrilled, which is why I haven't had the nerve to tell her about it."

Annie snorts. "You might want to say something before Christmas day then," she says with a laugh. Nina tries to smile in return.

"Yes," she replies. "I suppose I will have to confess," she says.

The two stare at one another for a long moment before Nina clears her throat and speaks again. "Okay, then. We should plan a menu. We will need a turkey, right? And cranberries? Aren't those things that Americans eat for holiday meals? It's been a long time since I prepared one."

Nina thinks back to her first Christmas in the United States when Andrew took her home to Florida to meet his family. His mother had eyed her suspiciously throughout the meal, watching her every reaction as she tried the new and foreign foods. And his father had peppered her with questions about Moscow, most of them ridiculously misinformed.

"So do people really fill their babies' bottles with vodka in the Soviet Union?" he'd asked, at which Andrew laughed, and Nina rifled through her confusion and limited vocabulary to try to come up with a reasonable answer.

"What about the mafia? Do they run the shots there? Wait...you're not a spy, are you sweetheart?"

He asked his questions and they all laughed, but a current of belief ran through each of his veiled jokes. They'd left that evening and had their first real argument when Nina demanded to know why Andrew didn't defend her, and he blustered on about her needing to learn to take a joke.

"Well," Annie says, dragging Nina from the memory. "James says he'd love to try Russian food, and you haven't made borsch in forever. Maybe you should make some for Christmas day. And we can have vereniki, and kutia, and black bread, and...do you think babushka would make her pampushki?"

Nina softens. The sweet doughnuts were Annie's favorite, and they had been the only thing that had ever joined her daughter and her mother together.

"Well, if I can find all the ingredients I need in the next few days, then I don't see why we can't do that. It might be nice to sit down to a hot meal from home." Annie nods.

"I'll only do this if you agree to one thing," Nina says. Annie's smile fades, and she crosses her arms.

"Alright?" she says, her voice guarded.

"I want you to help me in the kitchen," Nina says raising her chin. Annie smiles.

"Okay," she says. "I think that'll be fun."

"Good. Alright then. Let's make a list." Annie and Nina sit down at the table to plan, and as Nina pulls her chair up close to her daughter, she glances back at her mother's door, and her stomach flips as she thinks of the woman behind the closed door whom she knows nothing about.

---

The few days before Christmas pass in a whirl of activity as Nina and Annie frantically gather all the ingredients needed to pull together an authentic Russian meal. Nina keeps herself busy, refusing to stop long enough to let the lingering doubts and sadness that are always just below the surface wash over her. She hardly looks at her mother in the days leading up to their Christmas meal, and Elizaveta takes in the sight of her bustling daughter with sinking emotions. The tension leaves her exhausted.

"Mama?"

Christmas morning came and went with very little interaction between Nina and her mother. Nina pushes open Elizaveta's door to find her sitting in her chair in the corner of the room. Her face is pinched, eyes weary. "Are you okay?"

"Yes, fine," Elizaveta replies. "Just tired."

"Of course," Nina murmurs. She takes a step forward and clasps her hands in front of her. "Well," she begins. "Annie and I are just about ready for our Christmas meal. We even made *pampushki*. I wish you could have helped us, though." Nina clears her throat. She asked her mother to help them earlier, but Elizaveta had scoffed.

"You do not need me cluttering up the room," she'd said with a wave of her hand.

Nina takes one more step forward. "Mama, I wanted to let you know that Dr. Shevchenko is coming for our Christmas lunch today. He and I have been talking to one another...quite frequently, actually. And we've seen each other for several dinners."

Elizaveta stares hard at her daughter, her eyes narrowed as though she is fighting to concentrate on her words.

"I have...enjoyed my time with him," Nina says, clumsily tripping over her words as her cheeks flush. She clears her throat nervously.

Elizaveta nods her head once. "That is good," she says. Her voice sounds fatigued. "I told you he is a good, strong man. You must not to let him go."

Nina bites her lip and shakes her head. She claps her hands lightly together. "So," she says, ready to change the subject quickly. "Can I help you get dressed for our company?"

"Oh, I'm not going to join you for lunch," Elizaveta replies. She leans her head back and closes her eyes. "I am too tired."

"Oh, no, Mama!" Nina cries. "We want you there. Annie and I really do. We made all your favorite foods!"

Elizaveta shakes her head, not opening her eyes. "I don't want to, Ninochka," she says. Her voice is stubborn, like a toddler's, grumpy and gruff.

Nina sighs. She opens her mouth to speak again. There are so many questions she longs to ask, but there's never a right or easy way to ask them. Before she can speak, the doorbell rings, stealing the words from her lips.

"Well, Mama," she says quietly, "I hope you change your mind. It would be a shame not to have you with us."

Slowly, she pulls the door closed, taking a deep breath to clear her head before walking across the room and pulling open the front door. Her mouth spreads into a smile of relief when she sees Viktor.

"Merry Christmas," he says.

Nina smiles at Viktor as he steps inside. He leans down and kisses her on the cheek, then holds out the vase of flowers.

"You look lovely," he whispers in her ear. Nina shivers.

"You look very nice yourself," she says, stepping back and

taking in the sight of him. He is dressed in dark slacks, a crisp, blue shirt tucked neatly into his pants, revealing his strong shoulders and narrow waist. He follows Nina into the kitchen and nods as she holds up a glass of wine in his direction.

"Red or white?" she asks.

"Red, please," he answers. "It smells amazing in here," he says.

Nina smiles. "Thank you. Annie and I have been working on this meal all day. I finally sent her upstairs to put her feet up for a bit before the company arrives."

Viktor sits down on one of the stools at the counter and smiles at Nina. "So it sounds like things are improving between the two of you," he says.

Nina nods. "It has been a good week," she says.

Nina glances at her mother's door then turns back to Viktor. "Mama has been in a bit of a mood today. Things between her and Annie have only gotten worse. Mama has known about Annie's...condition...for over a month, but they still haven't spoken to one another about it. Mama wasn't too happy about having people over, either. She says she's not joining us for lunch." Nina opens her mouth to continue, to tell Viktor about what she found in her mother's closet, but finds she cannot formulate the discovery into words yet. She closes her mouth again and swallows hard.

Viktor glances over at Elizaveta's door. "Mind if I go talk to her?" he asks. Nina shrugs.

"You can try," she says. She walks him to the door and knocks softly.

"Mama?" she calls. "Dr. Shevchenko, uh...Viktor is here." Nina blushes again. "He'd like to come say hello. Is that okay?"

It's silent for a moment before the gruff reply floats through the door. "*Khorosho*. Fine."

"Good luck," Nina whispers as she pushes open the door. Viktor steps into the dim room and takes in the sight of Elizaveta sitting in her recliner. She looks frail, her lower half covered with a thick blanket. He walks to the bed and sits on the edge next to her chair.

"Hello Elizaveta Andreyevna," he says. "How are you doing today?"

"Humph." Elizaveta pulls her blanket up and nestles under it a little tighter. Viktor continues talking as if he hadn't heard her.

"It smells amazing out there, don't you think?" he asks. "It reminds me of my mother, of the way she could make our kitchen smell just like home through a few simple ingredients. I think my mother missed Russia most when she cooked borsch. There was something about the smell that made her long for the comfort of home."

Elizaveta locks eyes with Viktor and nods. "Yes, your Mama was right to feel that way," she replies. "The more the years go by, the more I long for home. I live here with the only family I have, but my heart longs for the family of my country. I am a torn woman. I miss the sounds and the smells and..." Her voice trails off as her eyes glaze over. Viktor waits for her to continue.

"Of course, everything is different now," she finally says, breaking her trance and looking up at him. Her eyes are sad, dark and brooding and far away. "The home of my childhood was not the home of my adulthood. And my home now would not be the same either. Everything changes." The tremor in her voice draws Viktor down, leaning in so he can better observe her eyes.

He reaches over and grabs Elizaveta's hand. "I would sure like it if you could join us for lunch today, Elizaveta Andreyevna," he says gently. "These familiar smells make me remember my Mama the way that you remember home. Maybe you and I could be a comfort to one another."

Elizaveta looks up at him and sighs. She is still for a long moment before replying. "Okay," she mumbles. "But only because you are handsome and you have nice eyes. Not because I want to."

Viktor smiles. "I suppose that's fair," he says.

"Tell my daughter I need her help getting dressed," Elizaveta demands. Viktor nods and pushes to a stand.

"*Spasibo bolshoya*," he says with a slight bow.

"You're welcome," Elizaveta replies.

Viktor walks out of the room and sidles up to Nina, grabbing her around the waist and resting his chin on her shoulder as she stirs the borsch in the large, metal pot.

"So, did she bite your head off?" Nina asks. "Because she's been barking at me for two days."

"Actually," Viktor replies, "she wants you to go help her get dressed so that she can join us for dinner."

Nina spins around and gapes at Viktor, who grins valiantly. "You are a miracle worker," she says. "But why does she need me to help her get dressed? She dresses herself every day."

Viktor shrugs. "I don't know, but her mood is tenuous," he replies. "If I were you I would go quickly."

Nina playfully smacks his arm, then walks around him to enter her mother's room.

"You decided to join us?" she asks as Elizaveta walks unsteadily to her closet. Elizaveta turns and nods stiffly at her daughter.

"Yes, I am going to join you because I think that Russian man in there is very handsome, and I want to make sure you don't ruin things with him."

Nina purses her lips together. "Okay, then. Well, Viktor says you need my help dressing. Is this true?" Elizaveta shakes her head.

"No, I can dress myself," she says. Nina shakes her head in confusion and turns to go.

"*Ninochka?*" Elizaveta asks. "I need to talk to you later about something...important."

The way she speaks makes the hair on Nina's arms stand up. She nods slowly. "Okay," she answers. "Of course, Mama. We can talk tonight."

Nina walks shakily out of the room and pulls the door closed behind her.

＊・＊・・＊・＊・＊・・・・・・＊・＊

They all pull their chairs to the table and look at one another awkwardly. The round, wooden table is small for a group this large. Nina sits looking at each of them, a plastic smile pasted on her face, entirely unaccustomed to entertaining this many people.

"Well," she says, her voice cutting through the awkward silence. "Thank you all for joining us today. It's been a while since we had guests." She pauses. "So, I guess all I can say now is Merry Christmas."

Everyone smiles. Nina gestures toward the table full of food. "Please," she says. "Eat. Pass me your bowls, and I will serve the borsch."

They pass their bowls to Nina, and she stands, walking into the kitchen. Viktor turns to James and his dad.

"So, Don and James, have either of you had a traditional borsch before?"

Don clears his throat and nods. "Actually, I have," he says. "My wife and I took a cruise once, and there was a kitchen of international cuisine. The borsch was my wife's favorite meal in that restaurant. Do you remember when she tried to make it at home?" he turns to ask James. The two lock eyes and fall into an uncomfortable silence.

"Anyway," Don says, shifting nervously in his seat, "I've had it before. James hasn't had a real borsch, though."

James shakes his head. "Nope," he says. "I'm looking forward to it."

Nina smiles and puts a steaming bowl down in front of him. "Well, I'm glad," she says with a warm smile. She places a bowl in front of Don, as well. "I hope it is comforting for both of you."

James looks down at the shallow bowl and takes in a deep breath. The bright red broth gives off an aroma that makes his stomach rumble, though the visual is more than he had expected.

"It's...colorful," he whispers to Annie out of the corner of his mouth. She smiles.

"Yep," she says. "And it's delicious. Here," she reaches across him, her hand brushing his as she grabs a bowl of sour cream. Taking a heaping spoonful, she drops a dollop of the sour cream in his bowl. Immediately, it begins to spread out, tiny little pieces of white breaking off like icebergs in an ocean of red and turning the broth a vibrant pink.

"That's the Russian way to eat borsch," she says. She puts sour cream in her own bowl and stirs it around slowly, the meat and cabbage bumping against her spoon. Drawing a large spoonful up to her mouth, she blows on it gently then takes a bite. She closes her eyes, the hint of a smile whispering across her face. "It's so good," she says.

James takes a deep breath, unsure about this new experience. He stirs in the sour cream, then lifts the spoon to his mouth and sips the liquid off the end. His eyes widen in surprise.

"Oh! It's good!" he cries. He takes another bite and closes his eyes as he swallows. "It's really, really good!" He looks around the table. "Like this is so good I want to rub it all over my face!"

Annie and Viktor laugh while Nina blinks in confusion.

"I...I don't understand," she stammers. "You will rub it on your face?" Annie laughs harder. James' dad shakes his head in disbelief.

"You would think I had never taken him out in public before," Don says to the group.

James takes another bite. "I'm sorry," he says, his cheeks

flushed. "I get excited about food. This stuff is really awesome. What's it made of?"

"Thank you, James," Nina says, nodding at the boy who had once made her so suspicious. "The main ingredient is beet. That is how you get the beautiful red color and the rich taste. It can be prepared different ways, but we like it with the meat, potatoes, fresh cabbage, carrots, tomato sauce, and a little onion. That's how my mama made it." Nina offers Elizaveta a small smile. Elizaveta blinks back at her daughter. She sits quiet in her chair, her borsch untouched.

Nina clears her throat in the uncomfortable silence and grabs her wine glass. "To new beginnings and new friends," she says, raising her glass high. "And *Na zdorovya*," she says, gesturing toward the food.

"What is *Na zdorovya*?" James whispers after they've all taken a sip of their drinks and put their glasses back on the table.

"It means 'to your health'," Annie translates. "It's the server's way of telling you to enjoy your food."

For several minutes, they're all silent, sipping the hot broth off of their spoons and relishing the bold mix of flavors.

"This is excellent, Nina," Don says, and Viktor nods beside him.

"Truly, it is," Viktor says. "It reminds me of my mother's borsch, and she was generally known to be the best cook on the planet."

Nina blushes. She looks at her mother who has finally taken a bite and laid her spoon back down next to her bowl.

"Mama?" she asks. "What do you think?"

Elizaveta looks over at Nina, blinking her eyes slowly. "It needs a little more salt," she answers. Nina's face drops, but she quickly brushes past the comment.

"Make sure you save room, everyone," she says. "I've also got vinegret, chicken, a chocolate torte, and pamposhki, which Annie helped me make today."

Annie smiles at her mom.

"What's vinegret?" James asks.

"It's a Slavic salad," Viktor answers. "It's made of beets, cabbage, peas, pickles, carrots, potatoes, and onions, and dressed with a little sunflower oil, and salt and pepper."

James swallows hard and tries to keep his face neutral. "Sounds great," he lies.

Viktor smiles and pats him on the back. "It's better than it sounds," he says.

James nods. "And pamposhki?" he asks.

"Oh, you will love it," Annie replies. "It's kind of like a do-nut, but it can be filled with potatoes or cheese. We filled ours with cheese. That's the way Babushka always made them." She offers her grandmother a shy glance. Elizaveta stares back, her eyes glassy. James watches the exchange between the two and clears his throat.

"Well, I cannot wait to keep eating," he says with a smile.

The meal passes slowly, with everyone relaxing and falling into natural conversation. Nina, Viktor, and Don all discuss matters surrounding healthcare, each of them playing a small part in that world.

Annie and James talk quietly among themselves about their latest book in English Lit.

"I love *The Crucible*," James tells her. "It's so fascinating be-cause it's based on actual history. Like, that kind of stuff hap-pened. Doesn't that sort of blow your mind?" Annie smiles and shakes her head.

"Of course you love it," she answers. "Is there a book you've read that you didn't like?"

James thinks for a moment. "*Pride and Prejudice*," he re-plies.

Annie laughs.

"I couldn't get into it," he continues. "I think, maybe, I have just a little too much testosterone to enjoy Jane Austen."

"Well, I guess I don't think that's a bad thing," she says with a snicker.

James grins, thoroughly enjoying Annie's relaxed smile and unguarded conversation.

An hour later, they all stand from the table and stretch.

"I'm stuffed," Don says. Nina chuckles.

"What are you laughing at?" he asks.

"When I first came to the US," she replies, "my husband would always say that after we ate. He would stand up, stretch, and say 'I'm stuffed', and I could never figure out what he meant. I spent the first year of our marriage trying to figure out what it was to be 'stuffed'. I kept imagining teddy bears with their stuffing, and it was such a funny picture for me that I would laugh every time he said it. The sentence still makes me smile."

Annie watches her mother closely as she tells her story. This was the first time she'd ever heard her mother talk freely about her first husband. It was different to see her speak so loosely.

"Well, James and I should head home," Don says. "There are big football games to watch today, right, son?"

"Oh," James replies, "right. The football games. Can't miss those." James turns to Annie and rolls his eyes. She giggles.

"Would you like us to help clean up before we go?" Don asks.

"Oh, no. But thank you," Nina replies. "This has been a lovely afternoon. I'm glad that you came to celebrate with us."

Don clears his throat. "Thank you for having us," he replies. "Today is a hard day. It was nice to take our minds off of things for a little while."

"You're welcome to stay longer if you'd like," Nina offers. Don shakes his head.

"No, thank you," he replies. He glances at James and gestures toward the door.

"See you later," James whispers. "Think of me as I suffer through the rest of this day."

Annie smiles and walks them to the door, waving goodbye as they duck into their car.

She turns and heads back to the kitchen, grabbing several of the plates off the table. A small pain in her abdomen causes her to gasp and fold over, dropping one of the bowls.

"Annie?"

Nina and Viktor rush over to her. Viktor takes her hand and helps her straighten back up.

"I'm fine," Annie says. "Really."

She blushes as the three adults all stare at her. Viktor walks her to the couch and has her sit down.

"Where does it hurt?" he asks, squatting down in front of her.

"Nowhere right now," she replies softly. She can feel her grandmother staring at her and she turns, locking eyes with the woman who makes her feel so alienated. But she doesn't find judgment in her eyes. Instead, she sees understanding. It's as though she sees her own reflection inside her babushka's concerned gaze.

"It was just one quick, sharp pain," she says, then she winces again.

"Can I put my hands on your stomach?" Viktor asks. Annie nods, blushing yet again. She wonders if she will ever get past the shame of this.

Viktor presses gently around the sides of her stomach. Another sharp pain jabs at her side and she winces again. Viktor smiles.

"It's okay," he says. "The baby is just kicking you, and he's got quite a kick."

"He?" Annie asks, her voice higher pitched.

"Or she," Viktor says. "Here, put your hand right here."

Annie puts her hand on her side and feels the thump against her ribs again. "I've felt some movement the last couple of weeks," she admits, avoiding eye contact with her mom. "But nothing like this." The baby kicks again, a sharp jab that takes her breath away. "That feels weird," she whispers.

Viktor nods. "I imagine it would," he says. "The baby has probably moved into a position that makes the kicks more noticeable." He looks over at Nina who stands beside the couch, her hand clutching at her heart.

"You should feel this," he says.

Annie finally looks up at her mom and nods slowly.

Nina takes a hesitant step forward and sits on the couch next to Annie. She places her hand on Annie's side, and a smile breaks wide her face as she feels the little kick again.

"That hurts!" Annie says. Nina smiles.

"It looks like this little one is a fan of borsch," she says.

"Annie, why don't you go upstairs and rest," Viktor says. "I'll help your mom clean up."

Annie looks at both of them. "Are you sure?" she asks.

Nina nods. "Yes, *dorogaya*," she murmurs. "Go ahead."

Annie stands up and smooths out her shirt, pulling it out away from her stomach self-consciously, still trying to conceal the ever widening bump that is growing more noticeable by the day. "Thank you," she says gratefully to Viktor. He nods in return.

Annie walks by her grandmother, who stands rooted in place next to the table. She watches her granddaughter walk to the stairs, and a piece of her heart trails behind the girl with whom she cannot really communicate. She wants to tell her everything. It's time. She needs them to know. The memories are pressing down with such force that she feels herself growing heavy. The weight of her silence is too much, and she needs to release the tension that's mounting inside.

She turns to Nina and opens her mouth to speak, but the words won't come out. She feels leaden, like she's being pressed down from all sides. She wants to reach out to them, but her arms fail to work. Only a passing moan crosses her lips as she sinks.

She doesn't hear Nina cry out, and by the time Viktor Shevchenko catches her, she can no longer even hold open her eyes.

# ELIZAVETA

*A silver willow by the shore*
*trails to the bright September waters.*
*My shadow, raised from the past,*
*Glides silently toward me.*
Anna Akhmatova

Sinking. That's the only way to describe what's happening. The water has enveloped me, and no matter how hard I kick, I can't break through the surface—I can't even find it. And just when I feel my lungs beginning to burn with the desperate need to breathe, I burst through the other side of the memory. I blink as I lay panting on the shoreline of the past. Pushing myself to a sitting position, I feel my hair matted to my head. When I brush it back, I catch sight of my arm and hold it out in front of me. It's smooth and tan, not yet weathered by age or spotted by the sun.

I squint, the light reflecting off the pond and nearly blinding me. I'm not really here; I know I can't be. But it feels real, and so for a moment, I relax. The breeze is blowing, carrying with it a scent so familiar that I feel the ache in my heart widening and tearing at my insides. It smells of fresh dill and cucumber. With that scent comes the sound of my mama's voice humming softly in the distance.

I turn my head and take in the sight of the house. It is small and wooden, the roof heavily slanted over rickety walls that don't look sturdy enough to withstand even the whisper of a breeze. I know this place. It's inside me, the memory of it. But right now it looks different. It's brighter than I remember and more welcoming. This was the house we stumbled into after a long walk. I remember the walk, but I don't remember why we were taking it.

I sit on the bank of the small pond for a long time trying to make sense of how I got here. I know this isn't where I belong. I know that this is a life I left, but for how long was I gone? I can't recall.

The wind blows, and I feel a tickle on my arm. I turn my head to the left and peer up through shielded eyes at the willow tree hanging over my shoulder. Its branches sway, the silver green leaves dancing in the late afternoon sunshine. It bends over the water, like a weary traveler who's desperate for a drink. I see the reflection in the ripples of the pond and lean forward to catch a closer glimpse. And that's when I see her.

She's young, with long, brown hair hanging in loose waves around her small face. Her eyes are wide and dark, her face somewhat distorted by the moving water, but still familiar to me. I know her. She is me...or she was me. She's the me who survived something terrible.

*What was it?*

She's the me who turned her face away while bad things happened.

*What were they?*

She's the me who lost so much, who said an unwilling goodbye to someone she loved, all wild-eyed and desperate—the girl who screamed a name into the empty space that was left behind, the void that would never again be filled.

*Whose name did she yell?*

She's the me who was both innocent and wise to the ways of the world, a rare blend of knowing too much and still not enough.

*Why?*

The girl whose reflection I saw in the pond had a different name, the name she answered to until the day she left home and decided to make a new life for herself. I'd almost forgotten that girl.

*Why did she do that again?*

"Victoria!"

The voice pierces my thoughts and I stumble to my feet, untangling them from the long, dirty brown dress that mama passed down to me once I grew big enough to fit in it.

*That was my name.*

# NINA

*A secret revealed
brings healing to the soul
when offered in confession.*

Nina paces back and forth in the hospital waiting room, clasping and unclasping her hands. She blinks hard, trying to push the memory of her mother's collapse out of her mind, but every time she turns, she faces that terrible moment again. It wasn't the fall that haunted her, though. It was the look on her mother's face just before she fell.

"Here, Mom. Take this."

Nina takes a small, Styrofoam cup of weak looking coffee from Annie's outstretched hand. "Thank you," she says. She follows Annie to the chairs by the window, then takes a sip of the coffee and flinches.

"Is it bad?" Annie asks. "I can get some more."

"No, no," Nina replies. "It's fine. It's just hot."

The two sit in silence for a long time. Finally, Nina turns to her daughter.

"Do you feel okay now?" she asks.

Annie nods. "Yes," she answers. "Fine." She runs her hand self-consciously over her abdomen. Nina watches the motion, then looks at Annie's young, innocent face. She shakes her head and sighs.

"I'm sorry, Annie," Nina whispers. Her eyes fill with tears. Annie turns to her mom.

"Why?" she asks.

"I failed you," Nina says. "I kept things from you, *important* things. I didn't think it mattered if you knew much about your father, and I didn't want you to be uncomfortable with my lack of information, so I just didn't talk. What a stupid, silly thing to do."

Nina's voice shakes unsteadily as she draws in another sip of the coffee, wincing as it scalds her tongue and throat.

"Mom, I—"

"No, I need to say this," Nina interrupts. She runs her hand through her hair. Her other hand trembles as she grips her coffee cup.

"I spent my entire life trying to figure out who my mother was," Nina begins. "To this day, I know nothing about my mama's past. I do not know the names of my grandparents, or where they came from. I don't know anything about my father. I don't even have a father as far as I know!" Nina sets her cup down on the table in front of them and shakes her head. She looks over at Annie who is silently taking in the sight of her usually calm and collected mother.

"I moved to America when I was twenty-five years old," Nina says. "Did I ever tell you that?"

Annie nods. "Yeah," she answers softly. "I remember you telling me once that you fell in love with an American man and moved to the U.S. after you finished the university. You told me that the marriage didn't last, but that the United States had worked out just fine."

Nina offers a weak smile and nods. "Yes, the U.S. did work out for me just fine. I met your father shortly after Andrew and I divorced. I didn't plan on marrying again so soon, but your dad was very persuasive."

"He was?" Annie asks. Her eyes light up at this new information. "How?"

"Well," Nina replies, "it is very silly when I say it out loud, but at the time it seemed romantic. He told me that he wanted to marry me, and he wouldn't take no for an answer."

"And did you want to marry him?" Annie asks.

Nina nods. "I did. He was so handsome and gentle. He was older than me. I was thirty-four and he was forty-eight, but he had never been married before. He said he'd been waiting for just the right woman to come along, and he found me. His very own 'Russian princess,' he would say." Nina blushes at the memory. Annie smiles.

"Anyway, I was embarrassed to be jumping into another marriage so soon, but sometimes the heart can't help but move in the direction that it's being tugged, so I agreed. We had a small ceremony at the courthouse, and a few months later..." Nina turns to Annie, her eyes bright. "A few months later, I found out I was pregnant."

Annie grabs her mom's hand.

"I was so excited to tell Richard," Nina says. She picks up her coffee cup and takes a sip. "He wanted children so badly. But the same day I got the news that I was expecting, he received the diagnosis of terminal cancer."

Annie's eyes well up at the thought of her mother, pregnant and alone as she watched her husband slowly die.

"I should have told you all these things a long time ago," Nina whispers. She pulls her hand from Annie's and wipes her eyes, swiping away the forbidden tears.

"Mom, sshh..." Annie leans into her mom, putting her arm around her shoulder protectively. "It's okay."

"It's not okay," Nina sniffs. "It's not okay because the truth is so much worse. I didn't come to America because I loved Andrew. I came to America because I wanted to get away from my mother. And I was determined that I would never parent the way that she parented me, but look what I have done." Nina gestures at Annie. "I've left you alone just like my mother did to me. And I drove you away the way that she drove me away."

"No, Mom. That's not what happened," Annie interjects.

Nina leans forward, dropping her head into her hands. Annie sighs and puts her hand on her mom's back.

"It is true that I wished I knew more about my father, and more about you. I wanted more information, but you didn't seem to want to share so I tried not to ask."

"I'm sorry," Nina whispers.

Annie shakes her head. "Mom, that wasn't what drove me away," she says. Nina looks up and meets Annie's eye.

"What was it then?" Nina asks.

Annie draws in a long breath and lets it out slowly. "Mom, you changed when Babushka came. Before she moved in with us, it was you and me. We rented cabins in the summers, and we explored the mountains. We talked and laughed and joked. We were like this really great duet, but then Babushka moved in and you shut down." Annie looks down at her hands.

"Mom, I'm not the one who left," she says softly. "You are. You just changed into a different person when Babushka came. Everything changed when she arrived."

Nina leans back in her chair and lets her mind drift over the years since her mother moved in, and it suddenly all makes sense. There had been no more summer trips, no more evenings giggling over old movies, no more spontaneous trips to the ice cream parlor on school nights. Annie was right; she had shut down when her mother moved to town. Nina sighs and turns to her daughter. She drinks in the sight of the young woman sitting next to her, the way her long blonde hair hangs in perfect, soft waves to the middle of her back. Annie's bright blue eyes meet hers, and she offers a small smile.

"I guess this whole mother-daughter thing never really gets easier, huh?" Annie asks.

"No, it really doesn't," Nina replies.

"I don't want Babushka to die," Annie says. Her voice trembles. "I feel like you and I are both missing something because we don't know anything about her. It's like we..." Annie pauses.

"It's like we can't know who we are until we find out who she is first," Nina says softly. Annie nods.

"Yeah," she whispers.

They're both contemplating the emptiness of an unknown past when Viktor walks through the door. Nina jumps out of her seat and rushes to him. He stops and looks gravely at them.

"What is it?" Nina asks, the words catching in her throat.

"Your mother had a stroke," he answers. Nina closes her eyes briefly, then opens them back up.

"How bad?"

"It was a hemorrhagic stroke," he replies gently. "There was a large area affected." Viktor reaches out and grabs Nina's hands. "She is in critical condition," he says gently. "The next forty-eight hours will be crucial."

Nina nods. "Okay," she says. She looks at Annie whose face has turned ashen. She puts an arm around Annie's shoulders.

"Can we see her?" Nina asks.

Viktor nods. "Yes, you can come back and see her. Just be prepared. She's hooked up to several machines. She doesn't look good, but she's stable for the moment."

The girls follow Viktor out into the hallway. Nina shivers. It's cold in the hospital. She crosses her arms over her chest and blinks at the sights and sounds around her. It's quiet. Christmas carols play softly from the speakers, and voices speak in hushed tones as nurses and doctors walk from one room to the next. Green garland hangs in waves down each side of the hall, with Christmas wreaths displayed on every door.

Annie's eyes scan their surroundings, and her mind drifts to James. She thinks of what it must have been like for him the year before, when he and his dad walked through similar hallways to find his mother and sister. Did he feel as numb as she does? Did the merriment of the Christmas decorations and songs feel like a slap in the face in this place that feels so full of sadness? Annie suddenly longs to see James, to call him and hear his voice. She's worried about him, alone at home with memories like that.

Viktor stops at room 322. He turns to Nina. She nods, and he pushes open the door.

The room is dim, the sound of a machine's whir and hiss drowning Kenny G's rendition of "Silent Night." Nina draws in a sharp breath at the sight of her mother lying in the hospital bed. She looks small, a blanket pulled up over her and tucked neatly into the mattress. A tube is in her mouth, taped to the side of her cheek and pulling her lip down. Her eyes are closed, her face relaxed. Despite the surroundings, her mother looks peaceful.

Annie grabs Nina's hand and squeezes it tight. Together they walk toward the bed. Nina leans over her mother and gently brushes a string of grey hair off her forehead.

"*Privyet, Mama*," Nina says softly. "I'm here," she says, the Russian words falling off her tongue like a lullaby.

Annie leans forward. "Babushka," she whispers. She forces the language that she's avoided for so many years to the front of her mind and tries to wrap her mouth around the unfamiliar syllables.

"I'm here, too," she says. "It's me," Annie looks up at her mom. "Nastia," she finishes.

"*Vsio budet khorosho*, Mama," Nina whispers. "You're going to be okay." She reaches over and grabs her mother's hand. "Viktor is here, and he is making sure they take good care of you. He's keeping the doctors from poking and prodding you too much, okay?" Nina chokes on her last words.

For several minutes they stand silently over the bed, watching Elizaveta's chest rise and fall in conjunction with the breathing machine. Finally, Viktor gestures toward the door.

Out in the hallway, he puts his arms around Nina and draws her into a tight embrace. Annie stands off to the side, blushing at this tender moment between her mom and a man she hardly knows. Viktor catches her eye and pulls back, clearing his throat.

"You two should head home," he says. "I'll keep an eye on her and call you if anything changes. You need to get some sleep."

"Oh, I don't know," Nina protests. "I should probably stay in case she wakes up. She will be disoriented, and you know how she gets when she feels out of control—"

Viktor holds up his hand and shakes his head. "She won't be waking up tonight, Nina," he says. "Take Annie home and get some rest. You both need it."

Nina sighs and clasps her hands together. "You promise you'll call me if anything changes?"

Viktor smiles. "I promise," he says.

Nina turns to Annie and notices the fatigue that has settled in her daughter's face. She looks back at Viktor and nods.

"Thank you," she whispers. "Can I just have a minute alone with Mama before we leave?"

"Of course," Viktor replies. He pushes open the door and lets Nina walk back in. She waits until it clicks shut behind her before walking to her mother's bedside.

"Mama?" she asks. She leans over so that her mouth is close to her mother's ear. "I'm sorry I ran away from you," she whispers. "I'm sorry I don't know enough, that I couldn't break through your barrier. I'm sorry, Mama, that I've spent these last years just tolerating you instead of really getting to know you. If you can hang on, I promise that I'll try harder. I won't hold so much of myself back, Mama." Nina brushes tears from the corners of her eyes and chuckles softly, imagining her mother's admonition if she caught her crying.

"Strong Russian women do not need to cry, *Ninochka*," she would say. Then she would quote Neksarov, the 19th century Russian poet. "You know that 'a Russian woman can stop a galloping horse and enter the burning house.' That is how strong we are. We don't have need for tears."

Nina smiles and shakes her head. She reaches down and puts her hand on top of Elizaveta's.

"Maybe a few tears wouldn't have been so terrible," she whispers. "*Spokoyne Noche*, Mama."

# ELIZAVETA

*I remember.*

I walk into the house and am instantly overwhelmed with emotion. The familiarity of the small space fills my soul, wiping clean any memory of the place that I came from. I am home. I didn't realize how much I had missed it.

"Victoria, please. Come help me would you?"

I turn and take in the sight of her. She's leaning over the large pot in the fireplace, stirring the soup slowly with her long-handled wooden spoon. She stands up and turns to me, and I gasp because I had forgotten how beautiful she was. Her eyes smile before her mouth, crinkling softly in the corners as light dances in the center.

"What's the matter, *dorogaya*?" she asks. "You look like you've seen a ghost."

"I have," I whisper.

Mama cocks her head to the side and looks hard at me. In just a few swift steps, she crosses the room and stands before me, placing her hand on my forehead. I close my eyes and lean into her touch.

"You don't feel hot," she murmurs. "Are you feeling sick?"

I shake my head no. Mama draws in a sharp breath.

"Well," she says. "If you're well, then I need you to help Tanya prepare the salad." She gestures to the left. I turn, and that's when I see her. My sister sits at the table, her young face staring up at me, large brown eyes framed by soft brown hair. She must be thirteen years old, innocent and sweet, though there's a hardness that permanently resides in her eyes.

*What caused that?* I wonder.

"Hi," I whisper. Tanya looks at me quizzically.

"Hi?" she says, confusion rippling through the air between us.

Mama points to the table. "Vika, please. Cut the radishes for me, and the cucumbers."

She points to Tanya. "And Tanyoosha, you are responsible for chopping the dill and cutting up the tomatoes."

I sit next to Tanya at the table and pull the plate of radishes toward me. The springtime breeze blows through the window, bringing with it the thin fabric that Mama tacked up to keep the sunlight from pouring in. The small curtain dances in the breeze, beating a rhythm of shadows across the room.

Tanya grabs a bunch of the freshly plucked dill and begins chopping, her tongue sticking out of the corner of her mouth. I slowly begin slicing the radishes, trying to place this time that I've landed in. Mama hums again at the pot, stirring occasionally between slicing potatoes.

"You're acting strange," Tanya murmurs. She glances up and catches my eye. Why do I feel such an ache in my gut at the sight of her? What happened that leaves me feeling permanently veiled from seeing her in this moment?

"Sorry," I respond. "I'm just a little tired today." It's true, what I've told her. I'm exhausted. My eyelids feel weighted, and my hands are clumsy. The dull knife slips across the cucumber and nicks my finger. I drop it and draw my wounded hand to my mouth.

"You okay?" Mama asks, stepping up behind me. I suck on my finger and nod my head. My finger doesn't hurt. I feel nothing, and taste nothing, but when I pull it from my lips I see blood pouring from the wound.

"Oh dear," Mama sighs. She grabs the towel that's tucked into her apron and presses it against my finger. "Hold it tight," she says. "The bleeding will stop soon." She turns to walk back to the fireplace where she drops large chunks of potatoes into a second pot of boiling water.

"We will have your father look at it when he gets home this afternoon," Mama says. My head snaps up.

"What did you say?" I gasp.

Mama looks at me with raised eyebrows. "I said your father will look at it when he returns home," she replies.

My head begins to spin, and I shut my eyes tight to quell the confusion that rips through me. "When he returns home from where?" I whisper. Tanya snorts next to me.

"What is wrong with you?" she asks. "When he returns home from the fields. He and Dima always get home in the evening."

And that's when I hear the snap. As Mama and Tanya stare at me, the room grows increasingly warm. I take it all in, the wooden walls, the fabric flapping in the window, the birds chirping and the water boiling. Then I look down at the table where Tanya and I sit, and that's when the color in the room starts to fade.

There is food on the table. Why do we have food? This memory suddenly feels out of place, as though it's a story drawn from imagination rather than reality. Did we always have food? No, of course we didn't. We never had enough food for a salad, or a hearty borsch. I never sat and watched the window fabric dance happily in the open frame. And I never heard my mother refer to my father in the present. My father resided only in the past tense.

This isn't a memory—it's a dream. Or maybe it's a nightmare, for the loss of this type of experience in my youth feels so very empty. It feels as though a knife has sliced right through me. I look down at my hand, and blood is pouring from the wound now. The room is spinning, and it's gone from hot to bone-chillingly cold.

I remember now where I came from. I remember who I was. And I remember why I left.

# ANNIE

"Hey you!"

Annie pulls her head from her locker and turns to James, a wide grin splitting her face.

"What're you doing?"

Annie sighs and turns back to her locker. "I'm looking for my Biology book. It's somewhere in the abyss." She gestures to her locker, strewn with papers and binders and books. James laughs. He leans forward and rifles through the locker, a look of mock horror painted on his face.

"You know, I think there are whole TV shows dedicated to people who can't throw stuff away," he says. Annie punches him in the shoulder.

James pulls his arm out and thrusts a book in the air. "Haha!" he says, triumphant. Annie raises one eyebrow and gestures with her chin.

"That's Civics," she says. He brings his arm down and looks at the book.

"Oh," he says with a shrug. "Well... need your Civics book?"

Annie smiles and nods. "I do, actually," she says, plucking it from his outstretched hand. "Thank you."

James shrugs and looks down at the floor. "What's this?" he asks, leaning forward to pick up a sheet of paper that fell. He turns it over and takes in the picture.

"Oh, that's nothing!" Annie cries. She reaches out to grab the picture, but James pulls it away.

"Did you draw this?" he asks.

Annie shifts from one foot to the next. Her cheeks are warm as she watches James study her drawing.

"How did you..." James stops and clears his throat.

"I saw a picture on your photo stream," Annie confesses. "Are you mad? I really didn't mean to draw them. It just sort of came out one day when I was in class."

James shakes his head. "I'm not mad," he says, his voice hoarse as he studies the picture of his mother and sister. Pencil drawn, the lines are smudged and faded, but the image is still so clear. She captured his mother well, the way her smile turned up a little higher on the right side than the left, and how her bangs hung across her forehead as though she'd left the house without brushing her hair that morning.

But it was the drawing of his little sister that really took his breath away. James blinks back tears as he takes in the way her eyes seem to dance. Annie had somehow managed to capture the mischievous way Lily had always grinned at the camera—like she knew a secret that no one else knew, and she couldn't wait to share it with you.

"Can I keep this?" James asks. He looks at Annie and she nods.

"Yes, of course," she says. "It's not my best drawing," she confesses.

James steps forward and kisses her, his mouth lightly brushing across hers. Annie pulls back, surprised.

"Sorry," James says, his cheeks deepening to a crimson. "It's just..." he looks back down at the drawing. "Annie, this is amazing." He looks up at her, his brown eyes swimming. Annie swallows a lump in her throat.

"I'm glad you like it," she whispers. They stare at one another for a long moment before laughter interrupts them.

"Aw, look how cute! The little Mama is so happy with her Baby Daddy."

Annie whips her head to the right to see the group of girls standing at their lockers across the hall. The tall one, Sarah, raises one eyebrow.

"So when are you due?" she asks.

Annie puts her hand self-consciously over her stomach. James grabs her arm and gives her a tug. "C'mon," he mutters. He slams her locker shut and pulls her with him.

The girls laugh as Annie stumbles behind James, blinking hard as she follows him down the hall. Dizzy, she grabs his arm to steady herself. They turn the corner and Annie stops, her feet frozen in place.

"People know," she says. Her voice is calm, monotone. There is no inflection, no emotion, but she feels the hollowness of her words. James drops her arm.

"Looks like it," he says.

Annie looks down at her stomach. It's February now, so the cold weather gives her more opportunity to dress in layers. But even beneath her bulky sweatshirt, the protrusion of her stomach is obvious.

"I knew people would find out eventually," she mutters. "I knew they'd start talking." She looks up at him, her eyes shining.

"They think you're the father," she whispers, a look of horror crossing her face. She puts her hands on her cheeks, hoping to cool them down, to stop the hallway from spinning so fast. "James, I'm sorry. I'm so sorry."

James shrugs. "Who cares?" he asks. "I don't even know those girls' names. I couldn't care less what they think of me."

"The girl talking was Sarah," Annie replies. "I've know her since we were kids. She came to my twelfth birthday party." Annie closes her eyes and shakes her head.

James sighs. "You don't have to apologize, Annie," he says. "And you really don't have to defend me. They can think whatever they want. We only have to see them for three more months, then we're out of here."

Annie swallows hard and looks down. "I'm due in two months," she says. "I'll have the baby before school is over."

James watches her, but doesn't respond.

"I have it narrowed down to two potential families to raise the baby," she says. "Did I tell you that yet?"

James shakes his head no.

"They both seem nice," Annie continues. "I don't really know how to choose. This is all so confusing and hard, and with my grandmother still in the hospital, my mom isn't really available to help me decide. I don't have anyone to talk to," she says.

James clears his throat. "What about Toby?" he asks, shifting from foot to foot uncomfortably. Annie winces.

"I called Toby last week to talk to him about it. He said he doesn't care. I haven't seen him since before Christmas."

The bell rings, and Annie jumps, the sound echoing like a clanging symbol beating against the insides of her brain.

"Well," James says. He looks down at the drawing in his hand, then looks back up at Annie. "If you need help deciding, or you just need to talk, I'm here, okay?"

Annie nods. "Okay," she whispers. She leans over and gives him a soft kiss on the cheek. "Thank you," she murmurs.

Annie turns and rushes down the hallway to her next class. James watches her go, his heart racing as he tries to process the overwhelming emotion that's bubbling in his chest. It feels like love, but he's not sure he really knows what that is. All he knows in that moment is that he would do anything to protect her.

# ELIZAVETA

*O, cold melody of my heart!*
*Why do you torture me?*

I'm trapped. For the second time in my life I am imprisoned, only this time it's not a physical confinement. I can feel my extremities on the outside world, but somewhere inside I am unable to break loose. People talk around me in words and syllables that don't make sense, a gibberish that leaves me exhausted. Shapes float in front of me on occasion, some of them almost recognizable, but then they fade, and I slip back into the past. It chased me for so long, and now it has caught me, clutching me tight into the vice-like grip of memories that are too terrible to bear.

Each time I slip back into it, I find myself back on the bank of the pond. Only it's not springtime anymore. It's winter, and I'm freezing. The willow tree isn't silver-green. It's barren, the branches pricking mercilessly at my arms and neck. It's mocking me, that tree. Reminding me that the shadow of my past cannot be avoided.

"Victoria!"

The voice pierces my thoughts, weary and drawn. I look to the left, following the sound of the voice, and I see it again. It's my home, the small, wooden roof heavily slanted over rickety walls that never really kept us warm in the winters. But after the long years in Siberia, none of us complained, because this house was the home we longed for when we lived in captivity. Mama said it was our answer to prayer, but I didn't understand what that meant; it was an answer to her prayers, perhaps, for I had never prayed.

I struggle to my feet, my joints screaming against the aching, bitter cold. I feel something turn inside me and look down, horrified. This is a new memory, one that I haven't yet been forced to relive. My stomach protrudes just enough that it unlocks this moment. I remember the feeling of life moving around inside of me. I look back at the house, and I know. This is the day that it all happened. This is the day that I've spent a lifetime trying to erase.

I look back at the water in the pond. It's frozen, but I can tell where the ice is thin. It would be so easy to walk out there, to step to the places that would crack and open up, swallowing me whole. But somehow I know it wouldn't matter. I'd still end up back here. I'd still be forced to relive this moment.

"*Vika!*"

Turning back, I slowly begin to make my way toward the house, a sense of dread building in my chest. I step inside and take sight of Mama standing over the fire, stirring a broth in the small pot. The broth is mostly water. There is one small potato tossed in, and half of an onion. The rest is simply melted snow, heated up and stirred into a loose soup that won't satisfy any of us.

There is no bread because the grain supplies are gone. Everything our village harvested in the last two years was given to a government who did not know how to use it. And the over-taxed ground yielded so much less than it had before. The war had devastated our land, leaving it dusty and dry, and with so many men gone, sacrificed to the Nazis and the gulags, those of us left behind were less confident on how to coax produce from the earth. So we found ourselves, once again, at the mercy of a ruthless government, taxed to the point of death, and starving because there was nothing left when it was all said and done.

Mama turns to face me, and I take in a sharp breath. Her face is drawn, her cheekbones clearly defined under dark eyes. I remember this now, the way my strong Mama had faded in the years following the gulag and Dima's departure. I remember the way that the light had faded in her eyes, and how her spoken prayers had changed from whispered psalms of praise to desperate pleas for deliverance. This is the Mama I find in today's memory. I look at her skeletal face, and my heart slows. Her features had hardened, yet still there was a gentleness in her eyes that hunger and heartache never did steal away.

"Darling, I need you to help me feed Tanya," Mama says. She turns to look at my sister who lies still in the bed. Tanya is young, and she's sick again. She was sick a lot that winter. I remember now how many times we were certain she would die, and each time Mama managed to nurse her back to life. Mama said it was because she prayed, and God saw fit to answer her.

I think it's simply a matter of luck, though I cannot decide if it's good luck or bad luck that would keep Tanya in this ice-cold hell.

I walk to my sister and sit down on the bed beside her. She looks up at me, blinking heavily in the dim light. There's a hardness permanently etched inside her eyes. It settled there the day we left Siberia, when we ripped her from Svetlana's arms and forced her to mold into the broken family that she didn't understand. She looks at me as though she's hoping for me to somehow free her, but I can't hold her gaze long enough to offer any kind of reassurance.

I stand up and turn to Mama, reaching for the bowl of broth in her hands. She looks back at me in horror. Her eyes drift to my stomach and then back to my face, and I know she's figured out my secret.

"You're pregnant," she whispers.

I don't answer because what can I say? I take the bowl

from her trembling hands and turn to sit next to Tanya. Blowing first on the steaming broth, I slowly tilt the spoon toward her upturned lips and let it drip into her mouth. She winces as it burns her tongue, then swallows. For several minutes, I feed her in silence. Finally, she relaxes against the blanket folded beneath her head and drifts to sleep. She ate only half the broth.

I stand up and take the bowl to the fire, trying to warm away the cold. It's just the three of us here. Just me, Mama, and Tanya. I remember it all now, everything I've been running from for so long. It's all right here, staring me in the face. I turn to look at my Mama who now sits quietly in a chair in the corner. I feel the hardening in my heart, the ice that settled in my veins and allowed me to make the unimaginable choice.

"You should eat the rest of the soup," she says softly.

I nod. Looking into the fire, I stand before it letting the heat nip at my cheeks. I fill the bowl up with more soup and take a sip. It's hot, scalding my tongue and throat. I swallow and still feel empty. I know that the feeling won't go away, even after I finish the bowl. The emptiness has never really left.

"Who is it?" Mama asks.

I turn to face her, the firelight flickering across her skin in a sorrowful dance. The kerchief on her head keeps her hair back so that the light perfectly frames her features.

"Kolya," I reply.

Kolya worked the land with me as a laborer on the soil that didn't belong to either of us. I didn't love him, and I knew he didn't love me, but he had decided to join the Red Army, to fight the Nazis and defend the Motherland, and he was scared. He had returned home after the war ended and confided in me the horrible things he had seen and experienced. It was one warm, autumn evening under the stars. He poured out his heart, and I wanted to comfort him, to somehow take away the pain that laced every word that came from his mouth. It was one night that meant nothing to either of us, and when it was over Kolya got up and left without even saying goodbye. For him, that was just another evening in a long string of evenings that would comprise his life. But for me, that evening would be the catalyst that changed everything.

"How far?" Mama asks.

I shrug. "I don't know," I reply.

Mama leans forward and puts her head in her hands. "*Dorogaya*," she whispers. "What will we do with a baby?"

My jaw tightens in defense. It's the question I've asked myself repeatedly in the months since I figured out my situation. I lift my shoulders up, then let them drop because I can't answer her question.

"How could you let this happen?" Mama asks. She looks up at me, and for the first time in my life I see anger flash across her face. My gentle Mama, always soft spoken and kind, looks at me through narrowed eyes. There's a fire that dances in the center, and I can't figure out if it's a reflection of the fire behind me, or if it's coming from inside her. Either way, I shrink back.

"You foolish, foolish girl," she seethes. "I can't find enough food to keep you and your sister sustained, and now there will be a baby?" Mama pushes up off the chair and shakes her head.

I raise my chin in defiance. "You don't have to worry about it, Mama," I say. "This is my responsibility. I will take care of it."

Mama laughs. It's a strange sound, to hear my Mama unleash such mirth. After so much happened, losing my father, surviving the gulag, losing Dima, and working herself to the bone every day, this would be the thing that broke her. Me.

I was the heartache that she wouldn't overcome. *Toska*.

"And how will you do it, Vika?" she asks. "You are nineteen years old, unmarried, and a laborer. More than that, you are a *kulak*. That is a special brand of disgrace that you will pass to this child. This world isn't good to women in our position. So what will you do now? How will you provide? How will you keep this child alive?" In two swift steps, Mama reaches me, her face so close to mine that I smell the hunger on her breath.

"My darling, you have no idea what it feels like to lose a child. You do not understand the devastation of not being able to provide for the ones who came from your womb. It's a heartache that never leaves you. Why did you do this? Why?" She looks at me, her eyes swimming with tears. "This isn't anything I ever wanted for you," she whispers. Her words are daggers. They cut through me, slicing into my core, filling me with such a sense of failure and dread.

*I can't stay here. I need to get out.*

I draw in a sharp breath and step away from her, shaking my head from side to side.

"Don't, Mama," I whisper. "Don't try to put shame and guilt upon me." I feel it then. The anger that had been bubbling just beneath the surface since my years inside the schoolhouse of the holding camp in Siberia begins to boil. "I'm only in this position because of our traitorous Papa." The words come out hot. Tanya stirs on the bed behind me, and Mama draws back as though I had struck her.

"What did you say?" she whispers.

"I spoke the truth. If my father had not been a *kulak*, none of us would be here. Dima would still be alive. And we never would have gone to that horrible place." My chin trembles violently, but I refuse to let the emotion break me. These are the words I wanted to say for years—the words I needed to say.

"You don't understand what you're saying, *dochka*," Mama whispers. "All these years, they have been difficult and painful, but God—"

"Do not speak to me of your God!" I hiss. "Don't mention His name in my presence. Your God has made you a traitor, too." My hands tremble as I back away from my mother. I reach the bed where Tanya lies, and I turn to look at my sister who stares back up at me, eyes too big for her thin, pale face. She looks horrified.

"Vika," Mama begins. She sounds tired now, defeated.

"No, Mama," I say. I kneel down and reach beneath the bed,

pulling out a small satchel. I open the small box next to the fireplace and quickly stuff a pair of socks, a shawl, and a thin pair of mittens into the bag. I tug it onto my shoulder and stand back up. "I'm leaving," I say, my voice soft and quiet. "I can't stay here any longer."

Mama's eyes fill with tears. "Vika," she says again, her voice no more than a tremor. She reaches out for me but I draw back, away from her grasp. "Please. My darling, do not leave. We'll figure this out together."

I shake my head, gritting my teeth as I take a step toward the door.

"Vika!" Mama cries. "Wait."

I stop and stare at her.

"Where will you go?"

I shrug my shoulders. "I don't know," I reply. "Maybe Moscow. Maybe Leningrad or Kiev."

Mama draws herself up and wipes her eyes with a shaking hand. She walks slowly to the bed and reaches beneath it, far into the back corner of the mattress. I watch in shock as she stands back up and turns toward me, holding in her shaking hand the small book of scriptures that Commander Nikolayev had given me so many years ago. She knew I had it all along.

"You should take this with you," she whispers. "You've hidden it for so long. Why stop now?"

My arms hang limp at my side as I stare at my broken mama. She reaches down and grabs my wrist, pushing the book into my reluctant hand.

"Take it," she insists, tears spilling onto her cheeks. "It will protect you."

I clutch the small book and feel my spirit begin to fall. Spinning on my heel, I run from the house, grabbing my thick, brown coat as I go and pushing into the darkness as her cries chase me out the door. I fight my way down the path, running and slipping over rocks and ice. It's dark tonight, one of those black, winter nights when the sky seems to blot out the moon, leaving the world hidden. Can a hidden world be seen by anyone? Could a stupid, pregnant, failure of a girl be visible in such a blackened land?

I trip on a tree root and fall hard, rolling down a small embankment. I land with a thud against a large boulder, knocking the wind out of my lungs. As I lay on the cold ground, gasping for breath, I feel a sharp pain in my back. I can't breathe, can't move. The pain rushes over me in waves, one after another, and the pressure mounts in my abdomen, and I know that I'm having the baby.

I push myself to my knees and try to stand, but the pain is coming so fast and hard that I can't move. I moan, holding my stomach, trying to stop what I know is happening.

"Mama," I cry through gritted teeth, hoping that somehow my plea will be carried by the wind to my mother's ears.

Finally, lying back against the rock, I give in to the pain and push. It's involuntary, this pushing. It's as though nature has taken over, and I am at her mercy. I push and groan, my throat growing raw as the pain works its way out of me. Reaching down, I remove my pants. I pull my knees to my chest and with one final cry, I feel life slipping from me. I catch the baby and pull it up to my chest, still connected to me. It's so small, this little life. I know in my heart there is no way this child can live. The world is too cruel a place for a life so small and inconsequential.

I can only make out a dim form in my arms. It squirms, and I pull it in a little tighter, wishing I could better stave off the cold. I feel one more release, and I know this child is no longer attached to me. Independent of my body, this child now has no protection in a world that never would have looked after it anyway. Running my hand down the tiny back, I trace every contour of the body in my hands. It's a girl. She makes tiny sounds, desperate little squeaks that beg for comfort.

I draw her in as close as I can and rock gently back and forth, wincing at the pain as my back rubs up against the rock.

"I'm sorry," I whisper. "I'm so sorry, little one." Her cries begin to fade. I rock some more. I don't feel the cold. I'm not fazed by the night sky. I am numb.

Over and over I beg her forgiveness. It doesn't take long for her body to grow still, and I know that it's over. I know that she didn't suffer. Perhaps that is the one comfort I take in the moments following her birth and death—the knowledge that I will spend a lifetime suffering in her place. I took that for her, and isn't that a mother's job?

I don't know how long I sit there with my daughter's life-less body. Perhaps it's minutes, or maybe hours. Time stops under that dark sky. I wish for it to simply swallow me up, but it doesn't. There will be no escaping the choices made that led me to this moment. I sit under the weight of them for as long as I can, and then I know it's time to go. There's nothing left to do but bury my daughter's body beneath a pile of stones on the side of the road. It takes so few to cover her.

I don't linger over her makeshift grave. I bury her quickly, then I leave. It's over. I trudge under the starless sky, my small bag bouncing against a raw back. I pull my arms tight around my waist, the emptiness inside so gnawing that I know I can't go back. I can't go on living life in this place. I have to get away, to try to erase this single moment in time because the horror of what just happened is a weight too great for me to bear. I can't live under the same roof as my Mama, listening to her prayers and her scriptures, and her soft humming in the corner. I can't look her in the eye and know that she and I share a similar pain—we both lost children. She was right. This devastation was too much.

I tremble violently, my shoulders quaking from fatigue, sorrow, and cold. I pull my arms in tighter to my chest and will myself to keep moving. I won't let this night become a reality. I will change it. I'll erase this from my memory. I'll go away and start a new life, forgetting this one entirely. Victoria no longer exists. She is buried with that tiny body beneath a small pile of stones on the side of the road.

I won't return to the pain of this night, because I know that if I do, it will surely kill me. I take a deep breath, drawing the icy air in my lungs and relishing the way it burns, then I let it out slowly. As I do, the world begins to spin. I stumble on the path, trying to figure out which way is up. I feel heavy, like something is pressing down on my shoulders. I push against the weight and hear a snap. I fall.

# NINA

*Morning, after the still of night,*
*dawns with a red-hued sky.*
*Dreams that stilled a heart with fright,*
*soften in the new day's cry.*

Nina walks down the corridor of the hospital, two cups of coffee held tightly in her hands. She heads to the nurse's station and holds one of the cups out.

"I thought you could use a little pick-me-up today," she says to Carol, the on-duty nurse who has been watching over her mother every day for the last three months. Carol looks up at Nina, her eyes wide.

"Did you get my phone call?" she asks. Nina's heart sinks. She reaches into her purse and pulls out her phone, noticing three missed calls.

She looks back up at Carol. "What is it?" she asks.

Carol smiles. "Nina, your mother is awake!" she says. Nina sets her cup of coffee down on the desk and turns toward her mother's room. It has been three months since her mother collapsed. Her vitals have been stable, but she has simply been asleep. Every day after work, Nina has come to the hospital and sat by her mother's bedside. Many afternoons, Annie joined her, studying and doing her homework at the small table in the corner of the room. And Viktor has been a constant by her side as she's talked to her mother. She read Pushkin and Pasternak, careful to not read too quickly because she could hear her mother's voice in her head.

*"Slow down, Ninochka. You cannot drive a poem like a car. You have to let it lead you."*

How many times had her mother made her stop and start again as a child when she read out loud? It used to drive her crazy, but in the months that she's been reading to her unresponsive mother, she's found herself longing for the criticism—anything to see some spark of life.

"Nina? Are you okay?"

Nina turns and gives Carol a half-hearted smile.

"Yes," she replies. "I'm just...nervous."

Carol leans forward, elbows pressing against the desk. "It's okay," she says. "Your mother is awake and responsive, but she isn't talking. That will take some time."

Nina smiles again, this time more genuinely. "Okay," she says.

Carol stands back up. "Also, Dr. Shevchenko is in the room with your mother right now," she says with a knowing smile. Nina blushes. As hard as she and Viktor have tried to remain professional when together in the hospital, their relationship hasn't been much of a secret.

With a deep breath, Nina walks toward her mother's room and pushes open the door. Viktor is sitting next to Elizaveta's bedside. Her hand is wrapped inside his, and with the other he holds up a tattered book, reading softly. Nina can't hear his words, but it doesn't matter. She doesn't need to because she is utterly taken with the sight of him. His broad back is bent slightly as he leans toward her mother. His long, white doctor's coat hangs down behind him, and his feet are tucked up against the bar of the stool. He looks comfortable and sturdy, almost as though he was supposed to be there all along. Nina is overwhelmed with the ease of the picture before her.

Sensing her presence, Viktor spins slightly on the stool,

catching Nina's eye and tossing her a soft smile. He nods his head toward her mother, who sits up in bed, blinking and turning her head slowly. Nina takes a few steps across the room and stands next to Viktor.

"*Zdrastvui*, Mama," she says softly. Elizaveta turns her head toward the sound of Nina's voice and looks hard at her face. Nina leans in closer so her mother can focus. Elizaveta's mouth opens and closes, her lips trying to form words that won't escape. Her eyes fill with tears, and she leans her head back against the pillow, looking up at the ceiling.

"Oh, Mama," Nina murmurs. She reaches over and smooths her mother's hair off her forehead. "It's okay. You don't have to try and talk right now."

Elizaveta moans, the anguished sound bleeding into Nina's heart. She turns to look at Viktor who moves his hand to Elizaveta's wrist, taking note of her pulse.

"What's wrong?" Nina asks.

"She wants to speak, but the stroke affected the part of her brain that allows for communication. I think she's scared," Viktor replies. "Her pulse is speeding up."

Leaning over her, Viktor looks in Elizaveta's eyes.

"It's okay, Elizaveta Andreyevna," he says. "You're alright. Just take a couple of deep breaths, okay?"

Elizaveta shakes her head, her lips still moving in a conversation that won't escape. Her voice comes out in guttural groans. Nina grabs her mother's hand and squeezes it tight.

"Mama, I'm right here," she says. She forces her words to come out calm, not wanting to alarm her mother any more. "Everything is going to be okay."

Elizaveta looks with wild eyes at Nina. Tears spill onto her cheeks, a river of sorrow streaking her weathered skin. Her hands flutter and shoulders begin to shake. Nina glances at Viktor, alarmed.

"I've never seen my mother cry," she says, the words coming out choked.

Viktor straightens up and walks to the door, sticking his head out into the hallway and calling for a nurse.

"I'm going to give her a sedative to calm her down," he says to Nina.

"You're going to put her back to sleep?" Nina asks, looking from her mother to Viktor and back again.

"It's mild," Viktor replies. "She won't sleep for long, but this will help her relax."

Carol walks in and the two of them move in a flurry around Elizaveta's bed, changing her IV bag, and making her more comfortable. As Viktor pushes the sedative into her IV, Elizaveta continues to quake. Her eyes shift to Nina's again, and she tries to form words. Her look is pleading. Her eyelids flutter as the sedative takes effect. Within a few moments, she has drifted back to sleep, her hands now still.

Carol walks by Nina and squeezes her shoulder reassuringly. "This is common," she says. "Lots of stroke victims wake up agitated when they realize they can't communicate. It will get better." She turns and offers a nod to Viktor, then steps out of the room. Nina leans against the wall and looks at him.

"She was fine when it was just you and her in the room," Nina says, her voice flat. "She didn't get upset until I got here." Viktor crosses the room and pulls her into his arms. Nina rests her head on his chest, suddenly feeling very heavy.

"She doesn't have things she wants to say to me," Viktor says. He kisses the top of her head gently. "It's you she wanted to talk to, and her brain can't send the proper signals to her mouth right now. It will get better."

Nina tilts her head back and looks at him. "Will it?" she asks. "Will I ever know my mother?"

Viktor kisses her forehead. "Maybe not how you want to know her," he responds. "But your Mama is strong. She's a fighter, and I don't think she's done yet. Just keep showing up. That's all you can do."

Nina closes her eyes and leans back into Viktor's chest. She feels safe there, perhaps for the first time in her life.

"*Ya tebya lyublyu*," Nina murmurs. The "I love you" flows so effortlessly from her lips that she doesn't realize she's said it at first. Then she gasps and pulls back, looking up at him as the color in her cheeks deepens. Viktor looks at her, tenderness written in his dark eyes.

"I love you, too," he says. "And I want to marry you."

Nina raises her eyebrows. "What?"

Viktor smiles. "I want to marry you," he repeats. "I want to spend the rest of my life with you. I can say it in two languages if you'd like." His eyes sparkle. "*Ti viidyesh za menya?*" he asks, in Russian this time.

Nina pauses for a moment to think. She swore after Richard died that she would never marry again. Love was too painful. It hurt too much when people left you behind, and she had spent a lifetime choking on the dust of those who left her. She turns to look at Elizaveta, now breathing peacefully, and she thinks of all the comments she heard over the years about her failure to marry a "good, strong Russian man." And now here she stands, feet away from her mother with a proposal hanging between her and just such a man. Nina laughs, the sound rippling from inside her and dancing into the stale room. Viktor smiles.

"What is it?" he asks.

"If my Mama were conscious and could talk, she'd be staring at me with her eyebrow raised. She'd probably have just answered "yes" for me, then she would have told me not to be a fool and let a real man slip away." Nina laughs again. She turns back to Viktor who looks at her with a twinkle in his eye.

"So is that a yes?" he asks.

Nina looks up at him and blinks back tears. "Yes," she answers with a nod. She smiles. "Yes, it's a yes!" Viktor scoops her up and spins her around with a kiss.

"Did you hear that, Elizaveta Andreyevna?" he asks, setting Nina down and looking at Elizaveta's still frame. "Your daughter just bagged herself a real man."

Nina laughs and playfully slaps his arm. She walks to her mother's bedside and leans over. "It's going to be okay, Mama," she says, joy replacing sorrow. "You have to get better now so you can see the fulfillment of your wish." She glances back at Viktor who stands with his arms crossed, an elated grin plastered across his face. "I'm going to marry a good, strong Russian man," Nina whispers.

Elizaveta's eyes flutter, as though she wants to open them but can't. They relax again, and Nina smiles, hope dancing in her heart for the first time since the day she left Russia for her new life in America.

# ELIZAVETA

*I am a whisperer.*

E very time I go to sleep, I am knocked back to a different memory. Remembering the night I left home unlocked everything about my past—all the things I'd spent decades running from are now here on the shore of my dreams, waiting to remind me of all the ways that I failed.

I saw her today. I saw my Nina, and I heard her voice, and I wanted to tell her everything. I'm tired of hiding. I'm tired of running. The skeleton of a little girl is buried beneath a pile of rocks, and I'm the one who left her there. I'm the one who abandoned a life on the side of a gravel path. I am a monster, and I can't hide it anymore.

When I tried to speak, I couldn't form the words. It was as though my tongue held them captive. After all these years of protecting my secrets, of burying them like I buried my daughter, now I *cannot* release them. Perhaps that is my punishment. Perhaps I must now live alone under the weight of my lies without the possibility of asking for forgiveness.

Just when I felt myself falling into a full-blown panic, the room began to spin. My body relaxed, and the words got swallowed back up, not to be shared. My eyelids grew heavy, so I closed them, and I let myself spiral back to the night I left home.

I'm back on the path now, stumbling along as the sun begins to peek over the horizon. I've walked all night long in
the frigid air, and I know that I will die if I don't find shelter.
The blood drips down my legs as I walk, a reminder that the
horror I experienced in the darkness of night was real. I didn't
imagine it. My body is numb, shocked by the events of the
last twenty-four hours. I consider sitting down on the wooded
ground and simply letting go, releasing myself from the nightmare. But then I see the barn up ahead, a lantern hanging outside the door, and I wonder if, just for a moment, I might be
able to find rest.

I stumble to the barn and pull open the door, stepping inside the four wooden walls. A man stands in the corner next to
one small, thin cow. He turns to face me.

"What do you want?" he asks. I try to speak, but the words
are frozen at the icy gates of my lips. The man's eyes run down
my body, taking in the sight of my dirty, bloody dress, blood
covered shoes, disheveled hair, and wild eyes. He sighs.

"You can't stay here," he says.

"*Pozhalusta,*" I whisper. It's the only word that I can speak,
so I say it again. "Please."

The man purses his lips and shifts his weight from one foot
to the next. "I could get in a lot of trouble hiding someone like
you here," he says.

"Please," I whisper. My lips are dry, my mouth desperately
parched. The word sounds cracked, like it's been rolled in saw-
dust and blown out with the wind.

The man sighs again. He motions with a single jerk of his
chin, and I stumble to the hay piled in the corner. Collaps-
ing onto it, I suddenly feel the weight of my fatigue. The man
walks up to me and squats down.

"What's your name?" he asks.

I open my mouth to answer, then pause. I can't tell him the
truth. I can't offer the name that has been mine up until this
point. I have to erase that past, to blot out the memory of the

days leading up to this one. My mind races as I try to decide how to answer him. He waits, the judgement in his stare leaving me flustered.

"Elizaveta Mishurova," I croak. I pick the name of one of the girls who was in the labor camp with me. Elizaveta had been older, and she was pretty in the way that I wanted to be pretty when I grew up. As a child, I would stare at her and hope that someday my face could look like hers. Whenever Tanya and I played house as kids, this was the pretend name I would choose. It was the identity that I longed for, and in that moment of stress it was the only name I could dig from my memory.

The man narrows his eyes and studies me closely. "Okay, Elizaveta," he says. Something in his voice sets off an alarm in my head. He is not a safe man.

I nod, crossing my arms over my chest to stop the trembling. He stands up. "I'll send my wife out to give you some food and different clothes. You need to change." He says the words disdainfully as he turns his face from mine.

"Thank you," I tremble. He waves his hand and walks out of the barn, pulling the door closed behind him. I look around in the dim, morning light. It's surprisingly warm inside the barn, or perhaps I am simply so cold that anything is better than before. The cow in the corner chews slowly, staring at me with sorrowful eyes that seem to understand and commiserate with my situation. She's bone thin, her ribs jutting through paper-like skin.

"*Privyet,*" I say quietly. She chews a hello in return. For a long while we watch one another until she finally turns away from me, exhausted from sharing my mental anguish. In the silence, I find myself suddenly overwhelmed with sadness. I burrow down into the prickly hay and start to cry, hot tears spilling down my cheeks and off my chin. I weep for my dead child, buried on the side of the road. I weep for my lost brother, my unknown father, and my mother and sister who I left behind without a goodbye. I weep for my lost innocence, re-linquished under the groping hands of Commander Nikolayev. I weep for everything I lost and all that I never really had. My sobs turn to wails as I process nineteen years of heartache.

I don't hear her walk in, and I don't notice as she stands and watches me cry. I don't know how long she witnessed my unleashing, but I jump when she finally clears her throat. Pushing to a sitting position, I wipe my face and try to calm my breathing.

"Hello." Her voice is gentle. She holds in her hands a tray, and over her arm hangs a garment.

"I've brought you some *chai*," she says. She walks to me and sets the tray at my feet. A tarnished tin cup of tea sits on the tray next to a plate of thick, black bread. I look at it, then back up at her.

"*Spasibo*," I whisper.

She leans down and hands me the dress and undergar-ments that are hanging over her arm. "Here," she says. "Take this as well. When you've changed, you can leave your dress by the door. I will try to wash it clean for you."

I don't reply, too stunned by her gentle kindness to know how to adequately respond. She stands up and pulls one more thing from her pocket. She holds the bundle of rags in her hand. She lays them down next to me.

"This is to help with the bleeding," she breathes. She kneels down, her eyes shifting from side to side. "You can't stay here long," she whispers. "It isn't safe." I make eye contact and nod slowly.

"Rest for now. My husband has to leave for the day. I will be back later to bring you your dress."

I nod, lips trembling. She stands up and nods her head, then turns and quickly walks out of the barn.

The day stretches on, fading from morning, to afternoon, then evening. Finally, darkness wraps around the barn. I spend the time in and out of a fitful sleep. Whenever I fall too deeply into my dreams, they are replaced with nightmares. I see my daughter, alone and buried beneath that pile of rocks. As I stare at her, she begins to move, to kick her legs and cry a weak, pitiful cry. She's alive, and I left her there alone in the cold. I shoot up in a wild panic, arms flailing as I gasp for air.

The woman stands before me, and I yelp. She holds up a hand and shakes her head. "It is only me," she says. "I didn't mean to frighten you." I blink in the grey haze of the early morning. A new day has dawned, time already rushing on forward as though nothing had changed.

My heart thrums against my chest, my stomach tied in a knot as I try to push the image of my tiny daughter out of my mind. The woman reaches out and hands me my dress. Somehow she has washed all the stains away. The garment lays clean and fresh, and I feel unworthy to wear it.

"You must change quickly," she says. "My husband will be home soon, and you cannot be here when he arrives."

I stand on shaky feet and take the dress. Turning my back to her, I quickly change, then hand her back the dress she let me borrow. She gives me fresh rags and some privacy as I change out my undergarments as well.

I'm lacing up my shoes when I hear the rumble of the car outside the barn. She turns to me, eyes wide, a look of apology washing over her tired features.

"Valya!" His voice comes out hard and angry. She ducks her head and steps from the barn. I hear them speaking in low voices and creep toward the wall to make out what they're saying.

"Just let her go," Valya pleads. "She is only a girl."

"She's a *kulak*," the man spits in reply. "And she hid in my barn. I'm not going to take the fall for her. She can go to the local authorities and tell them who she is and why she's running. We'll let them decide what to do with her."

I pull back in horror and look around wildly for a way to escape, but there is no other door but the one. I pick up my *katomka* and put it on my back, then smooth out my hair with trembling hands. The door opens and the man steps into the barn.

"Good, you're up," he says. His voice is gruff, but his eyes look tired. It's the look all of us share. Self preservation has a way of wearing down the body.

"You need to come with me," he barks. I nod and follow him slowly from the barn. Valya stands to the side, her head down. She doesn't look at me as I walk past.

The man and I climb into an old, rusty truck, doors moaning as we open them. After a few turns of the key, the engine finally starts, and we pull onto the gravel road in front of the barn. We ride in silence. I stare out the window, watching the trees move slowly past, feeling suddenly as though I may be suffocated by the rolling hills and open spaces. In ten minutes, we reach town, and he rolls to a stop in front of a worn down wooden building.

"Come," he barks.

I climb out of the car and follow him inside. A man sits at a table, a stack of papers in front of him. He looks up when we walk in and his eyebrows raise.

"Yes?" he says.

The man who brought me juts his head in my direction. "This runaway hid in my barn. She's given me a name, but I can't be sure it's her real name." He glances at me then, a sneer contorting the features of his face. Panic wells up inside me. I need to escape.

The man behind the desk leans back and crosses his arms. "What's your name, girl?" he asks.

"E...Elizaveta Mishurova," I answer. The man narrows his eyes.

"And where are you from?" he asks. I hang my head, unable to answer his question.

He stands up and walks around the table, stopping in front of me. He's drawn himself up to his full height, shoulders pushed back. He is tall and imposing. He reminds me of Commander Nikolayev. My shoulders begin to tremble.

"What are you running from?" he asks. His voice is cold, devoid of any emotion at all. I open my mouth to reply, then close it again. My whole body is now trembling. The man leans over me and his voice lowers.

"Do you know what we do with runaways?" he asks. I squeeze my eyes shut and remember standing at the fence outside the gulag looking for my papa. I remember the people who walked on the other side of the fence—skeletal and ghostly. I open my eyes and shift my gaze to his face, and I make the choice without even thinking. Perhaps I was always destined to walk this path. Maybe it was inevitable that one day I would make this choice, that I would turn my back on Family and embrace the predictability of State.

"I am fleeing my family," I whisper. "My mother is a traitor. She prays and speaks of God, and she is trying to force me to believe her lies. I can't stay with her. I want to serve my country."

As I speak, something inside me dies. Betraying the ones you love most will inevitably leave a scar, a mark on your soul so deep that it will take a lifetime to try to heal, but repairing such a tear isn't really possible.

The man stares at me, a look of amusement dancing through his eyes. "And how am I to know you're telling the truth?" he says. "How do I know you aren't some thief who is just trying to escape?"

I swallow hard and pull my *katomka* off my back. Reaching inside, my fingers grasp the small book of scriptures. I pull it out and hand it to him.

"This is her New Testament," I answer. He takes it from me and flips through the pages. "I stole it from her, hoping it would make her stop speaking of God and forcing her religion on me, but she won't stop. She's a traitor, and she is dangerous."

As soon as the words escape my lips I regret them. I wish I

could pull them back in and lock them up. The man's face widens into a sick smile, but I feel no relief, no sense of protection for my actions.

"It is a noble thing you're doing," he says, but the tremulous glee in his voice tells me that what I have done is the height of selfishness. He watches the color drain from my face and chuckles softly.

"And who is your mother?" he asks. I stand mute. He leans forward, his face so close to mine that I can smell the sardines on his breath. "It's too late to stop now," he says.

I whisper her name, and one hot tear escapes my eye. He shakes his head in disgust. "Stop crying," he mutters. "No one likes a weak-willed woman."

Walking to the chair behind his desk, he writes my mother's name down and the location of our home, which I whisper to him through quivering lips.

"I have a sister," I say. "She's younger and is often sick. Please, don't bring any harm to her."

The man shrugs his shoulders indifferently. "She's the child of a traitorous *kulak*, as are you," he glances up at me. "She'll have to decide where her allegiance lies just as you have." My heart sinks and my knees go weak. Time stops then, and keeps on moving all at the same time. The man gives me the chance to escape and, like a coward, I take it asking to be sent to Moscow. I long for the anonymity of the big city, to disappear inside a throng of people. I don't want to be seen or noticed. I want only to disappear.

One day later, I'm on a train heading north, my hands clutching new identification papers given to me "for my allegiance to our great country." In my *katomka* is the small book of scriptures that bought my freedom. The man had tossed it at me just before I stepped onto the train.

"A reminder of the price paid for your freedom," he'd said with a sneer as I clutched it in horror. Mama was right. That book had given me protection. But the protection had come at a cost for which I was not prepared.

I stare out the window at a land to which I know I'll never return. Tears prick at the corners of my eyes, but I blink them back. I won't cry. I feel nothing. No sense of loss. No hopeful expectation. I clutch in my hands the papers that now identify me as Elizaveta Andreyevna Mishurova, and I rehearse my story over and over. I am the daughter of intelligent parents who were killed in the war. It would be years before I started to believe my own story. On this day, I merely commit it to memory.

That was the day I tried to rewrite history—the day I decided that I would protect my story with all the strength I possessed, at whatever cost. I would never again be a *kulak*. Victoria was dead, buried beneath a small pile of rocks in the frozen ground where the silver willows weep. I would forget that girl, and I would forget that night, never again to mention or think of it.

That was the day I began speaking in whispers.

# ANNIE

Annie takes a breath and knocks on her mom's door.
"Come in!" Nina calls out. Annie pushes open the door and steps inside to find her mother wrapped in a towel.

"Good morning," she says with a smile.

"Good morning to you," she replies. Her mother has alternated between giddy and ecstatic since she and Viktor agreed to get married. The only time she saw the light fade from her mother's eyes was when the topic of Babushka came up. They had moved her to a rehab facility, and she was now consistently waking up each day, but her agitation grew whenever Nina walked into the room, making it even more difficult for her to try to communicate.

"What is it, my dear?" Nina calls from the closet. Annie stands outside the door as her mom dresses and takes a deep breath.

"I've picked a family," she says.

"What?" Nina asks, her voice muffled as she pulls a shirt over her head.

"I've picked a family," Annie repeats. Nina steps from the closet and studies Annie closely.

"Oh," she says, the smile slowly fading from her eyes.

Annie holds out a photo book. Nina takes it and slowly walks to the bed, flipping it open to look through the pages.

"Their names are Jack and Jenny," Annie says. "Totally American names, right?" she offers a tight-lipped smile. Nina sits down on the edge of the bed. She repeats the names over in her head. *Jack and Jenny.*

"They seem really great," Annie continues. "They have one child, a three year old girl, and they're super active. She's a schoolteacher, which I thought was kind of nice. And he does something in sales."

Nina flips through the book and takes in the sight of the smiling couple that has been chosen to raise her grandchild. Her heart constricts. There are pictures of them next to the ocean, standing on a beach in front of the Golden Gate Bridge, hiking in the Smoky Mountains. There's a picture of their home, a cute little house with a fenced back yard, a swing set, and a little girl with bouncing, blonde curls sitting on the swing. Jenny is petite, her wide smile indicating a bubbly personality, while Jack's smile reveals more of a serious nature.

Annie shifts from one foot to the other, running her hand up and down her stomach as she watches her mom flip through the book. Her abdomen is tight, sticking out awkwardly at an angle that is unmistakable and impossible to hide. The whispers and snickers of her classmates trail behind her in the halls now. She is *that* girl—the statistic—the pregnant teen. With only four weeks left until her due date and eight weeks of school left, Annie finds herself longing to just move past this point in her life. She's ready for this season to be over.

Nina clears her throat, willing the emotion out of the way. "So, you're sure about this?"

"What do you mean, sure?" Annie asks.

"I mean you're sure you want to let this child be raised by someone else—by people named Jack and Jenny?"

Annie gapes at her mom. "What's the alternative, Mom?" she asks. "I can't raise this baby by myself. Obviously! I can barely take care of myself. And what, are you going to help me?" Annie snorts.

"What's that supposed to mean?" Nina asks softly.

"It means, Mom, that you have plenty of other things to occupy your days. You couldn't take care of this baby any more than I could. You have Babushka, and you've made it more than clear to me that she's all you can handle. I almost feel sorry for Viktor. He has no idea that he won't be able to compete with Babushka for your attention."

Nina draws in a sharp breath. She and Annie stare hard into one another's eyes for a long time. Finally, Annie snatches the book from her and marches out of the room. She pauses at the door.

"I'm calling the agency today and telling them I choose Jack and Jenny," she says. She walks out and pulls the door closed behind her. For a brief moment she lingers in the hallway, regret churning in her chest at the bitterness she just unleashed on her mom. She turns to go back in, but quickly realizes she doesn't know what she would say because she had simply told the truth.

⋄⋅⋯⋅⋄⋅⋯⋅⋄⋅⋯⋅⋄⋅⋯⋅⋄

"Hey there."

Annie looks up at James and offers a half-hearted smile. He raises his eyebrows. "Well, that's the most pitiful greeting I've ever seen," he says. He slides around and falls into the seat next to her. Patting her knee, he gestures her to turn and face him.

"What's up?" he asks.

Annie shrugs. "I don't want to talk about it," she mumbles.

James cocks his head to the side. "Are you sure?" he asks. "Because I'm an excellent listener. And also, it may keep me from thinking about that awful book we're reading in Lit class right now. Why on earth would anyone assign *The Scarlet Letter* in the last quarter of school?! It's like torture."

Annie smiles, and the reaction feels good. "I've given up on that one," she says. "I'm not even trying to read it. I just looked up a synopsis online and studied the main points."

James clutches his heart and falls back into his seat. "You're not going to read it at all? That's sacrilegious...but also kind of brilliant. Can I copy your notes?"

Annie chuckles. Her smile quickly fades, and she looks down at her uneaten lunch. "I picked a family," she says softly. James leans in to listen over the din of the lunchroom.

"Oh yeah?" he asks.

Annie nods. "Yeah," she says. "I told my mom about it this morning, and she sort of freaked out. She asked me if I'm sure about this, and wouldn't I rather raise the child myself?"

James studies Annie's profile, the way that her nose slopes down softly, dotted with light freckles. "And that upset you?" he asks.

Annie nods. She turns to face him, her eyes full of tears. "This whole process is so weird," she says, blinking hard. "I've been looking through all these photo books of families that want to adopt. It's like I'm shopping for the people who are going to raise my kid, and it's so strange. But at least I was confident that I was making a good choice." Annie shakes her head and looks away. "My mom took that away this morning, though," she says. "Now instead of confident, I just feel selfish."

James grabs her hand and squeezes it.

"Are you sure I'm doing the right thing?" Annie asks. She doesn't look at him when she speaks the question, and the words float out into the lunchroom. She wonders if they were lost completely in the noise, but then James speaks softly.

"I can't really answer that," he says. "But I can tell you that I think you might be one of the bravest people I've ever known. And I can also tell you that as someone who has seen adoption firsthand, you aren't giving up."

"Annie," he waits for her to turn and face him. "It's pretty cool what you're doing, so don't convince yourself that it isn't. If anything, I would say that your willingness to give your child to people who are longing to be parents is the most selfless act humanly possible." James leans forward and looks into Annie's eyes.

"I mean, think about it. You're giving life twice. You're not only *having* the baby, but you're giving it a stable family."

A single tear spills out of Annie's eyes and runs down her cheek. James reaches up and wipes it away.

"And don't worry about your mom," he says. "I bet she'll come around."

Annie sighs. "It's always so hard with her," she says. "I thought we were doing better, especially recently since Babushka has been so sick. She and I have been talking more, and it seemed like it was going to be better between us. Then this morning happened." She shrugs.

James leans down and reaches into his backpack. He pulls out a brown paper bag and opens it up.

"Sandwich?" he asks. He holds up two peanut butter and jelly sandwiches. Annie laughs lightly.

"You don't have to feed me every day, you know," she says.

"Oh yes I do," James retorts. "I've got to make sure you're properly exposed to the great, American foods. Like P, B, and J...and mac and cheese." He pulls out a plastic container packed with mac and cheese. Handing her a plastic fork, he gives her a proud grin, entirely pleased with himself.

"Hang in there with your mom, Annie," he says, pulling the top off the container. "If I've learned anything since my mom and sister died, it's that parents aren't superhuman. It's like these life stresses put a chink in their adult armors, and suddenly they're real people with real emotions."

Annie takes a bite of mac and cheese and smiles at him. "Thanks," she says. "This is really good," she says gesturing to the bowl. James grins back.

"I told you!" he says. "This stuff is the nectar of the gods."

Annie leans over and kisses him gently on the cheek. "No really," she says shyly. "Thank you."

James clears his throat and gives her one short nod. For several minutes they eat in silence, their chairs pushes closer together than normal. Finally, James swallows and puts down his fork.

"So," he says, one eyebrow raised. "About those notes on *The Scarlet Letter*."

# NINA

*I long for home,*
*but what awaits me there?*
*Nothing but memories long past*
*and secrets untold.*

Nina closes the door softly behind her and turns to face her mother. Elizaveta sleeps peacefully in the small bed. The room is dark and quiet, the rehab center a nice change from the constant bustling of the hospital. Nina walks lightly to the side of the bed and lowers herself into the chair.

"*Privyet*, Mama," she says softly. Her voice carries into the gentle hum of the air conditioner. Nina takes in the sight of her mother's wispy, grey hair laying in strands across the thick pillow. Elizaveta looks calm and peaceful, but only when she sleeps. When she's awake, she's agitated and frustrated. Communicating has been her biggest challenge, though the nursing staff insists that she's doing better. Nina sighs.

"Mama, I wish I could talk to you," she says. "I've always wished I could talk to you. I've spent an entire lifetime wishing that I could share with you the things that were happening. But more than that, Mama, I wanted you to talk to me." Nina leans forward on her elbows. She thinks back to the very first time she kept a secret from her mother.

She had been eight years old, a student in the second form at school. It was the day of remembrance, when students honored the memory of the great father of their nation, Vladimir Illyich Lenin. They would go that day to the Mausoleum and lay flowers as a class outside the doors, paying homage to the man responsible for giving them the opportunity to live in such a great land.

"You must look your best today," Elizaveta whispered to Nina as she fixed her hair that morning, pulling it into a two tight ponytails and tying white ribbons around the thick rubber bands. Nina wore her uniform, freshly cleaned and pressed to perfection. Her white collar stuck out in sharp points from the top of her black dress, and Mama pinned her *Octybryonok* pin at the top near her shoulder, shining it with a kerchief so that Lenin's face gleamed against the small, red star. She tied Nina's shined shoes, smoothed her starched white apron, and together they marched through the icy, January streets to the school. Elizaveta was very serious that morning, more than usual. Her eyes were dark, her face stern. She squeezed Nina's hand so tightly it hurt, but Nina didn't say anything.

When they arrived at school, Elizaveta looked down with furrowed brow. "This is important, my dear," she said, her voice husky. "This is the day when you give thanks for this great land. You are fortunate to be educated here, Nina," she said, squatting down so that she was eye level with her daughter. "You are being raised as a good Soviet citizen. Be grateful in your heart." She thumped Nina's chest.

Nina walked into the classroom that morning with a knot in her stomach because her mother spoke words that she didn't understand. Even then, Nina remembers a part of herself that simply wanted to push against anything her mother said.

She took her seat in the middle of the classroom next to Nadya, the jewel of the class and the teacher's clear favorite. Nadya was smart and pretty, always answering questions correctly and receiving the highest marks on every assignment.

Nina, on the other hand, drew jeers from the teacher on more than one occasion for being "slow."

In the desk next to Nina sat Seryozha, the boy who drew even more disdain from their teacher than she did. He was a small boy who always wore his hair slicked to the side. He was missing his two front teeth, and he spent much of his school days picking his nose and wiping his treasures on the desk, which only drew more unwanted attention from the instructor.

Finally, after their morning recitations, the teacher instructed them all to get their coats and hats and to line up against the wall. As they walked out of the room, she handed each of them a single, red carnation. Then she took her place at the front of the line, and together they marched into the street.

It wasn't a long walk to Lenin's Mausoleum from the school, but it was far enough for Nina's feet to go numb from the blustery winter wind. Perfect Nadya walked in front of her, her head held high, seemingly unfazed by the cold. Seryozha slogged behind, wheezing as they walked at a brisk pace, trying to keep up with the rest of the line.

"I wish we didn't have to do this," he whined as they rounded the corner into the square. St. Basil's Cathedral loomed ahead, the vibrant spires standing out against the grey sky. "My Papa says Lenin wasn't even a good man," he whispered. "He says that Lenin killed lots of people, even some of my Papa's family."

Nina didn't know if Seryozha was talking to her or to himself, but she didn't turn around to look at him in case she might draw the attention of the teacher and receive a reprimand. Seryozha went on talking, his words settling uncomfortably in her ears.

"My Papa says that our nation would have been better without Lenin. And he says Brezhnev is a *durak*."

Nina sucked in her breath at Seryozha's words, his father's label of their current leader as a fool making her feel distinctly uncomfortable. She knew that what he said was dangerous.

It went against everything that her mama ever spoke. Nina also knew that Seryozha was Jewish, and that for some reason this made him bad. The teacher often spoke to him in anger when he answered a question wrong, calling him a sly Jew, which brought out a scowl on his face. Nina wondered as they marched toward Lenin's tomb that morning if that's why Seryozha's papa said such terrible things. Was it because he was Jewish?

"I'm not leaving this flower for Lenin," Seryozha mumbled behind her. The line slowed, but he didn't notice and ran into Nina's back, knocking her forward into Nadya who whirled around and tossed out a glare. Nina turned around and took in the sight of Seryozha, his nose running down to his lip, and his winter hat pulled so low that his eyes barely showed.

"Lenin was bad. My papa told me," he whispered. "I'm not dropping my flower. I'm just gonna pretend, then I will stick it in my coat." Nina turned back around, and in a split second made a decision that didn't make sense.

She decided to join Seryozha's secret rebellion. She didn't have a defense for why she decided to do it. She just made the choice, and it felt good to choose something for herself.

They approached the already growing mound of flowers outside the grey, cement building, and one by one, students dropped their flowers on the ground. The teacher stood off to the side, observing them all quietly. Nina slowly approached the mound, and just as she stepped to it, one of the students at the front of the line let out a laugh drawing the teacher's stern glance in his direction. Nina quickly stuffed the flower into her pocket and kept walking, her heart beating quickly from the thrill of independence.

As they marched away from the site, Nina turned her head slightly and glanced back at Seryozha, who grinned conspiratorially in return.

Nina felt sick to her stomach the rest of the day as she thought of the crumpled flower in the pocket of her coat. She was afraid of the consequences of getting caught, but that feeling seemed to be at war with the freedom she felt for making such a bold move of defiance.

When school was released, Nina walked out to find her mama waiting. Usually work prevented her from picking Nina up after school, but that day Elizaveta made an exception. She grabbed Nina's hand and guided her toward the tram.

"How was your day?" Elizaveta asked.

"Good," Nina answered. That was the truth. It had been a really good day. She had even answered a few questions correctly, receiving a nod of approval from the teacher.

"And how was your visit to honor Lenin?" Elizaveta asked. "Did you pay your respects?"

Nina thought of the flower in her pocket, and her heartbeat quickened. "Yes," she answered. "I paid respects."

Nina shakes her head and smiles at the memory. She had run to the bathroom that afternoon when she and her mother got back to the lab so Elizaveta could finish her work day, and she'd dropped the broken flower into the trash receptacle, her hands shaking from the fear of being caught. It was surprisingly easy to keep that secret from her mother, though. In fact, it made her feel almost excited to know that she could so easily hide a little piece of herself like that.

Nina sighs. That was the day she realized that she could hide things from her Mama. And the keeping of that one small secret gave her power. Even then, she knew Elizaveta to be a mystery. She sensed that there were pieces of her mother that had been withheld, and that she needed to reciprocate in order to preserve herself.

Nina's head snaps up when she hears the rustling of sheets. Elizaveta blinks in the dim light, her head moving slowly back and forth on the pillow. Nina reaches over and turns on the lamp beside her mother's table.

"Hi, Mama," she says softly. Elizaveta's head lolls to the side, and her eyes slowly focus on her daughter. Nina offers a gentle smile, all the while waiting for her Mama to start falling into her regular panic. She seems particularly agitated when Nina comes to visit. But today, her eyes are calm. She runs them over Nina's face.

"How are you feeling today?" Nina asks. Elizaveta licks her lips and opens her mouth. Nina reaches for the water on the nightstand and brings the straw to Elizaveta's lips. After a few sips, she lowers it back down.

"I hear that you were moving more on your own this morning," Nina says pleasantly. "That's wonderful, Mama! The nurses are all so pleased with your progress. And Viktor says you're looking stronger every day."

In fact, Viktor had said quite the opposite the night before when he and Nina had dinner. He'd told her that he had been hoping to see faster improvement from Elizaveta, but given her age and the severity of the stroke they should be pleased with whatever results they might get.

"Your Mama is tough, *Ninochka*," he said. "But she is also very old, and the body just doesn't respond at her age."

Elizaveta watches the way her daughter's eyes dance from her face to her hands and back again. She isn't telling the truth, but it's not surprising. Elizaveta is quite aware that she is slipping away. She's ready to make her confession now, but the illness has taken away her ability to do so. She just can't will the words to form. She opens her mouth to try to speak, but is immediately interrupted by the door opening.

"Well look who's awake," the on-duty nurse says. Elizaveta can't remember her name, but she likes this one. She doesn't talk too much. The others chat constantly, their English words sounding like a jumble of gibberish. Elizaveta only feels a sense of calm when Viktor is in the room, his Russian like honey to her soul. But this nurse is tolerable.

"How is my Elizaveta doing today?"

*Elizaveta.* The name she chose so long ago. The cloak she put on in order to bury Victoria. They don't really know who she is. None of them do. She has to tell them. Nina needs to know. She needs to understand that she was raised by an imposter—a *kulak* who would do anything to get ahead in life, even betray her family, take on a new identity and lie to everyone she ever met.

She presses her teeth to her lower lip and pushes the air out, forcing the word to come out in one, long hiss.

"What was that, Mama?" Nina asks, leaning forward. "Can you say it again?"

Elizaveta hisses out the word one more time.

"Can you understand her?" the nurse asks. Nina searches her mother's eyes.

"One more time, Mama," she pleads. Elizaveta takes a deep breath and slowly lets it out.

"Victoria," she whispers. Her eyes flutter, and she feels the strength beginning to fade. She hears Nina calling her, but she can't go back. Not right now. The confession will have to wait for another day.

# NINA

*Love.*
*The emotion of the addled,*
*or so they say.*
*And yet, I cannot escape*
*it's grip.*

Nina paces back and forth across the living room, her mind racing as she pieces together the strained moments of the last year. She glances up at the clock, then reaches for her phone on the kitchen counter.

Viktor answers on the second ring. "Hey there," he says, the smile in his voice evident.

"Can you come over?" Nina asks.

"Is everything alright?"

"No," Nine replies, her voice trembling. "I need to talk to you."

Fifteen minutes later, Nina opens the door to find Viktor on the front step, his brow furrowed in concern.

"What is it?" he asks. She opens the door wider as he walks inside, grabbing her hand as he passes.

"I just don't know what it all means," Nina says. "I'm so confused, and I'm tired, and my grandchild is going to grow up with parents named 'Jack and Jenny,' and I don't know what to do."

Viktor holds up his hand, cutting Nina off. "I'm going to need you to slow down," he says. "I have no idea what you're talking about."

Nina takes in a deep breath and lets it out slowly. "My Mama spoke today," she says. Viktor walks her to the couch and gently pulls her down beside him.

"And?" he prods.

"She only spoke one word," Nina says. "She said 'Victoria'."

Viktor leans back and looks at her intently.

"She said 'Victoria', and then she went back to sleep. I was so confused and upset that I just left after that. I didn't even go back to work, which is not good. I'm going to lose my job if I don't pull myself together, and then we'll really be in trouble. I can barely afford all the bills that are pouring in right now as it is."

Viktor grabs her hands and squeezes them tight. "One thing at a time," he says. Nina nods.

"I've been doing some research, you know," she says. "I've been reading about people who survived Stalin's purges—people like my Mama who lived through the years before the war. She fits the profile exactly."

"What profile?" Viktor asks.

"The profile of a *kulak*. She's secretive, offering practically no details of her past. She's never told me a single thing about her childhood. She always just dodged questions or ignored them totally. And lately, she has been acting so strange."

"Yes, but she's been sick, don't forget," Viktor interjects.

"I know. And I know that she is old and perhaps confused, but this is something different."

Nina sighs. She stands up and runs her hand through her hair. "It wasn't uncommon for *kulaks* to change their identities, you know," she says, switching to Russian so that she can speak more freely. "In fact, there's an actual name for my mother's generation. Did you know that?"

Viktor shakes his head.

"They are called 'The Whisperers'." Nina raises her eyebrows and stares hard at Viktor. "Do you see what this means?" she asks.

Viktor opens his mouth to answer, but is immediately interrupted.

"It means that my mother could very well be someone entirely different! Maybe the reason she never told me anything about my past is because she was afraid." Nina paces back and forth as Viktor watches silently.

"Maybe she was scared that she would be found a fraud and sent away. I just don't know what happened to her before I was born, and I hate it!" The pitch of Nina's voice raises as she continues to walk the floor.

"I feel lost without this information. I feel like Dima and Victoria are clues to a puzzle, but they're the only two pieces I've got, and that's just not enough to figure out the whole picture." Nina stops and turns to Viktor.

"What if I never find out?" she asks. Her breath comes out in short gasps as she feels her chest constrict. "What if I never know where she came from, which means I will never know where I came from?"

Viktor stands up and walks to Nina, placing his hands on her shoulders and looking at her gently. She lets out a small laugh.

"Are you sure you want to marry me?" she asks. "Because I think I might be going crazy."

Viktor smiles. He brushes the hair back off her forehead and kisses her. "I can handle a little crazy," he replies. "I'm Russian."

Nina smiles.

"Now," he says. "What is this about 'Jack and Jenny'?"

Nina sighs. "Annie told me this morning that she picked a family to adopt the baby. It's a couple named 'Jack and Jenny.'"

"And this is bothering you?" Viktor asks.

"No," Nina replies. She stops and shrugs. "Maybe," she says.

"I don't know." With a sigh, she flops onto the couch. Viktor sits back down next to her.

"Annie is so young," Nina mumbles. "Of course she doesn't need to start raising a child. I was thirty-five when I had her, and I didn't know what I was doing then. I would have been a mess at seventeen."

"So what's bothering you?" Viktor asks.

"I don't know!" Nina says, throwing her hands up. "I'm just having a hard time with all of this. That baby is going to be raised by a couple who probably know nothing about Russian life. The baby may never know anything about its Russian roots."

"And that upsets you?" Viktor asks.

"Yes!" Nina exclaims. "But I don't know why it upsets me. I've spent more than half my life in America. I feel as American as I do Russian. But, oh I don't know." Nina studies her hands. "I feel like somehow I'm betraying my country by letting this child go."

"Yes, but *dorogaya*," Viktor says gently. "This really isn't your decision. It's Annie's, and this is the decision she has made."

"I know," Nina replies.

"And more than anything, Annie needs your support," Viktor adds, his voice gentle. "The baby is going to be fine. It's going to be loved and cared for, and you don't know that they won't know anything about Russian life. But whether or not the child grows up learning of its Russian roots shouldn't be your main concern. You need to look out for Annie, because I imagine that she's got some difficult times ahead of her."

Nina draws in a deep breath and lets it out slowly. "You're right," she says. "I know you're right."

Viktor leans in, his face close as his eyes search hers. "You should be proud of her, you know," he says. "She's strong and independent, and she's making a brave, difficult choice. She had to learn that from someone." He kisses the tip of her nose. "I believe she got it from her mama."

Nina leans her forehead against his and closes her eyes. "I don't deserve you," she breathes.

"*Dorogaya*," Viktor whispers. "You are so much stronger than you give yourself credit for, and you deserve many things."

Nina leans into him, her head falling to his shoulder. "Let's get married soon," she whispers.

"I would marry you yesterday," Viktor responds.

NESTING DOLLS
<GRADIENT>

# ANNIE

A nnie pushes open the door and steps inside the cool room. Her babushka sits up in the bed, staring blankly at the wall in front of her. Annie briefly considers backing out, but Babushka turns and locks eyes, and she knows she's committed. She walks across the room and steps up to her grandmother's bedside.

"Hi, Baba," she says softly.

Elizaveta stares at her granddaughter. The golden glow of the dim, florescent lights highlight the top of Annie's head, casting a haze around her. Elizaveta's eyes drift to Annie's stomach, then move slowly back to her face. She lifts her hand and, finger shaking, points at Annie's protruding abdomen.

Annie runs her hand over her stomach self-consciously. "Yes, I'm doing alright," she says. Her grandmother's mouth turns up slightly. She reaches toward Annie's stomach. Annie steps closer, grabbing her grandmother's hand and sliding it to the side where the baby stretches and pushes uncomfortably against her skin. Elizaveta's eyes soften to the touch.

"I'm placing the baby for adoption, you know," Annie says. She speaks this in English, unable to wrap her mind around the Russian explanation for what she's planning to do. Elizaveta presses her hand against Annie's stomach and closes her eyes.

"I'm sorry I haven't tried harder to know you," Annie says softly. "I think I was jealous of you all these years. Mama couldn't focus on both of us when you arrived, and I got mad at her, and at you. I didn't want to try and get to know you, but I'm sorry about that."

Annie keeps talking despite the fact that Elizaveta's eyes are squeezed shut. Somehow it's easier to let the words just tumble out this way.

"Anyway," Annie continues. "I'm sorry that I was always so distant." She puts her hand on top of Elizaveta's. Elizaveta opens her eyes and looks at Annie.

"*Ya tebya lyublyu*," Annie whispers. I love you. It feels strange to say it out loud, but as soon as she does, Annie realizes that she means it. She does love her grandmother, despite all the years of questions and silence. Elizaveta cocks her head to the side, her mouth beginning to move and work its way around words.

"You," Elizaveta breathes, the Russian words slipping from her lips like drops of rain. "*Khrabraya. Khoroshava. Dobraya*," she whispers. "Brave. Good. Kind."

She drops her hand and leans back on her pillow, exhausted from the effort of communicating. Annie blinks hard as she reaches into her backpack and pulls out a drawing pad.

"I have something for you," she says. She slips the book open and pulls out a page. Slowly, she lays it down on the bed in front of Elizaveta.

It's a picture of a little girl and an old woman holding hands. It is drawn from behind, the old woman hunched over a cane, and the little girl standing next to her, long hair tumbling over slender, youthful shoulders. Their hands are clasped together, as though they are joined by something more than family. The simple pencil drawing reveals some unseen bond between the two. Elizaveta's heartbeat quickens at the sight of this drawing, so similar to the drawings she used to produce as a young woman. She raises her eyes to meet Annie's and points at the paper, then points at her granddaughter.

"*Da*," Annie replies. "I drew that. I draw a lot actually. I never really know that I'm doing it, though. It's strange. It happens when I'm distracted. And I don't usually show the pictures to anyone, but I drew this one this afternoon, and I knew I needed to show you."

Elizaveta slowly reaches down and, with shaking hands, picks up the drawing and hands it back to Annie.

"No," Annie says. "It's for you." She points at Elizaveta who pulls the picture back and hugs it to her chest. She reaches for Annie's hand and clasps it tightly. Annie squeezes back, then folds over and winces. Elizaveta looks at her in concern.

Annie stands back up and shakes her head. "That's been happening all day," she says. "I guess my body is just getting ready for..." she leans over again and draws in a sharp breath. Elizaveta tries to speak, willing the words to form on her tongue, but only grunts and syllables escape. She points at the Call button on the side of the bed, and Annie punches it. A few minutes later, a nurse comes into the room.

"What can I do for you, Miss Elizaveta?" she asks. She stops when she sees Annie folded over the side of the bed. Elizaveta grunts and gestures, the drawing fluttering from her hand and onto the floor.

"Honey, are you alright?" the nurse rushes to Annie's side. Annie looks up at her with a grimace and shakes her head.

"It hurts," she says. The nurse turns and runs into the hallway, returning a minute later with a wheelchair.

"We're calling 9-1-1," she says. "An ambulance will be here in a few minutes to take you to the hospital."

Annie nods and swallows hard as fear grips her. Another wave of pain washes over her and she cries out, reaching her arms across her stomach.

"I'm not due for another four weeks," she says through gritted teeth. "This is too early."

"Don't you worry, honey," the nurse says. She wheels Annie toward the door, slowly pushing it open and pulling the wheelchair into the open doorway. "The doctors will take good care of you."

"Can you call my mom?" Annie asks as tears well up in her eyes. The nurse nods her head.

"Already have someone doing that," she says. "You don't worry about anything, sugar. You're going to be just fine."

The door swings shut behind them, and Elizaveta is left alone. She stares at the picture lying on the floor out of her grasp, and she hears the voice in her head. It's her mother's voice, soft and gentle, singing the Cossack lullaby of her youth.

> *"A dream is wandering at night,*
> *A nap is following his way.*
> *A dream is asking, "Dear friend,*
> *Where shall we now stay?"*

# ELIZAVETA

*Motherhood: You did not absolve me.*

I stare at the picture for a long time, wishing that I could lean over and pick it up. From my bed, the outline of the drawing is blurred, but I have already memorized it. Why didn't I know that she shared my gift? Why, after so many years of living with her, did I not see the hidden talent? Could it be that the ability to keep secrets is passed down through the blood?

No, of course it couldn't be so, for Nina and Nastia have so little of my blood running through their veins. And yet, here is this evidence of a shared talent kept secret. I don't know what to do with this revelation. I can't talk about it with anyone, cannot explain to my granddaughter that she and I have something in common. I can do nothing but sit with my own thoughts and memories accusing me, offering no condolence, no forgiveness.

I turn my head toward the door where the nurse just wheeled Nastia out, and my heartbeat quickens. The memory of that cold night so many years ago haunts me. I feel the pain, hear my own screams, sense the phantom weight of my tiny daughter on my chest. I reach my hand toward the door, wishing that I could take this moment from her, that I could bring the pain and fear on myself, for isn't this partly my fault? My lies and my secrets all paved a path to this moment. The weight of that presses down on me until I can't breathe. The room starts spinning, and I'm gasping for breath. I hear the nurses running in just as the room goes dark, and I slide back into the past once more.

When I open my eyes to today's memory, I find myself back in my Moscow apartment. It's one week after Tanya left Nina on my doorstep. I was still staring at the door at that point, hoping that Igor would come through it and agree to tackle this challenge alongside me.

The baby was difficult, crying through the night with such a ferocious screech that the woman who lived below me came storming up to my flat at three in the morning and demanded I shut the child up or leave.

"Where did this child come from anyway?" she spat as I bounced Nina up and down in my arms, awkwardly trying to calm her down.

"She belongs to a friend of mine," I lied. I didn't have a story for how I ended up with a child, and I still hoped that Tanya would return.

"Well your friend needs to find someone more competent to watch over her child," the woman barked. "You are clearly starving that baby to death. What are you feeding it anyway?"

"Milk diluted with water," I replied. The woman snorted.

"The baby needs formula," she said. "Find a way to get some. Until then stop diluting the milk. Feed the child so it will stop screaming or leave this building."

I walked into the kitchen and pulled the glass bottle off the counter. I'd purchased it at the corner store along with the milk. I didn't want to ask anyone how to care for the child because I didn't want to explain how I came to have a child.

*"You are clearly starving that baby to death."*

My neighbor's words rang through my ears as I filled the bottle with what little milk I had left and placed it in a pot of boiling water on the stove to warm. I put my finger in her mouth and winced as she sucked ferociously on the tip. Every once in a while, she'd spit my finger out and let out an angry squawk to which I'd respond by giving her a fresh finger.

Finally, the milk was ready. I sat on the couch and put the bottle in her mouth and watched in awe as she drew in long gulps. By the end of the bottle, her little eyelids began to droop. She fell asleep in my arms, her tiny mouth open and relaxed. I stared at her for a long time that night, trying to decide what to do. I could take her back to Tanya, but that would require going back to the home where all the memories were buried, a home without Mama or Dima, a home without a single happy memory.

I could leave her on the steps of the children's home, but I knew in my heart that I couldn't betray my sister like that a second time. The only other option was to raise her myself, to take her as my own and give her the life that Tanya couldn't. She could have an education, and the freedom to move about in a world that didn't automatically count her out because of the geography of her birth.

I watched her sleep that night, and I decided that this would be my redemption. Raising this child would absolve me of the guilt of my past. I wasn't to be Nina's savior so much as she was to be mine.

I didn't know that such expectations were much too high for a child to meet.

# NINA

*Toska.*

Nina bursts through the doors and runs to the reception desk, Viktor right behind her.

"My daughter was brought here by ambulance," she said. The words were coming out fast making her Russian accent strong and difficult to understand. "Anastasia Abrams. She is having a baby."

The receptionist blinks at Nina. "I'm so sorry," she drawls. "Can you say that one more time?"

Nina growls and hits the counter. Viktor steps in and puts his hand over hers. "Her daughter arrived by ambulance a few minutes ago. She was in labor. Her name is Anastasia Abrams. Can you please tell us where she is right now?"

The receptionist types Annie's name into her computer then looks up. "She's is Labor and Delivery, Room 406. It's on the 4th floor."

Nina and Viktor spin around and race to the elevators. When the doors close and the din of the hospital is locked out, Nina swallows hard, the silence deafening.

"She's going to be okay," Viktor says softly.

"It's early for the baby to arrive," Nina replies. Viktor nods his head.

The elevator doors open, and Nina rushes out. Glancing at the sign, she turns to the left and heads toward room 406.

"I'll wait here!" Viktor calls. Nina stops and turns back to him. She raises her hand to her lips and kisses it.

"Thank you!" she says.

Moments later, Nina bursts through the door of Labor and Delivery room 406 to find her daughter lying on her side in tears. A nurse stands nearby monitoring the machine that measures contractions.

"Mama!" Annie cries. Nina rushes to her daughter and leans over, pushing her hair back off her face.

"Sshh, *dochenka*," she whispers. "I'm here." Nina glances at the nurse.

"How is she?" she asks.

The nurse nods. "She's at 9 centimeters and 90% effaced. The contractions are coming every minute and a half. This is going to be a fast labor." She glances at Annie, and then at Nina, her eyebrows raised. Nina immediately bristles.

"When will the doctor be here?" Nina asks.

"Any minute," the nurse replies.

"Good," Nina says. She turns her back to the nurse. "You may go now," she says. The nurse quickly walks out of the room, muttering something under her breath as she leaves.

"Mama," Annie moans. Nina grabs her hand and leans down. "Mama, it hurts," she gasps.

"Yes, my darling," Nina croons. "I know. Did they give you something for the pain?"

Annie shakes her head. "They said I'm too far along. It wouldn't work in time to help me."

Nina walks around the other side of the bed and pushes against Annie's back. Annie groans again as another wave of pain washes over her. "Mama!" she cries out. "Mama, help!"

Nina sings softly as she kneads at the muscles in her daughter's back. She sings the lullaby that she used to sing when Annie was little and got scared. It was the same song her mother sang to her when she couldn't sleep. Softly, gently she croons the lullaby in Annie's ear, soothing the fears of both of them.

*"A dream is wandering at night,*
*A nap is following his way.*
*A dream is asking, "Dear friend,*
*Where shall we now stay?"*

*"Where the house is warm,*
*Where the baby is small.*
*There, there we will stay,*
*Lull and hush the baby-doll."*

Annie reaches back and grabs her mother's hand. "I'm scared," she whispers.

Nina leans forward and brushes her lips across Annie's sweaty cheek. "I know," she says. She smooths Annie's hair back. "It's okay to be scared."

The doctor bustles into the room with the nurse on her heels. "Hello, Miss Annie!" he says cheerfully. "I hear it's time for you to have a baby."

Annie groans in reply and the doctor gently guides her to her back and checks her progress.

"Alright, my dear," he says. "This is happening very quickly. It's time to push."

Annie looks up at Nina with shining eyes. "I can't," she cries. "I can't do it. It's too hard. It hurts too much. Mama, I can't!"

The fear in her voice tears at Nina's heart. This is more than physical pain. She can see the emotional tearing taking place, her daughter's eyes bubbling with a heartache that Nina needs to reach. She puts her hands on either side of Annie's face and leans in close.

"You can do this," she says. "You can do this because you are brave. You're braver than I ever was at your age. I ran away from my problems, but you are facing them. You're strong, and good, and brave, and I am here with you. We'll do it together."

Annie searches her mother's eyes and nods her head. Taking a deep breath, she looks at the doctor.

"Ready?" he asks. Annie looks at Nina and nods. "Okay, then I need you to push hard, Annie!" he commands.

Annie squeezes her mom's hand and with three hard pushes, she feels the release as the baby slips from inside her and into the doctor's arms. Nina stands up to catch a glimpse of the tiny baby as the nurse whisks it from the doctor and lays it gingerly in a nearby incubator. Annie lays back on the pillow, panting.

"Is the baby okay?" she asks, her eyes searching the room as nurses bustle in and out. "I don't hear crying. Why don't I hear crying?"

Just then, the smallest cry pierces the room, the sound reverberating off the walls and into Nina's heart. She takes a step toward the incubator where the nurses are wiping off the baby and wrapping it in a blanket.

"Is it a girl or a boy?" Nina asks softly.

"It's a girl," the nurse answers. "And she is small. We need to run a few tests."

"It's a girl?" Annie asks from the bed. "Is she okay? Will she be okay?"

Nina turns back to her daughter with tears in her eyes and nods her head. "Yes, she will be okay. She's tiny and perfect. Do you want to see her?"

Annie hesitates. She searches her mom's face. "Should I see her?" she asks.

Nina reaches out and runs her hand over Annie's head. "I can't answer that for you, my darling," she says softly. "But if there's any part of you that wants to see her, then I think you should give yourself that gift. Because she's beautiful."

Annie nods. "I do want to see her," she whispers.

Nina turns to the nurse. "My daughter would like to see her baby."

The nurse looks from Nina to Annie. She leans down and wraps the tiny baby tightly in a blanket, then walks slowly to Annie's bed, holding the small bundle close to Annie's face. The baby is small with a shock of black hair and a tiny mouth. Her eyes are closed tightly, and her cry sounds like a little lamb. Annie reaches up and runs a finger over her soft head.

"Hello, little one," she whispers.

"I need to take the baby for a little while," the nurse says. "But I can bring her back when we're finished running the tests."

Annie drops her hand to her side and shakes her head. "You don't need to bring her back," she murmurs. Nina looks at her daughter, then shifts her eyes to the nurse and gives her a brief nod. The nurse lays the baby back in the incubator and wheels her out of the room.

Nina sits and holds Annie's hand in silence as the doctors and nurses finish cleaning her up and making her comfortable. Before long, the room clears out and the two sit alone, engulfed by the silence.

"Did you call Molly?" Annie asks.

"I did," Nina replies. "I told her that the baby was coming quickly, and she said she would call the adoptive family right away. They should be here by this evening."

Annie nods.

"Molly said that you could meet them if you'd like. And you can have as much time with the baby today and tomorrow as you need."

"I don't need any time," Annie interjects. "And I don't want to meet them."

Nina nods. "I understand, darling, but..."

"Mom, please. I can't. I don't want to talk about it right now, okay?"

"Okay," Nina responds. She stands up and leans in to kiss

her daughter on the cheek. "I am very, very proud of you," she whispers.

Annie stares stone-faced at the wall. She doesn't respond to her mother's words or touch. Nina takes in a deep breath and lets it out slowly.

"I'm going to get some tea and let Viktor know the baby arrived safely," she says. "Would you like anything?"

Annie shakes her head.

Nina turns and slowly walks out of the room. Running her hand over her eyes, she heads to the waiting area to talk with Viktor. She doesn't notice the young man walking nervously past her as she turns the corner and walks down the hallway.

Toby knocks three times on the door. He's just about to turn away when he hears a soft "Come in" from the other side. With a deep breath, he pushes open the doorway and takes in the sight of Annie lying under a thick blanket in a bed by the window. She looks small and lost.

"Hey," Toby says quietly. Annie shifts her gaze to his face and takes a minute to register his presence.

"Hi," she says. "How did you know I was here?"

"The social worker, uh, Molly, called me," Toby responds.

"Oh," Annie replies.

"Yeah," Toby responds. He stands awkwardly by the door as if contemplating an escape.

"It's a girl," she says softly.

"Okay," Toby replies.

"The adoptive parents are on their way to meet her now," Annie continues. Toby nods.

"Yeah," he says. "I signed all the paperwork."

Annie looks up at him in surprise. "You did?" she asks.

"Yeah. Molly met me in the lobby, and I got it done."

Annie leans back on the pillow. "It's happening so quick," she says. "It's weird."

Toby nods. "Did you see her? The, um...baby?"

Annie nods. "Yeah, just for a minute. Since she was early

and small they needed to take her to run tests, but I got to look at her. She was cute. She has black hair."

The two sit silently for a long minute before Toby reaches for the doorknob. "Annie," he says. "I'm sorry it happened this way."

Annie leans her head to the side and looks at him, her eyes full of heartache. "I'm sorry, too," she whispers.

"So I guess I'll see you around?" he asks. Annie nods, blinking back tears, knowing that they will never see one another again.

"Bye, Toby," she whispers.

He nods and pulls open the door, backing out quickly. Annie closes her eyes and tries to will herself to sleep in the hopes of pushing past this day and into the next. Immediately, the lump in her throat starts fighting against her skin, her eyes burning. She squeezes them tighter shut, trying to push out the image of the little girl she just birthed, but she can't escape it. Somehow, in the brief moment that she had to look at the baby, the tiny girl was seared into her for good.

Hot tears roll down her cheeks, and she claps her hands over her face. Something inside breaks, and she can't stop the overwhelming emotion roaring over her like a surprise summer storm.

"Mama," Annie whispers. She presses her hands into her eyes. "Mama." She says it over and over like a lifeline tethering her to the side of a precipice. She's begging her mother to hear her and respond.

"Annie?"

Annie looks up to find Nina standing in the doorway with two hot cups of coffee in her hand.

"Mama," she whispers. Nina rushes to her side, setting the coffee cups down on the bedside table and climbing into the bed next to her, pulling Annie into her arms.

"Sshhh, my darling," she whispers. "Sshh..."

Gasping for air, Annie clings at her mother's shirt, burying her face in her chest like she did as a child when the lightning flashed and she needed an escape from the terror of the storm. Nina rocks her gently, back and forth.

"Did…" Annie gasps, her words swallowed in grief. "Did I do the right thing?" She pushes back and searches Nina's face, begging for confirmation. "Is adoption the right choice, Mama?"

Nina pushes the hair off of Annie's face and wipes the tears that have streaked her splotched cheeks.

"Yes, my dear," she says. "I believe you are doing the right thing."

"But it's so hard," Annie sobs.

Nina nods. She pulls Annie back into the crook of her arm. "Yes, it is hard, *dorogaya*," she says. "But hard doesn't mean wrong. In fact, doing the right thing will rarely be easy. It will always be hard."

"Why does it hurt so bad, though?" Annie weeps.

Nina puts her lips on the top of her daughter's head and breathes the word out. "*Toska*," she whispers. "A mother's love can hardly be explained or understood. It can only be felt, and sometimes that love is the height of anguish."

"I don't feel like a mother," Annie says. "I only glanced at her, then I looked away. But I can't forget her face. I can't stop seeing it."

Nina blinks. "You don't need to run from it, Annichka," she says. "You may not *feel* like a mother, but you *are* a mother. That won't be taken away from you. You chose to give that little girl life, and then you chose to give her a family to provide for her the things you couldn't. I cannot think of a greater gift a mother could give to her child."

Annie nestles into her mother's chest a little further. Slowly, the tears quit falling from her eyes, and her breathing calms. Nina glances down to see that her daughter is sound asleep. She gently lays her on the pillow and climbs out of the bed. Walking to the door, she turns to glance back at Annie once more. It's dark outside now, the glow of the lights overhead illuminating Annie's bed in an amber halo. She remembers another time she looked at her daughter lying in a hospital bed.

Annie had been ten years old and had complained of a stomachache for days. But she was always complaining of aches and pains back then, and Nina had learned to tune out her whining. It wasn't until the school called that Nina began to suspect something might really be wrong with her daughter.

She'd rushed to the school to find Annie doubled over in pain and sobbing hysterically. They drove straight to the Emergency Room where Annie was whisked into surgery to remove her swollen appendix.

"If you had waited a few more hours, it would have burst," the doctor told her that evening. "She might not have survived."

For hours Nina sat by Annie's bed, sick with the thought that she almost did nothing—that her daughter could have died because she wasn't willing to really listen to her.

With a sigh, Nina pushes the door open and steps into the hallway. She walks numbly to the waiting room where Viktor sits in the corner quietly reading the newspaper. He looks up when she approaches and offers a gentle smile.

"How is she?" he asks.

"She's asleep," Nina responds. "I think I will stay here tonight just in case she needs me."

Viktor nods. "Of course," he says. "Can I get you anything?"

Nina shakes her head and runs her hand over her eyes. "I need to see my mother," she whispers. Viktor stands up and pulls her into his arms.

"I'll take you there first thing in the morning, okay?" he responds. Nina breathes in deeply, comforted by the warmth of his arms. He kisses the top of her head. "Get some rest," he says.

Leaning down, Viktor grabs his wallet and keys. When he straightens, Nina grabs his arm.

"When this has all settled down, I want to marry you," she says.

Viktor smiles and kisses her forehead. "It's a plan," he responds.

Nina watches him go, the ache in her chest softening as she soaks in his retreating figure. She remembers back to the last argument she had with her mother before she left with Andrew for America.

"You will regret this!" Elizaveta had barked as Nina packed. She was allowed to leave the country with only twenty kilograms in her bag. Her mother had hovered in the doorway, the ring on Nina's hand evidence that she'd already dismissed her mother's warnings and done the unthinkable—she had married an American, and now it was time to leave. Her new husband waited for her in America. He'd flown back to Russia and filled out the needed documents, made the necessary promises, and agreed to be her husband. Now he was back home, waiting for her to come and begin the new life that had been promised. And Elizaveta was making one last ditch effort to talk her out of it.

"Mama, I'm married," Nina had sighed, folding and refolding clothes to make them all fit. "I have to go."

"You don't! We can fix this," her mother barked. "We can tell them that you were wrong, you made a mistake. You don't really want to do this."

"But Mama, I do want to do this!" Nina cried, throwing her hands up in the air. "I married Andrew, and I want to go to America. I want to experience a new corner of the world!"

"But why that corner?" her mother yelled. "Why would you go to a land where everyone walks the streets with guns in their hands?"

Nina sighed. "Mama, you can't believe everything you read in *Pravda* or see on *Posledniye Izvestiya*," she said, gesturing her hand toward the small television currently playing the country's news channel. Elizaveta slumped against the doorway, her arms crossed over her chest like a petulant child not getting her way.

"You married a foreigner—an American," she said, softer now. "You need a strong Russian man to look after you. Russian men are the only real men in the world, you know. All the others are just boys pretending to be men."

Nina laughed at her mother, shaking her head. "How would you know, Mama? What man have you ever been with? I've never seen you with a Russian man, or heard you speak of a Russian man. If the Russian men are so wonderful, then why have you and I never had one around to look after us?"

That was their final conversation. After that, they spoke only short sentences as Nina finished up her packing and prepared to leave her country behind. There were more words to say, better words perhaps. But the damage had been done long before, and when she got into the taxi the next morning that would deliver her to the airport, she'd glanced up at the window of their flat and waited to see if her mother would lean out and wave goodbye. She didn't, and Nina knew she'd severed what little tie had remained between her and her mother.

Walking to the large window that overlooks the city, Nina takes in the lights. She focuses in on her reflection in the window. She's older now than she was then. Her face is more drawn, eyelids a little heavier. Gone is the innocence of that young girl who came to America, certain that she'd prove her mother wrong. In her place is a grown woman who is less sure now than she was twenty years ago—a woman who wants nothing more than to hear her mother say "I love you."

# ELIZAVETA

*It is time.*

She bustles through the room, talking as she moves. I don't understand her words, but I enjoy the soft way she speaks. Her voice is like a melody, gentle and sweet, not as harsh as some of the other nurses who clip through each sentence as though they've got a mouth full of metal.

Every once in a while she looks at me and smiles as though she's said something that I should find amusing. I try to push my mouth into a returning smile, but I'm not sure I'm successful. When Nina pushes open the door, the nurse turns and welcomes her in. The two speak softly, occasionally glancing my way as they share private information about my wellbeing. I sigh, frustrated at my inability to get up out of this bed and care for myself. I spent my entire life independent, needing no one to take care of me, and now I am confined to a strange bedroom entirely at the mercy of young nurses with names like 'Carol' and 'Jillian.' American names are so odd. I cross my hands over my stomach and look at Nina with raised eyebrows. She catches my eye and clears her throat.

"Hi, Mama," she says. She looks surprised, as though she's seeing me for the first time, and perhaps she is. Today is the first time I feel like myself since I fell all those months ago. I nod my head at her in return.

Nina pulls up a chair and sits next to the bed. There's a wary look in her eyes. She's waiting for me to get upset, but not today. Something inside feels calm this morning. I look back at her, studying her face. She looks tired.

Licking my lips, I let the word bubble on the tip of my tongue before forcing it out. "Nastia?" I ask.

Nina nods. "Yes, that's what I've come to talk to you about. She had the baby yesterday. It's a girl. She was very small. Only 6 pounds, which is almost 3 kilograms. But she will be just fine."

I listen quietly, my mind drifting to my granddaughter lying in a hospital bed, her arms empty. I feel something twist inside, a pain in my heart that's more than physical. My eyes fill with tears.

"Oh, Mama, it's okay," Nina says gently. She reaches awkwardly for my hand. "Annie is okay. She saw the baby for a brief moment, and she's considering meeting the adoptive parents now, which I think would be the best thing for her. I think she needs to see them and talk to them so that she can feel confident in her decision."

I slowly reach up and wipe my hand over my eyes, erasing any evidence of emotion. Turning my head to gaze out the window, I wish that I could get out all the words that seemed locked up inside.

"Mama?"

I shift back to look at Nina.

"Mama, are..." Nina sighs and stands up. She rubs her eyes and walks to the window, crossing her arms over her chest as she looks back at the morning sky all blue and alive, the clouds dancing past the hilltops in a morning praise. Nina doesn't look at me when she asks the question, and her voice is so soft that I have to strain to hear her.

"Mama, did you give birth to me?" Nina asks.

I lean back on the pillows and blink my eyes. For a long moment, the question hangs between us both. It's heavy and thick, and I feel the weight of her query pressing down on me. I shift my gaze back to Nina who has turned to face me, full of longing and fear. Slowly, I shake my head from side to side.

"*Nyet*," I whisper.

Nina's eyes fill with tears. She nods her head. I reach out my hand to her, to the little girl I raised, the one who left me and made her own path in this world. I remember the morning I held her for the first time, the horror I felt in knowing that she was a part of me that I would not be able to turn my back on. I look in her eyes, and I think of Tanya. Would she be pleased with the job I've done? Can I even take credit for any of the good in Nina?

Nina blinks hard as she places her hand in mine. "Who did?" she asks.

I close my eyes and take a deep breath. I see my sister standing there with us in the room. She isn't looking at me. She's looking at her daughter, at Nina. Her eyes are soft as she takes in the sight of this strong, grown woman.

"My. Sister." The words stagger out in a whisper. "Tatiana Kyrilovna Doroshenko. Tanya."

Nina sinks down onto the bed, her hand going limp in mine. With my free hand, I point to my chest.

"Victoria Kyrilovna Doroshenko. Vika."

The name falls from my mouth, so foreign and strange. It is my name, but it's the name that I abandoned so many years ago. I remember that girl now, but she doesn't feel like me. It seems that I did manage to rewrite my own history.

"Ekaterina Grigorevna Doroshenko," I whisper. "My mother."

Nina pushes away from the bed and takes several deep breaths.

"Dmitri Kirilovich Doroshenko. My brother. Dima."

Soft sobs escape Nina's throat as she watches me. I feel the strength beginning to ebb as I siphon off the names that I locked away so long ago. The room is going dim, and I don't have much time. I need to tell her one more thing.

"Kiril Andreyevich Doroshenko. My father." I need her to know. I need to give her this one last piece before the darkness pushes over me. "Died," I breathe. "Gulag. Kulak."

I sink then into the darkness, and for the first time in months I sleep peacefully. No memories, no heartache. Just rest. As I drift to sleep, a plea escapes my lips.

"Forgive me."

It passes from my soul with the hint of a sigh. I cannot be absolved of all my guilt, because the one I betrayed is not there to hear me. But as my soul quiets, I hear my mother's voice, soft and gentle, like a breeze through a meadow. She's whispering in my ear the way that she did as a child when she pressed up against me in the frigid nights.

"You are forgiven, my daughter. You are forgiven. Accept that because it's grace, and it's given for you. You just have to believe."

The freedom of my confession releases the weight that had clamped down on my soul all those years ago. I grasp at her words, my fingers lacing through them, breathing in a peace I have never known. I was foolish to think that I could choose State over Family. How could I have been so blinded to the truth?

She's humming over me now, the old lullaby that's so very familiar. Her voice is soft and warm. She sang this song to me often as a child. I remember.

I finally understand after all these years. I can hear Mama's song melt into my heart. It's the one she sang at night, when the icy winds of Siberia thrummed past our little hole in the ground.

> *A dream is wandering at night,*
> *A nap is following his way.*
> *A dream is asking, "Dear friend,*
> *Where shall we now stay?"*

*"Where the house is warm,*
*Where the baby is small.*
*There, there we will stay,*
*Lull and hush the baby-doll."*

She would sing this until our bodies relaxed against hers, then she whispered words to a God I never understood or wanted to know, and I accept now that perhaps she had been right all along. And so as the weight of my secrets float away, my spirit joins my mother's voice in a gentle whisper. I believe now, and it is well. After all these years, it is well.

# TEN YEARS LATER

You ready?"

Nina looks up as Viktor enters the kitchen. The tips of his hair are still wet, and a scent of aftershave trails behind him down the staircase. He steps up behind her and kisses her cheek.

"Almost," she replies. "I just need to finish the salad."

Using the edge of her knife, Nina slides the cut radishes off the cutting board and into the waiting bowl. She grabs two spoons and begins mixing it all together, the tomatoes and cucumbers combining with radishes and green onions to make a colorful and inviting summer salad. She tosses in fresh dill and the prepared bowl of *smetana*, then mixes it all together and inhales deeply and smiles.

"This smells like home," she says. Viktor grins, reaching over her shoulder and grabbing a cucumber out of the bowl.

"You say that every time you make this," he says.

"It's the only dish I really remember my mama making as a kid. I know we ate borsch and vereniki and plenty of blini, but every summer, this is the dish that mama didn't let go empty. She made a fresh batch of radish salad every single day."

Nina steps to the sink and rinses off the knife, then grabs a towel and wipes her hands.

"What time are we supposed to be there?" Viktor asks as

he reaches in the bowl and pulls out another bite. Nina smacks his hand and shakes her head as he grins sheepishly.

"We're meeting them at 4:00, then they'll come back here to have dinner with us. Annie wanted to let the baby get an early nap before they had to leave the house."

Nina glances out the window and takes in the sight of the perfect spring day. This is the tenth time they've visited Mama's graveside together as a family, and each year it feels more and more like a celebration. Nina thinks back to the morning that her mother passed away, just three days after she offered to Nina what felt like a last confession. She never opened her eyes again after the morning that she shared her real name. It was as though she was finally at peace enough to let go.

Nina spent the year following her mother's death researching old records, contacting researchers nationwide who specialized in searching for those lost to the generation of gulags. She looked for whatever information she might find on her family and came up empty. Based on her mother's last name and birthdate, a sketch of where she may have been born was formed, somewhere in central Ukraine, likely on a collective farm, the daughter of a wealthy peasant who became a threat to Stalin's paranoia.

She also pieced a vague story together based on the very few entries her mother made in the small journal Nina found after her death. Written by the unsteady hand of age, the journal told Nina that her mother had lived in a holding camp outside the gulag where she survived harsh winters. The details were sparse, but they were enough to paint a picture of the life her mother lived long ago, and they gave her some tangible evidence of her birth mother, Tanya. Nina would never really know where she came from, but somehow what she did know became enough.

"I've been thinking," Nina says as she and Viktor walk to the car. "Annie's daughter is ten years old now, almost the same age Annie was when my Mama came to stay with us.

Annie will probably receive a new update on her soon with a picture. I wonder what she's like. Last year, Jenny told us that she was becoming quite an accomplished ballerina. I wonder if she's still dancing..." Nina's voice drifts off as she considers the granddaughter being raised by another family.

Viktor inhales deeply, taking in the scent of the budding honeysuckle that grows on the side of the townhouse every spring. "Does it bother you still, not really knowing her?" he asks.

Nina cocks her head to the side and thinks. "No, not anymore," she says. "It did for a long time, but the more I've thought about my mother and what she did when her sister left me, the more at peace I am with Annie's choice. I don't really know what happened with my birth mother. I don't know why or how I ended up being raised by her sister, but I don't think it matters, because that's how it was supposed to be. I was supposed to be the daughter of Elizaveta Andreyevna Mishurova. Not her sister. And not Victoria Kyrilovna Doroshenko. For whatever reason, my mother needed to abandon that name and start over, and I *had* to be raised by the woman she became. I won't ever understand, but it's okay. Because it led me here, and it gave me Annie, and..." she stops as Viktor pulls open the door and turns to face him.

"It gave me you," she says.

Viktor smiles and leans in for a soft kiss. "Your big, strong, Russian man," he says in a thick accent the way her mother would say it. Nina laughs then slides into the car.

Twenty minutes later, they pull up to the cemetery and park in a spot near the small plot where her mother rests. As Nina pushes open her door, she looks up to the crest of the hill and sees Annie and James, the baby set firmly on Annie's hip. Beside James stands their three-year-old son. When he sees Nina, he breaks into a wide grin.

"Babushka!" he cries, running down the hill, his little legs barely keeping him upright. Nina squats down and catches him just as he trips and falls into her arms. His hands are sticky and his hair is a mess. Nina grins and kisses the top of his head.

"Hello, my beautiful boy," she croons in Russian. Sasha looks up at her and giggles.

"Mama taught me a new poem today!" he says.

"Oh really," Nina replies standing up and grabbing his hand. Viktor steps up beside them and ruffles the top of Sasha's head. "Let me hear it."

"*Beliye baranyi! Bili v barabanyi! Beliye baranyi! Bili v barabanyi!*"

Sasha marches in time to the beat of his poem as Nina and Viktor laugh at his enthusiasm. They reach the top of the hill where Annie and James greet them.

"He's doing well," Nina says. Annie grins.

"Well, he and I are kind of learning together," she replies. "Speaking comes pretty naturally, but reading and writing are harder. We're working on it, *pravda* Sasha?" she says switching to Russian. He grins back up at her.

"*Pravda!*" he shouts.

Nina reaches out for the baby, and Annie hands her over. "*Privyet*, Vika," she croons in her granddaughter's little ear. Victoria bounces and babbles, drool spilling down her chin. James reaches over to wipe her mouth, then leans in and gives Nina a kiss on the cheek.

"*Privyet*," he says. Nina raises her eyebrows.

"Are you learning Russian, too?" she asks.

"Well, I kind of feel like I have to now!" he answers with a laugh. "Otherwise these three are going to gang up on me, and I'll never know what's going on."

Laughing, the group makes its way to the graveside where they stop and stare at the small plaque marking where the matriarch of the family rests.

ELIZAVETA ANDREYEVNA MISHUROVA
VICTORIA KYRILOVNA DOROSHENKO

"I bet Babushka would like that we come out here every

year to visit her," Annie says softly. Nina cocks her head to the side and offers a wry smile.

"Maybe," she says. "Or maybe not. She wasn't much for being outdoors. I can almost hear her *tsk*-ing and asking me why we don't just stay inside and drink some *chai* instead of coming all the way out here."

Annie snickers. "You're probably right. She would have had some comment, I'm sure."

They stand silently for a few more minutes before Sasha breaks through the breeze and interrupts their thoughts.

"Babushka, *Ya khochu kushat*," he says, his Russian words lisped. "I want to eat!"

Nina smiles. "Okay, Sashenka," she says. "We can go back to my house now and eat. How does that sound? And Dyedushka bought you a new toy to play with!"

Sasha jumps up and down and claps his hand, grinning up at Viktor who smiles back, his eyes gleaming with pride. Viktor relishes his role as grandfather, doting on the children at every opportunity.

The group turns to leave but Nina remains. "I'll be there in a moment," she says. Annie reaches out for the baby, but Nina meets her eye.

"May I keep her with me?" she asks.

"Sure," Annie replies. She grabs James' hand, and the two of them turn and walk down the hill together, Sasha running ahead of them toward the car.

"Hi, Mama," Nina says softly. The birds overhead chirp in a springtime harmony that fits this perfect day. Nina holds Vika tight as she babbles and kicks her feet.

"This is your great-granddaughter. Her name is Victoria Elizabeth. Annie named her after you." Nina blinks back tears, pulling the baby in a little closer and putting her chin on top of her little head, her wispy, blonde curls blowing in the breeze.

"We are doing well, Mama. Annie and James are happy and healthy. Annie is even teaching her children Russian if you can believe that." Nina smiles at the thought of her mother nodding her head in approval.

"Viktor and I have been married for ten years now, and Mama, as much as I hate to admit it, you were right. There is something about a Russian man that is so much better. You would be pleased."

Nina looks down the hill at the rest of her family. Annie is wrestling Sasha into his car seat while James and Viktor stand to the side talking, probably about the latest book they're each reading. James is a literature teacher at the local high school, and he's passionate about his job. He and Viktor love to dissect the books they're reading, from the poetry of Pushkin to the theology of C.S. Lewis.

Nina turns once more to her mother's grave and blinks back tears. "Thanks again, Mama," she says. "Thanks for giving me a chance. I don't know what happened, but I know it must have been a huge sacrifice for you. I didn't tell you enough when you were alive, but Mama..." Nina stops and takes a deep breath. "Mama, I love you."

Turning, she makes her way down the hill to the family that's waiting, ducking under the willow tree that shades her mother's grave. Its branches whisper the wisp of a song that Nina can hear gliding away on the wings of the wind.

> *"A dream is wandering at night,*
> *A nap is following his way.*
> *A dream is asking, "Dear friend,*
> *Where shall we now stay?"*

# ACKNOWLEDGMENTS

No author can claim she did it all on her own. Every story takes a team of people to mold and shape the characters into something that truly resonates. I am most fortunate to have a rock star team who not only cheers me on but also believes in my abilities with unwavering faith. They are the people who make me brave. There are so many people to thank for helping me bring this particular story to life.

First and foremost, I must thank Bethany Hockenbury, my editor extraordinaire and dear friend who spent hours on this project, losing sleep and sacrificing time in her busy life to ensure the story was as concise as possible. Without Bethany, this book would have been a mess of misplaced commas, over-used adjectives, and underdeveloped characters. Bethany, you refuse to let me settle for mediocre. Thank you for pushing me toward excellence.

My dear friend and Ukrainian sister, Svetlana Tulupova, read the earliest version of this manuscript and offered profound insights into the life and history of those who were known as *kulaks*. Thank you, Sveta, for helping me bring Elizaveta's story to life. I am deeply grateful for the time you spent gathering details and data so that I could accurately depict that history. You are a gift.

Thank you, from the bottom of my heart, to Julia Kuznetsova-Radivlov for reading the manuscript and offering thoughts and perspective on life in 1980's Soviet Union. Both Julia and

Natalia Scarberry were key in offering the little details that give this book necessary authenticity. My dear friends, I am grateful to you both for your enthusiasm and willingness to help an American writer tackle Soviet history.

Emerson Cooper, you are a phenomenal talent. Thank you for so enthusiastically catching my vision for Annie, and for helping capture her through drawings. I am unendingly grateful to you for the time you put into this project, and I'm thankful that I have the unique privilege of calling you family. Keep drawing!

Thank you to Susie Finkbeiner, Jocelyn Green, and Catie Cordiero for listening to my ideas and encouraging me to keep writing and pushing forward in the story. I am deeply grateful to you all for your encouragement.

Thank you to Roseanna White for her expertise in layout and design, and for helping me make this final product a reality! I am so grateful.

Thank you to those who read early copies of the manuscript and offered thoughts, encouragement, and insights into the story so that I could make it stronger: Amy Hewitt, Katie Finklea, Becke Stuart, Barbara Stuart, and Wendy Speake.

Thank you to my friend and agent, Rachel McMillan, who is a wealth of knowledge in the industry of writing and publishing. I am in awe of your talent, Rachel, and thankful for your encouragement and support.

This story is more than just a work of fiction. In the depiction of Annie, I wrote a love letter to the beautiful, broken road of adoption. To all the birth mothers who make the difficult but brave decision to place their children for adoption, thank you. As one who has been touched by adoption in its many facets, I write from a place of deepest respect and humility.

To the men and women of the Russian Heritage Society in St. Petersberg, Florida: Thank you for accepting me so openly into your group, and for your overwhelming support. What a gift you all have been to me.

Finally, I must thank my family who make the entire process of writing a book possible. To my parents, Richard and Candy Martin, who first put me on a plane to the former Soviet Union as a teenager, and who have since supported me unwaveringly in my many adventures, thank you both. I am most blessed to be called your daughter.

To my children: Sloan, my firstborn and enthusiastic cheerleader. Thanks for cheering me on. You make me want to keep writing. Tia, my daughter who has taught me what it means to want something and chase it without fear of failure. You are one of the hardest workers I know. Landon, the child who models what it looks like to delight in your gifts and talents. Thank you for always making me smile. Annika, the surprise gift with big eyes and an even bigger heart. Thanks for still curling up in my lap and holding my hand in public. And to Sawyer, the child who is teaching me how to love in a whole new way. You just might be the bravest boy I know. I can't wait to see what the Lord has in store for you.

To Lee, the man who has faithfully stood by my side and pushed me to chase my dreams for nearly two decades now. I'm not sure he knew what he was getting into when he married the girl with big dreams and an even bigger imagination, but he's never once held me back from pursuing both. Thank you for loving me so well.

And finally, thank you to all of you, the readers who pick up books and look for new adventures on the page. It is a daunting task to try and dig through a history that is layered and complex. Thank you for picking up this book and reading it, and for trusting that I did my very best to bring you a story that was both engaging and historically factual. It is a great gift to be able to deliver stories into the hands of those who appreciate them.

# ALSO BY KELLI STUART

*Like a River From Its Course*

2017 Carol Award winner for Best Historical Fiction
2017 Christy-nominated Best Historical and Best Debut

"Gritty and Touching."
*~ Publisher's Weekly*